DATE			

FULL DRESS GRAY

ALSO BY LUCIAN K. TRUSCOTT IV

Dress Gray
Army Blue
Rules of the Road
Heart of War

LUCIAN K. TRUSCOTT IV

FULL

DRESS

GRAY

WILLIAM MORROW AND COMPANY, INC. / NEW YORK

It is the policy of William Morrow and Company, and its imprints and affiliates,
recognizing the importance of preserving what has been written, to print the books we
publish on acid-free paper, and we exert our best efforts to that end.

Library of Congress Cataloging-in-Publication Data

Truscott, Lucian K., 1947–
   Full dress gray / by Lucian K. Truscott, IV.
     p. cm.
   Sequel to: Dress gray.
   ISBN 0-688-15993-1 (akl. paper)
     1. United States Military Academy—Fiction. I. Title.
PS3570.R86F85 1998   98-4320
813'.54—dc21   CIP

Printed in the United States of America

First Edition

1 2 3 4 5 6 7 8 9 10

BOOK DESIGN BY JO ANNE METSCH

www.williammorrow.com

To my father
Lucian K. Truscott III
Colonel, USA, Ret.

ACKNOWLEDGMENTS

I have received advice and counsel from many people during the time I have worked on this book (some of whom wish to remain anonymous), but most appreciated were the invaluable and boundless memories, wisdom, and good humor of David H. Vaught, Gary Moyer, Kathy Pardue, Lieutenant Colonel Norm Grady, and Colonel Fred Black (Ret.) and most especially the nonpareil legal stylings of Major Doug Dribben, JAG extraordinaire.

LKTIV
Los Angeles

"The discipline which makes the soldiers of a free country reliable in battle is not to be gained by harsh or tyrannical treatment. On the contrary, such treatment is far more likely to destroy than to make an army. It is possible to impart instruction and to give commands in such manner and such a tone of voice to inspire in the soldier no feeling but an intense desire to obey, while the opposite manner and tone of voice cannot fail to excite strong resentment and a desire to disobey. The one mode or the other of dealing with subordinates springs from a corresponding spirit in the breast of the commander. He who feels the respect which is due to others cannot fail to inspire in them regard for himself, while he who feels, and hence manifests, disrespect toward others, especially his inferiors, cannot fail to inspire hatred against himself."

—MAJOR GENERAL JOHN M. SCHOFIELD,
in an address to the Corps of Cadets,
August 11, 1879

FULL DRESS GRAY

MOST PEOPLE spend their lives praying they'll never see the day that will force them to answer the question *Who am I?* This was not true of Rysam Parker Slaight. He could remember with absolute clarity even thirty years later how it happened.

It was just after graduation leave, and he was a second lieutenant, attending the Infantry Officers Basic Course at Fort Benning, Georgia. The first time the company formed up, he found himself standing in ranks next to a classmate who had just barely made it into the officer corps, having graduated a single slot from the bottom of the class. He was an awkward sort of fellow. His fatigues hung from his tall, gangly frame like loose tenting, and he had enormous feet, which splayed to the sides when he walked, a prominent, hooked nose that jutted from beneath the bill of his cap like the prow of a boat, and a beard so heavy that by noon, he looked like he hadn't bothered to shave at all that morning. At West Point, guys used to call him "Whizzer," or "The Whiz," precisely because as a cadet, he was anything but. Whizzer took the teasing in a jocular, forgiving way, and his natural-born enthusiasm for things military ended up converting most of the doubters, even those who figured right from the start that he didn't have what it took to get through four arduous years of Academy life. Guys in his regiment used to say he was goofy, but the Whiz was a good guy. Among cadets, this was a sobriquet that made up for a multitude of sins.

Now that he was an officer, the nickname had stuck, but the goofiness was gone. Whizzer was a lieutenant, just like everyone else in IOBC, and he was a regular officer in the United States Army. He had a new seriousness about him, and there was a reason for this: Whizzer had volunteered for an immediate assignment to Vietnam. In a very few months, as soon as he completed preliminary officer training, he would be an infantry platoon leader in combat.

Realizing that he didn't have much time before he departed for war, he had used his two-month leave before reporting for duty at Fort Benning to accomplish what were for him two important goals: He had married a hometown girl only a year out of high school, and he had grown a mustache. It may not seem that these two accomplishments represented a meaningful preparation for beginning a career in the Army, but a wife and a mustache were two things that he had been forbidden during his four long years as a cadet, and using the twisted logic of cadet thinking, it probably seemed to Whizzer that because they were denied to him as a cadet, they were essential to him as an officer.

So on that first day of IOBC when Whizzer showed up in ranks, there was parked beneath his nose a lush growth of facial hair expertly trimmed in regulation military manner extending to the corners of the mouth and not beyond. Classmates in the IOBC company, including Slaight, thought the mustache had transformed the Whiz. He looked, well, something approaching *military*. And he acted that way, too. He and his young wife had taken a dingy garden flat in the Camelia Apartments, just outside the gates of Fort Benning in Columbus, Georgia. He drove a brand new Corvette. His fatigues, at least very early in the morning before the stifling heat of a Georgia August day had wilted them, were starched stiffly, and his boots were expertly spit-shined, toes gleaming like black agates in the sun. The Whiz could thus be described as *strac,* a military word that bespoke expert attention to appearance and a superior military bearing.

But there was a problem. More than one, actually. Two captains had been assigned as "platoon advisors" to the platoon. This was for them "TDY," a temporary-duty assignment while they awaited slots in the next class of the Infantry Officers Advanced Course. These sterling exemplars of military proficiency took one look at their platoon in the Infantry Officers Basic Course and calculated that they wouldn't have fulfilled their natural duties as men and as officers if they hadn't run at least one of the "college boys" out of the program and thus out of the Army. They were not college boys, having graduated from high school, been drafted, and received their commissions in Officer Candidate School. One of the platoon advisors was a stockily built man who carried himself like a professional wrestler, his shoulders rolling menacingly as he walked. The other advisor was short and very slight. It was necessary for him to tilt back his head and look up to make eye contact with Whizzer, which he proceeded to do as the two captains zeroed in on him.

Specifically, they zeroed in on Whizzer's mustache. The captains walked up to him that first day in formation and ordered him to cut it off. Whizzer patiently explained that his mustache was legal, having been trimmed in the manner specified by Army regulations, and he had no intention of cutting it off. Out of the corner of his eye, Slaight saw the beginnings of a grin cross the face of the shorter of the two platoon advisors, the one everyone would come to call "Monkey Breath" because of the strong stench of cigarettes and coffee that was emitted every time he opened his mouth. The grin was replaced by a reddening scowl, and the captain turned on his heel and stalked away. Whizzer glanced at Slaight and shrugged, thinking it was over. Slaight knew it was not.

The platoon advisors appointed Whizzer student platoon leader, which meant that Whizzer marched the platoon to and from classes at the Infantry School. When the platoon reached its first class that morning and the command to fall out had been given, the platoon advisors told Whizzer to march over to a nearby tree, and in full view of the rest of the company they proceed to order Whizzer to give the tree marching commands such as "Platoon, attention!" "Column right, march!" "Platoon, halt!" It was harassment, pure and simple. While Whizzer's command voice was not among the most authoritative Slaight had encountered, everyone in the platoon had heard and acted upon Whizzer's commands without problems. Whizzer and the rest of the platoon soon got the message that his command voice wasn't the point, his mustache was. The platoon advisors were intent on making his life miserable until he cut it off.

Slaight was at the Officers Club when it came to him. He was having a beer with another classmate, whom everyone called "Airborne" because he had used one of his summer leaves while at West Point to attend Airborne School instead of taking a well-deserved vacation. Slaight told Airborne he felt like growing a mustache, so Whizzer's wasn't the only mustache in the platoon and the advisors would have to concentrate their hazing on two lieutenants instead of one. Airborne rubbed his upper lip thoughtfully. It turned out that just that morning he had begun to wonder what he'd look like with a mustache. Airborne decided he would grow one, too.

By the end of the week, out of the forty lieutenants in the platoon, thirty-nine had mustaches, the sole holdout being a graduate of the Citadel who thought the platoon advisors were well within their rights in their hazing of Whizzer.

The sprouting of thirty-eight new mustaches did not escape the attention of the platoon advisors. They relieved Whizzer of his student platoon command and gave the job to Slaight. When it turned out that his talents at marching the platoon to and from classes didn't need much work, their frustration grew. They assigned the student platoon command to Airborne. He was similarly well equipped to command the platoon. They fired Airborne and gave command of the platoon back to Whizzer. He had been working on his marching commands at home and took over, marching the platoon to and from classes with alacrity.

The platoon advisors had hit the wall. They were in charge of a platoon of mustache-wearing malcontents who had rallied behind the man they wanted to run out of the Infantry School. New measures would be necessary.

It was very early one morning during bayonet drill that they struck. Whizzer, they said, had been two minutes late to formation. Because of his egregious crime they ordered Whizzer to send his wife home to live with her mother and to move himself immediately into the Bachelor Officers Quarters where his movements could be more closely monitored. Whizzer contested their assertion that he had been late and noted that he had exactly six weeks left with his wife before he reported for duty in Vietnam. The platoon advisors were unmoved by Whizzer's career schedule. They reported Whizzer's purported crime to the battalion commander, and the colonel issued his order forthwith: Get rid of the wife and move into the BOQ or face a court martial.

Whizzer went home and told his nineteen-year-old wife what had happened. The next day, at a noon "tea" hosted by the wife of the battalion commander, Whizzer's wife walked up to the colonel's spouse and told her if she thought her husband could order her to go back home to live with her mother and take away the six weeks she had with Whizzer before he reported to Vietnam, she could go fuck herself.

The colonel's wife was not amused.

The following day, Whizzer was called into the colonel's office and dressed down for his wife's insubordination. Whizzer's wife had told him about the confrontation with the colonel's wife, and so Whizzer was prepared for the colonel's tirade. He told the colonel that since the First Amendment to the Constitution applied to lieutenants' wives as well as it did to colonels' wives, he had to assume that his wife was making use of her right to free speech to express her feelings to the colonel's wife, and he opined that the confrontation between their wives was not Army business. The colonel exploded. Whizzer stood his ground. The tempest swirled further, and an appointment was arranged for Whizzer to pay a visit to the Commanding General of Fort Benning several days later.

Whizzer invited Slaight home for dinner that evening. Over a meal of canned vegetables and a chicken casserole that tasted suspiciously of Campbell's mushroom soup, Whizzer and his wife explained the situation. It was clear to Whizzer that he was being railroaded out of the Army. Going to West Point and becoming an Army officer had been his dream since he was a young boy. What was he going to do?

Slaight pondered Whizzer's dilemma. It seemed that no matter which way he turned grim questions loomed, freighted with even grimmer answers. If Whizzer caved in and sent his wife home, he might be killed in Vietnam and never see her again. If he refused the order to move into the BOQ, they would court-martial him, and he would be dismissed from the service, and his dream would die. He was a loser either way.

Whizzer's appointment with the Commanding General couldn't be scheduled for three days because the company was going into the field on overnight maneuvers. During the time they were on maneuvers, the company was under the control of an infantry training battalion, so the services of the platoon advisors were not needed. Three days went by without their unwanted attentions.

When the company returned from the field, the platoon advisors were standing in the company area wearing starched fatigues, in contrast to the members of the platoon, who were unshaven, dirty, and bedraggled from forced marches, sleeping under ponchos on the ground, and eating C rations. When the platoon was dismissed, the platoon advisors walked past Whizzer and followed Slaight into the barracks. They caught up with him in the hallway on his way to turn in his M-16 and took him by the arm, one on each side, yanking him into a windowless supply room.

The platoon advisors shut the door and gave Slaight a direct verbal order to shave off his mustache. In their infinite wisdom, they had concluded that it was when Slaight grew his mustache that the rest of the platoon followed suit, and so if Slaight shaved off his mustache, the rest of the platoon would do as he did, and Whizzer would feel the peer pressure and shave his, too.

Slaight explained that he liked his mustache. He was going to keep it.

The smaller of the two platoon advisors, who spoke in a thin-lipped southern drawl, asked Slaight if he knew why Army regulations allowed mustaches.

Uh-oh. Here it comes, thought Slaight.

It's because of the niggers, said the platoon advisor. *They like to grow them thin mustaches because their women like the way it feels when they get their faces down there and eat them nigger pussies.*

Having explained to Slaight the origin of the Army regulation permitting mustaches, they now told him what would happen if he refused their order. They would make sure that he was graded at the bottom of the class in leadership, which counted for 50 percent of class standing at the Infantry School. This would grievously damage his career and he would begin his life as an infantry lieutenant way behind his classmates. Moreover, they would put a memo in his permanent personnel file warning future commanders that Slaight was a troublemaker.

Slaight stood there staring at them. He was still wearing his helmet from the field. It was heavy, and the airless supply room was stiflingly hot, and he could feel the sweat dripping from his chin strap onto the breast of his fatigue shirt.

The two captains stared straight back at him, waiting. Instinctively, he knew he had reached a turning point in his life. He could accede to the demands of the platoon advisors and graduate with distinction, or he could stand up to them and suffer the consequences. He took a deep breath and looked each of the men in the eye.

Back in my trailer, I have a photograph of my father holding me in his arms when I was one year old and he was a lieutenant in the infantry. In the photograph, he has a mustache. That was twenty-two years ago. Now I'm a lieutenant, and I have a mustache just like my father's, and I'm not cutting it off. Now listen to me, you two fucking assholes, and listen good. If I hear either one of you use the word nigger *again, in any context whatsoever, I will report to the Staff Judge Advocate of Fort Benning and bring charges against you under Article 133 of the UCMJ for conduct unbecoming an officer and a gentleman.*

Slaight pointed at the door.

Both of you redneck assholes get out of my sight. I don't want to hear another word from either of you until this course is completed.

The platoon advisors paused for a moment, then the little one looked at the stocky one and they turned around and left without another word.

Whizzer went to his meeting with the Commanding General and refused to send his wife home to her mother and move into the BOQ. The Commanding General concluded that Whizzer's having volunteered for an immediate assignment to Vietnam put him in a special category, and sent word back down to the company that Whizzer was to be permitted to remain in his off-post apartment with his wife.

When the platoon graduated from IOBC, the platoon advisors were as good as their word, and Slaight was ranked right at the very bottom of his class. This was not the career-ending disaster it might have been in another time, for ten thousand miles away there was a war going on. As an old sergeant had told Slaight one summer when he was assigned to a training company at Fort Knox, war has a way of changing everything.

Whizzer reported to his assignment in Vietnam six weeks later,

Slaight to his about eight months after that. Slaight never saw Whiz-zer again, though he heard on the grapevine that he had been a good platoon leader who got most of guys back alive.

More than thirty years would pass before Slaight was confronted again with the question he had answered that hot day in a supply room at Fort Benning, Georgia.

Who am I?

BOOK

ONE

CHAPTER 1

IT WAS the day after Labor Day, and it was hot. The new Superintendent of West Point had awakened at five A.M. and had gone for a run down Thayer Road. By the time he returned to Quarters 100, around six, the temperature was already in the eighties, headed quickly, he knew, into the nineties.

His wife, Samantha, greeted him at the back door with a bottle of cold water. "You're looking a little worse for the wear, General Slaight." She laughed as he collapsed weakly on a kitchen chair and drained the bottle. Sweat was pouring down his face, his graying hair was matted to his scalp, and his ARMY T-shirt was soaked clear through.

"It's going to be a scorcher," he said, panting.

"I wonder if you shouldn't put off the parade until the weekend," his wife mused. "I was watching the news. It's supposed to cool off by Saturday." She crossed the kitchen and switched on the coffeepot. Come December, they would celebrate their twenty-sixth wedding anniversary. Her hair was pinned up on the top of her head with some kind of clip, and she hadn't yet put on her makeup, but mornings had always been kind to her. She woke up with color in her cheeks and bright eyes and a wry, crinkly smile that hinted conspiratorially at her prevailing mood, which was usually one of ironic skepticism and a low toleration for army bullshit. Slaight watched her rinsing a couple of cups at the sink. She was a remarkably beautiful woman. There had been days when he thought that he regretted having married this sometimes difficult, demanding, and headstrong woman. But by nightfall his regret had inevitably faded into the kind of comfortable acceptance that landmarked marriages that had gone the distance like theirs. If time didn't heal every little wound of married life, it sure as hell served as a good Band-Aid.

"Don't think I can cancel the parade. It's the pass in review welcoming me to West Point, and the Corps practiced all last week. Gibson's been laying on this parade all summer," he said, referring to the Commandant of Cadets, Brigadier General Jack Gibson, the hard-charging infantry officer who was in charge of cadet military training and the disciplinary system. Beginning his third year as Com, the prematurely graying young general with the huge black eyebrows had been nicknamed "Black Jack" by cadets who had become accustomed to encountering his grim face during the Com's frequent surprise inspections of the barracks.

"Well, I think it's too hot," said Samantha, pouring herself and the general cups of coffee.

"I agree with you," he said. "But I'm afraid it's too late. The Chief of Staff is already on his way up here." He checked his watch. "We'd better get dressed. We're supposed to meet his plane up at Stewart Field at eight-forty-five."

"Tell me it wasn't Gibson who invited him. Please."

Slaight laughed. "Laying on a big welcome for the new Supe is his job, Sam."

"And I'll just bet he used the opportunity to its fullest advantage. His own." Disdain broke her words into individual syllables draped with irony as her voice slipped back into the cadences of her native New Orleans.

"I wouldn't put it past him. Gibson's a piece of work," said the general.

He stood up and pulled his wife close, kissing her lingeringly. She gave him a mock struggle and pulled away, touching the damp front of her robe. "Look at this. You're so stinky and sweaty, I'm going to have to put this straight into the wash."

He pulled off his T-shirt and stepped out of his running shorts.

Naked, grinning ear to ear, he handed his sweaty clothes to her. "Throw these in the wash while you're at it."

She dropped the wet wad of clothing like it was contaminated. "Do it yourself, General," she instructed. "What do you think that third star earned you? If you think rank is a vacation from shit details, you've got a big surprise coming, Superintendent Slaight."

She stopped in the kitchen door and gave his nude body a slow once-over and grinned. "Why am I getting this feeling that returning to West Point has brought out the boy in you?"

" 'Cause it has," said Slaight, sprinting toward her. She raced for the back stairs, taking them two at a time. He caught her at the landing, wrapping her tightly in his arms. "We've got time," he whispered. He kissed her again, holding the back of her neck as she reached up and unclipped her hair, letting it fall to her shoulders. He ran his fingers through the little bursts and streaks of silver that shone in the soft light filtering through the sheer curtains on the landing window, and he heard her sigh as she pulled away.

"Later, buster."

It was going to be a long hot day, but there were sure as hell worse ways to begin.

IT WAS only a short walk to the reviewing stand from Quarters 100, located on the west side of the Plain. It seemed to Slaight that every step he took deposited a shovelful of irony atop the neatly trimmed grass.

It was thirty years ago that he had been walking the area when he heard that Samantha's brother, David Hand, had been found dead by drowning up at Lake Popolopen, about a dozen miles northwest of West Point. The Academy had acted the way institutions act when they are confronted by uncomfortable if not potentially dangerous news. Hurriedly the death of a plebe had been swept under the proverbial rug, and life at the Academy had been returned to what passed for normal. Slaight had spent the rest of that year and a good portion of the next trying to find out what had happened to David Hand. When it was proven that he had been gay and had died at the hands of his cadet lover, the granite of what the cadets called their "rockbound highland home" had seemed to crack under the strain. Slaight had in fact been so disillusioned by the experience of going up against the institutional inertia of the Academy that he had told the then Superintendent, General Rylander, he was going to resign before graduation and forgo his commission as a second lieutenant of infantry.

Then something had happened. Judge Hand, the father of David and Samantha, walked into his barracks room the morning he was going to submit his resignation and sat down on the bed and told Slaight a story. He was a father with a son who all his life had dreamt of being a West Pointer and an Army officer, and now his son and his dreams were dead. It would break Judge Hand's heart to see another young man's dreams dashed against the hard reality of his son's tragic death.

As Judge Hand spoke, Slaight's friends Leroy Buck and John Lugar wandered into the room and stood over by the window. Listening to Judge Hand, Slaight looked over at his friends. Their faces wore the weary frowns of firsties—guys who had spent four years at West Point and had pretty much seen and heard it all. But their frowns dissolved as the Judge's personal pain flooded the room. When the Judge left, Buck and Lugar hung around, waiting for Slaight's reaction. He remembered now that there had been literally nothing he could think of to say. He had walked over to his desk and torn up his resignation. The next day, the three of them walked together to Michie Stadium and stood in the June sun and threw their cadet caps high into the air in the traditional celebration signaling that they were no longer cadets but second lieutenants in the United States Army.

Slaight remembered he was standing there holding hands with his lover, Irit Dov, when Samantha Hand and Judge Hand walked up to congratulate him.

"David would have wanted it this way," Samantha said.

Judge Hand cleared his throat and did his best to hold back the tears welling up in his eyes. "I'm . . . proud of you," he stammered. Then Samantha gave Second Lieutenant Slaight a quick kiss on the cheek and she and her father melted into the crowd surging around the new grads.

Irony upon irony. Now his wife, Sam walked with Lieutenant General Slaight as he strode across the grassy expanse of the Plain.

Behind the barracks walls, he could hear the cadet companies forming up.

"A Companayyyy... a-ten-SHUN! B Companayyyy... a-ten-SHUN! C Companayyyy... a-ten-SHUN!"

Soon the sunny exits of the sally ports through the barracks would be alight with the glistening buttons of cadet full dress gray coats as the Corps marched from the barracks and began the age-old tradition of passing in review for the Superintendent of the United States Military Academy. It was an onerous task that Slaight had performed literally hundreds of times as a cadet, and now, across the years, the generations would connect once again on the Plain. This time, he would stand atop the reviewing stand and they would pass in review for him.

The cadet who had shaken the stony foundations of the rock-bound highland home had returned to find the place changed. As he watched the cadet battalions pound through the sally ports, he could see the occasional dark expanse of cadet neck where female hair was pinned under the full dress hat of the cadet parade uniform. The old tennis courts across from the library were gone, and Thayer Road no longer bisected the Plain.

But so much had remained the same. It was bloody stinking West Point hot, the way Slaight remembered it had been in the Septembers of his cadet years—the kind of heat that wilted the crease in cadet dress white trousers the moment they were put on; heat that caused the wool jackets of the full dress gray uniform to smell like a barnyard. He looked up at the gothic chapel, standing high above the barracks atop its rocky promontory like a medieval military fantasy. The stone barracks across the Plain from him were as stately and austere as he remembered them. As battalions came on line across the broad expanse of the Plain, the cadets themselves were still ruddy-cheeked and ramrod straight, and they marched with a proud precision that paid homage to the generations who had done exactly what they were doing so many, many times before them.

Four thousand cadets in a row of four regiments broken down into three battalions each stood at attention before him. Not for nothing, Slaight mused, was it called the Long Gray Line.

Slaight was standing to the right of General Edward Jay Meuller,

the Chief of Staff of the Army. The Commandant, Brigadier General
Gibson, stood to his left. The Cadet First Captain took the report
from the Cadet Adjutant and spun around to face the reviewing
stand.

"Sir, the Corps of Cadets is all present and accounted for!" he
barked, as he executed a snappy salute with his saber. Slaight took
a single step forward.

"Pass in review!" he commanded.

The First Captain wheeled around and shouted, "Pass in review!"

Starting with the First Battalion of the First Regiment, cadet commanders barked the orders that would send their respective units
marching across the Plain in front of the reviewing stand. First came
the Brigade Staff, followed by the First Regimental Staff, which preceded the First Battalion Staff, which led the First Battalion. Slaight,
and indeed all of the officers on the reviewing stand and in the
bleachers, stood and saluted as each battalion executed its snappy
"Eyes . . . RIGHT!"

General Meuller, a robust, barrel-chested man with bushy white
eyebrows and twinkling blue eyes, waited until two battalions had
passed before he nudged Slaight with his elbow and whispered, "I
still can't get used to hearing a young woman give the command
'Battalion . . . a-ten-shun.' "

Slaight chuckled. He had been the tactical officer of a cadet company in 1977, the year after women had first been admitted to West
Point, and he had still been there in 1979 when the first female
battalion commander shouted her first orders at a parade on the
Plain. "It won't be long before one of these young women will be
standing up there in Michie Stadium with four stars on her shoulders
giving the graduation address, sir."

He heard a chuckle from General Meuller and caught a sideways
glimpse of Gibson's face reddening beneath the visor of his cap.

"I want to be there when that happens," said General Meuller.

"I'll make sure you're invited, sir."

Just then the battalion immediately in front of the reviewing stand
marched off and executed a column right, then proceeded down the
Plain toward the west. Lying on the Plain where the battalion had
stood was a cadet who had dropped from the heat.

"Still leave 'em on the Plain till it's over?" asked General Meuller, turning to General Gibson.

"Yes sir. Medics will be out there as soon as the last battalion passes in review."

"Happened to me when I was a plebe," said General Meuller. "Same kind of day. Walking out on that Plain was like stepping into a goddamned frying pan. Sweat was pourin' down my face, and I felt my knees shaking. Next thing I knew, I was on a stretcher. I took shit from the yearlings clear past Christmas."

Slaight stifled a laugh. "I always thought it was that damn full dress hat squeezing your head that did it," he whispered.

"There's another one dropped, sir," said Gibson, nodding at a second cadet facedown on the grass as another battalion marched off. The last battalion came on line, leaving a third cadet crumpled on the turf.

When the final battalion had passed in review and was headed back to the barracks, three teams of medics carried stretchers onto the Plain and began treating the prone cadets. Slaight invited General Meuller to stay for lunch in the mess hall, but as the general shook hands with the officers and wives who had joined them on the reviewing stand he begged off, citing a staff meeting he had to attend that afternoon to get ready for a White House briefing the next day. Slaight followed the Chief of Staff down the steps from the reviewing stand and stood there as Gibson escorted him to his staff car. Samantha joined him.

"Watch him," she snarled. "Gibson's going to escort him back to his plane." Sure enough, the Commandant climbed into the rear seat of the staff car next to General Meuller, and they watched as the car sped away toward the North Gate. "Asshole." Samantha spat the word between clenched teeth.

"Aww, c'mon, hon. He's got the Academy's best interests at heart," joked Slaight.

"Yeah, and bears use a Kohler toilet instead of the woods."

Slaight laughed. In the distance, he saw two medics help one of the fallen cadets to his feet. "C'mon," he said, taking Sam's hand. They started walking across the Plain toward the cadet who had dropped in front of the reviewing stand. There was a stretcher on the ground and two medics were bent over the cadet. One of them, a specialist with a mustache that struggled to cover his upper lip, making him look even younger than he probably was, had a look of panic on his face. Slaight broke into a run, Samantha close behind.

When they reached the medics, one of them was speaking excitedly into a handheld radio, calling for a doctor. Slaight looked down at the cadet. She was lying on her back, her eyes were open, and her face was drained of color. She opened her mouth, gave a little gasp, and shivered, as though she'd been hit with a blast of cold air. Then she was still. The medic with the mustache felt her pulse and pressed his ear close to her mouth.

"Cardiac arrest!" Quickly he began CPR. He pulled her head back and cleared her airway. Then he pinched closed her nostrils and started mouth-to-mouth. The other medic threw down the radio and started unbuttoning her full dress coat. He exposed her chest and started the rhythmic process of cardiac massage.

A siren sounded somewhere in the distance and grew louder. In a moment, an ambulance skidded to a halt next to them. Two medics and a doctor rushed forward carrying a portable defibrillator. The doctor, a young captain, rubbed the paddles together as the machine powered up. "Clear!" he shouted, placing the paddles on the sides of the young woman's chest. Her body jerked involuntarily as a jolt of electricity surged through her abdomen. The medic immediately restarted mouth-to-mouth while the doctor felt for a pulse. "Nothing. Let's try again." He rubbed the paddles together, watching the control panel of the defibrillator. A red light blinked off and a green light began flashing. "Clear!" he called. Then he gave the prostrate cadet another jolt.

Slaight squatted next to the cadet's body. Her eyes were glassy. He took her hand. Still kneeling, the doctor felt for a pulse, then he gently touched the shoulder of the medic. The medic stopped giving mouth-to-mouth. The doctor looked over at the Superintendent. He squinted into the bright sun and licked his lips. "She's gone, sir."

CHAPTER 2

S LAIGHT SAW two officers running toward him. They halted and snapped salutes.

"Colonel Rafferty, sir. I'm the Regimental Tac."

"Major O'Donnell, sir. H Company tactical officer. How is she?"

Slaight returned salute and glanced at the doctor, who was slipping the paddles into slots on either side of the defibrillator. "I don't think I caught your name, doctor."

He straightened up with a start. "Captain Miles, sir."

Slaight turned to the tactical officers. "Captain Miles has pronounced this young woman dead. May I ask her name?"

Major O'Donnell blinked his eyes repeatedly. His mouth opened, but no words came out.

"Major?" Slaight asked gently. "Are you okay?"

The major nodded vacantly. He coughed, bringing his hand to his mouth. "Sir, her name is Dorothy Hamner. She's a first-class cadet, from upstate New York."

"Thank you, Major." He turned to the regimental tac. "Colonel Rafferty, will you call the Provost Marshal and the Staff Judge Advocate? I want an immediate and thorough investigation of this incident."

"Yes sir." The two tactical officers stood there for a moment, looking down at the body of Cadet Dorothy Hamner.

"Gentlemen," Slaight said sternly. "Today."

"Yes sir," said Colonel Rafferty. They walked away at a brisk pace.

For the first time in several moments, Slaight became aware that Samantha was still standing next to him, her hands clasped together as if in prayer. "Sam, this is going to take some time."

She looked at him blankly. "It was too hot for a parade, Ry."

"I'll walk you back to the quarters." He took her hand, but she pulled quickly away.

"You've got work to do. If there's some way I can help, let me know. Maybe we should send a car for her mother and father."

"That's a good idea. Why don't you call Melissa and tell her to have a staff car standing by," he said, referring to his secretary.

"Sure." She took a step backward, then she reached for him. "Ry, this has never happened before, has it?"

"No. There's never been a cadet who died at parade. Never in the history of the Academy."

"It's so sad," she said. She touched his wrist, then she turned and headed across the Plain.

"Yes, it is," he said quietly to himself.

Even though the congressional appointment process ensures that West Point classes are composed of students from all fifty states and a wide variety of backgrounds, there are certain truths about West Pointers that apply nearly across the board. One of them is that returning to West Point as the Supe would be for most, but not all, a dream come true.

To be appointed Supe was to have the Army and the Academy itself recognize that your service to the nation as an Army officer had a strong component that came from West Point, and indeed that celebrated the Academy and all that it stood for. It meant that the Academy motto, "Duty, Honor, Country," was in your bones. It meant that your country trusted you to see to it that the principles of the Academy were conveyed to the cadets who would pass through its gates just as those principles had been conveyed to you when you were young and eager for an Army career. This was not something that Slaight took lightly. In fact, he knew the day they told him he was appointed Supe that his dedication to the cadets who were his charges would become his very reason for being.

And now he stood on the Plain on his first day as the Superintendent of the United States Military Academy in the blast-furnace heat of a September midday sun, and he could feel sweat darkening his dress white uniform, and he could feel the stares of those who surrounded the young woman lying dead upon the ground. Suddenly, even as the crowd around him grew larger and more curious and noisy, Slaight felt very, very alone.

Since 1802, the job had remained the same. There was only one Supe at a time, and now it was his turn.

He looked at the body of the young woman at his feet. In the history of West Point, no cadet had ever died at parade, and yet there she lay, on the morning of his first day as Supe. While it was in the nature of the job for an Army officer to live in the presence of death, it was never easy. As a cadet, there had been David Hand. As a young infantry lieutenant, he had lost two men in his stateside platoon, one to a heroin overdose and the other to a shotgun blast in the stomach, received as he attempted a drug buy in downtown Colorado Springs. Later, in Vietnam, his platoon had suffered multiple casualties, three of them deaths. He had classmates who had given their lives in Vietnam. He had classmates who had lost their lives to AIDS. As a battalion and brigade commander, he had consoled the parents of teenage children who had died in automobile accidents and accidental drownings. He had struggled to help his wife Samantha cope when her father, Judge Hand, died in his sleep in his Garden District house in New Orleans. Just two years before, while he was commanding an infantry division on maneuvers, a Blackhawk helicopter carrying twelve troops and two pilots had flown into a hillside in the midst of a sudden thundershower at night, killing everyone on board. In many ways, Slaight was as prepared as any man or woman could be when confronted with a sudden and unexpected death. And yet, as it had every other time someone died, death came as a violent shock to his system. It was as if he were greeting death anew every single time. It seemed that God had intended it to be that way.

For a fleeting moment, he felt twinned with her. She was lying on the Plain, as alone in death as he was standing there beside her in life. He shook off the feeling, because it was not true. She was gone, and he had just arrived. Her days as a cadet had ended and his as Supe were beginning.

He felt a hand on his shoulder and turned to find the round, bespectacled face of Colonel T. Clifford Bassett, head of the Department of Law. Bassett had been Slaight's military attorney when he was a cadet who was in a great deal of trouble with the Commandant of Cadets, General Hedges. And now here he was, a professor of law at the place that had confounded the two of them so many years before.

"Cliff. It's you," Slaight said absently.

"Is there something I can do, General?" asked Bassett.

Slaight thought quickly and led Bassett away from the crowd that had gathered around the body of the young woman. "Yes, there is," he said in a low voice. "You can tell me what you know about the Provost Marshal and the Staff Judge Advocate."

"Lieutenant Colonel Gene Percival's the Provost Marshal. He's . . . uh . . . competent. The SJA is Colonel Mike Lombardi. He's as sharp as they come."

"Do they get along?"

Bassett chuckled. "After a fashion."

"Here's what I'd like you to do. Lombardi's going to be in overall charge of investigating this tragedy, with Percival reporting to him. I'd appreciate it if you'd quietly ride herd on the two of them, let me know how you think they're doing. Could you do that?"

"A little unorthodox, but I'll certainly do what I can."

"Thing is, I don't know either of these guys, and you do. I want to make sure they dot the i's and cross the t's. We've got a dead female cadet, Cliff. The flare's going up on this one."

"You're right about that, I'm sure. I'll keep an ear to the ground for you."

"Thanks."

A staff car pulled up next to the ambulance and both rear doors opened.

"I'm going to slip off. I don't want to get in the way," said Bassett, moving through the crowd as two officers got out of the staff car and approached Slaight.

They saluted. "Colonel Lombardi, sir. SJA."

"Lieutenant Colonel Percival, sir. I'm the Provost Marshal."

Slaight returned salute. "An awkward time to be making your acquaintance, gentlemen. But here we are."

"I've got the CID Special Agent in Charge on the way, sir," said Percival. "His name is Chief Warrant Officer Jim Kerry. He's a good man."

A brace of MPs poured out of another staff car and began moving the crowd from the area. Slaight and the two colonels walked through the MP perimeter. Captain Miles had put away the defibrillator and was standing next to the body.

He saluted. "What do you want my people to do with the body, sir?"

Lieutenant Colonel Percival spoke first: "I've got the CID on the way, Major. Is this the position she fell in?"

Captain Miles turned to the medic with the mustache. "Specialist Thompson, is this the way you found her?"

"No sir. She was facedown."

"You turned her over to administer aid, am I correct?" asked Percival.

"Yes sir."

"All right then. Let's not disturb the body further until the CID has had a look."

"Do you want me to stand by, sir?" asked Captain Miles.

"Yes. Please keep your ambulance on hand. We're going to transport her up to the hospital for an autopsy before long."

"Yes sir," Miles replied.

Slaight signaled the colonels and stepped away from the body. "I want an interim written report on my desk by close of business today. Can you see to that, Colonel Lombardi?"

"Yes sir. Will do."

"I don't mind pointing out to you gentlemen that this incident is going to attract more than what is perhaps its fair share of attention. I'm going to personally notify the Chief of Staff, and I'm certain that the Pentagon will be hanging over your shoulders every step of the way. That's not to mention the press."

Lombardi's brow furrowed. "How do you want to handle them, sir? The press, I mean."

"We'll send them through the PAO as usual. There isn't any sign of foul play here. I think what we have on our hands here is a tragic accident, and we'll handle it the way we'd handle a training accident or a traffic fatality or any other kind of accidental death. Is that clear?''

"Yes sir," they chorused.

"I'll look for you at eighteen hundred hours, Colonel Lombardi."

"Yes sir. I'll be there."

Across the Plain, Slaight could see Samantha standing on the front porch of Quarters 100. When she saw him start across the Plain toward his office, she went inside.

Time has a way of slowing almost to a standstill in the midst of a crisis; this is especially true the older you get and the more rank you achieve. Sometimes Slaight thought that waiting was 90 percent of a general's job. It was one of his great frustrations. Once they put the stars on your shoulder, protocol dictated that you couldn't do it yourself anymore. He knew he'd spend the coming days and weeks waiting: waiting for the autopsy results. Waiting for the report from the CID Agent in Charge. Waiting for the recommendations of the Provost Marshal and the Staff Judge Advocate. He wished there was some way he could jump right on this thing and get it resolved and out of the way, but he knew there wasn't. And so he began the process of waiting for the others to do their jobs. His job would be to make sure they did them well.

CHAPTER 3

JACEY SLAIGHT looked up as the door to her room opened, and her roommate, Belle Carruthers, walked in wearing her bathrobe. She was a black woman with skin the color of polished mahogany, and she had an infectious smile that when she turned it on threw light into dark corners. She unwrapped the towel around her head and sat down on her bed.

"You should get out of that uniform and get yourself a shower, Jace. You look like you're gonna melt."

"Dorothy's dead, Belle," she said flatly.

"What?"

"I just got a call from the Tac. She died a few minutes ago."

"I can't believe it!"

"Get the plebes and have them run the rooms. I want you to call a meeting down in the sinks. As company commander, I'm going to have to make the announcement to the entire company."

"Right," said Belle. She tied her robe and went out the door. Belle was the Executive Officer, and part of her job was running the physical operations and scheduling for the company. She used plebes as messengers, a kind of human intercom. Soon, Jacey could hear plebe "minute callers" in the hallways, announcing the company meeting at the top of their lungs. Jacey unbuttoned her full dress gray coat and peeled off her sweat-soaked T-shirt. She grabbed a fresh one from her drawer and turned on the tap in the sink to wash her face. She looked in the mirror. Her auburn hair was braided into a tight twist and tucked up against the back of her head, the hairstyle that many female cadets chose instead of a short bob. She had prominent eyebrows and dark brown eyes and high cheekbones and a mouth that turned down slightly at the corners. Kids used to tell her she looked mad all the time, and the thing was, they were about half right. She had never been one who suffered fools gladly, and her high school years had been jam-packed with fools. One of the things she had liked about West Point right away was the fact that teenage foolishness wasn't tolerated, was in fact actively discouraged.

When she was a kid, she had never thought of herself as beautiful, or even attractive, and moving from one high school to another, she had never stayed in any one place long enough to fit in with the crowd. But by her yearling year at West Point, the soft contours of her childhood had been sharpened into the kind of dark allure that men, especially those a few years older than herself, found irresistible.

But having just returned from the steaming parade ground, irresistible she was not. She splashed water on her face and quickly ran a brush through her hair and pulled on the fresh T-shirt. Company meetings were informal gatherings, but it seemed only fitting to pay Dorothy Hamner the respect of appearing before her company mates in dress attire to make the announcement that she had died. She quickly zipped up her dress gray coat and headed for the stairs, but stopped herself outside her door. Just down the hall was Dorothy's room. She walked slowly to the door and knocked. She heard the voice of Dorothy's roommate, Carrie Tannenbaum: "Come in."

Jacey opened the door. "Carrie . . ."

"How's Dorothy? Is she okay?" Carrie was standing at the sink, washing her hands. Jacey took a step. Carrie's face crunched into a grimace of pain as she saw the look on Jacey's face.

"I'm sorry, Carrie. She's gone." Carrie collapsed to her knees. Jacey gently took her hand and led her to the bed, where they sat down. Carrie was sobbing softly as Jacey tried her best to comfort her. "It's so awful."

Carrie turned her head. Her cheeks were streaked with tears. "What happened?"

"They don't know yet."

The door opened, and Belle stepped into the room. "Everybody's ready downstairs, Jace."

Jacey squeezed Carrie's hand. "You don't have to come, Carrie. Just stay here. I'll be back in a few minutes to check on you."

"Thanks, Jacey," said Carrie.

Jacey followed Belle downstairs, where the hundred-and-some members of Company H-3 had gathered in the empty storage room that was used for company meetings. The plebes were seated stiffly on benches, all of them in proper uniforms of one kind or another. The upperclasses were standing in the back, or lounging against the side walls, and they were attired in everything from jogging clothes to bathrobes to old and tattered jean shorts and ARMY T-shirts. It was the prerogative of the upperclasses to bend and twist the collection of cadet uniforms into what passed for individuality. This was especially true of firsties, or seniors, who in their fourth year as cadets had turned the science of cadet dress into an art form.

Jacey looked toward the back of the room. Her boyfriend, Ashford Prudhomme, was leaning against a metal locker. He was wearing an Aussie bush hat and a pair of cutoff camouflage pants and a T-shirt with the "Screaming Eagle" of the 101st Airborne Division emblazoned on its front. He might have looked like a refugee from the Willis and Geiger catalog were it not for the crooked grin that crossed his handsome features.

Belle cleared her throat and announced in a loud voice, "May I have your attention, please? Jacey's got something to say to the company, and I'm going to ask for your undivided attention." She turned to Jacey and nodded.

"It's my sad duty to tell you that Dorothy Hamner died a few moments ago out on the Plain."

The room was completely silent. She heard whispers and one or two agonized moans, then a wail of pain filled the room as one of Dorothy's best friends, Stella Angelo, fell into the arms of the young woman next to her. Jacey pushed through the cadets gathered around her.

"I'm so sorry, Stella. We're all here for you."

Stella looked at her, red-faced, tears pouring down her cheeks. "I saw her fall. She was standing right in front of me. But she was moving, Jacey! I saw her! She was alive when we marched off!"

Jacey looked around at the other cadets. "Is that right? Did anyone else see her move?"

One or two cadets nodded. A plebe raised his hand. "Epstein? What do you want to say?" asked Jacey.

The plebe stood up. He was a skinny, awkward guy with a pimply face and red hair. "I saw her, too, ma'am. She fell straight down, then I saw her lift her head. She tried to say something, but I couldn't hear what it was."

"Anybody else?"

Another hand went up. Nancy Taylor was a yearling, a pretty girl with freckles and the alert, wide-set eyes of an outdoorswoman. "I heard her breathing real hard before she dropped."

"Like what, Nancy?" asked Jacey.

"It was like desperate panting, like it was hard for her to get a breath."

Jacey took Stella's hand. "Did Dorothy say anything to you in ranks before parade? I mean, like, that she wasn't feeling well?"

"She didn't say much. She was kind of quiet, but that's nothing new. Dorothy could be that way sometimes."

Jacey squeezed her hand. "There's going to be a CID investigation. Those of you who were close to Dorothy in ranks and saw what happened, I want you to remain in the barracks and make yourselves available to the investigators. Understand?" Heads nodded. "The rest of you, I don't want to hear any rumors spread around about Dorothy Hamner."

A hand went up. "What do you mean, spreading rumors, Jace?" asked a fellow firstie.

"I mean I don't want anybody in this company going around the battalion floating bogus theories about how Dorothy died. There's going to be an autopsy. There will be an investigation. Her parents are being notified. We'll know for sure what happened to her pretty soon, but until the investigation is finished, I don't want any speculation polluting the atmosphere. Understood?" Heads nodded. "All right, dismissed."

She found Belle waiting for her in the basement hall. Belle whispered, "Are you thinking what I'm thinking, Jace?"

Jacey answered, "Something's wrong. We've had parades on days when it was a lot hotter than it was today, Belle. Dorothy shouldn't have *died* out there."

"I'll see you back in the room."

"Be right with you," said Jacey. She waited until Belle had disappeared around the corner, then she stepped into one of the basement phone booths, dropped a quarter in, and dialed the office number of her law professor. "Captain Patterson, it's Jacey Slaight. Sir, we just got the news that the girl on the Plain, she's dead. She was one of my classmates, sir. In my company. The reason I'm calling is, I want to know what you think I should do."

She listened to his advice for several moments, then she thanked him, hung up the phone, and headed up the stairs to her room.

"Belle, round up a couple of plebes. I want everybody who was close to Dorothy in ranks to report to me immediately. We're going to take their statements and write them up. I want to get them when their recollections are as fresh as possible."

"You talked to Captain Patterson, didn't you?"

"Sure. Wouldn't you?"

"In a Brooklyn minute," said Belle, heading out the door.

CHAPTER 4

CHIEF WARRANT OFFICER Jim Kerry was a weary veteran of the Army's Criminal Investigation Division, the outfit on every Army post that served as adjunct professional criminologists to the Military Police. At forty-four, he had twenty-two years service, having entered the Army after two years in the sheriff's department in Leadville, Colorado. He had been one of those "wanna see the world" recruits who had been promised a tour in Germany when he enlisted, and it was originally his intention to serve out his enlistment, get out, return to Colorado, and run for sheriff, using his military experience in his campaign. But when his boss told him he could attend the Army's criminology school and emerge as a warrant officer, he jumped at the opportunity.

As a military assignment, West Point was supposed to be what they called in the Army a "good deal." It was a small post, populated in large measure by married officers and their families. The enlisted cadre numbered only a few hundred. Most of them had been handpicked for the assignment, so crime at the Academy was nearly nonexistent. CWO Kerry planned on serving out this last tour at West Point and retiring. There were openings in police departments up and down the Hudson Valley. He'd made a lot of friends, and his wife liked the area, since she came from northwest Connecticut, only an hour away.

When the call came that a cadet had dropped dead on parade, Kerry grabbed his black bag of crime-scene tools. The death of a female cadet meant it would be only a matter of hours before he felt the breath of the Pentagon on his neck.

He arrived at the Plain to find that the MPs had set up a neat perimeter around the incident site. The girl was on her back, right where she fell, according to the medics who had administered CPR. The doctor on the scene, a captain out of the University of Maryland whom Kerry had encountered once or twice around the hospital, told him that she had been turned over in order to administer CPR, and her full dress coat had been opened and her head tilted back to enable mouth-to-mouth. No one had touched her rifle or the rest of her uniform. Her full dress hat had apparently come off in her fall.

Kerry knelt down next to her. She was ashen, already turning blue. "How did she appear when you got here?" he asked the medics.

The one with the mustache spoke up. "She looked like she was in shock," he said in a squeaky, high-pitched voice.

"What's your name, soldier?"

"Singer, sir."

"Was her face flushed?"

"No sir. White as a sheet."

"How do you figure that, Captain Miles?" he asked the doctor.

Miles paused for a moment before he spoke. "I'm an emergency specialist. I haven't been in the Army long, but I've treated more cases of heat prostration than I'd care to think about. I've seen them as red as beets. I've seen them the color of blue denim. I've seen them so damp with sweat you'd think they just stepped out of a pool. I've seen them dry as a piece of sun-baked concrete. But I've never seen one like this. She was cold, and clammy."

"Any ideas?"

"I'm not even going to hazard a guess. We're going to have to wait for a full pathological workup."

"Anybody talk to the cadets who were standing nearby?"

"They're already back in the barracks," said a deep voice. Kerry turned to find a major standing over him. "I'm Major O'Donnell, her company Tactical Officer."

Kerry stood up and shook hands. "I'm going to want to talk to those cadets, sir," he said.

"I'll see to it they remain in the barracks today until you've interviewed everyone you need to."

"Thank you, sir."

He stooped down and lifted one of her hands. It was cold. He nodded to Captain Miles. "You can have your people move the body to the hospital, doc."

"Do you want me to notify Major Vernon?" he asked, referring to the pathologist assigned to the West Point hospital.

"I already gave her a call. She'll be waiting when you get there."

"Right," said Miles. The medics picked up the body of Dorothy Hamner, moved her to a stretcher, and carried her to the awaiting ambulance. Its siren shrieked as the ambulance pulled away, leaving Kerry standing in the middle of the circle of MPs on the Plain.

GENERAL SLAIGHT hung up the phone and reached for the insulated pitcher of ice water he kept on the corner of his desk. He poured a glassful and drained it quickly. His call to the father of the dead cadet had been painful, as those kinds of things usually are. What's the right way to tell a parent long distance that his child has died? He had made the same kind of call before, more times than he cared to remember. And of course he had written the requisite letters from Vietnam. It seemed as if it got harder every time.

The staff car would pick up the parents in Oneonta in the morning. They would proceed directly to the Supe's office, and from there to the hospital to make the formal identification. He had told his aide to call the hospital and speak to Major Vernon to make sure that the body could be released to the parents within forty-eight hours. They would spend tomorrow night in the Hotel Thayer and accompany the body back upstate the following day.

"Melissa, get me the Chief of Staff, will you?" Slaight called through the open door leading to his secretary's office. "I think he's probably still airborne on his way back to Washington. Call his office at the Pentagon. They'll patch you through to the plane."

"Will do," said Melissa.

Slaight heard the muffled sounds of her voice, talking to the Pentagon on the phone. Her name was Melissa Grant, and she was a retired master sergeant he had brought with him from his last assignment, commanding an infantry division out at Fort Riley, Kansas. Her husband was the motor sergeant down at the post motor pool and they had three kids, all of them under ten. She was a model of order and calm amid the chaos of everyday Army life.

He walked over to the window. Across Thayer Road cadets were flooding out of the barracks and into the mess hall for the noon meal. An announcement would be made from the Poop Deck that Cadet Dorothy Hamner had passed away on the Plain at parade that morning. The Corps of Cadets would bow their heads in a moment of silence, then the waiters would push carts full of trays out of the kitchen and the din of the cadet mess would return. For the Corps of Cadets, life would return to what passed for normal.

The Supe, however, had a creepy, tingly sensation at the back of his neck that told him things were going to be anything but normal at West Point until the cause of her death was established. In the thirty years it had taken him to become a lieutenant general, he had developed a finely tuned sense for which incidents would turn into a crisis, and which ones would not. He knew the incident on the Plain would test him, and moreover, it would test the Academy itself.

He wondered aloud, "I wonder if the old place is up to it?" He truly didn't know the answer to his own question. He had just begun his five-year term as Supe. Along with getting acquainted with the senior officers who ran the academic departments at the Academy, he had inspected the barracks and interviewed the new Cadet First Captain and his brigade staff. One night, in civilian clothes, he drove to Highland Falls and talked to a few off-duty firsties who were having a beer in one of the bars downtown. They didn't recognize him, so he heard what he assumed was something of the unvarnished truth from the cadets, and he had been relieved to make the discovery that their gripes mirrored fairly accurately his own when he was a cadet.

Even though West Point had gone through the revolution of admitting women in the mid-seventies, it was an institution that had changed very little over the years. Its mission had remained the same:

Knowledge of power and the way it was exercised in the United States Army was passed from one generation to the next. Slaight had experienced unit commands at company, battalion, brigade, and finally division levels, and he had watched West Point disgorge successive classes of brand new second lieutenants into the ranks of the officer corps. It comforted him to know that over the last thirty years, West Point had continued to provide the Army with reliable, dedicated, even inspired leaders.

Despite the changes it had gone through, West Point had remained true to its past. It was an institution of higher learning, and it conveyed bachelor degrees upon its graduates, but it was not a *college* in the ordinary sense of the word. When he was a plebe, the upperclassmen had told him over and over again that West Point was *a way of life,* and during his four years as a cadet, he had learned that the upperclassmen's assessment was true as far as it went.

But he had learned something else about West Point during the time he had struggled to discover who killed David Hand, and he had never forgotten it. West Point was a place of many, many questions and relatively few answers.

He came by this realization during his yearling year, when he spent nearly every night staying up late, sitting around the barracks room occupied by two disgruntled firsties, Mayer and Holman, cadet buck sergeants who introduced him to the phrase "believing the bullshit." This was cadet slang for blindly accepting what West Point called the "approved solution," whether to an engineering problem, or a military field exercise, or the confounding puzzles of everyday Army life. Slaight came to accept the premise that the questions that he confronted each day were many and profound, while the answers provided by the Academy were few and simplistic and sometimes just plain wrong—in other words, "bullshit."

So it was as a cadet that he had come to see West Point as a kind of separate reality. Within the walls there was a way of life that could be depicted accurately only in cadet slang. Plebes were "beanheads." Yearlings were "indifferent." Cows were "hard-asses." Firsties were "over it." You were "slugged" with demerits for misbehavior. Anything that was unexpectedly positive and without visible strings attached was "a good deal." Girls were "hens." To ramble with one's buddies and have a good time was to "motley." An attractive girl who didn't give you much grief was "a motley hen."

The stifling, confining nature of the Academy produced a glue holding cadets close together that went way beyond the conventional notions of bonding. To be a cadet was to be apart from the "real world" outside West Point's gates. This was a reality that would mark each and every graduate differently, but only slightly so, for they all had the shared experience of life behind the walls, where the world they knew had only one color, gray.

Slaight sat down at his desk and propped his feet on the edge of an open drawer. The notion that at age nineteen or so he had actually sat in a barracks room and talked for hours about the mysteries surrounding two entirely separate realities—the real world outside the gates and the false, hermetically sealed world within—seemed bizarre to him now that he was the man in charge of the cadet rooms in which he had no doubt that such discussions still took place. There was a phrase back in the sixties. It was a hippie saying, but inevitably it had filtered through the gates and into cadet consciousness: *What goes around, comes around.*

"Sir, I've got the Chief for you on line one." Melissa's voice boomed through the door, jarring him from his thoughts. He picked up the phone.

"General Meuller, this is General Slaight." He addressed the Chief of Staff formally, because protocol demanded it. Meuller was a four-star, and Slaight was a three-star. In the Army, rank ruled. "I thought you'd want to be informed as soon as possible that there was a serious incident today at the pass in review. The cadet who dropped on the Plain directly in front of the reviewing stand? It was a young woman, and she has died, sir."

The Chief of Staff asked him a couple of quick questions and he told him that the parents had been notified and the CID investigation was already under way. Then the Chief said something Slaight found extraordinary.

"I recommended you to the President as Supe for a reason, Ry. I've watched you navigate rocky roads before. I told the President you've got a solid chassis and a good set of shock absorbers on you. Now's the time to prove me right. We've got some problems with the Congress, Ry. This guy Thrunstone over at the House National Security Committee has been rattling his saber all over town, talking about cutting Army manpower, moving defense-budget money around so he and his pals can spend less on warm bodies and more on the weapons systems they like so much in the Congress. He has even been floating the idea of closing down the service academies or consolidating them. The last thing we need is for this incident to get blown out of shape and start whetting Thrunstone's appetite for wreaking havoc on our forces, or on the Academy. Are you getting my drift?"

"Yes sir."

"You're going to have to handle this thing just right. I don't want it blowing up in our faces."

"Yes sir."

"Very well. Keep me informed."

"Yes sir."

Slaight heard a click as the Chief of Staff hung up.

So that's it, he thought to himself. On his first official day as Supe, a female cadet dies at parade and the Chief of Staff informs him that a very powerful congressman is talking about shutting down West Point.

Welcome home.

CHAPTER 5

MAJOR ELIZABETH VERNON was a slightly built woman of thirty-seven years with dark brown hair and piercing blue eyes. She was an Army brat who had been born in Japan, graduated in one of the early classes of women at West Point, and served a couple of years in the Transportation Corps before earning a slot to attend New York University Medical School. She had done her first year of residency at Harlem Hospital before transferring to an Army hospital in Arizona. Her first specialty had been emergency medicine, and experience at patching up accident victims and nineteen-year-old corporals with stab wounds had led her naturally into pathology.

An assignment to the West Point hospital was the first time in her career that she had been put in charge of her own department. It wasn't much, actually—just three small rooms in the basement of the hospital. Her tiny office had a window to an outside alley near the top of the wall behind her desk, which afforded an excellent view of the underside of delivery trucks. Her staff consisted of a single nurse, Lieutenant Stephani Duffy, and a specialist clerk about as functional as the generation-old computer they'd been issued.

But she made do. Her lab room was a testament to what could be done with small spaces, a skill she had developed when she lived for a time in a travel trailer as a lieutenant. The autopsy room had a four-drawer refrigeration unit, and a single stainless steel pathology table was positioned beneath an operating room light she had scavenged when an influx of federal dollars had updated the operating rooms the year before.

West Point was a pretty quiet place for an Army pathologist. In over a year of duty at the hospital, her sleep had been disturbed only once by an emergency call. To be sure, there had been a few automobile-accident deaths, and over the winter, an outbreak of diarrhea at the post grade school had confounded parents and teachers alike, until Major Vernon traced its cause to a ditch behind one of the housing areas on post where children played after school. The ditch was contaminated with raw sewage, an accidental overflow from the post sewage-disposal plant that had occurred during heavy rains. They had cleaned up and fenced off the ditch, and the gradeschool kids' bowels returned to their normal digestive rhythms.

When Major Vernon received the call from Chief Warrant Officer Kerry that a female cadet had been stricken at parade and was dead, she had been flooded with memories of her days as a cadet. The cause was probably heatstroke, she quickly surmised. She remembered those incredibly hot parades during the summer and fall months, when the Hudson Valley would seem like a gigantic reflector oven. She had never dropped at a parade herself, but she had seen quite a few cadets crumple around her, male and female alike. While no one had ever died at parade, heat prostration was common enough that cadets even joked about it. If you dropped at parade, you were a "dropper." She prepared the autopsy room and awaited what she felt should be a rapid, uncomplicated examination.

The ambulance pulled up to the emergency-room entrance almost exactly an hour after the young woman had collapsed. Major Vernon knew this because she knew when the parade had been scheduled, and parades at West Point always went off on time. The body of the young woman was on the table five minutes later. The first thing they did was strip her and insert a rectal thermometer to get an immediate reading of her body temperature. If she had died about sixty minutes before, and if the cause had been respiratory arrest and heart stoppage due to heatstroke, she figured the body temperature would still be well above normal—103 or 104, down from a peak temperature that might have exceeded 107.

She removed the rectal thermometer. The young woman's temperature was two degrees below normal. There was not the slightest indication of heatstroke.

"Stephani, we've got a problem here," Major Vernon said to the nurse standing next to her. "Let's begin by reserving at least a unit of her blood. I have a feeling we're going to be using the lab quite a bit on this one."

"Yes ma'am," said Lieutenant Duffy, rolling the implement cart to the side of the table.

CHIEF WARRANT OFFICER Kerry drove the staff car up the ramp from Thayer Road and parked next to Sherman Barracks. There was a broad expanse of immaculate concrete between matching sets of barracks that had been built in 1960, when the Corps had begun an expansion from about three thousand cadets to its present strength of four thousand.

Kerry was directed by the Company H-3 Charge of Quarters, a yearling with negligible authority but plenty of chutzpah, to a room on the second floor. He knocked on the door, and the young woman he knew to be the Supe's daughter answered.

"I'm Jacey Slaight, the Company Commander. Please come in," she said. "This is my roommate, Belle Carruthers."

It wasn't often that Kerry had had occasion to visit a cadet room on official business. Disciplinary matters concerning the Corps of Cadets were either handled by the cadet chain of command or bumped up to the Tactical Department, where they came under the purview of the Commandant of Cadets. Only once in Kerry's experience had a cadet been arrested on post, and that was for speeding.

The room was a soberly decorated place, if decor could be said to have played a role at all. Recent changes to the cadet rule book had allowed the presence of a rug in the rooms of first-class cadets, but there wasn't one in this room. Uniforms were hung neatly in the wood closets at one end of the room, and matching metal desks faced the door at the far end. Single bunks were arranged on either side of the room, and they were expertly made up in the prescribed cadet fashion, which is to say, they looked as if no one had ever slept in them.

Jacey pointed to one of the bunks. "Please sit down, Chief Warrant Officer," she said formally.

Kerry looked down at the rigid surface of the blanket.

"It's okay," said Jacey. "Inspection's over."

He sat down and pulled a notebook from his pocket. "It's my job to run the investigation of the circumstances surrounding the death of Cadet Hamner. I want you to understand that even though I am an officer of the Criminal Investigation Division, this is not a criminal matter at the present time. However, a death on active duty is presumed to be a matter for law enforcement unless and until it is proven otherwise." He paused, looking directly at both of them. "Am I making myself understood?"

"Yes," said Jacey.

"I'm going to need to talk to any cadet who had knowledge of the circumstances involving Miss Hamner's collapse during parade. I'll need to talk to her roommate or roommates, and I'd like to hear any assessments you have of her as a member of your company." He shifted slightly on the bunk, trying to achieve a position that didn't cause him pain. He couldn't imagine how anyone could get to sleep lying on such an uncomfortable mattress. It wasn't so much a bed as it was a device designed for proper display of sheets and blankets. "Anything you can think of regarding Miss Hamner may prove helpful to us. I want you to feel free to say whatever's on your minds."

He saw them glance at each other before they spoke. It wasn't conspiratorial. Just nervous.

"I've spoken to the company about Dorothy," said Jacey. She picked up a stack of handwritten sheets and handed them to Kerry. "These are statements I took from everyone who was close to her both before and during the parade. I had them write down their recollections when they were as fresh as possible."

Kerry flipped through the pile of pages quickly. "You sound like you've been through this before," he said.

"Not really," said Jacey. "But they taught us in law class last year that witness recollections are stronger and more reliable the closer they're recorded to the event which precipitates them."

"Your law professor sounds like a pretty smart character."

"Captain Patterson is one of the best."

"I'll have a quick look at these statements and then I'd like to interview the cadets themselves."

"I'll have them waiting for you downstairs in the company meeting room." She looked over at her roommate. "Belle? Let's round them up. I'll meet you downstairs. I want them down there right away so we don't waste too much of Chief Warrant Officer Kerry's time."

"Sure," said Belle. She grabbed her cap and left. Jacey stopped at the door. "We want to do everything we can to help you find out what happened out there today."

Kerry watched her walk out the door without answering. This was one formidable young woman. It surprised him not in the least that her father was the Superintendent.

THE BODY of Cadet Dorothy Hamner had been dissected and lay faceup on the autopsy table. Her torso looked like someone had peeled away her skin to expose her soul, yet it was the mundane result of an ordinary autopsy that lay before Elizabeth Vernon and Stephani Duffy. The doctor had removed, examined, and sectioned the heart, removing material for microscopic examination later. But she could tell from her preliminary look at the heart itself that this had been a healthy young woman. A cursory look at the exterior of her lungs told Vernon Cadet Hamner had most likely never passed the working end of a cigarette between her lips. The lungs were of average size and weight.

She cut into and emptied the stomach, nearly filling a stainless steel specimen tray, to find the cadet mess hall breakfast in the process of digestion. There was no sign of vomit in the esophagus, nor were there signs of musculature strain, as if something had been vomited and blocked the airway, then been somehow exhaled and lost in the transportation of the body, a circumstance Vernon had come across in her career at least twice before.

In fact, absent any lab finding to the contrary, the gross exam of the body of the deceased produced what the doctor found to be not a terribly surprising result. She was a young woman in good health who had suffered a cardiac arrest of unknown origin.

Vernon removed and cut into one of the lungs. "Jesus, look at this," she said. Her major air passages were slightly constricted. "I'm going to section both lungs and have a look under the microscope. There's something going on here."

They worked on the lungs for about an hour, removing samples and sectioning and preserving them for later analysis. When she was finished with the lungs, Major Vernon said, "I want to have a look at the vaginal area before we close up the torso. Help me lift her legs."

Lieutenant Duffy and the major each grabbed a knee and bent it stiffly into shape, spreading the thighs in the process. The doctor took up a position at the foot of the autopsy table and carefully spread the young woman's labia.

"Look right here." She pointed to a red, swollen area at the opening of the vagina.

Lieutenant Duffy coughed and turned her head.

"Are you all right?" asked the major.

"Yes ma'am," answered Duffy.

"You want to stop for a minute?"

"No ma'am. I've been to the gynecologist. It's just, like, I've never *been* the gynecologist."

"Got you," acknowledged Vernon. "Do you want to take a minute?"

"No ma'am. I'll be okay."

"All right then, can you hold this area open for me? I want to get a couple of close-up photos of the abraded area."

Lieutenant Duffy used surgical clamps to hold open the vaginal entrance while Major Vernon photographed the area.

"I had a case like this back at Fort Huachuca," said Vernon. "A specialist got raped downtown. They beat her and drove her out in the desert and left her. Didn't find the body for two days. Turned out she never regained consciousness and died of exposure and lack of water. It was July. There's nothing hotter that Fort Huachuca in July."

"Yes ma'am, I've heard that," said Duffy. "I had a roommate from Phoenix in college."

"This young woman shows the same signs of vaginal trauma as the one in Arizona."

"Do you think she was raped?"

"I don't know. Female cadets stopped taking shit from male cadets years ago, and she would have reported a rape if it happened. But there's always a chance that she had been raped and chose not to report it immediately. After all, she died only four or five hours after awakening the next day. Maybe she was traumatized. Maybe she just needed some time. I guess now we'll never know what she was thinking."

"I wonder what really happened to her."

"Hand me a sterile slide, please, Stephani. We're going to find out." Vernon walked to a cabinet and came back with a speculum and inserted it in the vagina. "Swab, please."

Duffy handed her what looked like a long wooden Q-Tip, which she slid through the opening in the speculum, introducing it into the far reaches of the vagina. She took a sample and smeared it onto the slide.

"Again, please. One of each." She did the same thing with a new swab and a new slide, then repeated the procedure again. When she was finished with the slides, she used a suction device to remove a larger sample from the vagina, which she deposited in a test tube. Then she removed the speculum and they lowered the young woman's knees. Silently she began to stitch up the torso.

"We're going to have to send this stuff down to the Institute of Pathology at Walter Reed Army Medical Center. It's going to take a week or so to get the results, and until they come in, I want to keep this aspect of our inquiry quiet. Do you understand me?"

"Yes ma'am," said Lieutenant Duffy.

"I'll notify the Special Agent in Charge that we've shipped off these samples, but he's the only one I want informed until we get the results."

"Ma'am, can I ask why you want to keep this secret?"

"I don't want anyone getting wind of the fact that she has signs of sexual trauma. Somebody did this to her. I want that somebody to stew in his juice until we turn up the heat to boil."

CHAPTER 6

SAMANTHA SLAIGHT was sitting at her desk in what had once been a maid's room just off the pantry, which she had transformed into a private office. It was a small space, only about nine by nine feet square. There was a tiny adjoining bath, and her desk looked out a window onto the garden. She had arranged her office to be the place she went to run the family business, as it were: to pay the bills and answer mail and make the social plans that, because they comprised a fairly large part of the Superintendent's job, consumed an even greater part of her time. She didn't mind. Entertaining came naturally to a woman from New Orleans whose father had been a judge and, before that, a powerhouse in the city's legal and political communities, which were actually a single community in those days. She remembered that her mother still had a tiny office in the slave quarters behind their house in the French Quarter that she used for the same purpose. There was a cliché about southern belles and afternoon teas and cocktail parties and balls and ball gowns, but it didn't apply to New Orleans women, because most of the women her mother had known, and indeed her mother herself, were truly neither southern nor belles. New Orleans was located in the South but was not naturally of it. Samantha had once heard a cook who worked at Antoine's in the Quarter describe New Orleans in this way. He had a Creole accent, which mixed the weird Brook-lynese of the New Orleans working class with the rhythms of the Cajun French. Listening to him talk was like hearing an accordion in full wail: "See, there's this ocean nobody knows about, see, which begins way over there in the Mediterranean 'round 'bout Greece and Italy and France and Morocco and Tangier and such, and this ocean goes all way 'cross and ties into the Caribbean, see, 'round 'bout the islands of Martinique and Nevis and Antigua and St. Barts and such, and this ocean just keeps on goin' round the Florida Keys and then it heads right into the Gulf, see, and it goes right on up the Missis-sippi and it ends up right down there at the foot of Saint Peter Street, see?"

Precisely.

She was tapping at the keyboard on her laptop, sending an E-mail to a friend whose husband was over in Bosnia. Her friend had the geographical-widow blues after fifteen months during which her two teenagers had gone through the normal hormonal changes all teen-agers went through, made vastly more difficult by the absence of their father. The friend had E-mailed Samantha that she felt like a "cross between a maid and a shrink," a feeling Samantha had ex-perienced more than once. Samantha was writing the final lines of a hang-in-there-babe note when she heard the back door open. She leaned back in her chair and saw Jacey walk into the kitchen.

"Jace! In here!" she called from her office.

Jacey embraced her mother. "Mom, I had to come and talk to you. The girl who died today? She was in my company."

"Jace, I'm so sorry," Samantha said. "Let's get something to drink."

"I can't stay long," said Jacey. "I've got to get back to the com-pany. But I needed somebody to talk to, Mom. You don't mind, do you?"

"Of course not." Samantha poured them tall glasses of iced tea and they sat down on stools at a counter in the kitchen overlooking the garden. It was an extraordinary space, walled on three sides by elegantly trimmed hedges, planted with flowering shrubs and beds of perennials that began blooming in the early spring and still showed colors into late fall. Samantha ran her hands through her hair and gave her daughter an encouraging smile.

"Dorothy was a great kid, Mom. It's just so awful to think she's not there anymore."

Samantha put an arm around her daughter's shoulders. "Jacey, it's never easy when somebody dies. Remember when your grandfather passed away? It was so sudden and unexpected, I thought I'd never recover. It's the way people are, Jace. When somebody who's close to you dies, it's like a blow to your heart. You'll do all right, Jace. You'll see."

"It's still hard, Mom."

"Of course it is, darling. That's why you should talk to your dad. He knows about this kind of stuff. It's his job. It's been . . ." She took a deep breath, and her eyes wandered away from her daughter's face, across the garden, over to the barracks of North Area that loomed in the distance. "It's been his life, Jacey. There's no way you can go wrong talking to your father."

"Mom, that's why I had to talk to *you*. Don't you see? Daddy's the Supe now. People are watching everything I do. If I go running to my father, they're going to think I can't take it. I can't let that happen, Mom. I've got to deal with this on my own."

Sam leaned over and kissed Jacey on her cheek. "I understand, Jace. I know your father will, too. But just remember, if you need us—either of us—we're here."

"Thanks, Mom. You'll tell Daddy, won't you? I mean, I don't want him to think I'm avoiding him, but it's kind of like I have to. At least until we figure out how this is going to work, with me being a cadet and a company commander, and him being the Supe."

"It's going to work out okay, Jace. You'll see."

Jacey stood to leave, and Samantha marveled at the miracle that was her daughter. She and Ry had waited awhile before deciding to have a child, and now she was glad they had. To be able to experience your own daughter in full stride making her passage into adulthood was like nothing that she could have ever foreseen. She had always known that there was something really special between mothers and daughters, because she had felt that way about her own mother, now living alone and rattling around her huge Garden District house down in New Orleans like a pebble in a tin can. But you don't really know what it's like until you look back over the fence from the other side. Being a mother had its pain-in-the-ass component, but now came the payoff. She had ushered her daughter out the door into the care and feeding of West Point, and now she would be there when West Point ushered her through the gates into the care and feeding of the Army, and on to the care and feeding she would be doing on her own.

"Bye, Mom. And thanks."

"Bye, Jace. I love you."

The screen door shut with a gentle pop and silence settled over the house again. Never in her life had she spent so many hours listening to nothing more than the wind rustling leaves and whistling through the windows.

She missed the sometimes gentle, sometimes shattering din of young voices around the house, and there was a part of her that would never be able to see in the face of her daughter anything other than the innocence she glimpsed when she first held her baby girl in her arms. That was the thing about being a mother. At the close of the day she was left feeling that this was the biggest and best thing that had ever happened in her life, motherhood, and she suspected that at the close of her life the feeling would be exactly the same.

She thought of Dorothy Hamner's mother and the mothers of children who had been killed, interviewed on the news or the magazine shows. *Closure* was the word they used. Was this what they were seeking when they stood silent vigil in a courtroom, awaiting the conviction of a killer? Was it because they knew that the death of a child had left the door ajar, the door that would have led to the rest of the child's life?

The death of a daughter at Jacey's age . . . Samantha's imagination froze at the prospect of losing her own daughter. Inside her the sixth sense of motherhood raised a red flag. There were going to be consequences from the death of this young woman. Right now, she couldn't tell what they would be, but she knew they were out there, waiting.

CHAPTER 7

I T WAS because his secretary, Melissa Grant, had a formidable shit detector that Slaight had insisted she attend the briefing on the investigation given by the Provost Marshal and Staff Judge Advocate. When they arrived, Slaight put them quickly at ease, inviting them to take a pair of overstuffed armchairs that faced the dark brown leather sofa where he sat. Melissa was to one side, a yellow legal pad perched on her knee.

"What have you got for me?" Slaight asked.

Lieutenant Colonel Percival cleared his throat. "Chief Warrant Officer Jim Kerry is running things for the CID, sir. He's the Special Agent in Charge here on post. He has interviewed all of the cadets in Miss Hamner's company who witnessed her collapse on the Plain, sir, and he has forwarded his notes from the interviews to Major Vernon, who is conducting the autopsy. It's Kerry's feeling that the cadets' observations of Miss Hamner's behavior just previous to her collapse might help Major Vernon in her determination of cause of death. Agent Kerry reported that she was seen breathing heavily just before she fell, as if she couldn't catch her breath."

"Did the cadets in her company notice anything unusual about her before parade?"

"Apparently not. As you know, sir, your daughter is Hamner's company commander. She reported to him that Hamner's behavior was completely normal." He cleared his throat. "Incidentally, sir, Agent Kerry has told me that she was a big help. She personally took statements from all the cadets in the company who saw the young woman fall at parade."

"Thank you," said Slaight, allowing himself a twinge of pride.

"I've got a preliminary report from Major Vernon, sir," said Percival, reaching into his briefcase. He handed over a single sheet of paper, and Slaight scanned it quickly.

"This indicates that she has established a strong probability that the young woman did not die of heatstroke."

"Yes sir."

"What do you make of that, Colonel?"

"She indicates that we're going to have to wait for the results of certain lab tests she's running, sir, before we get anything solid."

"I understand that, Colonel Percival. I'm asking what you make of Vernon's initial determination that she apparently did not die from the effects of the heat. Another cause of death will emerge eventually. Do you have any speculation what that might be?"

"No sir."

"Let me ask you this. Has there been any evidence turned up over the last year concerning use of drugs by cadets?"

Percival glanced at Lombardi, who leaned forward in his chair. "The answer to that is negative, sir. As you probably know, we do urine tests on the Corps, the way they're done periodically on all active-duty soldiers in the Army these days. We haven't turned up any positive test results recently."

"What period of time are you talking about?"

"The last positive we got was two years ago from a new cadet candidate on the first day of Beast Barracks. He admitted having smoked marijuana several days before reporting to West Point. A determination was made that his behavior as a civilian was most probably an aberration, and he was admitted to the class, and he's still here. He stands in the top third of his class, and is a candidate for a cadet leadership position this semester."

"I see," said Slaight. "Anything else, gentlemen?"

"That's about it, sir," said Percival. "We've done everything we can do unless and until evidence of criminal wrongdoing results from Major Vernon's autopsy lab tests."

"How about the body?"

"Major Vernon will release it to the parents tomorrow afternoon, sir."

"Good." As Slaight stood, the colonels jumped to their feet in anticipation. They both reached for their hats and snapped salutes.

"Do me a favor, will you?" asked Slaight.

"Yes sir," Percival answered quickly.

"Inform me immediately if there are any developments—any at all. I'll tell my secretary to interrupt whatever I'm doing to take your call."

"Yes sir," said Percival. "Glad to, sir." Slaight waited until he could hear the sound of their leather heels on the stairs as they made their way quickly to street level.

"Melissa, get General Gibson on the phone for me, will you?"

"Right away, sir."

GENERAL GIBSON hung up his call from the Superintendent and looked out the windows of his office, on the top floor of Washington Hall. The windows looked north at the sweeping curve of the Hudson River as it snaked around Trophy Point.

Not even Slaight has a view like this, he thought to himself with satisfaction.

General Gibson was a handsome man, deeply tanned from the biweekly golf games he had made time for over the summer, with thick brush-cut graying hair. He had pale blue eyes and an intense way of looking at people when he spoke to them that was just shy of being intimidating. Yet when he turned on his smile, the word telegenic came to mind. Indeed, when Brigadier General Jack Gibson had been promoted to general a year ahead of the next man in his class and had been assigned straightaway to the Commandant's job, it had been taken in the Army as a sign that Gibson was one of that new breed of Army officers who could be counted on to represent the face of the modern Army to the nation. He was automatically seen as a man on a fast track to three or even four stars. Gibson himself had no doubt that he would achieve four-star rank. Indeed, he had his eye fixed firmly on the Army's top job: Chief of Staff. His mentor, a man named Cecil Avery who had served a term and a half on the National Security Council in the last Republican White House, and who was now ensconced in a so-called chair down at the Council on Foreign Relations waiting out the reign of the current Democratic occupant of the White House, had assured Gibson that if he could rein in his ambition in such a way that it did not stand beside him like another person in the room, he would be a shoo-in for Chief within five or six years.

Gibson had controlled his ambition with some inconvenience, for what would an Army officer amount to without the psychic sidearm you carried with you at all times? And yet, he knew Cecil Avery was right. Ambition was one of the weapons in your arsenal that you couldn't show. He knew the Army was funny that way. It was supposed to be a fraternity of warriors, soldiers who were trained to kill the enemy in as efficient a manner as possible, soldiers whose mission in life was to take the high ground and occupy it. Still, it seemed as if you could behave like a warrior against the enemy, but you had to behave like a damn gentleman with your fellow officers. You might be a killer by job description, but you were supposed to appear to your fellow officers and the rest of the world as a soldier-statesman, a man of quiet reserve and unquestionable ability, of patience and judgment, and in this day and age, even a dollop or two of political correctness.

That was the thing Gibson didn't like about Slaight. The new Superintendent was one of those politically correct bastards who owed his career to Meuller, the Chief of Staff, who, nearing the end of his term, was pushing the integration of women into the fighting force of the Army way too fast. Now there was a dead female at West Point, and he knew Slaight was going to go out of his way to assure Meuller and the top brass how much he and West Point *cared*. There would be a great show of politically correct backing and filling, and Gibson thought it was probable that careers would suffer because the young woman had died at parade, and that those with the suffering careers would be men. Watching Slaight ride herd over the investigation was going to make him sick.

Brigadier General Gibson had been born in North Carolina, and he liked to think of himself proudly as a son of the South. He had a brother who had gone to The Citadel, and an uncle who had graduated from VMI. His father had come from a tobacco-farming family, and, having received a law degree from the University of North Carolina, had worked the state's power structure expertly. He started out as an attorney for one of the major cigarette manufacturers, and was now counsel to the Governor and a major player in state politics.

You didn't come from a family like Jack Gibson's without having been steeped in the rituals and traditions of the Deep South. Gibson had driven a car with a Confederate flag license plate on the front bumper until a friendly brigade commander, himself a son of the South, pointed out to him that though about 40 percent of the Army's officer corps was comprised of southerners, 60 percent was not. He was bound to come across a general officer who did not share his love of the South's proudest symbol, the Confederate battle flag, and this political disagreement would end up affecting Gibson's Officer Efficiency Report, the Army's officer report card, which determined promotions, job assignments, and even changes of station.

So Gibson had removed the Confederate flag from his bumper. In doing so he had successfully concealed the most visible symbol of his hard-line conservative politics, which included his opinions about women in the Army. Gibson was one of those male officers who believed that skirts had no place on the battlefield. The presence of women in units that had contact with the front lines of combat was a trend that had progressed rapidly over the last ten years. Gibson felt women on the battlefield were detrimental to the combat effectiveness of the Army and a threat to the Army's ability to defend the nation.

Gibson's politics had made his assignment as Commandant of Cadets awkward, for West Point had somewhat ironically been on the front lines of female progress in the Army. Women had been admitted to the Corps of Cadets in 1976 and had thrived at the Academy. Even though West Point was a place that had been hidebound with tradition stretching back almost two hundred years, because of its high public visibility it was also a place that responded quickly to political pressure. If West Point had been seen as stiffly resistant to the admission of women, in the manner of The Citadel and VMI, the outcry would have been intense. Realizing this, West Point had put up a friendly public face and had moved quickly to integrate women into the Academy's theretofore male rhythms. And to what must have been the surprise of the next several Academy administrations, young American women had met the challenges of West Point, and then some. The Academy had produced one female first captain, and women filled leadership positions at all levels of cadet life. Female Academy graduates had served the Army with the same distinction as male graduates. While equality of the sexes would never be absolute in the Army, West Point had probably done more to advance it than any other military institution.

Brigadier General Gibson was aware of this, and so when he moved into the Commandant's office he immediately established himself as publicly friendly to the interests of women in the Academy.

In fact, a year previously, when he had escorted a crew from ABC TV's 20/20 through a tour of cadet life, he had made sure that the achievements of female cadets were featured prominently. The correspondent for 20/20 had been a woman, and he had played to her New York liberal media prejudices expertly. When the show aired, he came across as an exemplar of modern Army values. West Point was showing the way when it came to women in the Army, and Brigadier General Jack Gibson was leading the charge. There had been officers like Gibson in the Army before—men whose public personas belied private distaste for the political and social changes that had swept through the Army like a fast-moving train over the last thirty years. But Jack Gibson was really, really good at it. In another era, he would have made the cover of *Life* magazine. But a fifteen-minute segment on 20/20 was even better. Tens of millions of Americans had seen him on television and had apparently believed what they saw: a modern-day military man ready to become one of the top leaders in the twenty-first-century Army.

Gibson walked to his window. Down below, cadet joggers were circling the edge of the Plain, headed up Washington Road on the slow climb toward the North Gate. Over on Trophy Point, four MPs were folding the flag that they had lowered at Retreat. He picked up his cap and headed out the door.

*   *   *

SLAIGHT WAS seated behind his desk when Gibson was escorted into his office by Melissa Grant. Gibson snapped a salute and reported. Slaight returned salute and led the way to the sitting area across the office.

Neither man was happy that their first official meeting at the Academy concerned the death of a female cadet, but of the two, Slaight was probably the more unhappy, because if there was one man in the United States Army who knew the true political bent of the Commandant of Cadets, it was Slaight. He had been Gibson's commander ten years previously, when Slaight had been a lieutenant colonel and Gibson as a captain had commanded one of the companies in his mechanized infantry battalion. Female soldiers were already showing up in jobs that put them in direct contact with the entirely male infantry battalion Slaight and Gibson were in, and Gibson at that time had made no secret of his distaste for female soldiers and their presence in a combat division. In fact, Slaight recalled the Confederate flag Gibson had sported on his front bumper, and he recalled as well when it disappeared, along with the overt signs of Gibson's hostility to women in the Army. But reports from younger officers in Gibson's company kept filtering up to the battalion commander. Gibson held "manhood sessions" with his young charges at a country-and-western bar some distance from the post, at which copious quantities of beer were consumed and antifemale marching songs were sung. While all of the young officers went along with Gibson's program of machismo, several of them did so without enthusiasm. Among these were young West Point lieutenants who had graduated with female classmates and saw nothing wrong with the presence of women in the Army. So even as Gibson concealed his hostility to women from his superiors, his lieutenants concealed their disgust from him. The situation finally deteriorated to the point that Slaight felt it was necessary to call Gibson into his office and forbid the off-post shenanigans, an order with which Gibson vociferously disagreed.

It came as no surprise to Slaight when he learned that Gibson had successfully challenged the below-average Officer Efficiency Report Slaight had given him upon his departure from the battalion. Even then, Gibson made no secret of the fact that he had friends in high places, and apparently his friends had helped to quash Slaight's

OER, which would have ordinarily delayed Gibson's promotion to major.

Now the two former combatants faced each other across the coffee table in the office of the Superintendent of the United States Military Academy. Slaight dismissed Melissa and listened for the sound of the door closing when she left.

"I guess we go back a ways, huh, Jack?" said Slaight, trying to start the meeting on a lightly ironic note.

"I guess we do," responded Gibson without humor.

"Remember that time back at Carson when I was running the One-eighty-sixth, and you had C Company?"

"Yes sir."

"I'm hoping we can start our association here at the Academy with a clean slate. Is that agreeable to you?"

"Yes sir." Gibson's voice was flat and emotionless.

"It would have been preferable if our first meeting concerned the cadet intramural athletic program, or some other piece of ordinary Academy business. But instead we're looking at a situation that can go one of two ways. The death of the young woman this morning can be attributed to conditions beyond the Academy's ability to have predicted or controlled, in which case it will be seen as a tragic accident and we can move on. Or her death may be proven to have been caused by some kind of misdeed here at the Academy, in which case we've got real problems, Jack. You've been Com for two years. I'm sure you realize how serious this could turn out to be."

"General Slaight, I can assure you right now that there was no foul play involved in this young woman's death. I think it's pretty obvious that she couldn't take the heat, and she passed away because of this obvious weakness."

Here we go, thought Slaight.

"I hate to burst your bubble, Jack, but I've seen the initial autopsy report, and there has already been a determination made that this young woman didn't die from heatstroke. So you can stick your weaker-sex notions back in your pocket. If I hear any talk around the Academy that she died at parade on a very hot day because she was a woman, you're going to be answering to me. Is that clear?"

"Very," said Gibson, dropping the "sir" that should have been appended to his statement.

Slaight noticed the lack of respect from his Commandant and thought briefly of saying something, but decided to move on. "Let me tell you how this is going to work," he said pointedly to Gibson. "Tomorrow morning when the parents of Miss Hamner show up they will be greeted by you and me. Sometime later, there will be a movement of the body under Cadet Honor Guard from the post hospital to an awaiting hearse. I want the entire Third Regiment in full dress gray outside the hospital. I want that girl's body to be transferred into that hearse with all of the pomp and circumstance we can drum up, do I make myself clear?"

Gibson nodded. "Yes sir. Sir, the Corps has a full day of classes tomorrow. Do you want me to ask the Dean to excuse the Third Regiment from class for the day?"

"I'll handle that," said Slaight. "I want you to get something straight right now, Jack. As of today, this is *my* Corps of Cadets. That dead body out there on the Plain today is *my* dead body. Therefore you will treat the death of this young woman as a tragic accident and accord her the honors which are due from the Academy and the Corps of Cadets. Understood?"

"Perfectly."

"You have your marching orders," barked Slaight, pointing toward his office door. "Get moving."

Gibson stood, tossed off a salute, and left.

Outside the window, the Hudson was just catching the last rays of the setting sun. Even in the midst of the storm that he knew was gathering around the death of Dorothy Hamner, he felt calm. Back when he was a cadet, the notion that he would one day occupy the office of Superintendent with all of its history was so distant from his comprehension as to be unthinkable. And yet now, strangely, he could make sense of it. There had been a battle raging for the soul of the United States Army, and right now, at this very moment, guys like Meuller and Slaight were winning the battle. But just over the next hill—perhaps with the election of a President who was anti-woman in addition to being antigay, for example—were the legions of those who believed as Gibson believed. The turn-back-the-clock crowd, guys who believed the country could retreat to the "values" the country was imagined to have shared in 1950, and everything would begin working again, and moreover, would somehow work *better.*

Right now, he knew two things for sure: First of all, it was up to him to make the system work the way it was supposed to work. Secondly, he knew he would get exactly no help in that regard from his Commandant of Cadets.

But then again, what had his training led him to expect? A free ride? He looked out there at the Hudson and saw a tugboat pushing three empty barges upriver. The barges hit some kind of mean eddy as they approached Trophy Point and began aiming themselves at the western shore of the Hudson. Slaight watched, fascinated, as the captain reversed engines and the river surged beneath his tugboat, and gently, ever so gently, the three barges began to realign themselves, and he was able to proceed upriver.

Four years at West Point and thirty years of life in the Army had reminded him again and again of Newton's law that for every action, there is an equal and opposite reaction. Slaight watched the tug push the barges around the bend of Trophy Point and turned away from the window. "Are you ready to call it a day, Melissa?"

"Yes sir."

"Come on. I'll walk with you as far as the library."

Outside the Headquarters Building, a lone cadet carrying an armload of files fumbled a salute and said, "Good evening, sir," as they passed. Slaight returned salute. "Any thoughts?"

Her mouth formed a thin smile. "Well, sir, I didn't hear what went on between you and the Com. But I can tell you that Colonel Percival is either very naive or he's blowing smoke your way, sir."

"How do you figure?"

"Well, sir, for one thing, there are about six effective ways to beat a urine test, and any cadet with nimble fingers can pull them off the Internet in about two minutes."

They walked in silence for a moment, then Slaight said, "There were guys in my class who smoked marijuana. After graduation, I was one of them, briefly. I even inhaled."

She laughed. "Sir, everybody here at West Point came from somewhere else, and in most of those somewheres, use of drugs by schoolkids is a given."

"So the negative results on the urine tests Percival's talking about could be misleading."

"I'd bet my car on it, sir. Back in the division, I heard about guys who wouldn't use drugs for a month or so, then they'd store clean urine in anticipation of the tests."

Another cadet passed by, saluting smartly.

"Thanks, Melissa. I'll see you in the morning."

"Yes sir. Good evening, sir."

Quarters 100 was visible in its white clapboard glory across the Plain. As he strode across the grassy expanse of the parade ground, he tried to remember if he had ever entertained, even for an instant, perhaps as he bent into an icy wind one night on his way to see *The Graduate* over in the old theater in the gym, a fantasy that one day he would return to West Point as Supe.

He chuckled to himself. *Never.*

CHAPTER 8

ASH PRUDHOMME was waiting for Jacey in her room when she returned from supper. They had been seeing each other for about two years, and during that time, she had come to realize that he was a lot more than the sum of his parts, which were deceiving, to say the least. He was the son of a New Orleans grocery owner, and he had grown up in the apartment over the store in the French Quarter. It was a small place, as groceries went, but it had an excellent meat counter and a top-notch selection of wines and imported beers, so anybody who knew anything about food in the Quarter frequented Prudhomme's. Ash hadn't thought much about a military career when he was growing up, but when a West Point cadet came to his high school on a recruiting trip, he had been won over.

Adjustment to West Point discipline hadn't been easy for a boy from the French Quarter, but Ash had made the transition after a few dozen hours walking the area as a plebe convinced him that buckling under and doing what he was told was preferable to walking punishment tours with a rifle on his shoulder. Still, West Point hadn't completely stripped him of his Cajun ways. "You can take the boy out of the bayou, but you can't take the bayou out of the boy," was the way he put it to Jacey when she commented on his love of musicians like the Radiators and the Neville Brothers and Dr. John and Boozoo Chavis. Ash was the lead singer in one of the West Point rock and roll bands, and he had succeeded in teaching them some Zydeco songs, which they played to the distinctive two-step beat of Louisiana's Cajun country. The band was called Talent Show, after an old Replacements song that was also part of their repertoire. Being the singer for the band gave Ash a certain panache among his classmates, but he wasn't a guy who lacked much in that department anyway. He had the joie de vivre that seemed to be inbred among denizens of the Crescent City. Jacey's own mother was evidence enough that New Orleans imbued in its citizens a sense of style and love of the good life. "Let the good times roll" wasn't a cliché. Like West Point, it was a way of life.

It didn't surprise Jacey to find Ash seated behind her desk in the semidarkness of early evening. They usually got together and went for a jog before supper, but Dorothy's death had canceled that. She closed the door and put her cap on the top shelf in the closet, turning around to find herself in his arms. He kissed her and rubbed his nose against hers.

"You got time for something other than, like, a run up to the reservoir?"

"Not really," she replied. She felt his hands squeezing her ass and wriggled free. "C'mon, Ash. Someone might see us. It's PDA."

"I just love that phrase. PDA. Public display of affection, like there's something wrong with a guy touching a girl."

"You weren't exactly just touching me back there."

"I can't help it. You've got a delicious ass."

She switched on her desk lamp and sat down. There was a yellow phone-message slip on her desk from the Charge of Quarters. "Oh, jeez, my dad called."

"This is gonna be weird, with your dad being the Supe. Everybody's gonna be watching us."

"You don't think I've thought about that?"

"Hey! Hey! I'm not trying to start something." He pulled her toward him, kissing her.

"All the more reason you ought to learn to control your restless little libido," she retorted, releasing herself from his grasp.

He grinned. "I can see right now we're gonna have to scat out of here on the weekends, big time. Just between you and me, getting out of here and being alone with you is number one on my agenda.''

"Just remember we've only got every other weekend. I've got to trade off with Belle. One of us has to be here, even on weekends.''

"Bummer," he joked. "Why couldn't you have gotten company training officer, or another diddly-shit job?''

"Real funny, Ash. You've heard the complaints that I got company commander because the Tactical Department was filling its female quota.''

"C'mon. Gibson picked you because you're qualified.''

"Yeah, but it's gotten so hard to know what's what anymore. People are complaining that things have gotten to be way too PC, and I'm starting to agree with them.''

"Everybody knows you stand at the top of the class in the company, Jace. I haven't heard anybody saying you pulled down CO because you're a female.''

Jacey sat down on the bed next to him. "Yeah, but now I'm starting to hear I got my stripes 'cause they knew my father was going to be appointed Supe this year.''

"Everybody knows that's bullshit. You told me your old man and Gibson don't get along.''

There was a soft tap at the door and Belle walked in. "You two got your clothes on?''

"We were talking about Dorothy,'' said Jacey.

"I figured,'' said Belle.

"What do you think happened?'' asked Jacey.

"All I know is, she was one strac chick,'' said Belle. I don't see her dropping out there today from the heat.''

"I know. We've had parades on days that were a lot hotter,'' said Jacey. "I heard only three people dropped out there today. Remember that parade last year in May when twelve people dropped? And how many of them died? Zero.''

"Nobody's ever died at parade,'' said Ash. "This is so bizarre.''

"Well, we knew Dorothy, and we know she didn't die because today just happened to be her day.''

Ash glanced at Belle, and the two of them nodded their assent.

"Something bad happened to Dorothy,'' said Jacey. "I'm going to find out what it was.''

Belle grabbed her bathrobe and a towel and headed for the sinks. Ash lingered for a moment. "This is a weird way to begin firstie year, huh?"

"It sure is." She held his hand as they walked to the door. "She was one of us, Ash. She's not going to die in vain."

He looked into her eyes for a long moment as they stood at the closed door, and for a moment, she thought he was going to kiss her, but then he just nodded slowly, and he turned and left.

The phone rang. She knew who it was before she picked up.

"Hi, Jace. How's my doll?" asked her father.

"I'm okay, Daddy."

"Your mother's worried about you. So am I. It's a terrible thing, what happened to your company-mate. I'm sorry you find yourself in the middle of it."

"Please don't worry. I'll be all right. I mean, it's still such a shock."

"I know it is, Jace. We're doing everything we can to find out what happened to her."

"Can you tell me anything, Daddy? I mean, do they know what killed her?"

"We won't really know what happened until the full autopsy report is in. But they've determined this much. She didn't die from heat-stroke."

"I didn't think the heat killed her. None of us did. Dorothy wasn't . . ." She searched for the right word. "Weak. She wasn't weak."

"I'm sure we'll get the whole story in a few weeks."

"It's so weird, Daddy. I mean, I feel so alone."

"You're a company commander, Jace. You have been put in charge of other people's lives. When it comes right down to it, you're the one who's on the spot. It's a natural feeling, Jace. People are precious. When they leave so suddenly, they take part of you with them."

"I guess part of it's because you're the *Supe.* If I lean on you, people are going to think I'm weak."

There was a long pause as her father gathered his thoughts. "Well, we knew this wasn't going to be easy."

There was another pause as each of them tried to think of what to say next. Finally Jacey said, "Thanks, Daddy. Don't worry about me. I'm going to be okay."

"Just remember that you can pick up the phone anytime, and I'm here. So is your mom."

"Bye, Daddy." She hung up the phone.

If it wasn't the heat, it had to be something else.

CHAPTER 9

T HE LECTURE by the Chairman of the Honor Committee was scheduled for nine P.M. in Thayer Hall's South Auditorium. Slaight waited until the plebe class was seated before slipping into an empty seat in the back row. Every eye in the room was focused on the stage, so the entry of the Superintendent had gone unnoticed.

The Commandant of Cadets walked to the center of the stage and stood at parade rest, his feet spread, hands crossed behind his back.

"My name is Brigadier General Jack Gibson, and I'm the Commandant. It's both my duty and my pleasure tonight to introduce to the plebe class the Chairman of the Cadet Honor Committee. His name is Cadet Jerry Rose. He is a cadet captain from the Second Regiment. He comes from the heartland of our nation, from the state of Missouri, and I have known him since he was a yearling honor rep. It is one of the jobs of the Commandant to oversee the administration of the Cadet Honor Code, in concert with the Chairman of the Honor Committee. I want you to remember everything Mr. Rose has to say to you tonight, for what he tells you tonight may be the most important words you will ever hear in your life." He turned to his right. "Mr. Rose. The plebe class is yours."

Rose strode purposefully from the wings to the center of the stage.

At five feet eight inches, Rose was hardly an imposing figure, but he spoke with authority and conviction about West Point's most treasured asset, its Honor Code.

"As we begin the academic year, you plebes should understand one thing very clearly. The days of your training on the Honor Code during Beast Barracks are over. As of this moment, you are all members of the Corps of Cadets, and you will live by the strictures of the Code just like every other class here at West Point. This means you will not lie, cheat, or steal, and you will report anyone you know to have done so, even your own roommate. Now I realize that this may seem to be a harsh and unforgiving system, but you are in the Army now, and you live in a harsh and unforgiving world. The Honor Code is the thing which binds us together in the Corps of Cadets. Without honor, you will not succeed in our world. Without honor, you cannot assume the burdens of command which await you upon graduation. Without honor, you cannot fight and win the nation's wars. Without honor, you are nothing."

With that, Rose turned and strode from the stage. His lecture had been so brutal and brief it seemed as if the air had been sucked out of the room. The auditorim was utterly silent, and the plebes sat in their seats, staring rigidly at the empty stage until an announcement over the P.A. ordered them to return to the barracks.

As Slaight walked alone across the Plain back to Quarters 100, he found himself glad to see that the Honor Code was being treated with the same seriousness it had been when he was a cadet. There were many mysteries concealed beneath the layers of cadet life within West Point's walls. Cadets drew themselves close within the Corps and concealed from others the secrets of West Point life. The Honor Code and the way it was enforced by cadets at the Academy was perhaps the biggest secret of them all.

West Point could be a very deceiving place. On the surface, things looked almost perfect: lawns groomed, hedges trimmed, houses and barracks stately and imposing, well-groomed cadets striding purposefully back and forth to duties and class. But Slaight knew it was what happened just beneath the impressively ordered surface of the Academy that made the place tick—or fail to tick. The Honor Code was the heartbeat of the Academy. In a strange way, it required the gentle ministrations one tendered a good friendship, and like any good friendship, it was a two-way street. Without the cadets' mutual dependence on the honor of one another, the Honor Code would simply cease to exist, and so would West Point.

Slaight had heard worried talk among West Pointers over the years that West Point was turning into just another college. Many traditionalists were convinced that allowing women into West Point had ruined the place. But to presume that males had a hammerlock on the cadet motto, "Duty, Honor, Country," was to presume that it was necessary to exclude females in order for men to maintain their grip. Slaight found that notion not just silly, but dishonorable. The twenty-year history of the success of women at the Academy had proven the old grads wrong.

When Slaight reached the front porch of Quarters 100, he found Sam sitting outside. She pointed across the Plain behind him. A steady procession of cadets wearing their dress gray uniforms walked slowly through the sally ports. Slowly the grounds outside Central Area were filled with the entire Corps of Cadets, silent and still and gray.

Then came the mournful tones of taps, played by two buglers, one echoing just a phrase behind the other. The Corps of Cadets stood at attention and saluted to mark the passing of Dorothy Hamner, a fellow cadet. When the cadets lowered their salutes and turned and walked silently back through the sally ports into the barracks, Samantha said, "That was remarkable."

"Yes, it was," Slaight agreed.

Later, as he finally closed his eyes the night of his first official day as West Point's new Superintendent, his sleep was fitful, interrupted by the kinds of dreams that left you wondering in the morning if you had slept at all.

Elsewhere at the Academy, the sleep of others was similarly interrupted, but not by dreams.

CHAPTER 10

T HE ARMED FORCES Institute of Pathology was on the campus of Walter Reed Army Medical Center, out on Georgia Avenue in northwest Washington, D.C. Major Elizabeth Vernon had always found the building curious because it was windowless, built in the late 1940s as the nation's first atomic-bomb-proof building and envisioned as a model for future governmental buildings downtown. The invention of the hydrogen bomb quickly made such an innocently conceived notion obsolete, and it was the obsolescence of the pathology building that amused her. To think there was a time when men thought they could build bunkerlike structures that would withstand the splitting of the atom!

She parked her rental car and headed for Colonel Phillip Knight's second-floor office. He had been stationed at the Pathology Institute for most of his career. In addition to having trained Major Vernon, he was also responsible for the schooling of most of the pathologists in the Army, so he hadn't been surprised when she called him a few days previously and sought his help in the case of the young female cadet who had died during a parade at West Point.

Major Vernon saluted when she entered Colonel Knight's office, but he waved her off and reached across his desk to grasp her hand firmly in both of his. "Liz! How great to see you!" He wore rimless

half-glasses that gave him a look far more scholarly than his demeanor, which was rather jolly and carefree. She recalled that he
had a couple of kids in college, one of whom was probably in med
school by now, wanting to follow in her father's footsteps. She had
been over to the Knights' for dinner a few times, and remembered
the dinners fondly. Both Colonel Knight and his wife cooked, and
their dinner parties were an odd mix of very fussy, elaborate food
and an atmosphere so relaxed it bordered on chaotic.

"I've been pretty good, sir."

"Your return to West Point must be agreeing with you. You look
well. Have a seat." She sat down and laid her briefcase on the desk.
"You've got a problem, I understand."

"Yes sir. As I told you on the phone, I'm pretty well stymied on
this one."

"Why don't you fill me in on what you've got so far."

She opened the briefcase and removed the file on Dorothy Hamner. "Twenty-one-year-old female in apparent good health. No re-
curring medical problems to speak of in her three years at the
Academy. Goes out to parade on a hot day—"

"How hot?"

"The temperature was recorded as ninety-six degrees on the day
of her death."

"Wearing the woolen cadet dress uniform, I presume?"

"Yes sir, wool full dress gray coat over cotton trousers."

"And that silly hat."

"Yes sir."

"Were there any symptoms reported by fellow cadets previous to
her death?"

"Not that morning in barracks. The only symptoms that were reported were those immediately preceeding her loss of consciousness.
Shortness of breath, gasping. One cadet said her eyes bulged."

"You said her blood tests appeared to be normal."

"Yes sir."

Colonel Knight stood. "Let's get down to the lab." He led the way
downstairs to the well-equipped pathology lab Major Vernon remembered from her training. Several technicians in white lab coats were
working across the room. Major Vernon opened her sample case,

and the colonel took the first slide and slipped it under the microscope. He peered into the eyepiece and whistled softly.

"That was taken from the lower left lobe, but the rest of the samples look pretty much the same, sir."

"This is extraordinary inflammation. Are you certain there was no history of asthma?"

"Yes sir. I checked all of the Academy's medical records and spoke with her family physician on the phone."

"Let's have a look at another." She handed him a second slide and he viewed it for a moment before looking up. "If the rest of the lungs look like this, there's little doubt she suffered a massive respiratory failure. The question is, why? Let's have a look at those blood results."

She handed him the printout from the blood tests and he examined it carefully.

"She's got a slightly elevated blood-sugar level here."

"Yes sir, I noticed that, and I went back and checked a blood test that was done on her about a year ago, when she had a standard cadet physical exam. Her blood sugar was about the same, slightly elevated, so I didn't take much notice of it."

"Could be significant, and then again, it could be normal for this particular individual. Blood sugar can vary. Mine's a tad below normal." He ran his finger down the test results and looked up. "I see you didn't order a serum cortisol on her."

"No sir."

"It's not a standard test, but given the condition of her lungs, I'd say we'd better run one. Did you bring extra blood samples?"

"Yes sir." She reached in her briefcase, pulled out a small foam container and removed a test tube of Dorothy's blood. Colonel Knight called to one of the technicians and handed her the test tube.

"Run a serum cortisol level on this sample, please," he said. The technician took the test tube and went through a door into another part of the lab.

"You want to go for a walk while we wait for the test results?" asked the colonel.

"Sure."

He picked up a paper bag, and they exited the Pathology Institute and wandered down a winding path through Walter Reed's parklike grounds. Colonel Knight reached into the bag and pulled out a plastic Ziploc of peanuts and shook it. Instantly, three squirrels scampered down the trunk of an oak tree and gathered at his feet, squatting on their hindquarters and making little chirping sounds. He tossed each of them a peanut, and they took off in three separate directions. The two officers sat down on a shaded bench. The colonel tossed another peanut to one of the squirrels. "I come out here to think. It's quiet, and feeding these guys is just distracting enough to give your mind some time to wander."

"I'd forgotten how beautiful it is here," said Major Vernon.

"You need time in the day like this in our line of work." He chuckled. "Contemplating the whys and wherefores of dead folks all day gets a little old after a while."

"Did you ever wish you'd taken up another field of medicine?"

"Nope. This one suits me just fine. After all, it's the only kind of doctoring you can do where nobody ever dies on you."

Major Vernon laughed. "Even dermatologists get an occasional fatal case of melanoma."

"Podiatrists have a negligible mortality rate, although I met one guy who lost a patient to a far-gone case of gangrene."

"I guess a pretty dark sense of humor comes with the territory," said Major Vernon.

"It helps."

"Can I ask why the cortisol test occurred to you, sir?" asked Major Vernon.

"You may," he smiled.

She grinned. He had played the same game with her when she was going through training. He was waiting for her to answer her own question. "Okay. We've got severe lung inflammation which was present at the time of death and was not merely a contributing factor, but most probably causal. She was reported to be asymptomatic by her fellow cadets before parade. There's an interview with more than one cadet who reported that she was acting normally in ranks as they formed up in the area of barracks. You're figuring that the inflammation present at time of death didn't occur between the formation in the area of barracks and her death at parade maybe thirty minutes later."

"Correct."

"So some level of inflammation was probably present previously that morning."

"Correct."

"And if she was asymptomatic, she was treating the condition."

"Correct again."

"With prednisone, or some other corticosteroid."

"Correct. We'll get some kind of indication if our theory is right with the serum cortisol test results."

"If we're right, and she was treating herself with a corticosteroid, where was she getting it?"

"An off-post doctor, perhaps. It's available over the counter in foreign countries."

Major Vernon's eyes widened. "I studied her entire cadet file. She was stationed at Fort Bliss, Texas, over the summer for training. Across the river from Juarez."

"There you go." The cell phone on Colonel Knight's belt jingled and he unclipped the phone. "You've got the results? We'll be right there."

Colonel Knight and Major Vernon made their way back to the Pathology Institute and entered the downstairs lab. The specialist who ran the blood test handed Colonel Knight the results. He thanked her and quickly scanned the printout. "Yep. There's the cortisone, right off the scale. She was loaded up on the stuff." He handed the printout to Major Vernon.

"Jeez. How much do you figure she was taking?" asked Major Vernon.

"It's just a guess, but I'd have to say sixty milligrams or more."

"With a dose like that, why wasn't it working?"

"It was. She was asymptomatic an hour before death."

"Then she must have suffered a flare-up."

"Correct. And now the question is why she was treating herself outside normal military medical channels."

"That's an easy one. A lung condition as chronic as we found would disqualify her for commissioning. She was eight months away from graduation. The pressure she must have felt to make it through her senior year and graduate must have been incredible. She was hiding her condition and self-administering the corticosteroids to keep herself from being medically discharged.''

''That sounds about right to me.''

''So what are we going to do about our steroid-popping cadet, sir?''

Colonel Knight pondered the question for a moment. ''It would be nice if we had a diagnosis and could pinpoint exactly what condition she was suffering from. Your slides look an awful lot like asthma, which could account for the sudden flare-up she apparently suffered.''

''In what way?''

''An allergic reaction can exacerbate asthma, sometimes greatly so. Let's say she had an allergy to freshly mown grass, and they had just mowed the parade grounds that morning. That alone might have been enough to cause a flare-up. Then there's the possibility there was a bacteriological or viral cause of the flare-up.''

''I ran the standard cultures and found no sign of pneumonia or bronchitis, typical or atypical.''

''Did you take samples from her nasal passages and sinuses?''

''Yes sir. There was some mucus, but it was clear and not present in gross quantity.''

''So the likelihood of her having contracted one of the rhinoviruses is small, but not out of the question.''

''Yes sir.''

''There's the possibility that the corticosteroid she was taking interacted with another drug.''

''We didn't find any illicit substances in her blood test.''

''Wouldn't have to be illicit. Take Tums, for example.''

''*Tums?*''

''Antacids can bind steroids in the intestine so the drug is not well absorbed.''

''But she had an incredibly high cortisol level in her bloodstream at the time of death.''

''Yes, but the level of the drug in her lungs might have been much lower.''

''I'm not following you, sir.''

''The adrenal glands are thought to produce most of the naturally occurring cortisol within the body in the morning, which is why steroids are normally taken in the morning, so as to mimic the body's

production. But when you're on high doses of a steroid like prednisone, the adrenals virtually shut down. Her high cortisol level can
be attributed to several factors. Her time of death was what?''

"Ten A.M.''

"Let us suppose she took the prednisone, if that's what she took,
about two hours earlier. Suppose she had taken an antacid about the
same time. There would be reduced absorption into the bloodstream. Yet the dose she took the day before could still account for
her high blood level if it wasn't properly eliminated by the body.''

"How would that happen?''

"Constipation might do it, along with a reduced intake of fluids
and consequent reduced urination.''

"She had a full bladder at time of death and it appeared that she
hadn't had a bowel movement in more than twenty-four hours.''

"There you go.''

"But why would this lead to a lower level of drug in the lungs?''

"A dose of steroids usually lasts in the body several hours, but the
effects are far more long-lasting. Let's suppose she took a dose the
day before and the effects were tapering off the following morning.
She takes another dose that morning, but its absorption is blocked
or reduced by one or more of the factors we've discussed. The cortisol blood level would be fairly high, while the active presence in
the lungs, which would come primarily from the most recent dose,
could be low, or even negligible. If there was an allergic reaction
that tripped the flare-up, a low level of corticosteroids in the lungs
would leave them unable to fight the inflammation, and bingo—
you've got a respiratory emergency, failure to oxygenate the blood
stream, and cardiac arrest.''

"Can we prove that scenario?''

"Maybe, maybe not. But we've got something to go on. Was there
anything else you found that might help us?''

"Yes sir. I found an abraded area in the labia. I took a vaginal
sample and sent it down to Rockville, Maryland.''

"Did you request DNA analysis?''

"Yes sir.''

"We're backstopping Rockville on DNA these days. Let's get back
to the office. Maybe we've got some answers for you.''

Back in his office, Colonel Knight picked up the phone and

quickly dialed an interoffice number. "Ben? Phil Knight. Have you got a minute?" He leaned back and fiddled with the phone cord. "Did you log in a vaginal sample from a Major Vernon at West Point about a week ago?" Listening, Colonel Knight nodded to Major Vernon and gave her a thumbs up. "How far along are you? Two more weeks? Okay, thanks, Ben."

"Did I hear you say two weeks?" She sounded shocked.

"He said the process used to separate out different DNA from a single sample is very complicated. They just developed the process recently, and they're still feeling their way. He doesn't want to make any mistakes."

"So you'll call me when the test results are in?"

"Of course I will."

Major Vernon stood. "I think I'd better be getting back to the Academy, sir. They're chomping at the bit up there. Even though these are only partial results, they are significant, and the authorities are going to want an immediate briefing."

They shook hands and Colonel Knight walked her back to her rental car. "I'll give you a ring the minute I get the DNA results on your sample."

"Thanks, sir."

CHAPTER 11

EVEN THOUGH temperatures at West Point had reached into the high nineties at Labor Day, only two weeks later there was an icy chill in the night air, and fog had rolled off the Hudson across the Plain and pressed against the barracks threateningly. Every cadet knew what the gray mists outside the windows meant. Within a month or so, cadets would be going to class in overcoats and scarves with their collars turned up against the icy winds that blew down the Hudson.

An early meeting had prevented the Superintendent from taking his usual morning jog, so he waited until a few hours after supper to pull on a pair of sweats and head up Washington Road. Headlights poked through the fog ineffectually as cars crept along the damp street feeling their way through the soup. He passed a few cadets making their way back to the barracks before taps. They saluted sharply, making the safe assumption that he was probably an officer.

It comforted Slaight that the rhythms of life at West Point had not changed much since he was a cadet. The day began early, at six A.M., when the "Hellcats," the Army drum and bugle corps, blew reveille in each of the cadet areas of barracks. Even though cadets mercifully didn't have to report outside for reveille formation anymore, they were still saddled with making beds and cleaning rooms and preparing their living areas for inspection. Then came breakfast, when the entire Corps sat down together to eat in the mess hall, and then, at 7:15, began the academic day, which was a full one. Most cadets took two classes in the morning and two in the afternoon. The academic system was much the same as it had been when Sylvanus Thayer, the Academy's first really effective Superintendent, organized it nearly two hundred years ago. Classes were taught in small "sections" of fifteen to twenty cadets, and each cadet was tested and received a grade in every class, every day. This put cadets under intense pressure to study each night and be prepared for class the next day, because they knew beforehand that class performance counted. There was virtually no chance to relax, slough off your studies, and wait until the end of the semester to cram for exams, because you took an exam every day. It was one of West Point's true oddities that final-exam week at the end of each semester was a time of relaxation for many cadets, who hardly needed to cram for finals when they had crammed every night of the entire semester for daily exams in each of their subjects.

At the close of the academic day, cadets headed out of the barracks in every direction on their way to various athletic activities. Many participated in Corps Squad sports, like football or soccer or lacrosse or rugby or swimming or wrestling. Anyone not on a Corps Squad played intramural athletics, which ran the gamut from tennis and flag football to canoe racing and orienteering. After athletics came supper, and then back to the barracks for studies and cadet duties until taps at 11:00 P.M.

An important part of the West Point system was to test to the break-ing point cadets' abilities to organize their time and use it as efficiently as possible. That was why each day was so full and there was such pre-cious little free time. Cadets were expected to make hard choices about how to use their time. Those who chose well enjoyed success in their cadet careers. Those who chose poorly could easily end up fail-ing and being expelled from the Academy. The system was ruthless. One failing grade, in one course, one semester, was enough for expul-sion. Slaight had known one guy who flunked squash and less than a month later found himself in civilian clothes, headed back to his life in Kansas, or Ohio, or wherever he had come from.

On an impulse, instead of turning around at Washington Gate and heading straight home, Slaight took a turn and jogged down an alley behind the quarters known as Colonel's Row along Washington Road. The alley was dark, illuminated only by small light fixtures above each garage door. He had stopped behind a parked car to tie a loose shoelace when he heard the gentle hum of a garage-door opener and looked up. In the darkened garage, he saw two figures kissing passionately. Standing, he slipped and kicked loose gravel against the car's hubcap. At the sound, the figures inside the garage broke their embrace and ducked out of sight. The light over the garage door went out. For an instant, he thought he should identify himself so they wouldn't think he was an intruder; then he noticed the car parked inside the garage. It was a Porsche 911, one of only a few he'd seen on the post. He went ahead and jogged past the garage. The people inside must have crouched behind the car in the dark, because he couldn't see them. But he could see the West Point sticker on the bumper. The Porsche belonged to General Gibson, the Commandant of Cadets.

Slaight wondered if he had been recognized as he jogged past, but he thought not. He had his sweatshirt hood up, and without the garage light, the alley was totally dark. He hadn't seen their faces, but he could see enough from the light over the garage door to know that one was a stockily built man of medium height, and the other was a woman with light-colored, possibly blond, shoulder-length hair.

It was possible that someone else was driving the Com's car. He had a son who was going to college nearby in Connecticut. But the man kissing the woman in the garage fit the Commandant's body shape, and in the dim light, his hair looked just like Gibson's crew cut. He made a mental note of the quarters number over the garage.

By the time he got home, he had begun to question his sanity. What was he, anyway? A Peeping Tom? He stripped off his sweats and stepped into a hot shower. So what if Gibson was knocking off a piece? He laughed out loud.

"What's so funny, hon?" his wife asked.

He flipped the shower curtain aside. She was at the sink, brushing her teeth. "You'll never guess in a million years what I saw while I was out jogging tonight."

"I give up."

"I was running down the alley behind the quarters on Washington Road, and one of the garage doors opened, and I think I saw Gibson in there making out with somebody." He turned off the shower, grabbed a towel, and dried off.

"Gibson? You mean straitlaced-holier-than-thou Jack Gibson?"

"I couldn't see his face or hers, but the Porsche parked in the garage was definitely his, and the guy had a crew cut, real short."

"Whose quarters was it?"

"Number One-twenty-five. There wasn't any name."

"It's the Messicks'. Remember them? They were just down Grant Avenue from us at Leavenworth."

"Yeah, Dick is professor of social science. I saw him just the other day at a meeting of the Academic Board."

"I happen to know Dick is attending a conference at Princeton this week. He received his Ph.D. from Princeton, submitting some kind of paper he wrote."

"How do you know that?"

"Betty Jones told me at the Officers' Wives Club Luncheon yesterday. She said they're encouraging all of the professors to attend these academic conferences. It's part of the Academy's certification thing."

"Right. The Dean told me all about it when he briefed me a couple of weeks ago," he said.

"So you saw goody-two-shoes Gibson in a lip-lock with Helen Messick? *Very* interesting."

"I'm not sure. All I could see was that a man and a woman were kissing. There wasn't much light, but I think she had blond hair."

"Was it straight, or all poofed up?"

"It looked straight, about shoulder-length."

"That's Helen. She's been a bottle blonde at least since Leavenworth. Remember?" She finished brushing her teeth and moved aside so he could brush his.

"Yeah, I remember. Well, it sure wasn't a good-night peck on the cheek. When they heard me, they turned off the garage light and ducked out of sight. It was real obvious they didn't want anyone seeing them together."

"What are you going to do?"

He had a mouthful of toothpaste and pondered her question for a moment. He rinsed his mouth with water and quickly swirled water around the basin, wiping it clean, a habit he had picked up as a cadet and never dropped. "I feel kind of funny about it. I almost feel like I was invading their privacy. If I hadn't happened to be running down that alley, they would have done whatever they were doing, and nobody but them would know a thing about it."

"That's the nature of adultery, dear heart. It's supposed to be a secret. It's not just the sex. It's the feeling of getting away with it."

"You're probably right."

"Trust me. I *am* right. The problem is, now it's not a secret anymore. You know, and I know."

"Jeez, Sam, I'm not even really sure who I saw out there tonight."

She held out one hand, pointing into her palm with a finger. "A break, please? Could you give me a break and put it right here?"

He laughed. His wife was a piece of work.

She continued: "You're looking at Gibson's Porsche parked in Messick's garage, and you see a guy who looks like Jack Gibson, and a woman who looks like Helen Messick. Her husband's out of town, and all of their kids are grown up and out on their own. I'll make a bet with you. If Gibson and Helen Messick weren't doing the horizontal mambo in Quarters One-twenty-five tonight, I'll eat my hat."

"You don't even own a hat," he laughed.

"So I'll drive down to New York and buy one, and I'll come home and fry it up with some butter and onions and sit down at the kitchen counter and chew it up."

"Sounds like you don't think you're in much danger of losing the bet. What if I lose? What's my cost?"

"You take me to a romantic dinner at Cellar in the Sky."

"That place is *expensive.*"

She poked him playfully in the shoulder. "What's the matter? Scared you'll lose?"

"I am, actually. But not of paying for the dinner. Hell, I'll take you down there this weekend, win or lose. I've been wanting to go there ever since I saw it written up in *Gourmet* last year, remember?"

She got up on her tiptoes and kissed him. "You mean that? We can go this weekend?"

"It's a date." He splashed water on his face and looked in the mirror. "If you're right, and Gibson and Helen Messick are having an affair, I've got one hell of a problem on my hands."

"Oh, come on, Ry. You're not going to play morality police and throw the book at him, are you?"

"Not right now, I'm not. But what happens if he's stupid enough to keep it up? This is a very small post, Sam. They'll get stupid and somebody will see them."

"Somebody already did. You."

"It's hard for me to believe Gibson's stupid enough to throw his career in the toilet over Helen Messick. He is the single most ambitious officer in the Army."

"Well, he's messing around with Helen Messick."

He laughed. "Messing around with Messick. That's a good one."

"Freudian slip." She shrugged off her robe, stepped out of her slippers, sat down on the edge of the bed, and began brushing her hair, moving the brush slowly, a ritual she had gone through every night of their lives together. The look on her face was blissful. Her eyes were closed, and without makeup, her face had a soft glow of health and contentment. She was an amazingly beautiful woman, and as he watched her, he wondered what it would be like to be in a marriage that was so weak and troubled that you'd take a stupid chance like Gibson was taking. He felt like the luckiest man in the world.

He had run into Samantha Hand four years after graduating from West Point in a supermarket in New Orleans. She had been standing at the fish counter, buying soft-shell crabs, and had stood there for several moments watching her before he walked up, surprising her. They had lingered in the supermarket talking about food and wine and the restaurants they'd been to before each of them realized, practically at the same time, that an hour had passed. It had seemed the logical thing to do to go home with her and fry up the soft-shells and make a pan of dirty rice and a salad and share a nice bottle of Bordeaux, and later, when they had found themselves in her bed together, it seemed the logical thing to do to fall in love and get married, which they did just three months later. Everything was so damned *easy* with her. Being married to her was like the feeling you got when you slipped into an old and very comfortable pair of loafers. You hardly knew you were wearing them, and being with Sam, the feeling was so natural and instinctive, you hardly knew you were married. He had once heard a good friend describe his own marriage as a third person in the room. When Slaight expressed confusion, his friend had explained: "You know, there's you, and there's your wife, and over there, sitting in the corner watching everything you do, is the marriage." It was anything but that with Samantha. In the room of their marriage, all there was was the two of them.

"Speaking of slips," he said, walking around the end of the bed, "whatever happened to the little number with the leopard print you used to wear every once in a while? What's that you've got on tonight? All I can see is, it says GAP on the front of your shirt."

"Shut up," she said softly. "It wasn't a slip, it was a camisole, and at age fifty-one the days of getting dressed up in teeny little things to attract the attentions of my husband are well behind me. Or they should be, anyway." She grinned at him from beneath the covers, which were pulled up to her chin.

He climbed in next to her and snaked his leg across the bed, his ankle finding hers. He slipped a hand beneath the curve of her waist and pulled her to him. His lips found hers, and he kissed her eagerly.

She broke away and nibbled his neck as she felt his hands gently massage her. If there was anything that felt better than the way she felt at this moment—right here, right now—she didn't know what it was.

CHAPTER 12

MAJOR VERNON pulled into the lot next to the Provost Marshal's office and sat in her car for several moments pondering her dilemma. She had blood-test results but they were inconclusive as to the cause of Dorothy Hamner's death. DNA results on the vaginal sample were needed before she could request a cross-check against the West Point DNA database. She wondered if she should tell Percival about the vaginal sample and the DNA tests that were being run.

Almost as quickly as she'd asked herself the question, she settled on its answer. *No.* There was always a chance that Percival would write up a report of their meeting and forward it through administrative channels. Her military experience told her that was a sure way to produce a leak. If the multiple sex partners of Dorothy Hamner were cadets, she didn't want them to learn their identities were in danger of being found out, so she decided to stay quiet about the DNA evidence until it was in hand.

Percival's office was at the end of the hall. She announced herself to his secretary and waited. Soon the secretary ushered her into his office.

In a military way, Percival's office looked like it belonged to a cop. There was an MP helmet sitting on an end table next to the sofa, and a photo on the wall of Percival as a captain at the Brandenberg Gate in Berlin, before the Wall came down. He rose to greet her, walking around his desk. She snapped a salute, which he returned haphazardly. "Major Vernon, good to see you. You've got your autopsy finished, I presume."

"Partially, sir."

Percival looked briefly puzzled and then motioned for her to take a seat. He relaxed on a sofa as she fingered the clasp of her briefcase. "I've got initial results from Walter Reed, sir. The Armed Forces Institute of Pathology. It turns out that Cadet Hamner had a respiratory condition, sir. Her lungs shut down."

"I see."

"We don't know what caused the failure of her lungs, sir. But we do know that she was treating herself with a very powerful drug that she had to have been obtaining from a civilian doctor, because no medical records at the Academy reflect either her pathology or treatment."

"What kind of drug was she taking?"

"A corticosteroid, sir. Most probably prednisone. In large doses. Her blood cortisol level was off the chart."

"It sounds to me like the young woman took unauthorized drugs, and they killed her."

"That's the odd thing about this case. The drugs were keeping her alive, sir. She was *successfully* treating her disease, whatever it was, until the day she died."

"Then what killed her, Major?"

"We don't know yet, sir."

"Tell me what you do know. In detail, please."

"Sir, we know that the prednisone she took was controlling an inflammation in her lungs which was basically trying to shut down her lung function. We know that the drug was working, because everything we have learned about her behavior in the days and hours leading up to her death tells us that her breathing and lung function was normal. What we do *not* know is why on the morning of her death the drug failed to control her inflammation, which appears to have flared out of control and killed her."

"You must have some idea of what might have happened," Percival said, shifting uneasily on the sofa.

"Yes sir. I believe something else was introduced into her system and interacted with the prednisone and caused it to lose its efficacy and fail."

"Do you have any idea what it was?"

"No sir. But we're working on it."

"What does your instinct tell you, Major?"

"She could have taken a nonprescription medication which didn't show up in her blood the next day. She could have been drinking to excess . . ."

"Did you find a high blood-alcohol level?"

"No sir, but as you know, alcohol passes rather rapidly from the bloodstream . . ."

"Then how could booze have killed her the next day?"

"Because its interaction with the corticosteroids in her blood the day before her death may have been what reduced or destroyed their efficacy, sir."

"I'm going to have to report this news to the SJA." He reached for a phone and told his secretary to get him Colonel Lombardi. He spoke in low tones to Lombardi for a moment and hung up. "I'm going to send you over to see the SJA. Colonel Lombardi wants to be briefed on the results you've got so far."

Major Vernon snapped her briefcase shut and saluted.

Percival waited until he heard the door to the outer office close before he walked over and called to his secretary. "Mary? Why don't you take your coffee break now." He watched as she picked up her purse and left. Then he closed the door to his office, picked up his desk phone, punched an open line, and dialed.

"Sir? It's Percival. There's something I've got to tell you right away." He fiddled with some pencils on his desk, lining them in a neat row. He checked his watch. "Yes sir. Ten minutes, sir." He hung up the phone and, spying the raindrops on his window, grabbed his overcoat and the plastic cover for his cap on his way out the door.

BRIGADIER GENERAL Gibson had turned his chair around and was gazing out his window at the rain-swept Plain as Lieutenant Colonel Percival detailed his meeting with Major Vernon. When Percival finished, Gibson got up and walked over to a large chart on the wall, tapping it with his forefinger. "You see these numbers? They are up in every single measurable category there is at West Point. Overall grade point average? *Up.* Retention of new cadets in Beast Barracks? *Up.* Number of high-school honor society members in the new class? *Up.* Average SAT in the last two classes? *Up.* Attendance at Sunday services at all three chapels? *Up.* Donations to the United Fund? *Up.* Volunteers at cadet-run charities? *Up.*" He stood gazing at the chart for a moment, then he did a slow about-face. "This investigation is turning into a goddamned joke! She's got more than enough evidence to close out her autopsy and issue a cause of death! The damn girl was taking drugs! Without authorization! I don't give a good goddamn if they call it suicide or not, but that young woman killed herself!"

Percival didn't respond. He didn't even nod. He knew enough to know that some of the time—in fact, a lot of the time—generals weren't looking for a response.

Slowly, Gibson walked back to his desk and sat down. "You said you sent her over to see Lombardi?"

"Yes sir."

"And Lombardi will make a report to Slaight?"

"Yes sir."

"You're close to Lombardi. Find out what Slaight's reaction is."

"Yes sir."

"You realize we wouldn't even be sitting here having this conversation if it was a male cadet who died out there on the Plain."

"Yes sir."

"Every goddamned pain-in-the-ass thing that happens around here is because some goddamn female thinks she's been harassed, or charges some poor doofus with date rape, or calls her goddamned congressman because they're not selling her brand of tampon in the PX."

Percival had heard Gibson complain privately about women at West Point before. He put on a show in public, but behind closed doors, no one hated the presence of women at the Academy as much as Gibson.

Gibson swiveled his chair to face the Plain. "You're my point man on this thing, Percival. I'm depending on you." He raised his right hand, making a salutelike movement over his head.

CHAPTER 13

JACEY SLAIGHT was sitting in the half-darkness of her room staring at the screen saver scrolling across her computer monitor. Some guy over in the Fourth Regiment wrote the program and sold it on a 3.5-inch disk for ten dollars. The image was an animation of several cadets in dress gray uniform, walking punishment tours back and forth across the screen with M-14 rifles on their shoulders. Having walked more than a few such punishment tours herself, the screen saver made her laugh every time she saw it. Even though it was rumored that punishment tours were about to suffer the same fate as reveille and be ended, leave it to a cadet to figure out a way to plumb nostalgia, poke fun at the Academy, and make a few bucks, too. Absentmindedly, she tapped the "enter" key. The screen saver blinked off, bringing up her desktop. She clicked on WP NET, logged on to mail exchange, and quickly typed in her password. Nothing much happening in her mailbox. There was a message from a friend over in the First Regiment, asking if they were still on for volleyball the next day, and a note from Ash telling her he had borrowed her Mudhoney CD and would bring it back after band practice that night.

There was a computer on each and every cadet desk at West Point, and the inter-Corps net called "exchange mail" linked cadet computers with those in the academic departments and the Tactical Department. Exchange mail was private, in that you needed a password to access any cadet's E-mail. But like many limited nets, the inter-Corps net was overseen by the Academy and monitored by the "Goldcoats," a group of U.S. Army sergeants who actually wore gold lab coats, and who were responsible for installing and repairing cadet computers. It was also their job to randomly access cadet E-mail through the mail-exchange server and check its content for use of foul language, sexual harassment, and the like. Monitoring of inter-Corps E-mail had a predictable consequence. It drove those seeking privacy to the Internet, a means of communication that cadets could access and was not monitored by snooping Goldcoats.

Jacey turned off the computer and was about to go to bed when she heard a gentle knock at the door. A voice whispered, "Jacey, are you awake?"

"Sure. Come in."

The door opened. Carrie Tannenbaum, who had been Dorothy's roommate, stepped inside. "I didn't mean to disturb you, Jacey," she said.

"That's okay. I was just sitting here daydreaming."

Carrie closed the door softly behind her. She walked over to Jacey's desk. She was holding a 3.5-inch floppy. "I was going to save a letter I'd been working on tonight when I found this. It was in my box of blank floppies. I grabbed it and stuck it in the drive, and I went to hit 'save,' and this whole list of files came up. They're Dorothy's. They look like her E-mail files. She must have put it there."

"Let's go over to your room. Is that okay?" Jacey asked.

"Sure."

They walked down the hall to Carrie's room. Two weeks after Dorothy's death, she was still living alone. Dorothy's bed was a bare mattress, and her side of the closet was empty. The only thing that remained in the room that had been hers was her cadet-issue computer, still on her desk. Jacey flipped on the desk lamp and turned on the computer. In a moment, Windows booted, and Dorothy's desktop glowed on the monitor. It was standard: a word processor, Netscape, some proprietary engineering programs they had used Cow Year, and Norton Utilities. Jacey turned to Carrie. "What did you use to open the files?"

"Exchange mail."

Jacey loaded exchange mail and stuck the floppy in the 3.5-inch drive. She hit the "open file" icon and hit the A drive button. A password dialogue box appeared.

"Do you know her password?"

"Yeah. We traded passwords last year so we could check each other's E-mail if one of us was gone. It's . . . uh . . . was 'Catch-22.' She just loved that book."

Jacey typed in the password and Dorothy's mail files appeared. She quickly scanned the list of files. You couldn't tell much about them, because the file names were in a kind of truncated code.

Jacey pointed at the first message and clicked. A note from a friend in another regiment popped up. They were making plans for the weekend. She clicked on the next message. It was from a guy in the Fourth Regiment she had met during duty at Beast Barracks, summer training for the new plebe class. He invited her to the Saturday movie. Jacey went to the next message. It had also been sent during Beast Barracks, when Dorothy had been a platoon sergeant on the cadet upperclass detail. The message was directed to a squad leader in another company. Apparently, Dorothy had caught one of his plebes using a pay phone after taps. Jacey clicked on another message. It, too, addressed an issue during Beast Barracks.

She continued down the list of files, clicking on one after another, until she reached the end. They were all of an incidental nature.

"You said you found the disk in your box. Did you check any others?"

"Not yet."

"Let's have a look."

Carrie opened her bottom desk drawer and brought the file box of floppies to Jacey. It held fifty floppies. About half were labeled. The others, toward the back, were blank. Jacey started going through the blanks, popping each one into the drive and hitting "open file" on the A drive. One after another they turned up blank. She was maybe halfway through the blank floppies when she inserted one in the drive and opened the A drive, and up popped another list of files.

She started opening the individual files. They were messages that Dorothy had sent to other cadets and to faculty members. Some were replies to messages they had seen on the other disk. Others were chatty notes to friends in other companies and regiments. Jacey quickly made her way to the bottom of the list. There was nothing out of the ordinary in any of the messages. She popped the floppy out of the A drive and fingered it thoughtfully.

"Why do you think she put her floppies in your box?"

"I don't know," said Carrie.

"They couldn't have been misplaced, could they?"

"I don't think so. She had her own file box. The CID guys took it when they went through her stuff."

"Let's keep looking." She grabbed another floppy. Blank. Another and another and another, all blank. She was almost to the end of the blank floppies when she hit "open file" and a new list of files appeared. She studied the list. All of the previous file names had vaguely military acronyms. These were different. She opened the first file. It was a letter from her father thanking her for the weekend her parents had just spent at West Point attending a football game the previous fall. The next file was a letter back to her father, making plans for Thanksgiving. More letters to and from her father followed, leading up to Christmas, and then there were some very depressed-sounding short notes from January and February, lamenting the cold and dark months of "Gloom Period," the dreaded dead of winter, when it seemed to cadets across the Corps that spring would never come, academics would never let up, and their four years at West Point would never end.

Carrie stood up and stretched. "I'm going to wash up and get ready for bed."

"Okay. This is only going to take another minute or so," said Jacey.

Carrie grabbed a towel and headed out the door toward the women's rest room. Jacey put the pointer on the next file and opened it.

The message was from Ash to Dorothy, forwarding an E-mail from another cadet, who had lost Dorothy's E-mail address. Startled to see her boyfriend's name in Dorothy's E-mail, she held her breath as she scrolled down to the forwarded message. It was from Rick Favro. He's apologizing for not writing, he's been in Airborne School, and they haven't had five minutes to themselves all month, but he just finished his last jump, and graduation is the next day, and he's using a lieutenant's computer, one of the guys from his company who graduated in June and is now down at Benning going through the Infantry Officer Basic Course. Favro's telling her about their last jump, the night jump, and how cool it was, and how he was thinking about her as his chute opened, and he looked up and saw this big thing that looked like a huge white pillow against the night, and how it reminded him of the big pillows on the king-size bed in the hotel room they shared at a resort in the Catskills just before he left for Benning and she headed for Fort Knox for summer training.

Jacey took a breath. Where in the hell did *this* come from? Dorothy and Rick Favro, the Second Regimental Commander and Vice Chairman of the Honor Committee, one of the biggest dudes in the whole damn class? They're shacking up together, and Dorothy's not breathing a *word* of it to Carrie or to any of her other friends?

She hit the down arrow. Favro is telling her he wants to see her when they get back to West Point, but reorgy week's gonna be hell, and he's got rugby practice on Saturday and Sunday of Labor Day weekend, but Labor Day, there's going to be this party, and some people are going to be there. They're all big-time guys, every one of them: Norm Reade, the Brigade Adjutant. Andy Lessard, the First Regimental Commander. Glenn Ivar, the star running back on the football team. And Jerry Rose, the Chairman of the Honor Committee. All guys. No females. At least, no *cadet* females. Then Favro tells her all of the guys are bringing dates, and they're going to rent a cabin on a lake just west of the Academy, and there's going to be a couple of kegs, and everybody's going to go swimming and it's going to be great and he wants Dorothy to come.

Jacey tried to imagine Dorothy's elation. Quickly she went to the next message. It was Dorothy's reply to Favro. She was trying to contain herself, but she gave it all away when she said their weekend in the Catskills had been the best three days of her life. Of course she'd go with him.

Damn you, Dorothy! Couldn't you play just a *little* hard to get?

Jacey hurried to the next message. It was from Ash, asking if Dorothy had received the E-mail he forwarded from Favro. Next came Dorothy's response to Ash. She said she had, and she ended her message with a cheery salutation: "See you at the party on Labor Day!"

Okay. Okay. Jacey could feel blood rushing to her head. She was trying to get a grip. It was bad enough that her own boyfriend knew that Dorothy had gone to a keg party the day before her death. But her boyfriend had *been at the party,* and he hadn't said a word to her about it. Jacey had called the company meeting and she'd asked everyone if they knew anything about Dorothy that could help in the investigation of her death. What had been her mood? How had she been acting that morning? Over the last few days? Ash had been at some lake at a fucking *keg party* with her, and that wasn't relevant?

What the hell was he hiding?

CHAPTER 14

B Y ANY measure, Colonel T. Clifford Bassett was an unlikely
sort of career Army officer. His face was cherubic, almost perfectly round, and his squinty gray eyes crinkled at the corners when
he smiled, which was often. His torso was similarly rotund and with
his short legs, he moved in a kind of truncated scurry. He could
often be seen in the lower corridors of Thayer Hall, hustling from
one classroom to the next, stepping inside to listen briefly or fire off
a question tinged with irony and humor. The sharpness of his intel-
lect could have been frightening were it not for his relaxed, even
jovial demeanor.

He had attended Harvard Law School and had been drafted into
the Army during the war in Vietnam. To his great surprise, having
completed Army legal training, he found himself assigned to teach
law at West Point. From the first, he had intended to resign from
the Army when his three-year commitment was up, and he did, taking a job with a white-shoe law firm down in New York. But several
years as a junior associate running legal errands and doing back-
office research for senior partners who couldn't have found the Federal District Court House if they were deposited in front of it by a
limousine convinced him that the practice of big-time New York corporate law wasn't really in his blood. He took the shuttle down to

Washington and a cab to the Pentagon and stopped in at JAG branch personnel and asked what he had to do to get his commission back. "Sign here," he had been told, and so he did. He spent a few years in Staff Judge Advocate offices at Fort Benning and Fort Leonard Wood, and when a permanent associate professorship opened in the Department of Law at West Point, he jumped at the chance. The Academy welcomed him back eagerly, because even as a junior professor, he had brought to the rather dry West Point law classroom a delicious sense of humor and an infectious love of the law that had energized students and his fellow law professors alike.

He had been promoted to professor and head of the Department of Law several years previously and was enjoying the golden years of his career overseeing both the department and the overall practice of law at West Point. He was the senior JAG officer at the Academy, and reported directly to the Superintendent. It was an unusual arrangement. Usually, the Staff Judge Advocate was the senior legal officer on an Army post. But as with many other things military, West Point was different.

It wasn't the power of the position that made the job satisfying, however. Far more important to him was the sense of being part of a continuum, the yearly passage of knowledge from officer to cadet that had gone on at the Academy for almost two hundred years. Even after all his years teaching law at West Point, there was still a spine-tingling thrill in crossing intellectual swords with young and nimble minds when he taught the occasional class or delivered a lecture and took questions from cadets. They were impatient and curious and eager and edgy and skeptical, and on good days, they could throw off a superheated spark-filled energy that was invigorating and just plain downright fun.

When he learned that Ry Slaight, his former student and old friend, had been appointed Superintendent, it was a confirmation that he had made the right choice, having returned to the Army and taken the long, slow road that had delivered him to his present job. He knew it wasn't often in life that things worked out the way they had for him. He and his wife Fran lived in one of the large sets of professors' quarters along Thayer Road. The fact that West Point was only an hour from New York meant they could partake of the city's wide variety of cultural institutions they had enjoyed so much when they were living on the Upper West Side. What could be better than a night of Puccini, topped off with a late dinner at Joe's Shanghai, down on Pell Street, or listening to Wynton Marsalis at Lincoln Center, followed by a big bowl of bouillabaisse at Perry Bistro, down in the Village? He and his wife both loved great music and great food, and New York provided copious quantities of both.

Bassett recalled a time when he had invited Slaight and his date over for dinner on a Saturday night sometime during the winter of 1968. It was below-zero weather, and the roads were icy, and they were late, but they made it to the stone barn that Bassett had rented on the grounds of an old farm just north of West Point off Route 9W. Fran had made a huge pot of spaghetti, which everyone had consumed with gusto, and they had sat around the dining-room table talking long after the dessert had been consumed and the coffee had gone cold.

Along with sharing a love of good restaurants and good food, talk was a thing they had in common. Nothing made T. Clifford Bassett quite as happy as sitting around and throwing ideas back and forth and testing which ones stuck and which didn't. He had been certain, even then, that the same was true of Slaight.

Bassett had counseled Slaight during his firstie year, when he was going up against the system at West Point trying to find out who had killed David Hand, and he remembered with great alacrity how the system had almost chewed up Slaight and spit him out before he was able to prove Hand had been murdered by an upperclass cadet, a homosexual lover who was afraid Hand would expose their affair.

And now that Slaight was Supe, his former student was charged with defending that which he had once challenged with such vehemence. The irony was delicious.

So when General Slaight walked into Bassett's office in Building 606 late one afternoon, it hardly surprised him. Many times before, Cadet Slaight had walked into the much smaller windowless office he used to have in the basement of Thayer Hall.

The Superintendent sat down heavily in the chair facing the desk of the professor of law, and he rubbed his forehead with both hands, as if to remove worry or stimulate thought. Or maybe both.

"Cliff, I've got a problem," said General Slaight.

"The last time you came to my office you were rubbing your forehead the same way."

Slaight laughed at the memory. "Yeah. You're right."

"I've been watching Lombardi closely. So far, he's doing all the right things."

"It's not Lombardi. It's Gibson."

"Gibby?"

Slaight laughed at the sobriquet.

"What could possibly be wrong with a perfect specimen of officerly gentlemanhood like Brigadier General Gibson?" asked Bassett with a smile on his face about as wide as his shirt collar.

"I think he's having an affair with Helen Messick."

Bassett leaned back in his chair and interlaced his fingers across his ample middle. "My wife is of the same opinion."

Slaight's eyes widened. "How so?"

"Last spring, Fran's mother called from Ohio and offered to treat her and her sister to a long weekend in the city. They were going to take in some shows and visit the museums and eat at Gotham Bar and Grill and shop at Bergdorf's and generally indulge themselves. They took connecting rooms at the Plaza, and Fran was returning to her room one night that weekend when she saw Gibby and Mrs. Messick down the hall. He slipped his card into the slot and the two of them stumbled inside. Fran said they were pretty sloshed."

"Did he see her?"

"No. Even if he had, I doubt he would have recognized her. We don't exactly mix it up with the Gibsons, if you get what I mean."

Slaight laughed. "Neither do we." He looked out the narrow window in Bassett's office, which provided a sliver of a glimpse of the hills across the Hudson. "Do you have an idea if anyone else knows about them?"

"Fran running into them down at the Plaza was an odd coincidence. I don't think many officers or wives here at the Academy spend weekends at the Plaza. Gibson's in the clear, so far."

"Not any longer. I was out jogging the other night and saw them in Messick's garage. Found out the Colonel was away at some academic conference."

"They saw you?"

"They saw me, but they couldn't recognize me. It was dark, and I had my hood up."

"Interesting."

"So the problem is, what do I do with an adulterous brigadier general who also happens to be the Commandant of Cadets?"

"Well, I can certainly fill you in on the legal aspects of the situation. Even if you wanted to charge Gibson, which I would counsel against anyway, there isn't enough evidence to sustain a charge of adultery, or even one of conduct unbecoming an officer and a gentleman."

"I had an idea you were going to say that."

"Do you want the details?"

"May as well hear them. Even if we don't end up bringing charges against Gibson, something's going to pop on this thing. I can feel it."

"As it stands right now, Gibson is a beneficiary of the UCMJ's rather strict standards for proving such a charge. Observation of a man entering a hotel room with a woman who is not his wife is insufficient. Seeing them holding hands, or kissing, or embracing won't do either. In order to make a charge of adultery stick, you've got to have proof that intercourse took place. That would mean vaginal penetration by the penis of the offending officer. Not even sodomy would suffice. Absent an admission by one of the parties that this in fact had occurred, there would have to be photographs of the act, or description by a witness to the act. In either case, not very likely at all."

"That's what I thought."

"You could probably bring an Article One-thirty-three conduct-unbecoming charge and make it stick, but I'm not sure you want to jump into that particular vat of tar."

"I don't."

"There are other alternatives available to you as Superintendent, of course," said Bassett, looking pleased with himself.

"I could have him drive around to my office and brace him and tell him to knock it off, you mean," Slaight said, chuckling.

"Yes, you could do that."

"You're giving me one of those looks you used to give me in class, goddamnit."

Bassett removed his glasses and began cleaning them with a handkerchief. "There's something you've got to keep in mind when dealing with a man like Brigadier General Gibson. He has friends in high places, and he is not shy about using them."

"Yeah, I know about how Cecil Avery has been pushing his career."

"Cecil has helped to assemble quite a handy little cheering section at the Pentagon. His support is deep and wide at the crucial deputy-chief level, among lieutenant and major generals."

"I understand they're going to give him the One-oh-first Airborne Division when he leaves here," said Slaight.

"Onward and upward is the plan. Three stars, assignment as a corps commander or as troubleshooter in the hot spot of the month, then a cushy political job at NATO, then Chief of Staff or Chairman of the Joint Chiefs."

"He's an asshole."

"He's the Al Haig of the nineties, Ry, a very clever, very determined man. Don't sell him short."

Slaight sank back into his chair and rubbed his forehead. "You know what my real problem is? When the Army decided to make the post of Superintendent a five-year slot for a lieutenant general in contemplation of his retirement at the end of his tour of duty, they pretty much made the Supe a lame duck from day one."

"That has occurred to me," said Bassett.

"The theory was, they'd elevate the Supe to three stars and make him more independent, and it's worked, more or less. But independence has a steep downside in an institution as hierarchical as the Army. Those above you in the chain of command don't trust you because they realize if your career is in its final years, you don't need them. But they maintained the Commandant as a slot for a hard-charger, someone they could depend on."

Bassett chuckled. "Someone who was dependent on them, you mean. That's what's interesting about armies. They defy the laws of nature. In armies, the fittest insure that those less fit depend on *them* for their survival."

"Wonderful. Gibson's following his dick around, and I'm following him, hoping like hell his dick doesn't get him lost."

"You'd better pray that he succeeds in keeping his affair a secret, because if word gets around this post that he's screwing around, he'll take you down with him. They'll say it's your fault, that you weren't running a tight ship, that you'd let moral standards slip."

Slaight started laughing. "And . . . I waited thirty . . . years . . . for this!" he sputtered between guffaws.

Bassett joined in the laughter. It was hilarious. God had set a trap and he'd walked straight into it. It was another of His marvelous jokes. You spent a lifetime getting power that, firmly in your grasp, just reminded you every day how small it was and how little it meant.

CHAPTER 15

JACEY HAD spent the day brooding about what she had learned from Dorothy's E-mail and had concluded that there just wasn't an easy way to approach Ash. What she needed to ask him was: Why? Why hadn't he told her about the party on Labor Day? Why hadn't he told her he had been at a party with Dorothy less than twenty-four hours before she died?

She had so many other questions. Was he trying to hide something? Had he taken someone else to the party? Was it some kind of a guy thing, where he and all these big-time six-stripers didn't want her around? That couldn't be it. She was friends with them, and as a cadet captain, she was one of them, and her boyfriend was one of them. It had been her dream since she was a little girl, looking through her father's West Point yearbooks. She thought those guys in their uniforms with all the stripes on their shoulders looked so *cool*. When they changed the law to allow women into West Point, all she wanted to do was become a cadet, earn those stripes, and be one of the cadet commanders. And now she was. The only difference between her and the others who commanded companies and battalions at West Point was that her father was the Supe.

But so what? That didn't change who she was. They were still her friends. Or were they? Was there something going on at that party they didn't want *the Supe's daughter* to know about?

She walked into the company Orderly Room. "Hey, have you seen Ash?"

"I think he and the band are rehearsing up in Building Seven-twenty."

"Thanks." She walked out of the barracks and turned up the stairs leading to a building that had once housed Cadet Supply and the tacs for the Third Regiment. Cadet bands had commandeered a room in the basement as a rehearsal space. She could hear them as she climbed the stairs. They were playing something by the Replacements, and Ash was singing. It was a sweet song, and she stopped outside the building listening for a moment. He had a real feel for the song. It was about a girl, a lonely girl who danced alone, twirling by herself in nightclubs. No one can get close to her, and even if they do, they can't figure out who she is. She heard him singing her favorite lines, and he knew how to deliver them, as if the girl is forever just out of reach, and he knows why she's like that, and the saddest thing is, there's nothing he can do about it. The way he sang it, the song had a trancelike quality, and she felt herself falling into the web spun by the words and the pealing, lilting notes of the lead guitar . . .

Suddenly, she heard a loud clang as the drummer broke a stick on the cymbal, and the rest of the instruments trailed away, and Ash said, let's try it again from the top, and the drummer said he didn't have any extra drum sticks, and she heard Ash curse, and she could hear them packing up their instruments. She opened the door. Ash looked over.

"Hey, Jace, where you been?"

"Around."

Ash stuck his mike stand in the corner and walked over to her. "Want to go down to the Firstie Club for a beer?"

"Why not?"

He turned to the rest of the band. "You guys coming?" There were a couple of nods. "See you down there." He zipped up his dress gray coat and perched his cap jauntily at the back of his head. When they stepped outside, it felt to Jacey like the temperature had dropped about twenty degrees. She shivered and pulled her sweater closed.

"You want to get a coat?" he asked.

"No, let's walk."

They made their way down the narrow stairs. At the bottom, he stopped. "Remember when we used to walk down Bremerton Road and stop and kiss in the dark behind the mess hall?"

"Yeah."

"Want to go around that way?"

"No."

They started walking toward Thayer Road. "You're a woman of few words tonight."

They were stopped across from the library. Cadets carrying armloads of books were pushing through its huge oaken doors.

"I read Dorothy's E-mail, Ash. I know you and Favro and Reade and Lessard and Ivar and Rose had a keg party on Labor Day out at some lake. What I don't know is, why did you freeze me out? Why didn't you take me? And why didn't you tell me Dorothy was there?"

He reached for her hand, but she pulled away. "We'd better go somewhere and talk."

"We can talk right here."

"Jace, there's a lot more to this than you know."

"Really?" She made a show of checking her watch. "We've got time. Why don't you start at the beginning and fill me in."

He looked around. They were alone. A brisk wind was coming off the river. "Let's go back to your room."

"Belle is studying."

"Then we'll go to mine."

"I'm not moving until you tell me why you betrayed me."

"Betrayed you? How do you figure that?"

"I asked every member of the company to come forward with what they knew about Dorothy just before she died. You were there at the company meeting. You heard me. You knew I was looking for anything that would help us find out why Dorothy died. And you were with her at a keg party the day before she died and you didn't tell me? You held back, Ash. That's betrayal, in case you're having trouble with the definition of the word." He stood there, shifting from one foot to the other, like he was cold. But he wasn't cold, and she knew it. "What's the matter, Ash? Are you covering up something, or covering up *for* someone?"

"Look, Jace. Nothing happened. You've got to believe that."

"If nothing happened at the party, then why didn't you come right out and tell me about it?"

"You know who was there. Rose is the Honor Chairman. Favro's Second Regimental Commander, he's Honor Vice Chair. Reade's Brigade Adjutant. Lessard's First Regimental CO, and he's an Honor rep, and Ivar—"

"Ivar gained over a thousand yards last year."

"Yeah. It was like, Dorothy drops dead, and if it got out that she was partying, and somehow it turned out . . ." He stopped and turned to her pleadingly.

She finished the sentence for him: "If something happened to her at the party which contributed to her death, there'd be major trouble, and some big-time stud cadets would get damaged if not canned, and the hallowed Honor Committee would be left without its hallowed Chairman, and in general, a world of shit would rain down on shoulders upon which shit has never fallen. Does that sum it up?"

"Yeah."

"So to stand up for your buddies, you decided it was necessary to cut me out of the loop. Didn't you trust me, Ash? Was that it?"

"I trust you, Jace, but—"

"Your buddies don't."

"Your dad's the Supe, Jace. It's different than it was last year."

She stared at him in the darkness, trying to make out his eyes. "Bullshit. My father being Supe wouldn't mean squat if you took me to the keg party and all everybody did was drink beer and go swimming in the lake and grab a room and execute the horizontal workout. That describes every cadet party we've been to. What was different this time, Ash? Why was this party off limits to me? Did something happen you don't want me to know about?"

"Nothing happened. Dorothy wasn't even drinking. I can swear to that. I was drawing most of the beers. You're right about it not being any different than any other cadet party. We had a cabin. Guys had dates. You know."

"So you had a date? Is that it, Ash? You were fucking somebody else at the party?"

"No. No. You've got it wrong."

"Then why didn't you take me, Ash?"

He paused, scraping his foot across the grass. "The guys didn't want you at the party because of your dad. They were afraid, you know, if guys got rowdy and stuff, you would tell your father and somebody might get in trouble."

"That is so totally wrong, and you know it."

"I tried arguing with them about it, but Favro and those guys, they just said no."

"You could have skipped the party. Why didn't you?"

"I don't know. I wasn't thinking."

"I think something happened at the party you're not telling me about."

"You're wrong, Jace. Nothing happened. I swear."

"Then why didn't you tell me about Dorothy being at the party? You're running around in circles. I can't follow you."

"The guys are afraid it will get to General Gibson. Don't you see, Jace? He *made* us. You, me, Favro, Reade, Rose, Lessard, every one of us. Gibson *picked us*. He gave us our stripes. He's the one who's restoring West Point's values. He's the one who has raised standards at the Academy higher than they've ever been. We can't let him down. We *owe him*, Jace."

He stood there silently looking into her eyes. For Jacey, time came to a standstill. Her mind wandered, flooded with the images and memories.

They had stopped on a grassy area across from Cullum Hall. Her father had told her they used to hang a wall of curtains all the way around the field during football practice, so scouts from rival teams couldn't drive onto Academy grounds and shoot sixteen-millimeter footage of Army plays. Now her eyes found Cullum Hall, just across the road. On the walls inside hung memorials to past superintendents and professors and commandants and graduates who had been killed in action. Absently, it occurred to her that one day a plaque would be mounted there memorializing her own father. Her eyes drifted to the night sky, dazzled with stars. The awful thing was, she agreed with him. Gibson was the *man*. He embodied the warrior spirit that was supposed to infuse every corpuscle of cadet blood.

"So you didn't tell me about Dorothy being at the party because you're afraid you'd be letting down General Gibson? I don't believe it, Ash. If you worship him so much, don't you think he'll listen to you when you tell him the same thing you've told me? That she was there, but nothing happened at the party? I don't get it, Ash."

Suddenly, an image of Dorothy formed in her mind, reminding her what had brought them to the open field across from Cullum Hall. "This isn't about Gibson, it's about Dorothy! You're hiding something, Ash. And you're afraid. We've been together all this time, and I can't figure you out. It's like I don't even know who you are anymore."

Ash dropped his head slowly, his eyes finding the ground. "The thing of it is, you're the Supe's daughter. Gibson's a powerful guy, Jace. In our world, the Corps of Cadets, the Com rules. We don't have your father to protect us."

As a smile formed slowly on her face, she wondered if he could see her in the darkness. Probably not, and probably just as well. "You know what I learned from Dorothy's death? People can die, even people you love, and West Point just sits here on the Hudson and goes on without them. I've got news for you, Ash. The Academy was here nearly two hundred years before we first passed through the gates. It'll be here two hundred years after we're gone. West Point's a living thing, Ash. The Com doesn't rule West Point. He's just another temporary caretaker, like my dad."

He nodded like he understood, but she knew that he hadn't. He was scared, and guys who are scared will do almost anything to make their fear go away.

She gave him a wave. "So long, Ash."

"I made a mistake, Jace. I told you I was sorry. I don't want to lose you."

"Making mistakes is okay, Ash. It happens. But you made excuses. I'm the Supe's daughter, remember? I don't buy excuses."

She walked away into the darkness toward the barracks, leaving him standing alone. When she knew she was far enough away that he couldn't see her, she turned and looked back. The guy who had just been singing with such empathy and passion about the lost and lonely girl looked like a lost and lonely boy.

Her step quickened. She passed Grant Hall and turned up the ramp to New South Area. Not for the first time in the life of a young woman who had lived in twenty different houses and apartments by the time she departed for West Point at eighteen, the barracks looked like home.

CHAPTER 16

WALKING BACK to the barracks, Ash was still in shock. It was the depth of Jacey's anger that surprised him, threw him off balance. He knew he had fucked up. It was just that he hadn't thought he fucked up big-time. But she did. She sure made that clear enough.

One of the things that attracted him to Jacey in the first place was that she had guts and she wasn't afraid to speak her mind. She was smart and funny and pretty and sexy and all that other stuff, but it was her courage that really grabbed him. You could feel it when you got close to her, like heat from a fire inside her. She had physical courage, which made her every bit as skilled at some of the toughest parts of their military training as any of the guys were. She rappelled down the side of a cliff like a mountain goat, springing easily from one rocky outcropping to another with graceful leaps and sideways jeté's that were balletlike. She could hump a pack with the best of them. She was among the top ten or fifteen cadets in the whole company in the two-mile run. During night training, she was unafraid to venture into pitch-blackness, following a compass course or her own instincts. One night, leading a patrol, she had fallen down a steep ravine that was invisible in the darkness, and Ash and the others on the patrol had stood there at the top like dummies. They couldn't see her. They could barely make out the ravine itself. They had no idea what had become of her until they heard her down there, yelling back up to them to come on down, which they did, and she continued the patrol from there, following the ravine to a little knoll she had found on the map. From the knoll she had figured a way to the objective, which they reached about two hours before they had been expected, so their attack against the "enemy" force was a real surprise. Her performance that night was one of the accomplishments that had earned her four stripes and a company command.

Ash could not take lightly her anger or her passion. He was paying the price of guilt for his mistake, and it was a steep one. Yet there was another, more complicated emotion he was dealing with. Even though he was the one who had screwed up, he found it impossible to accept the brutal dismissal she had dealt him. He was angry at himself and at her. But mostly at her. Guys weren't supposed to put up with shit like that from girls. Just because you screwed up didn't mean you had to lie down and take whatever she dished out. Hell, West Point taught you that from day one. You're a warrior. You don't take shit from *anybody.*

When he got back to the barracks, he stopped at her room to see if they couldn't talk it out, but Belle said Jacey didn't want to see him. Later on he called her, and when she answered, she said something like, "I've said all I have to say to you," and slammed the phone down.

He was *really* pissed, and the thing that pissed him off the most was when she told him he was scared of Gibson. She didn't understand that they lived in the real world, and Gibson ran the particular real world they lived in, and you had to respect that. You had to respect power, and Gibson had a shitload of power. That was what she didn't get. He and Favro and the rest of the guys didn't fear Gibson, they *respected* him. The closest he could come to understanding why she didn't get it was that she was a general's daughter. He tried to point out the difference between them, but she didn't listen. She was so convinced he had betrayed her that she turned down the reason thing and turned up the female thing.

When he hung up the phone he immediately called Rose and told him Jacey knew about the party and that Dorothy was there. Rose told him to meet up in the organ-practice room at the chapel.

Not many cadets knew that there was a little set of stairs behind a door at the side of the Cadet Chapel that led to a small room in the attic. You went up the narrow stairs, and at the top there was a door, and when you opened the door, there was this little room with an organ at one end and a bunch of wooden handles sticking out of the wall over on the right. There were some little firing-slit-type windows on one side, and you could look down and see the whole area of barracks from up there. A guy who was in the choir and also rang the chapel bells on Sunday mornings told him the wooden handles were just like the ones up in the belfry; they used them to practice. He tried it. You'd hit the handle, and you heard a little bell that imitated the sound of one of the big ones in the belfry. He and Jacey used to go up there at night when they were cows. It was quiet and totally private.

Rose was already there when Ash reached the practice room, and the others soon followed: Favro and Reade and Lessard and Ivar. Every guy in the room had the chiseled features of a male model. It was like an unwritten rule at West Point. You didn't see many guys wearing six stripes who fell very far outside the all-American-boy norm. Like nearly every other cadet, they were in excellent shape.

Ash was standing there with his hands in his pockets looking out one of the little windows when he heard Rose's voice. He turned around.

"Prudhomme tells me Jacey Slaight knows about the party."

"She fucking *knows*?" It was Ivar, the running back on the football team. It was the conceit of skilled athletes to believe that because of their physical prowess and the popularity that flowed from it, they had the most to lose when something went wrong in their lives.

Rose held a finger to his lips, silencing Ivar. "You never know who's around," he whispered. Then, to Ash: "How much does she know?"

"She knows about the party and that Dorothy was there. She's really far gone, because I didn't tell her about it. She thinks I betrayed her."

"How did she find out?"

"She got ahold of Dorothy's E-mail."

"Shit." Favro paced back and forth along the row of wood handles. "There was stuff from me, if she saved it."

"Well, it's there all right, because Jacey read it. All of it."

"Oh, Christ, that's all we need," said Lessard.

"Wait a minute. We're jumping way ahead of ourselves here," said Rose in measured tones. He was the most powerful man in the room. As Chairman of the Honor Committee, his power transcended battalions and regiments. It was Corps-wide. "What'd you tell her about the party?"

"I told her the truth. We had a couple of kegs, we rented a cabin, we went swimming, guys had dates. She's been to enough cadet parties to know the score. I even told her Dorothy wasn't drinking. But I mean, she knows stuff was going on . . ."

"What kind of stuff are you talking about?" asked Rose.

"People were fucking in the cabin. She's been to cadet parties. She knows what goes on."

"Did she tell you anything else about the E-mail?"

"No. The only thing she was pissed about was me not telling her about the party, 'cause she said the investigation is trying to look at everything that happened to Dorothy in the hours and days before she died."

Rose looked over at Favro, and then the two of them exchanged glances with Reade.

"I'm not sure there's a whole lot to worry about here," said Rose. "All we were doing out there at the lake was drinking beer and partying. Listen, Ash, I want to thank you for telling us about Jacey. We owe you one."

The others in the room stood around Ash in a semicircle. It was clear that they were indicating he should leave. "I guess I'll be going," he said, a little uncertainly.

"Don't worry about it. We'll handle it," said Rose. "Thanks again, man."

"Sure." As he headed down the stairs, Ash heard the door click closed behind him.

Favro was pacing the room. "Christ, Jacey's gonna take Dorothy's E-mail to her daddy, and all hell's gonna break loose."

Reade walked into the middle of the room and addressed the others like he was playing the role of adjutant at parade. "We've got to do something. We can't let her go blowing us out of the water. We've got to talk some sense into her."

Ivar was rolling his shoulders and fidgeting and scratching his crotch.

Rose walked over to him and threw an arm over his massive shoulder. "Listen, man, I think you ought to get back to the barracks and get some sleep. You've got a big game coming up. You don't have anything to worry about. All you were doing was hanging out and having some brews and swinging on that rope swing and dropping into the water, remember?"

Ivar nodded.

Rose's tone was soothing. "Leave it to me. I'll make sure nothing happens to you. I'm going to talk to Jacey myself. She'll understand."

Ivar's face brightened. "You mean it, man?"

"Sure. Get some rest. I want to see your numbers up another hundred yards on Saturday, man. I don't want you worrying and breaking your concentration."

"Okay, man." Ivar moved to the door. "See you guys," he said maneuvering his broad shoulders through the narrow door. Reade stepped over and closed it behind him.

Now there were just four remaining in the organ practice room: Rose, Favro, Reade, and Lessard.

Favro was still pacing. "Jesus fuckin' Christ, Rose, the bitch is going to fuck everything up for us."

"Yeah, man. We've got to do something," Lessard whined.

Rose walked slowly into the middle of the room. "You *idiots* have got to get your wits about you and look at this thing logically. What's she got? She knows we had a party. Big deal. She's been to our parties. What's she going to do? Go to her daddy and tell him there are these guys she parties with, and Dorothy went to one of their parties and then she dropped dead? I don't think so."

Favro stopped pacing and turned to face him.

"Now listen to me," said Rose. "She's got some stuff off Dorothy's E-mail she's going to have to take to the CID, or she'll be derelict in her duty, and I think we all know that's not going to happen. I think we can assume that the CID is going to question us. So what?

We can handle it. All we've got to do is get our stories straight."

"What are you gonna tell the CID?" asked Reade in a tone of desperation.

"We tell them we had a party and Dorothy Hamner was one of the girls who were there. We don't know anything about why she died the next day at parade. What are they going to do? There's no way they can prove any different."

"We're going to have to tell Gibson," said Lessard. "This whole thing could come apart. The Supe's going to be calling him in, and he's got to be prepped. Slaight's going to ask him what all of his six-stripers were doing out there at Greenwood Lake with the dead girl."

"You let me deal with Gibson. That's *my* job," instructed Rose.

"You think Gibson can handle Slaight?" asked Reade.

Rose snapped his fingers. "Like that."

Favro had been looking out one of the windows. He turned around. "What's going to happen if Jacey figures out that five or six members of the Honor Committee were at the party? Don't you think this thing is cutting a little close to the bone? I mean, it's not about Dorothy Hamner. We've got a lot to lose if she puts two and two together and she stops worrying about the dead girl and starts looking at *us*."

"Trust me. Nothing's going to happen," commanded Rose. "Everything we did was under the orders of the Commandant of Cadets. We're covered."

"I wish I was as confident about that as you are, Rose. But I'm not."

"You don't know Gibson like I do. Do you think he'd ask us to do anything which dishonored West Point? He's the one who's trying to *save* West Point, Favro."

"I know what he stands for, Rose. But I'm starting to get the feeling he's standing on our backs. You tell me why we should trust him to protect us."

"Because he's an honorable man and because there isn't a tougher son of a bitch on the face of this earth. We are his *warriors,* Favro. We follow orders without question. Every single weakling we ran out of here on Honor failed to measure up to the warrior standards General Gibson has returned to West Point. Not only have we done our duty, we have upheld the ethos of the warrior. Only the strong survive. We are strong. We are warriors. General Gibson would die before he would allow us to be dishonored.''

"I sure as hell hope you're right about Gibson," said Favro.

"I know I'm right."

Reade checked his watch. "We'd better get going. Taps is in ten minutes."

Rose walked to the door and then turned to face the others. "I'll talk to Gibson. He'll know what to do."

The others nodded their heads in agreement. Rose opened the door of the organ-practice room and they filed down the stairs, one after the other, behind the Chairman of the Honor Committee.

CHAPTER 17

S LAIGHT CALLED to Melissa through the open door of his office. "Get me General Gibson, will you?"

"Right away, sir."

In a moment his phone buzzed, and he picked up. "Jack, have you got a moment? Something has come up I need to talk to you about. Okay. Ten minutes."

Melissa was standing in the door. "More coffee, sir? I'll put on a fresh pot."

"I think you'd better. Gibson's going to need a jolt when this is over."

Slaight picked up his copy of the *Times*. There was a front-page story on the findings of yet another Pentagon commission on women in the military. This one was chaired by a former senator from Kansas. Problems between young men and women in basic training had persuaded the commission to recommend to the Secretary of Defense that all basic and advanced individual training in the services should be segregated.

Brilliant, he thought, recalling the problems he had encountered between black and white soldiers when he had first entered the Army as a lieutenant back in 1969. He served as a platoon leader in an infantry division that had suffered race riots, racial beatings, and several racially motivated slayings. He recalled one murder that had happened in his brigade. Four white soldiers had jumped a black soldier on guard one night and beat him to death with baseball bats. They caught the four eventually, and they were tried and convicted of murder, but that didn't stop the killing. Three more soldiers would die in racial incidents before he was transferred, and the place he went next was hardly better.

He marveled at the commission's recommendation that training should be segregated by sex, and thought back to what would have happened if a similar commission had recommended that the races be segregated when race was such a painful problem in the military. The lid would have blown off the country, that's what would have happened. The return of racial segregation to the military would have produced riots that made Watts and Newark look like playground tussles.

He heard a tap at the door and looked up to find Melissa escorting Gibson into the office. He stood up as Gibson saluted. He pointed to one of the armchairs. "Have a seat, Jack. Coffee?"

Gibson nodded. "I'd like that, sir."

Slaight made a mental note that at least a modicum of respect had returned to Gibson's manner. Melissa poured coffee and they sat down, again facing each other across the coffee table. Melissa left, closing the door behind her.

"I've thought this thing over, and there isn't any good way to go about the business we have this morning, so I'm going to cut out the bullshit and get right down to it. I know you're having an affair with Helen Messick, and I want you to knock it off."

Gibson sipped his coffee. If he had been startled, he didn't show it. "I don't know what you're talking about."

"All right then, maybe I can refresh your memory. I'm the one who saw the two of you in her garage Monday night."

"I was at home Monday night. My wife will back me up."

"We'll deal with your wife when the time comes, Jack, but I can tell you that your Porsche was most definitely in Helen's garage, and a man who looked just like you was standing there next to it kissing Helen Messick. It has been reported to me that you were seen with her late at night entering a hotel room in New York City. Is that any help to you?"

Gibson put down his coffee cup and glared at Slaight. "You don't have shit on me, General, and even if you did, you wouldn't bring charges.''

Slaight chuckled. "I knew you'd stonewall me, Jack. You're right. I won't bring charges against you because I don't want to drag West Point through an adultery investigation. But I'm here to tell you that I know what you're up to with Helen Messick, and I am giving you a direct order to knock it off. Is that clear enough for you?''

"Quite clear.''

"Let me tell you what's going to happen if it comes to my attention that you continue to carry on an affair with Helen Messick. I'll fix it so the star currently perched on your uniform epaulet is the last star you'll get. Do you understand me?''

"I don't cotton to threats. Not from you, General. Not from anybody.''

"I'm not threatening you, Jack. I am *promising* that you will end your career as a brigadier general, and that your next commander will know exactly how you carried out your duties as Commandant here at West Point. I am *promising* you that while I will not drag West Point's good name through the mud, I will be delighted to sully your name in every precinct of command which exists in this Army. And if you don't think I can do this to you, then you didn't pay much attention when I was your battalion commander. I'll do it, Jack, and I'll take great pleasure from it.''

Gibson leaned back in his chair and cracked a little smile. "You don't know who you're dealing with.''

"Oh, yes, I do. You're Cecil Avery's pet general, and you're buddies with Congressman Thrunstone, and you think you've got the Pentagon wired, and you think your career's on fire and not even a goddamned hurricane could put it out. Well, I'm not a hurricane, Jack. All I am is a lieutenant general who has ordered you to cease your affair with Helen Messick. But you'd better get this straight before you walk out of my office. I'm the Superintendent of West Point, and when I give orders, I expect them to be obeyed, and if my orders are not obeyed, I will do what I have just promised you. I'll cut you down like a sapling, Jack, and there won't be a goddamned thing you can do about it. Now get the hell out of my office.''

Gibson started to say something, but Slaight pointed silently at the door. Gibson walked out without a salute.

CHAPTER 18

GENERAL SLAIGHT opened the Scott Place gate to the garden and made his way down its winding pathways to find his wife sitting on the back patio with a large metal bowl between her knees shelling peas. He kissed the top of her head. "Where'd you find those, Sam?"

"Farm stand up in Vails Gate. Last of the season. I thought I'd throw them in a pan with scallops and a little white wine and cream and mint and toss in some linguini and see what happens."

"Hmmmmm. I know what will happen. It'll disappear down a couple of gullets in about ten seconds."

She laughed. "Does anybody like food more than you?"

"Cliff Bassett."

"Besides him."

He thought for a moment. "You."

"I'm not even in the same county as you. You're like the fifty-first state of food. There should be a star on the flag for your stomach."

He cracked up. She was right. As a cadet he had set records for inhaling incredible quantities of food. He and Buck and Luger used to go down to New York to a little hole in the wall called Puglia's just off Mulberry Street, where for about three dollars you could eat enough eggplant parmigiana and throw back enough coarse Sicilian red to bring on the DTs the next day. While his palate had become more refined over the years, the simple fact was, he just plain liked to eat.

"Where are the scallops?"

"In the fridge."

"I'll slice 'em up and get a pot of water going for the pasta."

"Not yet you won't. I haven't had a spritzer yet. And you look like you could use a martini. Why don't you get cleaned up and come back with the drinks?"

In a few minutes her husband reappeared looking refreshed. "You took a shower," she said approvingly.

"And brushed my teeth and cleaned my nails, sir," Slaight barked, imitating one of the reports plebes were required to give nightly to their squad leaders in his day. They laughed. He was carrying a tray of drinks and hors d'oeuvres. She followed him to a wrought-iron table and chairs that were tucked into a little grove of boxwood at the back of the garden. They sat down, and he handed her a spritzer. He picked up his martini and took a long sip.

"Boston P.D. picked up four of our hockey players around three A.M. last night down in the Combat Zone. They had a preseason game with Boston College earlier and skipped out of the team hotel and decided they needed to see what the inside of a strip club looked like. There was an altercation with the club's bouncers. One of our boys has a broken jaw, but apparently the bouncers fared much worse. Three of them were hospitalized."

"They arrested the cadets?"

"Yeah. I had the SJA airmail two of his best JAGs up there this morning, and they're working on it. I think what's going to happen is, the strip club will press charges, and the cadets will press countercharges, and the cops will drop the whole thing if we get the cadets out of Boston and promise they'll never return to the Combat Zone."

"Sounds like a fair deal to me," Sam said, spreading some soft cheese on a cracker. "What's going to happen to the hockey players when they get back here?"

"I'm sure they'll face at least a regimental board. I don't think they'll be spending much time on the ice this winter. Not wearing skates, anyway."

"Well, it could have turned out a lot worse. That's a bad area in Boston. They could have gotten themselves killed."

He swirled the ice around in the martini pitcher and poured himself another glass. "So how was your day?"

"I took Helen Messick with me to the farm stand this morning. We had lunch afterward."

"Really? Did she call you?"

"I called her. She's a lonely woman, Ry. That husband of hers is no prize, and I don't see Gibson providing much in the way of warmth and affection."

"You didn't sound like you felt very sorry for her before."

"I thought about it some. I wanted to leave the door open a crack for her, you know, Ry? She's not a bad person. I even kind of like her."

He leaned over and kissed her. "Again," she commanded when he pulled away. This time he grabbed her under her arms and lifted her into his lap and held the back of her head with both hands and kissed her nose and her cheeks and her chin and her neck and her lips, and when they parted, she licked her lips, and said, "I don't like martinis, but you taste *good.*"

They sat there for a while like that, sipping their drinks. "I wonder what's going to happen to Jace when she leaves here next year. I wonder if she'll find a guy like you and end up as a middle-aged woman who feels as lucky as I feel right now."

Slaight ran his fingers along one of the elegant blue veins that showed through the skin of her forearm. "Sometimes I feel like I don't really know my own daughter."

"What do you mean?" asked Sam.

"I didn't get to see her half as much as you did when she was growing up. I was always working long Army hours, and there were those times when I was overseas in Korea, or gone for six months on some damn temporary duty. Even when I was home for a stretch, I didn't do the stuff you did, like drive her to soccer, or pick her up from ballet lessons, or go shopping with her at the mall. I think I missed out on a lot."

"Well, you're not a mother, you're a father. But we had vacations, and you used to take her on those long drives between duty stations. Remember? You insisted that I fly and get there early and do the

whole quarters thing. I always thought you wanted that time to yourself with her.''

"I did.''

"You're a good father. She loves you very much, Ry.''

"I know, but I still feel like there's something missing between us.
I don't think she feels like she can talk to me the way she talks to
you.''

"Trust me. It's a girl thing.''

"I guess you're right.''

"You know I am.'' She rolled off his lap and stood up. "Are you
interested in sautéing some scallops and peas while I boil us up some
pasta?''

"You bet I am.''

"Do you think we should call Jacey and see if she wants to come
over?''

Following behind her, he reached up and grabbed her ass. "Nope.
I want you all to myself.'' She laughed and ran ahead of him into
the kitchen. He stopped at the screen door and stood there for a
moment, watching her lean over to reach for a pot at the back of a
cabinet. He'd seen her do it literally thousands of times in kitchens
big and small, in quarters they had lived in quite literally all over the
world, and it was like he could remember every time she had ever
opened a cabinet and reached for a pot. There was one thing you
could say about the kind of long-term marriage they had. The years
piled memory atop memory until finally you found yourself standing
there on a hill and the view you had was of your life together. He
knew that in cities like New York and Los Angeles, people paid millions of dollars to live in penthouses or houses in the Hollywood
Hills with views of the city.

Suddenly, he felt lucky. The price he'd paid for his view could
only be measured in years, and he was thankful for every one of
them.

CHAPTER 19

O N THE afternoon after the meeting at the organ-practice room, Rose called the office of the Commandant and requested a meeting. Gibson instructed his secretary to tell Rose to meet at his office after supper the next day. The Com had a suspicion this was not going to turn out to be one of their regular meetings about the Honor Committee.

Rose entered the Com's office, snapped a salute, and sat down stiffly in a chair across the desk from the Com.

"What's on your mind, Jerry?"

"Sir, we've got a problem. Jacey Slaight found out Dorothy Hamner was at our Labor Day party."

"Who told you that?"

"Prudhomme, sir. He was at the party, too."

"Who brought Hamner to the party?"

"Favro, sir."

"So she went to your party. I don't see the problem, Rose."

"Three of us had sex with her, sir."

"You idiots gang-banged Hamner? What in hell were you thinking?"

"We didn't gang-bang her, sir."

"So who fucked her?"

"Sir, it was me and Favro and Ivar."

Gibson rolled his eyes. "Did she put up any resistance?"

"No sir."

"So none of you forced yourself on the girl, is that correct?"

"Yes sir."

Gibson leaned back in his desk chair. "You realize what you little bastards have done? You let your dicks do your thinking for you, and you put everything we have worked for in jeopardy."

"Sir, I realize we made a mistake, but I think there's a way we can recover from it."

An odd, guttural sound surged from somewhere deep in Gibson's chest, startling Rose. The Commandant's eyes bulged, his upper body jerked forward, and when he pointed his cigar at Rose, it was shaking. "You think you can handle this, do you, Mr. Rose?"

"Uh, yes sir . . ."

"I don't know what I was thinking when I hand-picked you for Honor Chairman. It's a goddamned miracle you can find your way back to your own room at night."

Rose stared at the Com, eyes unblinking. He'd never seen Gibson explode like this before. He sat there considering his options. Neither of them were particularly savory. He could take the position that a West Point sexual group-grope was nothing new at the Academy and would fall into the wastebasket of "What else is new?" But he knew well the downside. Politically correct feminists at the Academy would call for their scalps.

His other option was to apply some pressure of his own to Gibson. There was a strange thing about ranking cadets and officers at West Point. They needed each other, and often it was difficult for either side to know how much.

Rose chose the second option. What did he have to lose? His career hadn't even really begun. Gibson, on the other hand, was what the Army called a "fast-burner," a man in a hurry. For this reason Rose felt he held the upper hand by the thinnest of margins.

He began slowly and deliberately: "General Gibson, I came here this evening to tell you that several of us have made a mistake. We can deal with the mistake we made, but I'm not sure West Point can handle this thing if it gets out of hand."

Gibson snarled, "What the hell do you mean by that?"

"Sir, if it's revealed that we had a party and that several of us had sex with Dorothy Hamner, it will be damaging, but not fatally. The fact she didn't charge anyone with date rape is evidence enough that the sex was consensual. The wild card in this thing is Jacey Slaight. She's got Dorothy Hamner's E-mail, and I am not certain what it contains."

"You mean there were messages to this girl from some of our people?"

"Favro sent her E-mail messages, sir, and Jacey Slaight has them. She knows who was at the party. She's getting too close to us, sir. I know she's not going to stop with Dorothy Hamner. She'll keep digging and digging. She's going to figure out everyone at the party was on the Honor Committee, and if she starts snooping around and discovers that we've been using the committee to cleanse the Corps of unworthy people, we've got a problem that I know I cannot handle."

"Listen to me, Rose, and listen good. Slaight's daughter won't find out a thing if you keep our people lined up on this thing. Do you hear me? This calls for airtight discipline. Everything we did with the committee was done to reestablish the warrior culture here at West Point. The committee did its duty when it sent those who did not measure up to our standards back to civilian life where they belonged. You and the others are to be commended, Rose. You have upheld the ancient warrior values of West Point. You have helped to turn us back from the dangerous slide West Point was making into weakness and disorder. Do you understand me, Rose? You've got to get our people to stand together!"

"Sir, I can assure you that we'll stand up and do everything we can to stop her, but she's the Supe's daughter, sir. She's got a direct line straight to the top. If it were anyone else in the Corps, I could give you an ironclad guarantee that we could handle it. But not Jacey Slaight, sir. This Dorothy Hamner thing has driven her crazy. She's out of control."

"You're telling me because this goddamned female dropped dead out on the Plain, everything we've worked for is in jeopardy."

"Sir, what I'm saying is we can shut this thing down, but we're going to need some help. I will talk to Jacey Slaight, but I am not certain I will be able to convince her to pull in her horns."

"So you want me to do it for you."

"Sir, you're the Commandant. You have resources we don't have."

Gibson swiveled his desk chair around, facing the windows. He lit a cigar and remained in that position for what seemed to Rose like several moments. When he turned back around and spoke, his voice was steady but half an octave lower. It was clear to Rose that Gibson didn't know where this was taking him, and it made him nervous.

"I'm going to need something on Slaight's daughter. I want you to handle it yourself. Favro is a hothead, and Ivar is good for only one thing: yardage. Lessard's too easily frightened, and Reade is a pompous, strutting peacock. That's why I made him Adjutant. What about Prudhomme? How much does he know about us?"

"He doesn't know anything, sir."

"Are you certain of that?"

"Positive, sir."

"What's his relationship with Slaight's daughter?"

"She broke up with him, sir. He's pretty angry at her right now."

"Pump him for everything you can get on her. You've got to come up with some dirt on her that I can use against that SOB Slaight over in the Headquarters Building. He's the one we've got to worry about. I've heard he's going to appoint a female dean. He's fixing to turn this place over to a bunch of politically correct pantywaists, and I'm going to stop him."

"Yes sir." Rose relaxed. His ploy had worked. The Com thought that he, Rose, was carrying water for the Commandant, when in fact it was the other way around. Gibson was going at Slaight through his daughter, and he needed Rose to do it for him.

"Maybe it's not such a bad thing that Slaight's daughter has injected herself into the middle of this thing. It puts her right in our crosshairs. If we can bring down his daughter, we can bring him down. And not so incidentally, everything we've worked to accomplish here at West Point will be protected as well."

"Sir, you can trust me to get Jacey Slaight for you."

Gibson took a satisfying pull on his cigar. He was pleased with the Chairman of the Honor Committee. He was indeed a cadet in his own image: cunning, ruthless, and smart. "I'm counting on you, Jerry."

Rose saluted General Gibson, picked up his cap, and left. The moment Gibson heard Rose descending the stairs, he picked up the phone and dialed the number in Washington, D.C., belonging to his friend and mentor, Cecil Avery.

"Cecil? It's Jack Gibson. I need you to get a message to Congressman Thrunstone for me. He's coming up to the Point this weekend for the game with Southern Illinois. I want Thrunstone to know that I don't trust Slaight and neither should he. Slaight's carrying water for that piece of shit Meuller. He's on the wrong side of every issue we care about. Tell Thrunstone I believe Slaight is a danger to our Army and a danger to our nation. He's hell-bent on moving females into every nook and cranny of the Army. I want Thrunstone to understand that Slaight is one of the politically correct assholes who are weakening our standards, weakening our Army, and weakening our national defense. Thanks, Cecil."

Gibson hung up the phone and allowed himself a satisfied smile. The Superintendent's visit with the Chairman of the House National Security Committee would be spun in a way he was certain that Slaight would never expect.

BOOK

TWO

T HERE WAS no direct route to take from West Point to Oneonta, so Jacey decided on Route 28 west out of Kingston
through the Catskills. She hadn't made that drive since the previous
winter, when, as a member of the Ski Patrol, she used to take weekend trips up to Belleayre or Hunter Mountain for training. She
passed through the familiar little towns of Mount Tremper and Phoe-
nicia and Highmount, and from there journeyed into an even more
sparsely populated area of the state. Ten or fifteen miles would pass
before the next little town emerged from within the trees. Finally
she drove beneath the I-88 underpass into Oneonta.

It was a college town with a state university and a private liberal-
arts school located a few miles from one another. Leafy streets were
lined with turn-of-the-century houses, and the downtown business
district was still intact, not having been seriously challenged by a mall
sited in a field on the edge of town. Oneonta reminded her of the
towns outside the gates of the Army posts on which she had grown
up. Like an Army town, it was a one-industry kind of place. You could
drive its streets and imagine pipe-smoking English professors behind
every fifth door.

She found the Hamner house on a cul-de-sac near the state university. It was a split-level that had probably been built sometime in

the early 1960s in the spasm of domestic-dwelling modernity that somehow concluded that houses should have both a "family" room and a "living" room, that these two spaces should be on separate floors, and that the main entrance to the home should provide you with your choice of rooms. You could descend the half-stairs into the "family" room or ascend similar stairs into the "living" room. Jacey had lived in a split-level when she was in high school and her father had been stationed in the D.C. area, and she had concluded that its architectural style had probably reflected the state of the American family when the house was built. Houses were split and families were split and kids were confronted every day with choices of families and lifestyles and a dozen other decisions that should never have been theirs to make in the first place. The second half of the twentieth century had been a schizophrenic age, and even the dwellings in which families as well as floor space were split reflected this.

She parked on the street and knocked at the side door under the carport. Mrs. Hamner answered. Jacey had met her several times over the years. The last time had been when the Hamners came to the Academy to claim Dorothy's body, and Jacey's company had provided the honor guard that carried the casket to the hearse. Mrs. Hamner looked younger than the mothers of the other cadets Jacey knew. She had thought maybe Dorothy had been born when her mother was about seventeen or eighteen. But the youthful glow Mrs. Hamner had shown before was gone now. She had lost weight. Her face was thin and drawn, and there were lines at the corners of her mouth that hadn't been there last year.

"Jacey, please, come in. It was good of you to call." Mrs. Hamner gave her a clinging hug. When she pulled away, she turned quickly toward the kitchen sink. "Would you like a cup of coffee, or maybe some tea?"

"Yes ma'am, tea would be great," Jacey said.

When Jacey had found Dorothy's private E-mail on floppy disks that she had hidden in her roommate's file box, she wondered if there weren't more disks that Dorothy had taken home. She had called Mrs. Hamner and asked if she could drive up and bring a few things of Dorothy's that had been inadvertently left behind. On the phone, Mrs. Hamner had seemed eager to see her. Dorothy had been an only child. Jacey could only imagine her loneliness and depth of loss.

As Mrs. Hamner busied herself making tea, they chatted awkwardly about West Point football. The Hamners were big fans and had attended every game while Dorothy was alive. The victory over UVA last Saturday had been a delightful surprise, Mrs. Hamner said. They had wished the game had been televised. She guessed they'd have to wait for the Army–Navy game to see the cadets play again. They wouldn't be attending any more games at Michie Stadium. The memories were too painful. Her voice caught and she leaned both hands against the sink. For a moment, Jacey thought she was going to cry and moved to comfort her. But Mrs. Hamner recovered her composure and poured two cups of tea, and they sat down at the kitchen table.

Jacey had spent the drive to Oneonta trying to figure out the best way to handle the situation, but there wasn't a best way, or even a better way. She reached into her purse and pulled out the envelope containing the E-mail disks and put it on the table. "Carrie found these in one of her storage files, Mrs. Hamner. They are floppy disks that contain Dorothy's private E-mail. We thought you might like to have them, since some of them are letters she wrote home, and letters she received from you and her father."

Mrs. Hamner took a deep breath, her eyes wide. Then she held up her hands defensively. "It's . . . it's too painful. You keep them. Her father and I have our memories. That's all we want . . . our memories."

Jacey picked up the envelope and was going to put it back into her purse when she thought better of it and placed the envelope back on the table. "Mrs. Hamner, I wasn't exactly straight with you on the phone when I called from West Point. Returning these private E-mail disks isn't the only reason I wanted to come up here and talk to you. There is a third disk we found that may be important in finding out why Dorothy died. We found messages about a party she attended the day before she died. I think something may have happened to Dorothy at the party which contributed to her death."

Mrs. Hamner folded her hands in her lap and looked out the kitchen window. "Dorothy told me about the party. She was so excited. She had a new boyfriend. She was just beginning her senior year. She had her whole life in front of her . . .'' Mrs. Hamner's voice trailed away, and she raised her hands to her lips as if in prayer. ''She took such delight in her life at West Point. It's hard for me to believe that she won't ever walk through the door again with a big smile on her face carrying a bag of laundry for me to do for her.''

Jacey took a sip of tea and waited. Mrs. Hamner reached for the envelope and the floppies spilled out onto the table. She looked over at Jacey, a great sadness seeming to deepen and darken her eyes. ''Dorothy's computer is upstairs in her room. Neither her father or I have touched anything of hers since she died.''

''Ma'am, I can hardly imagine how painful this is for you, but I'd like to have a look at Dorothy's computer. It's important to me, Mrs. Hamner, because she was my friend, and I need to know what happened to her. Do you understand? I promise you nothing is going to happen that will harm Dorothy's reputation. I promise you that, Mrs. Hamner.''

Mrs. Hamner's eyes welled up with tears and she grasped Jacey's hand in both of hers. ''You were a great friend to Dorothy. I just know she's looking down at us right now, and she knows how much you care about her.''

Jacey felt tears in her own eyes, and they sat there for a moment holding hands across the table. Then Mrs. Hamner stood up and, still holding her hand, led the way down a short hall and up a short flight of stairs.

''This is Dorothy's room,'' she said, opening a door. She flipped on an overhead light. The room was filled with Dorothy's things from high school: awards for being in a regional champion band, a boyfriend's letter sweater, photographs from proms, pom-poms, and all of the other stuff girls accumulate in their teens. Strangely missing was any evidence that Dorothy was a cadet. Mrs. Hamner must have realized that Jacey had noticed this, and said, ''We keep Dorothy's West Point things downstairs in the family room.''

''I had a room just like this,'' said Jacey. She saw the corner of a laptop computer sticking out from beneath a huge teddy bear on a desk across the room. ''Is that Dorothy's laptop?''

''Yes,'' said Mrs. Hamner. ''My husband uses it, too. That's how we sent our E-mail things to Dorothy. But neither of us has touched it since she died. Everything in her room is just as she left it the last time she was home.''

Jacey picked up the teddy bear, put it on the bed, and sat down at the desk. She opened the laptop and switched it on.

Mrs. Hamner was still standing in the door. ''I know Dorothy used to sit there when she was at home and work on her E-mail, because every once in a while she'd come downstairs and tell me some funny joke they were passing around on the Internet. You go ahead. I'm going back downstairs.''

The laptop powered up, and Jacey scanned the desktop. She hit the icon for Netscape and used Dorothy's password, ''catch22,'' to open her mail. Unlike her computer at school, the laptop seemed to have most of her E-mail on the hard drive. The ''in-box'' file contained about fifty messages. Jacey hit the ''sent'' button and found that that file contained just over a hundred messages.

Jacey's finger hit the touchpad and she started opening the messages in the ''sent'' file, which had been written on the laptop by Jacey and her father. The messages from her father responded to E-mail Jacey had sent from West Point. It was mostly chatty stuff between daughter and parents, responding to Dorothy's complaints about midterm exams, congratulating her on the brigade championship her orienteering team had won. Dorothy had written quite a few E-mails the previous summer when she had been home, messages to classmates and friends from West Point, talking about boys and parties, lamenting the days that were disappearing as their return to the Academy loomed at the end of their summer leaves. And there were some messages she had sent to friends she'd had in high school, who were scattered around the state and the country at various colleges. There was nothing in the ''sent'' file about the Labor Day party, and none of the E-mail she had sent from home had been to Favro. At least, none of it stored on the hard drive, anyway.

Jacey closed the ''sent'' file and opened the list of messages in her in-box. It was loaded down with messages Dorothy had sent her parents from West Point, making plans for weekend visits home and arranging for several visits her parents had made to West Point for football and basketball games the previous year. There were responses from her friends to the E-mails she had sent the previous summer. Jacey found two of her own E-mails to Dorothy, which she had sent on her laptop during summer training.

She went through the rest of the message list and found Dorothy's E-mails to her parents, and more personal stuff to her friends. When she reached the bottom of the in-box, she noticed the date and time of the final message. It was three days before Labor Day. There were no messages after that. Jacey sat there staring at the last message that had been logged onto the laptop in Dorothy's room at home.

What if her parents didn't check their E-mail regularly?

She hit the "get messages" button and waited. Sure enough, two new messages popped up in the in-box. Both were from Dorothy.

Jacey opened the first message. It had been sent two days before Labor Day. Dorothy was excited about the party and clearly smitten with Rick Favro. She told her mother about a new dress she'd bought that she planned on wearing to the party. She'd gotten her hair cut just before returning to the Academy. It was a letter from a girl who was falling in love.

Jacey closed the first message and opened the second. She checked the time and date. It had been sent at 4:04 in the morning on the day after Labor Day, the day Dorothy died!

Mom: I tried calling you just now, but you weren't home. I guess you had to work early today. I need to talk to you. Something happened, and I don't know what to do about it. I'll call you later today, after the parade. Love, Dorothy.

Jacey sat there staring at the laptop's screen. So something *did* happen to her, and it must have happened at the party, or else why would she be trying to call her mother so early in the morning? She searched quickly through Dorothy's drawer, found an empty floppy disk, saved the last E-mail Dorothy had written to the disk, and shut down the laptop.

Downstairs, she found Mrs. Hamner sitting with her cup of tea, staring out the kitchen window. She couldn't figure a good way to tell her what she had found, so she decided to let it go. The people who could do something about it were at West Point anyway.

"Mrs. Hamner? I think I'd better be going now."

Mrs. Hamner stood and and took Jacey's hand. "Did you find anything?"

"Not really, ma'am."

"Well, thank you for driving up here. I know Dorothy would appreciate what you're doing."

Mrs. Hamner opened the back door and stood there in the tranquillity of an upstate fall afternoon with a cool breeze gently ruffling her skirt. She looked at Jacey with her darkened eyes, then she leaned forward and kissed Jacey on the forehead in the way Jacey remembered her kissing Dorothy one weekend in Beast Barracks when they were plebes. Mrs. Hamner gave Jacey's hand a little squeeze, and Jacey stepped outside and heard the screen door snap shut behind her.

Jacey had a long drive ahead of her and some thinking to do, and as she started the car, she turned on the radio and found an oldies station that was playing Chuck Berry. He was singing about cruising and playing the radio with no particular place to go, and suddenly Jacey felt a wave wash over her and she felt a longing for the time in her life when she had a room just like Dorothy's. For all of her youthful frights and anxieties and panics, she knew that she hadn't had a worry in the world. She remembered how she had sat up at night in her room with her friends in their nightgowns at slumber parties, how they had whispered secrets to one another and giggled and gasped, and then Monday would come and all the secrets would have been told and they would gather in the school hallways waiting for new secrets to be whispered, eager to share and compare the mysteries of each unfolding moment of their lives as time rushed by in way too big a hurry, edging them into the future where new secrets, bigger secrets, deeper mysteries awaited.

She knew she was there right now. This was the future and she was living it. She knew a secret, a big one, and she didn't know where it would take her, or what she'd find when she got there. She backed down the drive and headed out of the cul-de-sac. At the corner, she gunned the engine and turned up the radio. They were playing something by the Box Tops; she couldn't remember the title, but the lead singer kept wailing over and over that *every road is a lonely street . . .*

She stopped at the turn for Route 28 as a big semi thundered past, headed south, its running lights twinkling in the dusk. Alex Chilton's angst-tinged moan filled her ears, and she switched on her headlights, slipped the clutch, and aimed the car down the road behind the truck. The Box Tops had it right: Every road *is* a lonely street.

CHAPTER 21

MELISSA CALLED out to Slaight. "Chief of Staff for you on line one, sir."

He picked up the phone. "General Slaight, sir."

"Ry, I just got a call from an aide to Congressman Thrunstone, somebody by the name of Wasserstein. Seems like Thrunstone wants to come up there next weekend for the Southern Illinois game."

"We'll be happy to have him, sir. He's on the Board of Visitors, isn't he?" asked Slaight, referring to the group of congressmen who served as a kind of Board of Trustees for the Academy.

"He was, until he took over the National Security Committee in 'ninety-four. Listen, Ry. We've been hearing some whispers from over on Capitol Hill that Thrunstone has been talking quietly about sponsoring a bill to either close down the service academies or consolidate Army, Navy, and Air Force into one national military college. He's been telling people he wants to save post–cold war defense dollars, but we hear differently. What he's really up to is putting a scare into the Army's senior leadership so we'll go along with him on Army manpower cutbacks. He wants to shift a lot of Army money over to Air Force and Navy weapons programs, and we're fighting him on it. Now I don't want you to bring any of this up with him, because he hasn't gone public with his plans to close down the military academies. I just want you to be aware of what you're up against."

"All politicians are minefields, sir, but I'll be especially careful to watch my step around Thrunstone."

"Don't sell this guy short, Ry. He's smart, he's charming, and he's ruthless."

"I understand, sir."

"Let me hear from you as soon as he's gone."

"Will do, sir."

Slaight hung up the phone and reached for his personal address book. If there was one person in the country who could fill him in on Congressman Thrunstone, it was his old classmate Leroy Buck. Slaight knew that Buck had been watching Thrunstone since he was in the State Legislature in Illinois, because Buck had been involved in southern Illinois politics all his life, and in fact had lost a race against Thrunstone for a State Senate seat back in the early 1970s.

Buck had been Slaight's roommate and best friend when they were cadets, and he had played a key role in helping track down the killer of David Hand. Buck had not been what you'd call a typical cadet, and he turned out to be a less than typical officer. He ended up resigning from the Army less than two years after graduation over a dispute with the lieutenant general who commanded Fort Bragg, North Carolina.

It seemed that Buck and another West Point classmate, a black guy by the name of Modell, had encountered many white owners and managers of apartment buildings in Fayetteville, the civilian community near Fort Bragg, who refused to rent to black soldiers, and that included black officers. There were a few places in the "black section" of Fayetteville that Modell could have rented, but they were run-down and much further from the post than he wanted to live. So Buck and Modell ran a "salt-and-pepper" team on the white apartment owners. Modell would show up for an apartment advertised in the paper only to be told it had just been rented. When Buck showed up to rent the same apartment only moments later, magically it would be available.

They compiled a list of about twenty apartment complexes in this manner and turned the list over to the authorities at Fort Bragg, asking that the apartment owners be instructed that it was illegal to refuse to rent to black soldiers, or any other black citizens for that matter. After weeks of haggling with the lesser lights of the command structure of Fort Bragg, they ended up standing before the Commanding General, who let them know that he had no intention of disrupting the local community. Buck and Modell informed the general that they had studied the Fair Housing Act of 1968 at West Point and knew the Act had a provision that required the military to enforce the law by denying the payment of military housing funds to landlords who discriminated. The Commanding General went ballistic. They later discovered that it was his intention to run for governor when he retired the following year, and so his unwillingness to confront racism in Fayetteville was tinged with political ambition. Buck and Modell stood their ground and found themselves asked to resign from the Army, which, while solving Modell's housing problem, brought their careers to an abrupt end. Slaight had always believed that the Army had suffered a far greater loss than either Buck or Modell.

Slaight dialed a number in southern Illinois and a voice answered, "Midwest Financial Services."

"Buck, what are you up to?" he asked.

"Slaight, goddammit. What the hell's goin' on? You sound like you're callin' from next door."

"I'm sitting here in my office taking in my view of the Hudson. How about you?"

"I'm sitting here working on some fool's problem with his back taxes. What's on your mind?"

"I've got your congressman coming up here to visit on Saturday for the Southern Illinois game."

"You don't mean the distinguished silver-tongued devil Chuck Thrunstone, do you?"

"One and the same."

"That SOB's a crafty one, I'll tell you that much. If they cut 'em any sharper than Thrunstone these days, I haven't heard about 'em."

"Fill me in on his background, will you?"

"Well, you know he was a state rep for quite a few years, then he ran for State Senate and beat my ass. He stayed there until he rode the Reagan landslide of 1980 into the Congress. He's been carrying the district by sixty percent or more based on the farm programs he helped to shove through when he was on the Ag Committee. It surprised the hell out of a lot of people here in Illinois when he quit Ag to run the National Security Committee."

"General Meuller just called and told me Thrunstone has been making some noises about sponsoring a bill to close down the service academies. What do you think he's up to? I mean, West Point is not exactly a huge item in the defense budget, and he's saying he wants to save defense dollars."

"It's not a budgetary thing. It's something else."

Even over the airphone, Slaight could almost hear the gears turning in Buck's brain. "What kind of a guy is he?" Slaight asked.

"Kinda rare breed. Rural Republican who uses suburban Republican tactics and raises major bucks every time he runs. He outspent his opponent nearly two to one last time around, using a good deal of money from defense industries. On a personal level, people say he's okay. People 'round here like him 'cause he comes across as a good old boy. He works the American Legion halls and the small town potluck church dinners like a pro, which he is. He's been in politics his whole life."

"You got to know him personally, back when you ran against him, didn't you?"

"Yeah." There was a strange pause, as if Buck was collecting thoughts he didn't really want to revisit. "I used to kind of like him back before he switched parties. He did a lot of good for the state back then. Then he turned into one of those pro-Nixon Democrats, and he switched parties, and that was when I ran against him. Me and another guy ran a candidate against him for the House four years ago. He killed us with right-wing Willie Horton–style TV attack ads, and that soured me on him for good."

"So it's just politics? I mean, between you and him."

"It's never *just* politics, Ry. It's *all* politics. It's in the air. Only trouble is out here in Illinois, me and Thrunstone have got to breathe the same goddamned air."

Slaight laughed. Not a single edge had been filed off Leroy Buck over all these years. "What's your best guess about what he's up to rattling his saber against the service academies?"

Buck turned from the phone to someone in his office and told them to hold a call. When he came back on, he sounded animated.

"This whole thing with the military has turned so goddamned political. Did you see that article about the study some college professor did?"

"Yeah, I saw it. Amazing."

"What'd he say? Twenty years ago about a third of officers were registered Republicans. Now two-thirds of them have no problem telling this guy they're Republicans? Christ, Ry. The Army is turning itself into an interest group of the fuckin' Republican Party."

"I personally think his figures are off. The guys I know, especially senior officers, are about ninety percent Republicans. But if it's like you say, and the Army has transformed itself into an interest group of the Republicans, why isn't Thrunstone backing them up?"

"Here's what the problem is. When an organization that has been traditionally apolitical up and decides to get political, then a couple of things are gonna happen. One, the organization is gonna end up owing the politicians, and two, sooner or later the politicians are gonna take the interest group for granted. Look at the Democrats and the way they treat black supporters. Same thing is happening with the Army. They've become so solidly Republican, politicians like Thrunstone can take them for granted."

"So Thrunstone's not afraid of the generals, because he knows they've got noplace else to turn."

"That's right. He can look for other ways to get 'em to come around, other than cozying up to 'em at military-defense conventions like the Association of the United States Army. Those generals down there in the Pentagon have got incredible influence over how defense dollars are spent. If they blink their left eye, a billion goes this way, and if they blink their right eye, a billion can end up going that way. It's a fuckin' nightmare, Ry. Unless I'm way off base, I think Thrunstone wants to insure he's got a stranglehold on the dollars left in the shrinking defense budget. He's gonna want those dollars spent where him and his buddies can reap the political benefits of defense jobs, and he's willin' to scare the generals to make sure that happens."

"He wants an advantage when he deals with the generals on the next five-year defense budget."

"And General Meuller is lookin' for a way to deny him that advantage, which is why you heard from him this morning."

"One last question, Buck. How do you think I should play this thing when Thrunstone gets up here?"

"Thrunstone's a good old boy, and I wouldn't trust that good old boys' club over there in the Capitol Building any further than I could spit. Know why?"

Slaight just waited, for he knew Buck would answer his own question.

"The trouble with good old boys' clubs is they're old, full of boys, and there ain't anything good about 'em at all, least of all that silver-tongued devil, Thrunstone."

Slaight lost it. He nearly pulled the laugh muscle in his chest. "You're saying I should pull some Stick shit," he said when he had recovered, referring to a classmate of theirs who was so tall and skinny he had been rapidly christened "The Stick" by his classmates.

"Yeah. Sit back and listen. He's not gonna give up much, but you'll know more when he's gone than you know right now."

"Thanks, man," Slaight said. "I owe you one."

"So come on out here in the spring and I'll put a goddamned shovel in your hands, and you can help me turn some peat moss and manure into my garden."

"I will," said Slaight. "See you, Buck."

CHAPTER 22

APTAIN PATTERSON'S office was at the far end of a corridor in Building 606, which had once housed the old cadet hospital building. Jacey had called him that afternoon, told him she had some questions, and asked if she could see him. He suggested she stop by after supper, when he would be finished with the day's business.

Captain Patterson had been her professor of law during the previous year. He had cut a handsome figure, standing before fifteen cadets in class, darting brilliantly in and out of arcane corners of military law, questioning them intently on the lesson before handing out written exams. The great thing about the way they taught military law at West Point was that every day, you had to sit down and write out an answer to a complicated question involving a proposition founded in the legal texts you were supposed to have studied the night before. Jacey had excelled at the exams, and she soon found herself in the First Section, at the top of her class in military law, where she encountered Captain Patterson. Everyone who had him for a law ''P'' considered him one of the smartest, funniest professors they'd ever had, and so did Jacey, which was why she called him when she returned from Dorothy's mother's house, carrying the explosive copy of Dorothy's last E-mail message to her mother.

The corridor was empty. She found him seated at his desk grading papers.

"Sir," she interrupted, standing in his open door.

He looked up. "Miss Slaight. Come in. Have a seat."

Jacey removed a law book from the only chair in the room and sat down. Quickly, Patterson stacked the papers he had been grading to one side, revealing his desk's burnished mahogany surface. He folded his hands and looked into eyes that, while they had always belonged to Jacey Slaight, now belonged as well to the daughter of the Superintendent of West Point. Something was going on inside her, and whatever it was, it went beyond her father's assignment to West Point. "What brings you over here to the Department of Law? I thought we were finished with you last year," he said jokingly.

"Sir, I need your advice."

"What kind of advice?" he asked, gently.

"Legal advice. It's a long story, sir."

He took a yellow legal pad from his drawer and made a note at the top. "Why don't you start at the beginning and give me the details as clearly and concisely as you can."

"Yes sir."

"And why don't you drop the 'sir' business. The way things work here at West Point, professors in the Department of Law can serve as attorneys for cadets and other military personnel on the post. The moment you walked into this office and requested legal advice from me, you effectively became my client, and you are protected by attorney-client privilege, so we may as well take advantage of it, don't you think?"

She allowed herself a little smile. She'd picked right. Captain Patterson was the guy.

She started with the shock of Dorothy's death on the Plain. Then she went through the hours immediately afterward—the company meeting, turning over the statements to Chief Warrant Officer Kerry, the whole thing. She told him about the night Carrie found E-mail disks, that later she had confronted Ash about the party, and that he had told her nothing out of the ordinary had happened, but she still couldn't understand why he had betrayed her by not telling her Dorothy had been there. Then she told him she had driven up to

Oneonta the day before and talked to Dorothy's mother, and how she found the rest of Dorothy's E-mail on the laptop in her bedroom.

Patterson interrupted her. "I'm going to assume that what you found in her E-mail is the reason you came to see me."

"Yes sir."

"So tell me about Miss Hamner's E-mail."

Jacey went through what she had found, right through paraphrasing the content of Dorothy's last E-mail message to her mother. Patterson was making notes and didn't look up.

"Have you told anyone what you've discovered?"

"Not yet. That's why I wanted to see you. I want to know what I should do."

Patterson stopped taking notes and looked at the first-class cadet seated across the desk from him. It wasn't so long ago that he had been a first-class cadet, although he had never had occasion to visit the office of a law "P" needing legal advice. If truth be told, he had cruised through West Point, and a couple of years after he graduated, he had no problem transferring out of the artillery into the JAG Corps and getting the Army to put him through three years of law school at NYU. When, two years later, they had offered him a slot in the Department of Law at West Point, he had jumped at the chance.

He knew precisely what had brought him to this exact moment in his life: a long, uninterrupted string of good deals. Now he realized the good deals were over. This young woman, Jacey Slaight, who just happened to be the Supe's daughter, had come to him for advice, and he knew from listening to what she had to say that his life was about to change.

He remembered having drinks one night in a Village bar with one of his NYU law professors, a guy he had really come to admire. "You know what's really shitty about the practice of law, Harper?" the law professor had asked.

Unable to think of anything negative about practicing law, since he had yet to practice it, Patterson had answered, "No."

"All you do is sit there and listen to other people's problems."

Now Captain Patterson knew intimately what the professor had meant. The thing was, your life was bound to change if you did the job right, because your client's problem became your problem as well.

"Well, I can begin by reminding you that under the UCMJ, you are bound by the law to report what you've found to the authorities. In this case, that would be the CID agent in charge. My advice to you is, take everything you've got to Agent Kerry."

"I knew you were going to say that."

"If you already knew that was your obligation, why did you think it was necessary to see me?"

"Because I'm afraid of what's going to happen."

"What do you mean?"

"I think this thing is going to blow into a huge scandal. If that happens, it's going to hurt my father. He's only been here a few weeks, and whatever happened with those guys and Dorothy, whatever crap they threatened her with the Honor Code, all of it started last year, and now my father's going to get loaded down with the consequences."

"This is going to sound cold and unfeeling, Jacey, but that's what happens to you when you're a general and they give you an important job. You pick up the crap that others left behind. It's just the way things work in the Army."

"But it's so unfair! Isn't there some other way we can handle it? I mean, can't you and I go to see the Commandant and tell him what I've found? Maybe he'll know what to do. He could call everybody in and question them. If Rose or Favro or any of the others did anything wrong, the Commandant would know how to handle it. Can't we do this without everything blowing up in my father's face?"

Patterson understood now that Jacey wasn't as troubled by what she had found as she was by its potential consequences. He wished there was some way he could tell her he'd handle it, and that everything was going to be okay, but there wasn't. The gears of the system of military justice had already begun to turn. If she didn't do the right thing, she would be ground up in the gears along with everyone else guilty of wrongdoing.

"It doesn't work that way, Jacey. For one thing, the system here at West Point is fairly unique and specific in dividing authority between the Commandant and the Superintendent. The Com is in charge of cadet discipline under Regulations USCC."

"The Blue Book of cadet regs."

"Right. And your father is charged with the authority to convene courts-martial, which means that he is in overall charge of the military justice system under the Uniform Code of Military Justice, the UCMJ. Those are two very different areas of authority, and what you're talking about comes under the UCMJ, not under cadet regs. If we went to the Com, he would be bound under the law to report directly to the Superintendent. There's no way to protect your father. The law puts him directly on the firing line."

"It's still unfair. He's not responsible for things that happened before he became Supe."

"No, but he's responsible for making sure that those events are investigated, and that the proper persons are brought to justice, if in fact it is found that crimes were committed. From what you've told me, I think there is reason to believe that a crime may have been committed. You can't suborn a felony, Jacey. You've got to take your evidence to the CID."

"Well, if I can't go to the Com, why can't I just take what I've found to my father? He deserves to know if things are going to start coming apart around here."

"If you do that, he'll be directly involved in the investigation, and if it comes down to a court-martial, he'll be accused of having exercised command influence over the investigation. They'll throw the charges out, and whoever's charged will go scot-free."

"It's like being caught in a trap. I can't do anything right."

"You can play by the rules and go through the proper channels. You can do what the law requires. And that's all you can do."

"There's something else, besides my father." She paused for a moment, twisting a small piece of paper in her hands. "I don't know what Ash's involvement is."

"From what you just told me, you're not too happy with him, so I don't understand why that should be a great concern for you."

"It's not that simple. We were together for two years."

"What does your instinct tell you? Do you think he's involved?"

She thought for a moment. "I don't think so, but I can't be sure."

"Why don't you talk to him about it? Tell him what you're going to do."

"Won't I be running the risk of him tipping the others?"

"Yes. But if your gut tells you he just screwed up the way guys sometimes do, then I don't think you've got much to worry about. If you think he's got something to hide, though, then I'd keep him out of it and go straight to Agent Kerry. That's a judgment call you're going to have to make, Jacey. I can't help you with that one."

She stopped twisting the piece of paper and dropped it in the trash can next to his desk. "I was pretty sure of what you were going to tell me, but I had to see if there wasn't some way my father could be kept out of it. Thanks, Captain Patterson. You really helped me."

"I'm not so sure I was that big of a help, but if there's anything else I can do, just let me know. I could go down to see Agent Kerry with you, if that would help."

"That's okay. I can handle it."

Patterson studied her for a moment. Something was missing. "There's another element here, isn't there, Jacey?" he asked. "The thing with your father . . . you're afraid if there's a big scandal, and it comes out that you're the one who pulled the trigger, the Corps of Cadets is going to think that you turned on fellow cadets and went running to your father. Isn't that right?"

She could feel her cheeks flush. He *was* the smartest "P" she'd ever had. "It's crossed my mind, yes."

"You're in an unenviable position, Jacey. You're damned if you do and damned if you don't. Under usual circumstances, you would have a few years of command under your belt before you found yourself caught up like this. But with your father as Supe, you're trapped. The only way out is to follow the law. That's the best advice I can give you. If you follow the law, there may be some cadets who are friendly to those who are implicated, and they're going to resent you, but the vast majority of the Corps will understand that you did your duty. You've got to trust the system at least that much, Jacey."

"I know you're right, but it's hard."

"Doing the right thing can sometimes be the hardest thing you've ever done in your life. I'm afraid this is one of those times."

"I know it is. I'm not looking forward to what I've got to do, I can tell you that much."

He walked her to the door. "If you want to talk, just give me a ring." He grinned. "In fact, as your attorney, I *advise you* to call me with any questions you have."

She smiled back. "Thanks again, Captain Patterson."

As she walked down the empty corridor, Patterson stood in the door watching her. She was a remarkable young woman, that was for sure. As she turned down the stairs, a figure wearing a gray jacket stepped out of a darkened door at the end of the hall and followed her. It was a cadet. Patterson wasn't certain, but it looked an awful lot like the cadet was following her. Patterson turned back to his office, grabbed the Academy phone book, looked up Jacey's number, and quickly dialed. No answer. Her roommate wasn't in the room. He flipped the pages of the phone book and found the number for her company orderly room. When a cadet answered, he told him to have Jacey call him the moment she entered the barracks.

Jacey had just reached Thayer Road when she heard footsteps behind her. She turned to find Rose trying to catch up with her. She kept walking, but Rose fell in beside her.

"Want to stop in Grant Hall for a coffee?" Rose said, nearly out of breath.

"Not really. I'm busy."

"I know you were just in Patterson's office."

Jacey turned to face him. "What were you doing? Following me?"

"No."

"Oh, you just happened to be up in Building 606 in the totally empty Department of Law tonight. Is that it?"

"There's something I think the two of us had better talk over."

"If you're referring to the fact that Dorothy Hamner was a guest at your party out at the lake, you can save your breath, Rose. I'm turning over everything I've got to Chief Warrant Officer Kerry."

"I don't think that would be a very good idea, Jacey."

"Why not, Rose?"

"You know how things work around here. If we get mentioned in the same breath with Dorothy Hamner, careers could be damaged."

"That's your problem. You and the rest of the big shots invited her to the party."

"It's not as simple as that, and you know it, Jacey. If we get questioned by the CID, how is that going to look on our records?"

"I don't know, Rose. Depends on what you tell them."

"The mere fact that we become involved in the investigation won't look good, Jacey. I'm telling you, there's no reason for you to go to the CID, because nothing happened at the party. Why don't you just leave it alone?''

"I think I'll just leave it up to Chief Warrant Officer Kerry. He's the one in charge of the investigation. He can make the determination as to whether or not what happened at the party has a bearing on Dorothy's death.''

Rose's jaw hardened, and he stepped closer to her. "You're going to end up causing more trouble than you know. And most of it's going to come down on your father.''

"I don't see how that could be the case, Rose. I know this much for certain. *He* wasn't at the party with Dorothy Hamner. *You* were.''

"You're going to be sorry if you push this thing.''

"Oh, I'm real scared, Rose," she taunted. "What's going to happen to me? A big bad bogeyman is going to come and get me?''

"You think because you're the Supe's daughter you can get away with this kind of shit. You're going to learn differently. I can promise you that.''

"What are you afraid of, Rose? What's got you so scared?'' He turned and started walking away from her, and she called after him, "You know what, Rose? I'm going to find out what you're so scared of, and when I do, you're going to be the first one to know.''

He kept walking, and she turned and walked up the ramp to the barracks. As she passed the orderly room, the Cadet in Charge of Quarters called through the open door: "Jacey! Somebody just called for you!''

She went into the orderly room, a bare space with a desk and a phone behind a counter. A bulletin board on the wall had queries like NEED RIDE TO NYC pinned on it, and there were some intramural awards the company had won mounted on the wall above.

"Who called?''

"Captain Patterson. He said you should call him the minute you got back.''

"Thanks.'' She went up the stairs and walked down the hall to her room. The door was ajar. Belle had told her at dinner that she was going to the gym to work out. She called through the open door: "Belle?''

There was no answer. She pushed open the door, turned on the overhead lights, and went inside. She looked around. It didn't seem as if anyone had been in the room until she reached her desk. All three drawers were open. She searched quickly through her top drawer for the floppy disks containing Dorothy's E-mail.

They were gone.

She picked up the phone and dialed Captain Patterson's number.

"Captain Patterson, it's Jacey Slaight."

"I think I saw someone following you when you left my office."

"It was Rose. He stopped me out on Thayer Road and tried to talk me out of going to the CID."

"It sounds like he's getting rather nervous."

"He's scared shitless. But you won't believe this. When I got back to my room, all my drawers were open. Somebody stole the floppies with Dorothy's E-mail on them."

"They got them all?"

"Yes."

"They know you're on to them, and they're playing for keeps, Jacey. I'd be careful if I were you."

"Do you still think I ought to talk to Ash?"

"Why don't you find out where he was while you were gone? It's possible he was the one who stole the disks. He would know his way around your room, wouldn't he?"

"Yeah. That's a good idea. I'll check on it."

"You don't have a copy of the E-mails?"

"No. The last thing I expected was that someone in the Corps of Cadets would steal them."

"It sounds to me like the time when you could trust your classmates is behind you. If I were you, I would start operating on that assumption."

"Thanks. I will."

"Call me after you've spoken to Agent Kerry, will you?"

"Okay. I've got to go. I'm going to look around for Ash. I need to know if he was a part of this. Thanks again, Captain Patterson."

She hung up. Out there on Thayer Road only moments before, she had realized Rose was frightened enough to threaten her. Now she knew how far he was willing to take it. She couldn't prove it yet, but she was certain that the Chairman of the Honor Committee had ordered someone to steal Dorothy's floppies. Every guy at the party was on the Honor Committee . . .

So that was it. The whole thing was about the Honor Committee. That's what they're trying to hide.

She grabbed her purse and headed out the door. She took the stairs two at a time and ran into the orderly room. "Where's Ash?" she asked.

"Up at Building Seven-twenty with the band."

"How long has he been up there?"

"He came back from supper and I saw him leaving with his harmonica and his amp, and I haven't seen him since."

"Thanks." She ran out the door and headed up the steps to Building 720. When she reached the parking lot next to the building she was out of breath, so she stopped for a moment and leaned forward with her hands on her knees, panting. She could hear the band down in the basement. Ash was singing another old Replacements song, shouting the refrain over and over: *I'm so . . . I'm so . . . unsatisfied.* She pushed open the basement door and stepped inside. Ash saw her and raised his hand, and the band stopped playing.

"Ash. We've got to talk."

He looked at the rest of the guys in the band and checked his watch. "This might take a while. Maybe we ought to knock off for the night."

"Sure thing," said the drummer.

"How's it going, Jace?" called the lead guitarist.

"Okay, Randy. You guys sound good. Been practicing long?"

"Since supper," said the lead guitarist.

"It shows." She gave the guys in the band a wave and Ash followed her outside. She closed the basement door and faced him in the dim light from a streetlamp across the parking lot. "Ash, I've got to ask you this one question, and you've got to tell me the truth. Randy said you guys have been practicing since supper. Is that right? Have you been up here practicing ever since supper?"

"Yeah, why?"

"You're telling me the truth, Ash? I'm serious. I can walk back in there and ask them, and I'll do it, Ash, if I think you're lying to me."

"I'm not lying. We've been practicing . . ." He checked his watch again. "Over two hours. What's up, Jace? How come you want to know if I've been here with the band?"

"Because somebody went into my room tonight after supper and stole the floppies with Dorothy's E-mail on them. That's why."

The shock on his face told her everything she needed to know. He knew nothing about it.

"Jace, I've got to tell you something. Last week, after you got so mad at me for not telling you about the party, I called Rose and I told him and I told the others that you knew, and that you had found her E-mail disks."

"I knew it. I just knew it."

"I was mad, Jace. Don't you understand? I know I screwed up not telling you about the party, but I just didn't think it was such a big deal. And you treated me like I'd done something terrible. You even accused me of fucking around on you, and Jace, you know I didn't do that."

She looked at him, and she knew he was telling the truth. It was like Patterson had said: Sometimes guys just screw up. "Well, it *is* a big deal, Ash. It's a big enough deal that your pal Rose, the Chairman of the Honor Committee, had somebody steal Dorothy's E-mail from my desk drawer."

"How do you know he's behind it?"

"Because I was over at Patterson's office tonight, and Patterson saw him following me. And after I left, Rose caught up with me on Thayer Road and he threatened me. He told me I'll be sorry if I keep pushing this thing. That's how he referred to it. *This thing.*"

"Jesus. I had no idea."

"What's going on, Ash? He's the Chairman of the Honor Committee! And he's scared to death! What is it that he's afraid of?"

"Well, there's Gibson . . ."

"Screw Gibson! This has got nothing to do with Gibson! It's all about the Honor Committee! I know it is, Ash, because I found another E-mail I haven't told you about. Early on the morning Dorothy died she sent a message to her mother. She said something happened to her at the party. She wanted to talk to her mother about it. Ash, she was trying to call her mother at four in the morning. She was scared. I'm sure of it."

"Christ."

"What do you know about these guys, Ash? Are Rose and the rest of them messing around with the Honor Code? I need to know the truth."

"I feel like the stupidest idiot in the world right now, because all I can tell you is, I don't know a thing. And the thing is, I should. I'm the regimental Honor rep. If those guys on the Honor Committee are threatening people with Honor violations, I ought to know about it. But I don't."

"What do you think is going on?"

"I don't know, but I'll tell you something right now. I'm sure as hell going to find out."

Jacey grabbed his hand. "I need to know that I can trust you, Ash. I mean it. This time, you can't go off and call Rose and tell him and the rest of your buddies everything I've told you. If you do that, the whole thing will be blown, Ash. So tell me. Can I trust you, like we've trusted each other for two years?"

He took her other hand in his and he looked directly into her eyes. "Jace, let me tell you something. When you walked away from me last week and you told me good-bye, it was the lowest I've ever felt in my life. I mean, I knew I'd blown it, and the years we've spent together just went up in smoke, and I was standing there, and I was so angry at you and angry at myself, I didn't know what to do. I'm going to help you. If they're fucking around with the *Honor Code*, Jace, we'll bring them down. It's *our* Honor Code. It's the whole reason I wanted to come to West Point, because I knew this is the last place on earth where honor comes before everything else. That's why I worked so hard to become an Honor rep. It's why I wanted to be regimental rep. It's the only thing I've ever really believed in, Jace."

"This isn't going to be easy," she said.

"I know."

"If this whole thing is about the Honor Code, they've got one hell of a lot to lose. I'm going to need your help."

"You've got it. You know they're going to fight us every step of the way."

"They've already started. The very cadets who are supposed to enforce the code against lying, cheating, and stealing just came into my room and stole those floppy disks. What else have they done? What are they trying to hide? This whole thing is going to come right down on my father's head."

"You're right. It's his watch. He's on the spot. Maybe you'd better warn him."

"I can't. Captain Patterson said I've got to go through channels. If I go to my father, they'll accuse him of exercising command influence in the investigation."

"Oh, man. This thing is a nightmare."

"Tell me about it."

"So what's next?"

"I'm going to see Agent Kerry."

"If you want, I'll go with you."

She found his eyes. "That's the nicest thing I've heard in a long time, Ash, but I don't think that's a good idea."

"Why not?"

"You're on the Honor Committee. You've got access to committee files and reports. You guys are friends. They trust you. If they find out you're talking to Agent Kerry, they're going to shut you out."

"You're right."

She moved close to him and took his hand. "C'mon, let's get back to the barracks."

CHAPTER 23

C OLONEL KNIGHT had called Major Vernon the night before with news that the DNA results were in, so the next morning she took the first shuttle out of La Guardia and a cab from the airport and was standing outside the Armed Forces Institute of Pathology when he drove into the parking lot.

"Fancy meeting you here," he said when he got out of his car.

"I didn't see much sense in wasting any time, sir."

"Let's get with it then." They took the stairs to the third floor. Lieutenant Colonel Benjamin Hallberg was waiting for them. He was tall and thin and looked as though he had once played basketball, which he had, as a Princeton undergrad. The sleeves of his lab coat were far too short and he had the goofy, aw-shucks body language of an athlete. His shoulders jerked back and forth when he walked, and his eyes searched the room restlessly, as if he was constantly prepared for a fast break.

"Ben, I want you to meet Liz Vernon." Her hand disappeared in his, and she had to look up to make eye contact.

"Nice to meet you, sir," she said.

"I recognized your name when we received the sample. Phil has told me about you."

She glanced at Colonel Knight. "I'm flattered, I guess," she said.

Colonel Knight grinned. "What have you got for us, Ben?"

Lieutenant Colonel Hallberg opened a file and pulled out a thick computer printout. He looked at Major Vernon. "Well, it took us two weeks, but we finally dislodged the results from the lab at Rockville. This was a twenty-one-year-old female cadet at West Point, right?"

"Yes sir."

"Was she a rape victim?"

"That's part of our problem. We don't know, sir," said Major Vernon.

"We separated three different DNA profiles besides the victim's from your vaginal sample."

There was an eerie stillness in the room as this news sank in. Finally Colonel Knight broke the silence. "Liz, you said you found evidence of labial abrasion. Don't you think this contributes to the conclusion that the young woman was raped?"

She thought for a moment before she spoke. "I'd say it ups that possibility by a factor of three, sir."

"Can you describe the abrasion for me?" asked Hallberg.

Major Vernon reached into her briefcase and handed each of the men copies of autopsy photographs. "The redness and swelling is on the left side. When I first observed it, the abraded area resembled another labial abrasion I found on another deceased victim which resulted from violent penetration. I've done several examinations of violent rape victims since then. There is usually a lot more tissue damage and inflammation is far more pronounced. However, the abrasion I found is consistent with rape, and your DNA analysis proving she had three sexual partners certainly points us in that direction. But there are mitigating factors here. She made no complaint of rape, and according to the senior criminal investigator, her behavior on the morning of her death was described by her roommate and by other cadets as quiet, but otherwise normal."

"Don't you think it's likely that she was raped and chose to conceal that fact from her friends?" asked Colonel Knight. "She may have been suffering from posttraumatic shock."

"There's also the possibility that she had been drugged and had no memory of the experience," Hallberg interjected. "Some of the so-called date rape drugs like Rohypnol can have that effect. Did Rohypnol show up in her blood tests?"

"No," said Major Vernon. "But there are other drugs out there that have the same effect as Rohypnol, and most of them wouldn't show up because the illegal labs keep one or two steps ahead of law enforcement by changing the chemical makeup of the drugs, and they're successful in keeping pathologists in the dark as well, because we can't keep up with their chemical formulations. Therefore we can't test for them."

"You're talking about designer drugs?" asked Knight.

"Right, sir."

"So where do you stand with the rest of your examination?" asked Lieutenant Colonel Hallberg.

"She suffered a massive respiratory failure," interjected Colonel Knight. "And one of the things Liz is looking into is the young woman's behavior in the days previous to her death. Your results certainly open a rather large door." He turned to Major Vernon. "You can cross-check Ben's DNA profiles against the DNA profiles of cadets. If the three men she had sex with were cadets, you'll come up with three matches."

"I wasn't aware West Point had a DNA database," said Major Vernon.

"It doesn't," said Lieutenant Colonel Hallberg. "All the DNA profiles are kept down here at Rockville. The profiles are intended for battlefield identification of body parts when a physical ID can't be done."

"Have military DNA records ever been used for this purpose before?" asked Major Vernon.

"You mean in the investigation of the death of a third party? I don't think so."

She tapped one of her fingers on the clasp of her briefcase. "Well, I guess there's got to be a first time for everything."

AS SHE flew back to La Guardia on the shuttle, Major Vernon knew one thing for sure: DNA was dynamite. A convicted rapist-murderer on death row in Texas had just been pardoned and released by a reluctant governor of Texas after DNA evidence proved without even the tiniest sliver of doubt that he could not have raped, much less murdered the victim of the crime. A leading expert in the field had recently announced advances in the accuracy of DNA analysis. It could now be established that the chances were up to ten billion to one that a sample's DNA did or did not come from one particular individual. There weren't even ten billion people on the planet. The science of DNA was fast approaching the apogee of the absolute.

That's why she knew she was going to have problems at West Point. They wanted a simple cause of death that was easy to understand— a slide they could lay on an overhead projector and put up on a screen showing a squiggly little thing blown up huge and hideous. They wanted a *germ*. What they did not want were *names*, and names were what they would get from the genetic profiles she was bringing back with her from Washington.

It was true that the names would have to be associated with the rest of the medical evidence in her briefcase. Cadet Dorothy Hamner had been loaded with corticosteroids, and this had contributed to her death. But something else had complicated her condition. The thing about the genetic profiles in her briefcase was that they belonged to young men who might hold a secret that Major Vernon had not been able to uncover. They might know what had been introduced into her system that caused her lungs to become inflamed and simply shut down and stop working.

She knew that Percival wouldn't know what to do, because DNA was a ticklish area, especially DNA that had been taken from individuals under governmental orders. He would turn right around and go to his superior, Colonel Lombardi, the SJA. But the problem was, nobody in the Army liked to be the bringer of bad tidings, least of all Percival.

LATER THAT afternoon, as she unsnapped the clasp on her briefcase, Percival lived up to her expectations. "Don't tell me you ran more tests."

"Yes sir." Major Vernon pulled the thick DNA file from the briefcase and rested the closed case on her knees. "As a routine part of the autopsy, I did a pelvic exam on Miss Hamner. She showed signs of vaginal trauma, so I took vaginal samples. Miss Hamner had had sex with multiple partners within twelve to eighteen hours of her death, sir.''

Lieutenant Colonel Percival leaned back against his desk chair and ran a palm roughly across his crew cut. "Just what we need," he muttered.

Major Vernon shot him a sideways glance and turned her attention to the file. "We know she had multiple sex partners, because a DNA analysis of the seminal fluid drawn from Miss Hamner's vagina produced three separate profiles. We can ID the profiles, sir. We can put names on them."

"How in the hell are you going to do that?"

"By cross-checking the seminal DNA pofiles against the DNA profiles we've taken from male cadets here at West Point."

"What's the purpose behind such a massive search of privileged information, Major? You're going to need a serious justification to make that fly."

"There are two strong reasons to order the search, sir. The first is that the vaginal trauma to Miss Hamner indicates that she may have been raped. She was a very conservative young woman from a small town in upstate New York. According to her roommate and other friends in her company, she had never shown any interest in the kind of sexual experimentation which would be indicated by three sex partners in a single night. Her vaginal area showed signs of abrasion and swelling, and these are consistent with forced sex. With evidence that no less than three men had sex with her, it's a reasonable assumption that she was raped. The second reason is, there's a very strong likelihood that one or more of the men who had sex with her may have knowledge about what she ingested that interacted with the corticosteroid in her bloodstream, causing her lungs to fail, sir. There is a strong reason to believe these men may be able to testify as to her cause of death."

"I'm going to have to call in the SJA on this."

"Do you want me to report to him like I did before, sir? This DNA stuff is pretty complicated."

"That won't be necessary. I'll go see him myself. You are to put your autopsy on hold until I get back to you, is that clear?"

"Yes sir."

Percival pushed his chair back from his desk. "All right then . . ."

"Sir, there's one other thing. Considering the nature of this issue, I think it would enhance our ability to conclude the investigation satisfactorily if knowledge of the DNA results were limited to myself, you, Colonel Lombardi, and the Superintendent."

"Are you trying to tell me how to do my job, Major?"

"No sir. I am merely suggesting that if word gets out that we can identify the individuals who had sex with Miss Hamner, it will give them an advantage if we reach the point where we call them in for questioning, sir."

"I am aware of that possibility, Major, I assure you."

"Thank you, sir, that's all I have."

"You are dismissed."

Downstairs, Major Vernon got into her car and pulled out of her parking space. Percival's reaction to the DNA news had been hostile. He had cut her out of the loop by not sending her to report to Colonel Lombardi, and she didn't like being told to put her investigation "on hold." When it came right down to it, she didn't trust Percival. At the stop sign, she had a crazy thought.

Why don't I follow him, see if he goes to see Lombardi like he said?

She looked in her rearview mirror. Percival was coming out of the Provost Marshal's building, heading for his car. Major Vernon turned right and pulled her car around the corner of a building. By leaning out of her window, she could see him get into his car in the parking lot. He backed out and pulled up to the stop sign. Instead of turning left, toward the SJA's office, he turned right. She waited until he reached the corner and pulled in behind him. She checked her watch. There was a chance he was going to lunch, but somehow she doubted it.

She watched from a spot next to Clinton Field as Percival pulled into visitor parking across from the Officers' Club. He got out of his car. Instead of walking across Cullum Road to the club, he continued down Cullum Road toward the library. She cut her engine and followed him on foot. Percival passed the library and crossed Thayer Road, entering Central Area. She walked to the corner of Pershing Barracks and watched as he entered Washington Hall at the entrance that led to the Commandant's office.

She knew from the short time it took him to reach his car that he had not bothered to call Lombardi. Now here he was, going straight to the Com with everything she'd just told him about the DNA results from the autopsy. She racked her brain, trying to recall how the Commandant fit into the chain of command.

He didn't.

The chain of command held that Percival was supposed to report to Lombardi, the SJA, and Lombardi was supposed to report directly to the Superintendent. But Percival wasn't going through the chain of command, he was going *around it.*

CHAPTER 24

SLAIGHT HAD spent most of the week on the mundane matters of Academy life. The investigation of Dorothy Hamner's death seemed to be stalled. Gibson wasn't misbehaving in any manner that was visible. The Corps of Cadets was caught up in the excitement of a winning football season. West Point's Black Knights hadn't lost once in four weeks. The only thing that hung over the head of the Superintendent was the visit of Congressman Thrunstone the next day.

As they finished a soup-and-salad lunch on the back porch, Sam noticed that he was staring out across the backyard without seeing. "Looking forward to the weekend?" she joked.

He nodded absently. "In a big way."

"You'll figure something out. Didn't Leroy give you some help?"

"Lots."

"What did he tell you? Watch and listen? That would be so like Leroy."

"That, and he filled me in on Thrunstone's whole story. He's a piece of work."

"So what are you going to do? Just between you and me, I don't see you keeping your mouth shut all day tomorrow."

"I don't know. I've got to think about it." He pushed his chair back from the table and kissed her. "I'd better get going. Supes aren't supposed to take two-hour lunches."

"Hell, you're the boss now. You can do what you want," she teased.

"Within reason. Thanks for the feast, doll." He grabbed his cap and headed for the front door. Outside, the day was brisk and the trees around Trophy Point had begun to change colors. He started down the stairs and turned around and went back inside.

"Sam?" he called from the door. She appeared at the end of the hall. "Do me a favor, will you? Call Melissa and tell her I've gone for a walk."

Sam smiled and gave him a wave that said she'd known all along what he'd do.

Slaight headed down the steps of Quarters 100 once again, this time turning north toward the cemetery.

The West Point Cemetery was located behind the Old Cadet Chapel, about a half mile up Washington Road from Trophy Point. Slaight had an affection for the Old Cadet Chapel that dated to his days as a cadet, when, even though he was a nondenominational Protestant, he had opted to be on what was quaintly referred to as "the Jewish Chapel Squad." This was back in the days of mandatory chapel, when all cadets, whatever their faith, were compelled to attend one of three churches each and every Sunday of their lives at West Point: Protestant, Catholic, or Jewish. It was claimed that the services in the Old Cadet Chapel were nondenominational Protestant, but in fact they reflected the very conservative religious and political beliefs of the Lutheran minister who was then Cadet Chaplain and whose sermons reflected a belief that God was most certainly a capitalist, most probably an American, and possibly Republican. The Jewish services, on the other hand, were of the Reform variety. Once a month a rabbi drove up to the Academy from Great Neck in his Ferrari. He was of the opinion that God, while probably a capitalist, was most certainly a Democrat. On the other three weeks of the month, cadets themselves gave the service, complete with the mellifluous vocal tones of the Jewish Chapel Choir, of which Slaight was a member in good standing. That the Jewish Chapel Squad attended services on the Christian sabbath rather than on the Jewish sabbath reflected the strictures of mandatory chapel, which held that at West Point, the Academy's rules prevailed over those of God.

It was after Jewish Chapel Squad services on Sunday mornings that Slaight had discovered the cemetery. He used to wander back there among the headstones, reading the names of graduates, thinking back over the long, bloody history of the United States that had brought so many of them to this place on the Hudson River first as eager boys, and finally as dead bodies.

One Thursday afternoon during the fall of his plebe year, he had come face-to-face with the process by which Academy graduates found their final resting place at West Point. His Tactical Officer called him to his office and informed him in very disapproving tones that he was to be excused from all duties for the next two days so he could escort the widow of a West Point graduate who had recently been killed in Vietnam. The Tactical Officer was of the opinion that plebes, like children, were best seen and not heard, and he would much rather have provided a first-classman, a cadet captain, to escort the widow. That she had specifically asked for Slaight had not made the Tactical Officer happy at all, but she had insisted, and so against his better judgment the Tac had sprung Slaight loose with a long and very profane admonition that he'd better not fuck up and bring discredit upon the Corps.

Slaight was instructed to meet the widow the next morning, Friday, at the Thayer Hotel, and attend to her needs until the funeral was over on Saturday and she had departed the Academy.

As General Slaight entered the cemetery on a crisp fall afteroon as Superintendent, he recalled that he had stood in the office of his Tactical Officer wondering who he could have known in his short life who would call upon him at a time like this. Then the Tac told him that her name was Virginia Parker Connolly.

Cadet Slaight remembered Virginia Parker. As a ninth-grader, she had been his ballroom dancing teacher when he was in the seventh grade. He had had a massive crush on her, which he had imagined she reciprocated, but the two-year age difference in junior high school was an insurmountable obstacle that neither of them dared cross. Now, apparently, she remembered him, too.

It seemed like meeting her in the Thayer Hotel had happened yesterday. The lobby had a high, wood-beamed ceiling and a mezzanine running around its perimeter. On that Friday morning, with most of the Corps of Cadets in class and their dates for the weekend still hours away from arrival at the hotel, the lobby was a silent, churchlike space. He found Virginia waiting for him on one of the sofas across from the reception desk. He remembered being struck by the fact that she had hardly changed, forgetting that only four years had passed since they had first met. She stood as he approached, and they embraced. He remembered being frightened of being written up for Public Display of Affection, because no cadet, under any circumstances, was supposed to touch a female in public, except to offer her his arm. But the violation went blessedly unreported and, slightly more confidently, he held her hand as she told him of being notified by a ring of her doorbell and the presence of an Army captain that her husband, Walker Connolly, a lieutenant just a year out of West Point, had been killed in action in Vietnam. They had been married at the West Point Chapel the week after he had graduated, and with his duty assignments at Ranger School and Airborne School, they had spent only eight months together before he left for Vietnam.

Slaight the plebe had the odd impression that her grief was tempered by the short time she had known her husband. As she spoke of him, it seemed as if they had barely known each other, and it turned out to be true. They had started dating when he was a firstie, and had married a few months later. Her anguish was sudden and hot and angry and very youthful, like that of a child whose doll had been lost and could not be recovered. He guessed that there would always be a part of her that would never understand why this had happened to her. *Why me? Why now?* To these tormented questions, he had no answer. All he could do was listen.

Her parents were not due to arrive at the Academy until that evening, and her husband's parents were coming from Hawaii and wouldn't get there until the next morning. As far as she knew, only a few of his classmates would be able to make the funeral. Many were in Vietnam, and the rest were scattered widely around the world at their first duty assignments. Few of them, as second lieutenants, had the kind of money or time it then took to travel long distances by air. The funeral was scheduled for the next afternoon, and so, for the time being, they were on their own.

Cadet Slaight asked her if she wanted to see where her husband would be buried, and lacking transportation, all they could do was walk the two miles to the cemetery. So, offering her his arm in the prescribed cadet manner, he led her off down Thayer Road.

The trees were turning, the air crisp, the sky the color of faded blue denim. As they walked, she told him that she had arranged to arrive at the Academy a day early so she could get her bearings before relatives and friends arrived. He suspected that she also wanted someone to talk to—someone she knew, someone she could trust and yet in whom she had relatively little invested emotionally. There were questions she had already begun to ask, and she had others. Long silences were interrupted by awkward inquiries about West Point, which he tried to answer bravely, so as not to disturb any memories she had of her husband's experiences there. But he soon realized that she knew the score. Her husband had despised his four years at West Point, and yet he had marched off to the sound of the guns ten thousand miles away, as any honorable officer would, and this was the thing that confused her. How could you hate West Point, hate being a cadet, hate Army training like Ranger School and Airborne School so much, and yet give your life for it?

He struggled for an answer. West Point was not a place you were supposed to enjoy in the way that students enjoyed colleges like Princeton or Vassar. It was a place that trained warriors, and the training was unpleasant and hard and often just plain ugly. Knowing his own father and grandfather while not quite knowing himself, he realized that you didn't have to love either West Point or the Army to love and want to serve your country.

They walked along Thayer Road and the river glistened bluish-gray below them. In the distance, the Hudson Valley seemed to stretch northward forever. He knew that she was asking deeply painful questions, and he was mouthing abstract and probably patently stupid answers, but she did not protest. It seemed as if the process itself was enough.

The walk up Thayer Road . . . the brooding questions and the hesitant answers . . . her hand grasping the rough wool of his dress gray jacket . . . the incredible aloneness of having known each other when they were so young and now enduring together what for each of them, but most especially for her, were terribly adult moments . . . all of it came flooding back as the Superintendent walked once again among the graves of the West Point Cemetery. General Slaight reached a little hill toward the back of the cemetery and turned to look south.

He remembered that as he walked down Thayer Road with Virginia on his arm, he felt lost, as if he didn't know which way to go. She seemed to have sensed this: He felt her hand grip his arm more tightly, she moved closer to him, and the feeling passed. He pulled himself together and held his head high, and he noticed that reaching the area of barracks she did the same, and together they walked past Grant Hall and Thayer Hall and Central Area, crossed the Plain, passed the Dean's Quarters, continued north along Washington Road to the Old Cadet Chapel, turned into its circular drive, and walked around the west side of the old stone structure into the West Point Cemetery itself. They passed the graves of those who were killed in World War II, and then those killed in Korea, and then they entered a part of the cemetery that had yet to be filled with headstones. It was as if a part of the grounds of West Point had been reserved for the next war, and that war was here now, in Vietnam, and men were dying once again in a faraway land, and there at the end of an empty row was a freshly dug grave, its reddish-brown dirt piled high and uncovered next to it.

They walked the final steps to her husband's grave site, and Virginia stood at its edge and looked down. "This is where he is always going to be," she said in a very matter-of-fact voice that betrayed neither sorrow nor pride. Actually seeing the hole in the ground had made real something that for her had been only an idea until then, and for reasons Slaight could not fathom, it comforted her that if she hadn't known where he had been for the last few months, or exactly where he had died, at least she would know forever and for certain where she could find him now.

He asked her if she wanted to see the inside of the Old Cadet Chapel, and she said no, that would come soon enough. And so with seemingly nothing else to do, they started the long walk back to the Thayer Hotel. This time, when they passed the area of barracks, cadets were crossing Thayer Road, returning to their rooms from class. As they passed Grant Hall, one of the upperclass cadets in Slaight's company caught sight of him walking down the sidewalk with Virginia on his arm. He turned and marched toward them.

"Halt, mister!" he commanded. They stopped, still arm-in-arm. "Plebes are not permitted to escort females on weekdays! Drive yourself up to my room immediately, mister!"

"Sir, I am escorting Mrs. Connolly under orders of the Tactical Officer. Her husband was killed in action in Vietnam two weeks ago, sir."

The upperclassman stood there on Thayer Road realizing that he had been caught in a moment of foolish impertinence, and not knowing quite what to do, his eyes wandered for a moment, from Virginia to Slaight and back to Virginia. Then she touched him lightly on the shoulder and said, "It's okay. I understand. It's just . . . West Point." The upperclassman mouthed silently the words, "I'm sorry," and turned up the ramp to the barracks.

When Slaight and Virginia had passed the old hospital and were back on the part of Thayer Road that passed the stately old quarters of the staff and faculty, she turned to him and said, "You know, it's funny, but he reminded me a lot of my husband."

The next day, Slaight accompanied Virginia and her parents in the staff car from the Thayer Hotel to the Old Cadet Chapel. His parents had been friends for many years with hers, but there was little to talk about during the drive down Thayer Road. When the service was over, he walked with her arm-in-arm behind her husband's casket as it was carried from the Chapel to the grave site. He stood to one side of Virginia, with her father and mother on the other, during the graveside service. When the Color Guard had finished folding the American flag into its traditional triangle, it was to Slaight that the captain in charge of the Color Guard passed the flag. He in turn handed the flag to Virginia, and the gathering of maybe two dozen parents and soldiers and cadets from Walker Connolly's old company stood silently as taps was sounded and a team of riflemen fired a final salute.

Later that night, Virginia called Slaight's company. The Charge of Quarters rushed up to Slaight's room, and he raced downstairs to the Orderly Room to take the call. She was down at Grant Hall and wanted to see him before she left early the next morning. Slaight raced back to his room and put on his dress gray uniform and hurried down the ramp from the barracks to Grant Hall. He found her sitting in one of the alcoves, under a photograph of General Robert E. Lee. She patted the sofa next to her and he sat down.

"Do you remember when we used to dance to those records like 'Earth Angel' and 'Stagger Lee' and you used to hold me tight and I would put my chin on your shoulder and it felt like we were in another world, far, far away, like there was no one else on earth but the two of us, and we were so close we could feel each other's hearts beating?"

He nodded.

"I want you to hold me like that again."

They stood, and he held her close and she began to rock gently back and forth as if she could hear music and they were dancing and they were just kids again and nothing awful had yet happened to either one of them in their lives. In that moment he caught a fleeting glimpse of the future, even as they tried desperately to relive their past. He knew that without a doubt his youth was over, gone for good, and that from this moment forward, everything in his life would be different. He had tried the day before to put into words something that he had only begun to suspect, that the world was not a nice place, that men could not help themselves, that not even the gift of love could keep them from evil, that life would be a struggle to reconcile the goodness of love and the evil of existence, and that the struggle would never end. And then she stopped rocking from side to side, and she pulled gently apart from him, and she looked into his eyes, and he knew that she already knew all of this. There was nothing he could say to her, nor was there anything she could say to him, that would make a difference in their lives.

She touched his hand. "I'll be going now. Thank you for everything." She walked from the alcove out the door of Grant Hall onto Thayer Road, and he never saw or heard from her again.

General Slaight walked past the last gravestone on his way out of the cemetery, heading south toward his office. As he recalled, years had gone by before he realized that within the space of only a few moments in that alcove in Grant Hall they had left one world and entered another, and they didn't need each other anymore.

* * *

ONE REASON General Slaight arranged to meet Congressman Chuck Thrunstone at Grant Hall in the alcove where General Robert E. Lee's portrait was hung was that the congressman was a "Civil War buff," a term loaded with meaning even in the genteel precincts of southern Illinois that the congressman represented. Slaight allowed him to discourse at length (and with severely limited historical accuracy, he noted) on the character and career of the general from Virginia who had attended West Point and entered the United States Army, only to make the choice later in his career to serve as the Commander of the Armies of the Confederacy against many of his West Point classmates in the War Between the States. Indeed, Thrunstone's recitation of General Lee's career had a ring of "those were the good old days, weren't they?"

Slaight did not bother reminding the congressman that the good old days of General Lee were also the bad old days of slavery because the congressman made it quite evident that to his way of thinking, at least, Lee had not been saddled with command of an Army that suffered the ills the congressman believed faced today's Army.

It was understood on the E-Ring of the Pentagon, in the office of the Chief of Staff of the Army anyway, that Congressman Thrunstone was a man distressed about what he liked to call the "direction" of the modern American Army. His unhappiness was thought by senior Army leaders to have been caused by the congressman's conviction that such viruses as "political correctness" and "affirmative action" and "feminism" had infected the armed services, and none of the services was more guilty of these perceived shortcomings, not to say crimes, than the United States Army. Word was passed from the office of the Secretary of the Army to the office of the Chief of Staff of the Army to the office of the Superintendent of West Point that the congressman from Illinois was to be handled like a chunk of C-4 explosive with a short fuse. For perhaps the first time in the experience of senior Army commanders, the Chairman of the House National Security Committee was perceived to be hostile to their interests. This was a development that had come as something of a surprise to the Pentagon, especially considering that the Chairman was a very conservative Republican, a politician of a stripe on which the Army had always thought it could depend.

But the real reason Slaight chose the alcove in Grant Hall had to do with his own memories. Eschewing protocol, Slaight had arranged to meet the congressman unaccompanied by his aide or other Academy hangers-on. The congressman had of course made no such arrangements, and was attended by a woman in charge of his public relations; his congressional chief of staff; the head of the committee's military liaison, by which was meant the chief-bringer-of-bad-tidings-to-the-Pentagon; and his chief legislative aide. A brace of black Lincoln Town Cars idled at the curb outside Grant Hall at the whim of the congressman, with his attendants milling about nearby. When the congressman was finished paying his respects to General Lee, Slaight led him out of Grant Hall and turned immediately up Thayer Road, walking north toward the Plain. The congressman's staff lingered behind, fluttering around the Town Cars, wondering what to do. Where was that damn general taking him? Worse still, what was the damn general telling the congressman, and far, far worse than that, what was the congressman telling the damn general?

The scene that ensued behind them was what Slaight used to call a clusterfuck. The congressman's staff was spazzing like plebes: Should they get into their cars and idle down the street at a discreet distance behind the Supe and their boss? Should they follow on foot, perhaps a bit closer, trying to hear what they were saying? Should they wait with the Town Cars until the congressman signaled them to follow? Should they take the unthinkable risk of interrupting him and come right out and ask the congressman what they should do?

As Slaight led the way down Thayer Road, chatting with Congressman Thrunstone, he knew exactly what was happening behind him, because it had been his intention to cause the clusterfuck and take advantage of the panic and indecision of the staffers. He wanted to remove the congressman from his handlers and quite literally have him to himself. The congressman, a voluble, garrulous sort with red cheeks and a huge shock of professionally coiffed and blow-dried silver-gray hair, was unaware of what was happening behind him. It was not his business to worry about his staff. It was their business to worry about him.

Thrunstone felt safe, because to his way of thinking, he was walking upon real estate owned by the federal government. As the Chairman of the National Security Committee, it was by rights *his* real estate, and the federal dollars upon which it depended were *his* federal dollars. As one of the chief congressional overseers of the federal defense budget, wasn't he the man who was courted by the various interest groups seeking dollars from the defense budget? And wasn't West Point, at this moment in its history, just another interest group pursing the almighty defense dollar?

He felt completely at ease on what was for him relatively foreign soil. Power had a way of doing that for you. You spent most of your life riding in cramped station wagons from an American Legion hall to a county fair to a country church potluck supper, shaking sweaty hands, eating fried chicken and barbequed ribs, listening to people complain about the quality of the blacktopping that in the last election had been promised for some county road out in a godforsaken corner of your district, and finally, after years and years and years of this, you found yourself with a polished mahogany gavel in hand presiding over the expenditure of 250 or so *billion* federal dollars, which you and only a handful of other good old boys like yourself had the power to dispense. What was it that Jewish guy said in that whacko movie a few years back? It's *good* to be the king.

It was a nice morning. Later, there would be a football game. Up at Michie Stadium, West Point would play the congressman's alma mater, the University of Southern Illinois. Between now and then, he had been assured, there would be lunch in the cadet mess hall. On a day like this one, with a relaxed schedule of hearty Army chow and rousing college football, what did the Chairman of the National Security Committee have to worry about?

Strolling across the Plain, the Superintendent and the congressman chatted about the upcoming football game. Southern Illinois was favored, by seven to eight points in some newspapers, and the congressman joked that if he was a betting man, he would have put some money on his alma mater.

"But of course as Chairman of the National Security Committee, you have to remain neutral, don't you, sir?" the Supe joked back.

The congressman chuckled. "You're not implying that I would deny funds to the Military Academy in order to gain advantage for Southern Illinois in a football game, are you, General?"

Slaight laughed out loud. A nerve, or perhaps several nerves, had been touched. "No sir. West Point's football program is self-sustaining, as I'm sure you are aware."

"Of course I am," said Thrunstone. They were walking north along Washington Road, away from the area of barracks. Thrunstone glanced behind him. A few cadets were back there on the Plain, placing tiny flags that would help to position cadet battalions for the parade that day. Tourists could be seen out on Trophy Point, taking photographs of each other. It occurred to him for the first time that they were alone. "Where are we headed, General?" he asked.

"I thought you might like to visit the cemetery, sir," Slaight said with a calm but direct tone. It was as much a command as a suggestion. "It's not usually a part of the standard West Point tour, but I thought, with American Army personnel serving all over the world, and with a lot of our young men and women over in Bosnia and the Middle East, not to mention those who went to war in years past, that you might want to see where some of them have ended up, Congressman."

There was quite a long silence, and they walked the better part of a block before Thrunstone spoke. "I wasn't aware this was on the agenda established between our offices, General."

"There was no agenda established between our offices, sir. There's about an hour before the parade, sir. I guess you could say that we're taking advantage of what we call free time here at West Point."

As they walked further, Slaight pointed up Mills Road in the direction of the Jewish Chapel that had been built entirely with private donations. He pointed out several projects that the Academy had under way with the generous donations of West Point's alumni.

"I attended the dedication of the Jewish Chapel. I'm aware the Alumni Association has a fund drive going on. It sounds to me like you've got a point to make, General," said the congressman.

They had arrived at the drive leading to the Old Cadet Chapel, and Slaight stopped. "I know that you are very busy down in Washington, and that you don't get a chance to get up here very often, sir. Your visits to West Point in the past have usually been in conjunction with the Board of Visitors, of which you were a member. As the new Superintendent of West Point, I'm curious about the purpose of your visit to West Point this time, and I figured if we took a walk and got a chance to know each other, you might enlighten me."

A thin smile formed slowly on Thrunstone's face. "General Meuller had a talk with you, did he?"

"No sir, he did not."

"It was Kobe," he said, referring to Secretary of the Army Thomas Kobe.

"No sir. I haven't spoken to Secretary Kobe since I've been Superintendent."

"Then you're up here freelancing, General Slaight? You're quizzing the chairman of the National Security Committee on your own?"

Now it was Slaight's turn to smile. "The Army has seen fit to turn the leadership of the Military Academy over to me for the next three years, sir. I feel like it's part of my duty as Superintendent to understand where West Point stands with the man who holds our purse strings. You are that man, Congressman. It's in my interest to know who you are and what you stand for, and it's in your interest to know who I am and what I stand for. That's the way the game is played, isn't it, sir?"

The congressman's thin smile widened, and then he laughed out loud. "You know what? I like your style." His eyes twinkled mischievously. "I wonder where the Army's been keeping you, General."

They strolled down the drive to the Old Cadet Chapel and ducked inside for a few moments. When they emerged, Slaight led the way into the cemetery and, guessing correctly that the congressman had never been there, pointed out a few graves. General Lucius Clay, buried just over there, commanded the Berlin airlift. General George Armstrong Custer, of the Battle of Little Big Horn, not far beyond. They strolled further. There was the grave of Colonel Bartley M. Harloe, who as an Army engineer built National Airport in Washington and most of the locks on the Mississippi River. They passed the grave of Arthur Bonifas, who had been an upperclassman in Slaight's company when Slaight was a plebe. Bonifas had been killed by North Koreans on the DMZ in an incident that had passed out of many memories, but not from the memories of those who had known him. When they reached Lieutenant Walker Connolly's grave, they stopped. Slaight told the congressman that the war in Vietnam had hardly begun when he had been killed leading a foot patrol in the delta. The congressman asked Slaight if he had known him, and Slaight replied, no, he had not. "I've known personally only a few of the men who are buried here, sir. But I know many of their histories, for their lives and their deaths are the history of West Point, and each in his own way, of our nation."

Slaight noticed Thrunstone checking his watch and led the way out of the cemetery. When they reached the circular drive in front of the Old Cadet Chapel, the congressman's Lincoln Town Cars were idling at the curb. One of the doors opened, and an aide jumped out. "Call for you, sir!" he shouted, holding a cell phone. Congressman Thrunstone excused himself and climbed into the backseat of the Town Car, and the aide closed the door. Thrunstone grabbed the phone, listened for a moment, grunted an assent, and handed the phone back to the aide. Then he reached over the front seat and grabbed the shoulder of the man sitting there.

"You're supposed to be head of my goddamned Pentagon liaison, Wasserstein!" he barked. "You take this car and you and Ford get your asses back to Washington and work up a file on that son of a bitch. I want to know who he fucks, where he shits, and what color his goddamned turds are, you hear me?"

Wasserstein's eyes blinked wildly. "Who, sir?"

"Slaight, goddammit!" said Congressman Thrunstone, pointing out the darkened windows of the Town Car at the Superintendent of West Point standing alone in front of the Old Cadet Chapel.

The door of the Town Car opened, and Thrunstone stepped out, his face bathed in a wide smile. "My wife wanted to know what I want for supper. Isn't that funny? I'm up here at West Point, and she's down there in Washington, and supper's about ten hours away, and already it's on her mind. I'm sure you know how it is with wives, General."

"Yes sir," said Slaight, "I know how it is."

J ACEY CALLED Agent Kerry the morning after she discovered that Dorothy's E-mail floppy disks had been stolen from her room and learned from his Military Police assistant that Kerry had been pulled off the investigation of Dorothy's death temporarily to testify at a court-martial down at Fort Belvoir, Virginia, as an expert witness. He would be back after the weekend, the MP had said.

Her parents invited her to watch the Army–Southern Illinois game from the Supe's box at Michie Stadium, but Jacey decided to sit with her company down in the cadet stands and was glad she had when Army trounced Southern Illinois twenty-four to six. It was great having a winning football team. Weekends at West Point became one long celebration. Spirits were high, and the whole Corps walked around the Academy sharing one huge grin.

She and Ash ran into each other on Saturday night after the game at the First Class Club, an informal gathering spot that served as a kind of adjunct officer's club for seniors. He asked her if she wanted to go across the river for brunch on Sunday, but she passed. She wanted to believe the things he had told her in the parking lot of Building 720, but the theft of evidence from her room had put her on edge.

Now it was Monday morning and Jacey was about to leave her room when she heard a knock on the door. "Come in," she said.

Ash opened the door. He was wearing his class uniform. "I just wanted to wish you good luck this morning with Kerry."

"Thanks, Ash."

"I did some thinking about this stuff over the weekend. Whatever it takes, I'm going the distance, Jace. You just tell me what you need and I'll get it for you."

"Thanks."

He hesitated for a moment, then stepped into the hallway and closed the door behind him.

Outside, a bright sun had warmed the area of barracks. Cadets were wearing light cotton jackets on their way to class as Jacey walked down Thayer Road to the Provost Marshal's building.

Kerry ushered her into his office. His manner was blunt. "So what have you got for me?"

"It's what I don't have we should discuss first," said Jacey.

Agent Kerry leaned forward in his chair and picked up a pen. "What do you mean by that?"

"Someone stole the floppy disks containing Dorothy Hamner's E-mail from my desk drawer Thursday night."

"Wait a minute. We took everything off her computer, including her E-mail. How did you come by this evidence?"

Jacey explained how Carrie had found Dorothy's disks in her file box, how they'd gone through her E-mail messages, how she had traveled to Oneonta to see her mother and had retrieved Dorothy's last E-mail message to her mother.

"What did it say?"

Jacey handed him a sheet of paper. "This is as close as I can recall it."

Agent Kerry read her handwritten recollection of the message, letting go a low whistle between his teeth as he reached the bottom of the page. He looked up at her. "Maybe you'd better tell me what else you found on her E-mail, as best as you can recall."

Jacey laid out everything she could remember from the E-mail disks they had found in Carrie's file box, including the names of the guys who had been at the party at the lake. When she was finished, Agent Kerry again picked up her handwritten recollection of Dorothy's last E-mail and scanned it. "What do you think is going on here, Miss Slaight?"

"Every guy at that party was on the Honor Committee. I think somehow, in some way, these guys have been misusing the Honor Code."

"You think this whole thing is about the Honor Code?"

"Yes, I do. I think Dorothy became aware of what they were doing and they did something to her. It's right there in her E-mail message."

"This is hardly enough to draw that conclusion."

"They must have done something to frighten her, or why would she be trying to call her mother at four in the morning if she wasn't really upset or scared?"

"What if all she was upset about was breaking up with her boyfriend? Girls call their mothers all the time when stuff like that happens."

"If that's all it was, why would they go to the trouble of stealing the disks out of my desk?"

"I'm going to need more to go on than speculation. From what you recall from her E-mail, she was very much in love with this guy Favro. Her message to her mother is interesting but inconclusive. What I'm trying to tell you, Miss Slaight, is that you've opened up a door for us here, but there's not much I can see in there. You get my drift?"

"Well then, look at it this way. Dorothy *died,* Agent Kerry. If these guys were with her the night before, why haven't they come forward and told you everything they know about her behavior in the hours just before she died?"

"You think they've got something to cover up."

"That is why Rose stopped me outside my barracks. He said if I kept pushing on this thing, I'd be sorry. It was a threat, Agent Kerry. They're covering up something, and they're scared, and guys who are scared are capable of doing stupid things."

CHAPTER 26

IT WAS just before lunch when Melissa buzzed him. Bassett was on the line. He knew of a new place in Cornwall, north of the Academy, only a few minutes away. It was just a little roadside spot, but the owners—Italians who had fled downtown Newburgh— were supposed to have excellent fried calamari served with a spicy marinara sauce and a fantastic Caesar salad swimming with sardines, laden with crunchy stalks of romaine, and drenched in the real thing, the raw-egg and Parmesan dressing that had made the salad famous before it had been watered down and mass-marketed to the passing masses at chain restaurants whose menus stated that they featured "our famous Caesar salad." Anything on a menu preceded by the words *our famous* was like being warned you were about to be served freeze-dried scrambled eggs in a mess hall. There were two things dishes were "famous" for: They were either forgettable or dangerous to your health.

Bassett suggested they forgo the Supe's staff car and meet instead at his privileged parking behind Building 606, where the beat-up Buicks and occasional six-year-old BMWs of the full colonels were parked. Slaight found Bassett's own battered BMW parked in the spot marked PROF LAW. Soon Bassett ambled across the lot and unlocked the doors.

The BMW had seen better days. The visors were cracked and peeling and so was the dash. "Why don't you get yourself one of those sun visor things?" asked Slaight, as Bassett backed out of his spot.

"You're the Supe. Why don't you build us a covered garage?" Bassett joked back.

The professor of law was one of those drivers who kept one hand on the wheel, but only as an afterthought. The other hand moved through the air like the wand of a conductor, bobbing this way and that as Bassett gave about 30 percent of his attention to the road and the other 70 percent to whatever was on his mind. It was the first time in years that Slaight had ridden with Bassett driving, and it brought back memories of the last time. He had been a cadet, and he'd been at Bassett's house for dinner, and Bassett was driving him back to the Academy, all the while his hands flying around the inside of the car like they had lives of their own, which they did. When they had pulled up outside of Grant Hall, Slaight recalled thinking that if Bassett could successfully drive him back to the barracks, then the least he could do was successfully figure out who killed David Hand.

Bassett made a turn off 9W onto a side road that was a back way around Vails Gate. On the right was a little white cottage with about twenty cars parked in front. Bassett found a spot down at the far end of the line of cars and they made their way to the front door, where they were escorted to a table in what must have once been a pantry. There were pipes overhead, and every time somebody flushed the toilet on the other side of the wall next to them, you could hear it.

Bassett dipped a piece of bread in a little pot of olive oil and devoured it eagerly. "I thought you might be interested in knowing that your chief law-enforcement officer, Lieutenant Colonel Percival, has been serving as a funnel of information to the Commandant of Cadets."

"How'd you find that out?"

"Well, two sources, actually. One of the clerks who used to work in my office is now pushing papers for Gibson. He, uh, reports to me informally on the comings and goings within the Commandant's office. It seems that Percival showed up there late last week without an appointment. The clerk heard Gibson screaming through the closed door. He made out the words 'that fucking bitch' and 'that fucking Vernon.' I naturally assumed they were talking about our pathologist, Major Elizabeth Vernon, but I had no idea of the nature of their conversation until Major Vernon herself showed up in my office this morning."

The waiter delivered two glasses of ice water and stood by, awaiting their orders. Bassett ordered calamari and Slaight ordered the Caesar salad, and they agreed to split a main course of ravioli stuffed with veal and broccoli, which Bassett guaranteed would be more than enough for the both of them. When the waiter departed, he continued: "Vernon was one of my students in military law when she was a cadet. She was one of those students who are a delight to teach. Fran and I became friendly with her and had her over for dinner several times. Major Vernon made a report to Percival last week and became concerned when she wasn't immediately sent to see Colonel Lombardi, so she followed Percival when he left his office. He went straight to Gibson with a report Major Vernon had just made to him. It seems that Dorothy Hamner had sex with multiple partners shortly before her death. Major Vernon has isolated three separate DNA profiles from a sample taken during the autopsy. She asked Percival to limit knowledge of the DNA profiles to the chain of command, which would mean himself, Colonel Lombardi, and you. When she discovered he went straight to Gibson, she reported it to me, knowing I would take the information straight to you."

"Smart," said Slaight. "I know about the DNA. I met with Lombardi this morning."

The waiter delivered the calamari and the salad, and Bassett speared a crusty set of tentacles, coated them with marinara sauce, and popped them in his mouth. "Man, you've got to try this stuff."

Slaight stuck his fork in a tubular chunk of calamari and did the same thing. "That is *good.*"

"So what did Lombardi have to say?" asked Bassett.

"He said Major Vernon wants to cross-check her DNA samples against the DNA profiles we've got on male cadets. She told Lombardi if they turn out to be cadets, she can identify the individuals who had sex with the deceased girl just before she died."

"She wants you to order what amounts to a search of the data bank on cadet DNA."

"That about sums it up."

"We know where Percival stands on the matter. What was Lombardi's counsel?"

"He's against it as well. He said that even if we end up ID'ing the cadets, they could refuse to answer questions on the grounds that the search was unconstitutional, and we'd end up with a scandal instead of helpful information."

"As a matter of fact, he's got something of a point there. What can and cannot be done with DNA taken from members of the military is an area of the law that hasn't been tested. But I'm pretty sure there's a regulation in there that DNA samples taken under the battlefield ID requirement cannot be used in a criminal procedure. Remember the two marines who refused to be tested, when the whole DNA profiling began? They took the position that they didn't want to be profiled for the purposes of battlefield identification because there was a chance their DNA might end up being used against them for other purposes. They said the test was an invasion of privacy."

"I remember now."

"They were found guilty and discharged for refusal of a direct order. The military court found that the marines had a legitimate interest in being able to ID the dead on the battlefield, which superseded their right to privacy."

"That was the argument the Pentagon used in the chapel case, wasn't it? Didn't they say that the goverment's interest in seeing to it that cadets received religious training superseded the cadets' rights to freedom of religion under the First Amendment?"

"The analogy is close, but the cases are different in this way. The DNA test is in fact simply another form of inspection, which soldiers are required to submit to every day, so the military had only to establish there was a legitimate and rational reason for the inspection. In the chapel case, the government lost because the test was far more profound. Faced with the stricture of the First Amendment against the establishment of religion, it was up to the government to establish a *compelling* reason to require church attendance of cadets. The government lost the case on several grounds, but a major element of the court's reasoning was that they couldn't credibly define what the government's compelling interest was. The government put on witnesses who said that it was absolutely necessary that cadets attend church every Sunday if they were to become effective and honorable officers. You may recall that the plaintiffs called the government's bluff. If attending church was in fact a requirement to become a lieutenant, then why didn't the government similarly compel attendance by ROTC cadets?''

"But you're saying this DNA thing is different."

"Correct. In the chapel case the cadets were able to prove that the government's arguments were bogus because the requirement to attend chapel was limited to the service academies, and did not extend to all officers commissioned into the service. In the present case, the government is saying that they have a legitimate interest in being able to ID scraps of human bones and other fragments on the battlefield and so DNA typing should be required across the board. Every member of the armed forces is required to be DNA-profiled. They are not acting in an arbitrarily selective manner here."

"These are complicated matters, aren't they?"

"That's why they pay you the big bucks," Bassett joked. "You're the guy wearing the stars. It's your call."

"What do you think I ought to do, Cliff?"

"Well, the regs are a little muddy here. While by law they preclude usage of the DNA samples in a criminal procedure, you don't have a crime yet. No one has been charged. All Major Vernon is attempting to do is establish cause of death. You can make an argument that this is a health and safety issue. Cadet Hamner dropped dead at parade on a hot day. There are parades held in hot weather all the time at West Point. You don't want any more cadet deaths out there on the Plain. What if Major Vernon discovers that Miss Hamner died because, say, she drank too much coffee in the mess hall that morning? With that information in hand, you could ban coffee on hot days when there's going to be a parade. The health and safety of the cadets is arguably your highest priority as Superintendent."

"So you think I ought to order the search."

"Go ahead and do it. There's a chance the DNA in the sample will turn out to belong to civilians. If it turns out to be cadet DNA, and we ID them, they'll be called in and questioned. They'll be afforded all of their rights, and if they refuse to answer, the legal process will run its course, if indeed there's a course to be run. I just don't see that there's a downside. You can always defend your decision to execute the search on the health and safety grounds."

Slaight ran his thumbnail between the two black stripes down the side of his uniform trousers.

"Cliff, do you remember back when I was a cadet and I came to see you about that Honor Code business? Officers were using the Honor Code to enforce discipline. They would ask cadets leading questions. If you told the truth, you got punished. But if you failed the tell the truth, they found you on Honor. I remember you told me it wouldn't be the last time in my life that I would face a situation where you were damned if you did, and damned if you didn't."

Bassett laughed. "Here we are, back where we started."

Slaight picked up his fork and stabbed another ring of calamari. "It's tough, Cliff. What is it they say about DNA? It's the building block of human life. I don't think we should trifle with our genetic identities. Maybe our genes will end up being the last bastion of privacy we have."

Bassett looked over at his old friend. "Like I said, that's why they pay you the big bucks, Ry. But I've got to warn you not to overthink this thing. When you get to be our age, there are limits to the advantage which can be gained from pondering the damn thing to death."

Slaight laughed. He knew exactly what his friend meant. When you're young, going at problems from every possible direction is fun, and you can only gain from it. But there was an old Academy adage they used to tell plebes:

You're not being paid to think, mister. You're being paid to act.

The waiter delivered the order of ravioli and divided it between two bowls. As Slaight dug into the pillows of pasta floating in a rich meat broth, he made up his mind. It was time to act. "I've decided to order the search."

"I think you ought to be careful with Gibson. There's a reason he's gotten Percival to leak the results of the investigation to him. He's trying to stay ahead of you. He's trying to find a way to influence the results of the investigation before they reach your desk. I don't know what his motives are—"

"Let's talk about Gibson for a moment, Cliff," Slaight interrupted. "We've got a dead body here at West Point. Why do you think he is trying to influence the investigation?"

"I guess you never tried to figure out who killed David Hand, and you never came up against a Commandant of Cadets whose name was Hedges, did you?" said Bassett sarcastically. "Gibson is responding to the investigation of the death of Miss Hamner in exactly the same way Hedges responded to your investigation of the death of David Hand. He doesn't want anyone messing with *his* cadets. They belong to him, don't you see, Ry? It's plain old *turf,* only this time the turf is human beings. He's trying to protect his ownership of them."

"Well, Gibson's going to get a lesson about who's running things at West Point if he keeps up this crap."

"He can make real trouble for you, Ry. He's got a pipeline leading directly to Thrunstone. If Thrunstone decides you're the Antichrist, you had better believe the members of his National Security Committee will plaster 'Slaight's the Antichrist' posters all over their districts and shout it from the rooftops."

"You know what? I don't give a damn. I'm going to push, and they can push back. If Gibson wants to play hardball, then I guess we'll see who's got the best bat."

Each of them chomped away on their ravioli for a few moments, then Bassett looked up at Slaight and caught his attention. "This isn't about who's got the upper hand, Ry. What this is about is the future of West Point."

CHAPTER 27

T HE GATHERING that afternoon at four P.M. in the office of
the Superintendent of the United States Military Academy included the entire law-enforcement chain of command at West Point:
Lieutenant Colonel Percival, the Provost Marshal; Colonel Lombardi,
the Staff Judge Advocate; Chief Warrant Officer Kerry, the CID Special Agent in Charge of the investigation; and Major Vernon, the
pathologist.

They sat around a small conference table at the far end of the
Supe's office. There was no one else present. Not a secretary, not an
aide, not even the Commandant. Gibson had been excluded because
he fell outside the official chain of command in law-enforcement
matters. Besides, Slaight knew Percival had been leaking every development in the investigation to him, and he didn't trust Gibson's
motives. Slaight made a show of closing the door to his office. He
walked over to his desk and punched the button on his phone for
his secretary.

"Yes sir." Melissa's voice boomed over the speakerphone.

"Hold my calls. I don't want to be disturbed unless there is an
emergency."

"Understood, sir."

Slaight walked directly to the head of the conference table and leaned forward, placing his hands on top of the table with his fingers splayed. Glancing down, his eye caught one of the blue veins criss-crossing the backs of his hands. It was pulsing.

"What I have to say to you people does not leave this room. Is that clear?"

Heads nodded, more than one a bit uncertainly.

"I'll say again: Is that clear?"

There was a chorus of "Yes sir's."

He took his seat at the head of the table, but he didn't lean back. He sat forward on the edge of the chair and looked from one person at the table to another.

"You are aware of the current status of the autopsy conducted by Major Vernon. We do not yet have a positive cause of death, but we do know that Cadet Hamner did *not* die from heatstroke, and we know that she had sex with multiple partners less than twenty-four hours before her death. Major Vernon has DNA typing from the three males who had sex with Miss Hamner. I'm going to order a search of the DNA profiles of all male cadets at West Point and direct Major Vernon to conduct a cross-check in order to see if there are any matches. Questions?"

Colonel Lombardi cleared his throat. "Sir, there's a regulation on the books which precludes such a search. It's part of the act that was passed which authorized the collection of DNA material for battle-field identification. I can look it up, sir—"

"You don't have to, Colonel," interrupted Slaight. He picked up a sheaf of papers. "I've got it right here, and I have studied it. I contend that as the Superintendent, I've got latitude. I'm ordering the DNA cross-check because we've got a health and safety issue on our hands here. A young woman died out there on the Plain during a parade. It was hot. There were some four thousand other cadets out there with her. Others dropped from the heat. None of them died. In fact, we have never had a death at West Point which resulted from a parade."

He waited until the last sentence sunk in. He was looking around the table to see who showed signs of nervousness or concern. They were poker-faced. The subject was the death of a twenty-one-year-old woman, and yet there was no emotion shown by a single person at the table.

"It is my intention as Superintendent that we never again have a cadet die during a parade. To that end, I am ordering the DNA search. It's the contention of Major Vernon that anyone who came in contact with Cadet Hamner within twenty-four hours of her death could be of help in the determination of the cause of her death. If we can find out what killed her, then we can prevent it from ever happening again." Again, he paused for effect, looking around the table. Every face was blank.

"I have spoken to Cadet Hamner's mother and father. They live up in Oneonta. Her father owns a gas station. Her mother runs a gift shop and works as a nurse's aide. They are good people, and when they sent their daughter to West Point, the last thing in the world they expected was that before she graduated to become an Army officer, her body would be shipped home in a goddamned box."

He turned to Colonel Lombardi. "I understand your concerns about the regulations, Colonel. As SJA, that's your job. But let me make clear to you that every year, about one thousand families like Dorothy Hamner's entrust their sons and daughters to us for four years. We are not going to let down Dorothy's parents, and we're not going to let down the parents of the kids who have been entrusted to us. If I have to step on a few toes in order to go about my duty insuring that these young people make their way from the first day of Beast to graduation at Michie Stadium, then so be it." He paused, giving Lombardi the time to respond. He didn't.

"We are going to find out what killed that young woman if it's the last thing I do as Superintendent, is that clear?"

Not a word.

"Now I'm going to caution each of you once again that what I've said here is not to leave this room, and I'll tell you why. There's always a chance that Dorothy Hamner died of a disease or natural causes. In that case, I don't want even a whisper of her sexual history to become part of the record of the investigation. There is also a possibility that the three individuals who had sex with Miss Hamner are cadets who had nothing to do with the circumstances of her death, and if that is the case, I do not want either them or Miss Hamner discredited. There is one more reason. If in fact it turns out that Miss Hamner's sexual partners were cadets, I do not want them forewarned that evidence has been gathered which might implicate them. Is that understood?''

Heads nodded around the table.

Slaight grasped the arms of his chair in preparation to stand up, but everyone at the table beat him to it. Some things in the Army never changed. A three-star general still got respect.

CHAPTER 28

O VER THE years, Samantha Hand Slaight had been many things to many people—a wife and a mother and a daughter and a schoolteacher who still substituted at the high school downtown in Highland Falls—but she had also been something else, something special. She had been an *Army wife*. She had learned to survive the constant change of stations, usually once every couple of years, but sometimes yearly, and just after they had first married, they had moved twice a year for two years. By the time she supervised the packing and loading of everything they owned into yet another semi-trailer for the move to Quarters 100 at West Point, she and Ry had lived in something like twenty-six different apartments or houses in the past twenty-seven years.

She had learned the myriad alleyways of military politics—how, as the wife of a lieutenant, you deal with the wife of the colonel, and later how, as the wife of the colonel, you deal with the wives of the lieutenants, and how, as the wife of a soldier of any rank, you deal with his commanding officer. She had developed a set of antennae as finely tuned as any. You had to smell trouble before trouble arrived. You had to find your way in the total darkness of an assignment to a new post with new commanders and new commanders' wives. You had to watch your husband's back at the same time you watched your own back, because as Ry had gained rank and responsibility, starting back when he was a major, moving on through lieutenant colonel, colonel, brigadier general, major general, and now lieutenant general, the knives were out every step of the way. The Army liked to think of itself as a society of warriors, and at least when it came to their careers, they certainly behaved like the warriors they dreamt themselves to be. Army officers were out for each other's blood from the moment they woke up to the instant they lost consciousness at night.

Yet having developed such a finely honed sixth sense about the Army and her place in it, she had discovered her antennae were as much a burden as a boon. Her ability to see into and through situations and people extended right into her own family, where a good deal of the time it got in the way or simply didn't belong. She found herself longing for the days when her husband went through a few days with a dark mood, or her daughter woke up on the proverbial wrong side of the bed, and well, that was just that. But now she could see his dark moods coming, and her daughter was as transparent to her as a glass of water.

And so when Ry had told her there was a major development in the Dorothy Hamner case, she had sensed that it was one that might not produce good news. And when Jacey had called the next day, she had heard the hollow tone in her voice signaling that her daughter felt very much alone right now. She also knew, because Jacey had told her as much, that her daughter was hesitant to talk to her father. Part of it was the investigation of the death of Jacey's friend Dorothy. But Sam also knew that a larger part was undoubtedly the fact that Jacey was a cadet and Ry was the Supe, and their respective ranks and stations in life were getting in the way of his being her father and her being his daughter.

What do you do when you find your antennae tingling with danger signals? Cook dinner. Get everyone around the table and let the forks fall where they may.

So she called Jacey and invited her over, and she told Ry to clear his schedule for the night and make sure he was home by six o'clock, because their daughter was coming home for dinner. Ry, who had indeed plunged into one of his darker moods, seemed to brighten at the prospect. Jacey sounded excited. The first thing she asked was,

"What are we having, Mom?" Sam told her spaghetti and meatballs, one of her favorite meals since she was a little girl. "Count me in!" she yelled into the phone.

Sam had the meatballs simmering in a nicely thickened red sauce and a pot of water ready for the pasta when Ry came into the kitchen unbuttoning his uniform jacket. He kissed the back of her neck and dipped a finger into the sauce. "Needs salt," he announced.

"It does not," she replied.

"Does too."

"So add salt on your plate. Not everyone in the world thinks food ought to have the salt content of movie-theater popcorn."

He laughed. "Okay. You got me." He looked around. "Where's Jace?"

"She called and said she'd be a few minutes late. She had orienteering this afternoon. It always takes them a while to get everyone rounded up and on the trucks to get back."

He laughed. "I remember those truck rides back from the deep boonies," he said.

"Why don't you open a bottle of wine?"

"Good idea." He picked a bottle of Chianti from the wine rack in the corner, opened it, and poured them each a glass. He took a sip. "This is great. Where'd you get it?"

"That little place over in Cold Spring. I took Helen Messick to lunch over there today. We stopped in the wine shop afterward."

"You're seeing quite a bit of her. How is she?"

"Same old Helen. We told Leavenworth stories. She can be pretty funny when she wants to be. I had a good time."

"I don't suppose the subject of the Commandant came up."

"Nope. I didn't expect it would."

"I think they're playing it cool since I dressed him down."

"I certainly didn't see any ripples in her pond today."

He took another sip of wine. "I'm going to grab a shower before Jace gets here."

"Okay." She smashed a couple of cloves of garlic and tossed them into a plastic container. Then she drizzled olive oil and white wine vinegar over the garlic, added a handful of crumbled blue cheese, a few tablespoons of yogurt, and one of mayonnaise, snapped the lid on the container, and gave it a good shake. She had just opened the container when she heard the back door. Jacey gave her mother a kiss on the cheek and stuck her finger into the dressing."

"Needs salt," she pronounced.

"You and your father and your salt. I swear."

"Where's Dad?"

"Upstairs changing. Do you want a glass of wine?"

"Sure."

Jacey poured herself a glass of Chianti. "This is wonderful."

"Hand me the lettuce, would you, Jace? It's in the bottom drawer of the fridge."

Jacey handed the lettuce to her mother, who divided it among three salad plates. "So what's new, Big Ma?"

"We're supposed to leave tomorrow for the Washington State game on Saturday. It's going to be a lo-o-ong weekend, I guess."

"I don't know what West Point's doing playing teams all the way across the country."

"It's the new league they formed."

"Yeah, but it still doesn't make much sense to me. I mean, hardly anybody but the team and the cheerleaders gets to go."

"And the Supe and the Supe's wife."

They heard Ry coming down the back stairs. He saw Jacey and quickly wrapped her up in a big hug. "Good to see you, doll."

"You too, Dad. Mom tells me you-all are going to the Washington State game."

"Duty calls."

"You sound real enthused."

"I'm eager to see the cadets whip Washington, but I don't look forward to the flights. I'm getting too old to be flying coast-to-coast and back in three days."

"Why don't you send me in your place?" Jacey teased.

"I'd love to." He took another sip of wine. "You two will never guess who has decided to retire. Don Frank. He told me today. He wanted me to have a jump start on picking a new Dean to replace him."

"Don Frank? I thought he'd stay here till they carried him away on a stretcher," said Sam.

"He's been a cool dean," said Jacey. "He hired some more new female professors last year."

"Did he recommend anyone to replace him?" asked Sam.

"He said I ought to talk to Roberta Graves."

"I remember Roberta. She's at the War College, isn't she?"

"Yeah, and she just got her first star. She would be one hell of a pick, that's for sure. She's smart as hell, she's well-connected, and she's written three books on military history."

"Do you think you could get her approved?"

"I know I can sell her to Meuller, and I'm sure he can get the President to make the appointment. I'm pretty sure she would make it through the Senate Armed Services Committee if there isn't any opposition to her from within the Army."

"Gibson will go all out against her," said Sam.

"He already has," said Slaight.

"What? General Gibson has put females in leadership positions all over the Corps. He made me company commander."

"He puts up a good front, Jace, but behind the scenes, he's the worst nightmare Army women could have. General Frank told me Gibson fought every one of the female professors he sought to appoint last year," said her father.

"I didn't know that."

"The Academic Board doesn't exactly advertise its disputes to the world outside the oak-paneled room where we meet."

"I don't understand. He's never said anything against women at West Point."

"Not out loud, he hasn't. But he hasn't made a secret of his opposition to increasing the number of women in the Army. Down at the Pentagon, they count him among those who are hard-core opponents of women taking combat roles. He even opposed women being allowed into Air Defense Artillery."

"That's strange," said Jacey, "because he's really popular among cadets, male and female alike."

Sam handed each of them a salad. "Let's take these to the table." In the dining room, Sam placed a salt shaker and oak pepper mill next to Ry's place at the head of the table and lit the candles.

"You guys still have candlelight dinners all the time?" asked Jacey.

"Every night. Your mom insists on it," said Ry.

"That's way cool. So retro."

"It's a nice way to end the day," said Sam, giving her table an admiring glance. It had long been one of her rules. Every night she set a table that she wouldn't be ashamed to share with anyone who walked through the door. Dinner was the one hour of the day when you could sit down in one place and relax and enjoy the wine and the food and the conversation that flowed therefrom.

"You guys let me know when dinner's ready. I've got the newspapers to catch up on. I've had a long day." Slaight walked across the hall to the study.

Sam and Jacey went back into the kitchen and Sam turned on the pasta water. When it came to a boil, she dropped most of a package of spaghetti into the pot and swirled the water until all of the strands of pasta had separated and the water had come back to a full boil. She stayed next to the stove, awaiting the inevitable foam that would rise to the lip of the pan.

"How many times have you cooked this dish, Mom?"

Sam thought for a moment. "Maybe a hundred."

"I thought you'd say more."

"I guess it is more. I started making spaghetti and meatballs before you were born, that's for sure."

"So that's over twenty-one years ago. If you only cooked it five times a year, you're already over a hundred, just in my lifetime."

"So, two hundred."

Jacey laughed and hugged her mother. " 'Course, then there were the times Dad cooked it."

"Yeah, I forgot about those. I guess that makes probably three hundred, between us."

"Almost a year of your life you have spent eating spaghetti and meatballs for dinner."

"You could look at it that way. Or you could say, the other damn forty-nine years I was eating something else."

Jacey high-fived her mother. "Your father forgot his glass of wine. Would you take it in there to him? And tell him the pasta's on," Sam said.

Jacey carried the wine into a wood-paneled study and put it down next to her father. He was sitting in a large wing-backed chair near the fireplace, reading the papers. She walked along the bookcases, scanning the titles, finally reaching for a book on a high shelf. *"The Man Who Kept the Secrets,"* she read aloud, opening the book.

"It's about the CIA director, Richard Helms," said her father, looking up from the paper.

"Did you ever meet him?"

He chuckled. "He departed the CIA about the time I was departing the Republic of Vietnam for the last time."

"Is it a good book?"

"Excellent."

"Can I borrow it, Daddy?"

"Of course you can. Only one condition."

"What's that?"

"You've got to come over here and have dinner with us on the evening you return it."

She grinned. "Mom said to tell you we're almost ready."

He put his papers aside and stood up. "Let's give her a hand," he said, placing his hand on his daughter's shoulder. Together they walked back to the kitchen. Sam was shaking the final drops of water from the pasta in a colander. She used tongs to serve three large bowls of spaghetti. Jacey grabbed a hot pad, took the pot of meatballs and sauce over to the counter, and spooned a healthy serving into each bowl. The three of them carried their bowls of pasta and glasses of wine to the table. Slaight had tucked the Chianti under his arm, and he poured a measure into each of their glasses before he sat down and raised his glass in a toast.

"Beat Washington State!"

"All right!" said Jacey.

Sam grinned. West Point definitely brought out the kid . . . in both of them.

The customary moments of silence followed, as they dug into the meatballs and pasta, gulping sips of wine between bites. Finally Jacey looked up at her mother. "It's great! It's . . . almost sweet. What'd you do different?"

"Fresh oregano and fresh basil. Dried is much stronger and more bitter. Fresh herbs have a subtle flavor."

Slaight looked up. "More wine?" Jacey held out her glass, and he poured another dollop. He looked down the table at his wife. "I'm okay for now," she said. He speared a few pieces of lettuce on his fork and swirled them in the dressing on his plate. "Great blue-cheese dressing, Sam."

"I just copy that stuff we used to get from Trader Joe's when we lived at Fort Ord in California."

"This is better."

"Definitely," said Jacey.

They munched in silence for another moment or two, then Slaight swallowed the last of his glass of wine and reached for the bottle of Chianti only to find it empty. "I'm going to open another bottle," he announced as he headed for the kitchen. When he returned, Jacey looked up from twirling her pasta.

"I talked to Chief Warrant Officer Kerry. We found copies of Dorothy's E-mail hidden in her room on floppy disks. I got some more off of her laptop in her bedroom in her parents' house. She wrote to her mother the morning she died that something had happened to her at a party the night before. She sounded scared."

"You told this to the CID?"

"Yes, Daddy. I told Agent Kerry everything I know."

"We've entered a dangerous area in military law here, Jacey. As the Superintendent, I am allowed to be kept abreast of the investigation, but I cannot get ahead of the investigation. I am not permitted to be a finder of fact, because I am the one who may be called upon to make a decision about whether or not anyone will be court-martialed. So it's vital, Jace, that you have reported everything you've told me to the proper authorities."

"I have, Daddy."

"That makes it okay, doesn't it, Ry?" asked Sam.

"For the time being. But if you discover anything else independently, you must report it to Agent Kerry before you inform me. You understand that, don't you, Jace?"

"Yes Daddy."

"All right then, why don't you start at the beginning, and tell me everything you told the CID."

Jacey filled in the gaps in the story. When she was finished, her mother said, "Ry, I don't like this."

"Neither do I," said Slaight without hesitation. "Jacey, I'm going to take you into my confidence and tell you something that I probably shouldn't be telling you. I'm going to tell you this because I want you to steer clear of the cadets who were at the party. Do you understand me?"

"I understand, Daddy."

"I think you've taken your involvement in the investigation about as far as it should go. I want you to let the authorities handle it from now on. From what you've told me, and from what I found out, at least three cadets here at West Point are going to find themselves in some very hot water pretty soon. Major Vernon received the results of a DNA test she ran as part of her autopsy of Dorothy Hamner. The test reveals that she had sex with three different men within twenty-four hours of her death. I've ordered a cross-check of Major Vernon's DNA evidence against the DNA profiles we have on male cadets. That means if the men she had sex with were cadets, we'll have their names in a few days."

"Daddy, that's why they're so scared! They must have raped her!"

"Jacey, I'm going to say it again. I don't want you involved in this any further."

"But I'm already involved, Daddy. Ash is going to examine Honor Committee records for patterns of abuse, and I'm going to help him. If they've been messing around with the Honor Code, we're going to find out."

"You've got to listen to your father, Jacey," said Sam.

"Are you guys forgetting that the Honor Code belongs to the Corps of Cadets? The Code is what makes us who we are. We're not college students, we're *cadets*, and we're not going to let them destroy it."

Sam looked from her daughter to her husband. The two of them were so much alike, it astounded her. Sitting there in the dining room of Quarters 100, she may as well have been sitting in Grant Hall with Ry thirty years ago, going over the evidence in the death of her brother. There had been nothing that could stop him back then, and there would be nothing that would stop her now.

"Ry," she implored, *"tell her to stop."* She looked across the table at him. There was a mix of sadness and pride in his eyes. She remembered the look, because she had seen it the first time he came home from being a company commander, after he had made decisions he knew would profoundly affect the lives of soldiers under his command, decisions he was unsure about, but which he knew he had to make. And she had seen it literally hundreds of times since.

He swirled the last of the wine in his glass. "Sam, I can't pull rank on Jacey and give her an order. I've warned her that this is a volatile situation and it should be left to the authorities. That's as far as I'm going to go."

Jacey reached for her mother's hand. "Even if he told me to stop, Mom, I wouldn't. I can't. Don't you see?"

"Now you're both going to tell me this is for almighty West Point." She stood up. "Well, *God damn* West Point!" She walked straight into the kitchen with Jacey at her heels.

"Mom, you don't tell me everything I can and can't do anymore. I'm on my own now. It's just the way it is."

"I understand that, Jace, but it doesn't make it any easier for me." Sam reached for her daughter, pressing her against her bosom. She knew that mothers had worried about daughters since time began, and that this moment was just one teeny-tiny blip in that great continuum, but it sure as hell hurt.

"We love you, Jace."

"I love you, Mom, and I love Dad, too. I know it's hard for you, but you've got to trust me. You know?"

Sam looked into her daughter's eyes. "I know, Jace. But I want you to be careful. Promise me you'll be careful."

"I will, Mom. I promise."

Sam held her tight, thinking back to all the nights she had cuddled her daughter . . . nights she was sick with a fever . . . nights she woke up from a bad dream . . . nights the boy she had a crush on didn't call. But this was different. Even though her daughter lived only a few hundred yards away in the cadet barracks, she may as well have been halfway around the world, because it was true. She was on her own now.

CHAPTER 2 9

CROSS-CHECKING HER DNA profiles against those of the male
cadets at West Point turned out to be a far more complicated
process than Major Vernon had anticipated. The DNA profiles of
cadets at the Academy were stored at the armed forces DNA database
in Rockville Center, Maryland, where they had been lumped together with the rest of the DNA profiles on active-duty military personnel. There were just about 1.5 million people in uniform. Culling
the male cadet DNA profiles was going to take some work. She went
at it step by step.

First she logged into the military network and accessed the Rockville Center database. She clicked away, asking the database to spit
out the Military Academy profiles. Not available as a separate file or
category, the computer answered. She made pass after pass at sin-
gling out the cadet data from the rest of the DNA database without
success.

After grabbing a quick lunch, she picked up the phone and called
down to Rockville. She spent about forty-five minutes on hold and
went through about four levels of civilian bureaucracy before she
located a human being by the name of Linda who knew how the
system worked. First Linda wanted to know Major Vernon's authorization. So Vernon hung up the phone and called Melissa at the

Supe's office, who quickly faxed the formal order authorizing the search to Major Vernon, who turned around and faxed it to Linda down in Maryland. Having covered her ass with actual paperwork signed by a three-star general, Linda grew cooperative.

"What we have to do is, we have to come up with a code we can feed into the computer that will pull your data out of the system. Do you know the code?"

"For what?" asked Major Vernon, completely puzzled.

"The code for cadets. I mean, like, the code that identifies cadets at West Point."

"I'll have to get back to you," she told Linda. She made a few calls around the post—to the personnel division over at HQ USMA, to the personnel office at HQ Corps of Cadets—and nothing turned up. Then it came to her. What are the basic identifiers of every individual in the Army? She had learned it as a plebe. The Code of Conduct said that if you're captured by the enemy, you are to give no information to the enemy beyond your name, rank, and serial number.

Providing the name of every cadet at West Point would be a time-consuming process. Equally tedious would be listing all cadet serial numbers. Which left *rank*. "Cadet" is actually a rank within the Army's structure, falling between second lieutenant and warrant officer. There is also a federal pay line for cadets, half of a second lieutenant's base pay. She picked up the phone and called finance at HQ USMA and got a sergeant first class on the line. She asked him for the code identifying the rank of "Cadet" in the Army's finance system.

"Easy," the sergeant said. He read her a five digit code, three numbers and two letters. "That's the pay line for cadets."

She thanked him, dialed Linda down in Maryland, and gave her the federal pay code for "Cadet." Linda asked her to hold the line for a moment. She could hear Linda's fingers flying across a keyboard 250 miles away. "Okay, I've figured out how to break it out." She explained to Major Vernon how to use the federal pay code to instruct the database to spit out the cadet DNA-profile data. Major Vernon thanked her profusely and hung up the phone. She poured herself a cup of coffee and sat down at her terminal. Once again, she accessed the Rockville Center database and typed in the code, along with the instructions Linda had provided. Her screen showed the blinking "wait" signal for a few long moments. Then the data started coming through the high-speed ISDN link. She took the entire download and popped it in a data file on a Syquist drive. The data included male and female DNA profiles, but that didn't matter. She'd just go ahead and run the check across the whole damn thing. She popped up the three DNA profiles she had separated out from Dorothy Hamner's vaginal sample and instructed the computer to search for a match between the file in its memory against the file on the Syquist drive. She hit "enter" and sat back. The Syquist drive whirred away, and she watched data fly down her screen. There was nothing quite like watching a computer hard at work. As she had suspected before the longer portion of the process had begun, the actual cross-check took less than five minutes. There they were:

Cadet Gerald Rose
Cadet Richard Favro
Cadet Glenn Ivar

"This is going to be cute," she said to herself out loud, recognizing each of the names on the screen. "We've got the Cadet Honor Chairman in the number one slot. In slot number two, we've got the Vice Chairman of the Honor Committee. And slot three is occupied by none other than the biggest ground-gaining running back West Point has seen in the last ten years."

She did some rearranging of the data on the screen and hit the print button. Next to her, a laser printer whirred to life and a single page slid forth. She picked up the page and carefully examined it. There was no way she could display all of the DNA data that matched her samples from Dorothy's vagina to the DNA profiles of the three cadets, but she had instructed the computer to use its own shorthand. In one column, she had listed the samples as ONE, TWO, and THREE with their DNA ID codes. In the column immediately adjacent, she had instructed the computer to print out the names of the cadets, along with their DNA ID codes.

A monkey wearing sunglasses in a dark room could see the match. She picked up the phone and dialed the number for Chief Warrant Officer Kerry.

"Jim, I ran the cross-check and I've got the names for you."

"Let me come to you," he said, and she heard the click as the phone went dead.

She looked at her watch. Five-forty-five. Her five-minute cross-check had taken just under five hours.

CHAPTER 30

WHEN PERCIVAL informed him that the DNA cross-check had identified the three cadets who had had sex with the dead girl, General Gibson called the Chairman of the Honor Committee and warned him. He left it at that. If he had told Rose to make sure they got their stories straight, or had contacted either of the others, and it turned out that somehow those idiots had contributed to the death of the girl, it would look like obstruction of justice.

He knew that all three of them, Rose, Ivar, and Favro, would be called in by the CID Special Agent in Charge and questioned about their behavior at the party on Labor Day. If what Rose had told him was true, that they were a little drunk, she was a willing particpant, and all they'd done was knock off a piece, there wasn't much to worry about. The problem was, cadets were unpredictable creatures. There was always the chance that something else had happened at the party Rose had not told him about. Rose was a conniving little bastard, and Gibson knew this well; he had maneuvered Rose into the postion of Cadet Honor Chairman precisely *because* he was a cunning little bastard. That was the thing about young men like Rose, with gigantic ambition and a limited grasp of their own conscience: You could control them because you knew what their motives were.

With one exception: sex. Years of experience in the gender-integrated Army had taught Gibson one thing. When it came to the libido, everything was up for grabs, especially when it came to the libidos of twenty- and twenty-one-year-olds. There was no way of knowing what had gone on between the three male cadets and Dorothy Hamner, and so for the time being, anyway, the cadets were on their own. The interrogations would take place. All Gibson could do about that situation was wait for the system to take its course and have what little faith he could generate that his three young charges may have fucked the girl, but they hadn't fucked up.

Gibson had not given Rose time during the brief phone call to make his report on the Jacey Slaight situation. He assumed that Rose had done what he said he was going to do and had figured out some way to get to her. Gibson wasn't concerned about Jacey Slaight's obsession with the death of her friend Dorothy Hamner. In fact, the Academy's own investigation was now going to find out much more than she already knew. What concerned Gibson about Jacey Slaight was the fact that he couldn't control her. She was smart and she was angry and he suspected that like most women, she could be dangerously vindictive. If she started sticking her nose into the affairs of the Honor Committee . . . Gibson fairly shuddered at the thought.

AFTER TAKING the call from the Commandant, Rose immediately got ahold of Favro and Ivar during a midperiod between classes that morning. They met in his private cadet room. Rose closed the door and locked it. He passed the word that the three of them had been identified by DNA evidence taken from Dorothy Hamner, and all of them could expect a visit from the CID. They had long since gotten their stories straight. It was just like he'd told the Com. They were drunk, she was coming on to them, and one thing led to another. The CID would ask for details. They would tell the Agent in Charge that they were in the rented cottage at the lake, and she had started doing a striptease, and they were all digging it, and when she got down to her panties and took them off and walked over to Rose and put them on his head, well, he took that as a signal, and they went into the adjoining bedroom, and they did it. When he came out, the others went in, first Favro, then Ivar. Later, they'd all ridden back to the Academy in the same car, Rose's car. They were all as stunned as anyone else the next day when they heard the announcement in the mess hall that she was dead.

Rose wondered if he should tell Favro and Ivar that he had stolen the E-mail disks from Jacey's room, but he quickly decided that was a piece of information that belonged to him alone.

Rose hadn't told General Gibson that he had Dorothy's E-mail disks because he didn't trust the Commandant. He wanted to wait and see how Gibson behaved when the heat got turned up. Gibson had warned him the moment he had gotten the news that the DNA cross-check had named them. He wasn't showing signs as yet of distancing himself from them. Still, you didn't get to be a general by looking out for many asses other than your own. So Rose would continue to hold the E-mail disks in abeyance. They were "hip-pocket" power. Rose would wait until the Commandant had trouble of his own. He knew Gibson was already having trouble with General Slaight. It was just a matter of time before his problems got worse. Rose would wait until exactly the right moment, and then he would take two of the E-mail disks to Gibson and report that he had been tipped that Jacey Slaight had them, and that he had then seized them. He would charge that Jacey was sitting on the E-mail disks because they contained exculpatory love letters between Dorothy and Favro. Gibson would be able to make the case to Slaight that his own daughter was guilty of withholding evidence and obstructing an official investigation. Rose knew that having come to Gibson's aid, he and the Commandant would be glued even closer together. He wanted to make it impossible for Gibson to cut him loose. His Honor Committee had passed judgment on cadets who stood entirely alone, without powerful sponsors, and he had watched as they passed through the South Gate in civilian clothes. He was determined that such a fate would not befall him.

The third disk, the one with the letter Dorothy wrote to her mother, he would hip-pocket for good. No one would ever read those words. Rose had made sure of that the night he melted the plastic floppy with a cigarette lighter and chucked it in a Dumpster.

CHAPTER 31

IT WAS nearly close of business on Friday and the weekend was almost upon them by the time Chief Warrant Officer Kerry got the names of the three cadets from Major Vernon. He waited until Monday before calling in the three cadets for questioning. He decided to interrogate them separately in a small, windowless room in the basement of the building housing the Provost Marshal's office. He'd make it as intimidating as possible, taking them out of their cadet barracks onto his turf, and see how far that got him.

He wanted to start with Ivar. He had looked up his cadet records and found he was close to the bottom of his class. Kerry thought Ivar might let something slip he could use against the others. But his request for an interview with Ivar fell on deaf ears. He had just returned from the Washington State game, and the team had been given a day of rest to get over jet lag. You should never underestimate the power of the Directorate of Athletics at West Point, he reminded himself. He took on Favro instead.

Cadet Rick Favro was a regimental commander and Vice Chairman of the Honor Committee. He was smart, but he lacked guile. Kerry had looked up Favro's records, too. His father owned a huge construction firm in Chicago that had built half the buildings along Michigan Avenue. This was a kid who had never bounced a check, had never lacked for anything in his life. When he walked into the windowless room in the basement, his sense of fear and dread was palpable.

He questioned Favro for about a half hour, and during that time, all he got out of him was that they'd had a typical cadet drinking party, things got a little wild, his girlfriend had started taking her clothes off in front of the three of them, one thing led to another, and they had all ended up in the sack with her. Then Kerry started boring in.

"You didn't mind it that these other guys were fucking your girl-friend?"

Favro looked straight at him. "I was pretty drunk. I don't remember getting angry at the time."

"How much of a girlfriend was she, Mr. Favro?"

For the first time, Favro showed nervousness. "We were just dating."

"Just dating. How many dates?"

"I don't know. We hadn't been dating long. A few, I guess."

Kerry watched with interest as he saw Favro begin to work on the germ of an idea.

"Maybe that's why I didn't end up mad at the other guys. I guess Dorothy and I really weren't that close. I mean, it wasn't like we were in love with each other or anything like that."

"Was Dorothy Hamner what we used to call a loose woman? Did she have a reputation for being easy?"

"I wouldn't say so."

"So you were surprised when she started stripping."

"Yes. I'd say that I was."

"Did you try to stop her?"

"Like I said, we were all pretty drunk. Maybe I was a little drunker than the others."

"How many drinks had you consumed?"

"We were drinking beer. We had a couple of kegs. I wasn't keeping count."

"But you drank a lot of beer."

"A whole lot."

"How would you describe the alcohol consumption of the others?"

"Dorothy wasn't drinking."

"What about Ivar and Rose?"

"They were pretty drunk."

"I don't understand, Mr. Favro. Ivar, he's a big-time running back, and he's got practice the next day. Rose, you told me he was the one who drove the car back to the Academy."

"I guess they weren't drinking as much as I was."

"And Dorothy Hamner wasn't drinking at all. So how do you reconcile these facts with your previous statement to me that . . ." He flipped through his notes and found the quote. " 'We were all pretty drunk and one thing led to another.' "

Favro considered the question for a moment before he answered. "I guess I was referring mostly to myself."

"By saying 'we.' "

"Yes."

"But the facts were otherwise, were they not?"

"Yes."

"And so when you first described to me the scene at the party you misspoke. Would that be fair?"

"Yes."

"Why so, Mr. Favro? You are the Vice Chairman of the Honor Committee, are you not?"

Now Favro squirmed noticeably in his chair, which was of the metal folding variety, not comfortable at all. "Like I said, I was pretty drunk. My memory of the whole thing isn't the greatest."

"But you have remembered so far the following: that, one, Dorothy wasn't drinking at all; that, two, Ivar wasn't drinking as much as you were; that, three, Rose wasn't drinking nearly as much as you were because he drove back to the Academy. So how, Mr. Favro, do you reconcile your drunken, faulty memory with the three specific recollections I just enumerated for you?"

Favro looked at a spot on the wall above Kerry's head for a long moment. Kerry had witnessed that behavior many times before. He called it the "prayerful stare." It was like he was waiting for divine intervention.

"All I can tell you is, I was real drunk, and everybody was drinking—"

"Except Dorothy," Kerry interrupted.

"Except Dorothy. And things started to just get kind of wild, and what happened, happened."

"How do you explain this to me, Mr. Favro? You invite a girl, a fellow first-class cadet, to a party as your date. She's the daughter of a gas-station owner in upstate New York. According to everything I've heard from her classmates in her company, she very badly wanted to be a career officer in the United States Army. She was described to me by her own roommate as a very conservative Catholic. She was strongly opposed to abortion. She told her roommate she voted Republican in the last election. She volunteered up in Wallkill at an orphanage before Christmas and Easter every year. So you take this girl from a small upstate New York town to a party, and she doesn't take a single drink, and suddenly, she starts performing a striptease and has sex with you and two of your friends."

Favro dropped his prayerful stare and looked straight at Kerry. "I don't know why it happened the way it did. It just happened."

"It just happened."

"Right."

"Was she taking drugs, Mr. Favro? Could that explain her behavior?"

"No."

"She wasn't drinking and she wasn't taking drugs, and yet she just up and took her clothes off and had sex with you and two of your classmates."

"I guess she had her reasons."

"But we'll never know those reasons now, will we, Mr. Favro? Because now Dorothy Hamner is buried in upstate New York."

Favro showed no emotion at all. In fact, his voice turned hard and cold. "I think it's worth noting, Mr. Kerry, that Dorothy Hamner did not file any charges against me or any of the others the next day. What happened between the four of us was consensual. If it hadn't been, she would have filed charges, and you would have been questioning me a long time ago."

Kerry took his time making a note of what Favro had just said. He thought briefly about bringing up Dorothy's last E-mail message to her mother, but decided it wasn't conclusive enough to warrant a new line of questions. He was relatively certain that Favro had at least been told of its contents and was probably prepared with an answer.

"I take it those are your final words on the subject of Miss Hamner," Kerry said without looking up.

"You are correct."

"Then you're dismissed, Mr. Favro."

THE FOLLOWING day, Kerry requested that the football team van deliver Ivar to the Provost Marshal's building immediately after he finished practice. When he walked in, Ivar's face was still flushed with the glow of physical exertion. Kerry sat him down on the same folding metal chair. He was huge, by cadet standards. Around 240, six-three, with enormous hands and a neck as big around as a telephone pole.

He got the same line from Ivar he'd gotten from Favro. It was obvious that they had gotten their stories straight, because the language was even similar. *We were all a little drunk . . . things started to get wild . . .*

The next thing Ivar knew he was in bed with her. He added a detail. She and Favro had been "playing around" in the backseat of Rose's car on the way back to the Academy.

"So she and Favro still seemed to be together, even after what happened."

"Yeah. You could say that."

"I find the whole thing rather curious, Mr. Ivar. If you were dating a girl, especially a fellow cadet, would you invite her to a party and then share her sexually with your friends?"

Ivar hadn't seen this one coming. Kerry could see him struggling for an answer he hadn't been prepared for. "I don't know . . ."

"Do you have a girlfriend, Mr. Ivar?"

"Sure. Back home."

"What's her name?"

"Karen."

"I'll ask you again. Would you invite Karen to a party and then share her sexually with your friends?"

"No."

"Then why do you figure that Favro did?"

"I don't know."

"Did you discuss it with him? Did you ever ask him why he allowed you to have sex with his girlfriend?"

"No."

"I find that incredible, Mr. Ivar. Here we have a situation where a bunch of guys get together and they're at a party and a girl who's one of their own classmates starts stripping her clothes off and then she has sex with the guys, and you're telling me that you and Favro never talked about this?"

"I've been pretty busy with football."

"I see. Mr. Ivar, you have written off this behavior, at least in part, to drunkenness. But you did not have that much to drink, did you?"

"I guess not."

"And neither did Rose, did he? Wasn't he the one who drove the car back to the Academy?"

"Yeah."

"Yeah, he drove the car, or yeah, he wasn't drinking that much?"

"Both yeahs."

"And Dorothy Hamner wasn't drinking, was she?"

"I didn't see her drinking."

"Was she taking drugs, Mr. Ivar?"

"I didn't see her taking any drugs."

"That's a qualified answer, Mr. Ivar. I'll ask you another way. Do you know if she was taking drugs?"

"No."

"Do you believe she was?"

"No."

"How do you explain the scene you've described, Mr. Ivar? You've been a cadet for more than three years now. Has anything like this ever happened to you before?"

"No."

"So what's your explanation?"

Ivar looked confused for a moment, then his face brightened. "All I know is, she didn't file any complaints. I mean, if she objected to what happened, wouldn't she have gone to the MPs, or to the Tac?"

"Perhaps she didn't have the time."

"She had all that night and most of the next morning."

"Before she died, you mean."

"Yeah."

Kerry folded shut his notebook. If these guys were the warriors of our nation's future, then the country had some worries about its safety. "That will be all, Mr. Ivar."

KERRY HAD saved Rose for last. He had spent extra time going over Rose's cadet records, and he'd made a few calls. This guy was a piece of work. He came from rather humble beginnings on Long Island. His father was a minor functionary in the Nassau County Republican machine. His mother managed a dry cleaner's. From the day Rose arrived at West Point he had thrived. He was in the top 2 percent of his class academically. Physically, he wasn't a standout, but his record in intramurals included stints coaching championship company teams in sports such as cross-country and cadet triathlon. He had ridden a rank-rocket to six stripes and the chairmanship of the Cadet Honor Committee. It was evident from Rose's file that his chief sponsor was the Commandant of Cadets. For some CID agents, this would mean that he was an individual who should be handled with kid gloves. But not Jim Kerry.

Unlike the other cadets, who had been wearing their class uniforms, Rose arrived after supper in his dress gray uniform and took his seat on the folding metal chair in a relaxed position, unzipping the bottom of his dress coat and crossing his legs. Rose didn't give him the same song-and-dance about drunkenness leading to things getting wild and one thing leading to another, which told Kerry that he had consulted with Favro and Ivar and was prepared for the line of questioning they had faced. Instead, Rose said while he was well acquainted with Favro and Ivar, he didn't know Miss Hamner at all, and so he did not have even the foggiest notion why she had behaved the way that she did. Then he cheerfully admitted that he had gone first with her because Miss Hamner had taken her panties off and wrapped them over his head, and had used them to pull him toward the bedroom.

"I don't know many cadets who would turn down an invitation like that one, do you, Mr. Kerry?" Rose asked cheerfully.

"No, but neither do I know many cadets who had sex with a dead girl less than twenty-four hours before she died. In fact, I know only three, and you are one of them, Mr. Rose, which is why you are here."

"Can I ask the purpose of this inquiry, Mr. Kerry? It is official, I presume, or I wouldn't have been asked to come to the Provost Marshal's building. Is this a criminal matter?"

"Not yet, it isn't."

"Then why are you asking me and the others about having had consensual sex with a young woman? She filed no complaints against us, neither a disciplinary complaint with the Tactical Department nor a criminal complaint with the law-enforcement authorities at West Point."

"We are in the process of seeking to determine her cause of death, Mr. Rose."

"I thought she died from heatstroke."

"That possibility has been discounted."

This statement set Rose back on his heels, but only for a moment. "Well, Mr. Kerry, I really don't have anything to say about how Dorothy Hamner died. She wasn't drinking at our party. The last time I heard, having sex, even three different times, with three different guys, doesn't kill you."

"That is an impertinent, improper, and disrespectful remark, Mr. Rose."

Rose let his face fall a little. "I'm sorry. I just don't understand why I'm here if what you're trying to do is determine her cause of death."

"You could confirm something for me, Mr. Rose. The other cadets, Favro and Ivar, told me that Dorothy Hamner wasn't taking drugs at the party. Is that your recollection as well?"

"Yes it is."

"Were you with her all or most of the time?"

"She was around. I think I'd have noticed if she was taking drugs."

"Why is that, Mr. Rose? She could have gone into the bathroom and closed and locked the door."

"What I mean is, she wasn't acting funny."

"You wouldn't say that a young woman from a conservative background in a small upstate New York town taking her clothes off and having sex with three fellow cadets is acting funny, I take it."

"No, I wouldn't."

"Have you ever had such an experience before, Mr. Rose? When you and another cadet or cadets had sex with the same woman at a party or another cadet gathering?"

"Once or twice."

"So this was nothing new to you."

"It doesn't happen all the time, but it happens. We're adults, Mr. Kerry. Guys go to whorehouses down in the city, too. Some of them come back with a case of the clap. I'm sure you are aware of that."

"I am."

"Boys will be boys. You were one."

"Indeed I was."

"Then I think our business is complete. I don't know why Dorothy Hamner died. I'm sure the autopsy will turn up something."

"Your business may be complete, Mr. Rose. But mine has just begun."

Rose stood up and walked to the door. "Good luck with your business, Mr. Kerry."

He is hiding something, thought Agent Jim Kerry. And I'm going to find out what it is.

CHAPTER 32

JACEY WAS alone at her desk going through company paperwork when the door opened and Ash walked in.

"I've got some news. I heard Kerry questioned Favro yesterday and Rose and Ivar today."

"I can't believe she did it willingly, Ash. Dorothy would never have sex with three guys, one right after the other. You knew her. She was so innocent. They raped her. I just know they did."

"Yeah, but how do you go about proving it was rape? It's not enough to say Dorothy was a great kid."

"When I talked to Kerry, I told him we think the Honor Code is involved, but he said he doesn't have authority to start poking around in the Honor Committee. That's a Corps of Cadets matter, he said. The only way he could get clearance to look into the workings of the Honor Committee would be if he could tie the Honor Committee directly to Dorothy's death."

"Well, the three guys who screwed her are all Honor reps. That's a start."

"But not enough."

"Well, maybe we can give him some help. I checked out the regimental Honor records today."

"You did?"

"As regimental rep, I've got access to the files of the Honor Committee. I didn't want anybody thinking I was up to something, so I just pulled my regimental files and went through them. I even asked Rose to remind me how the cases were filed. I told him I was trying to find a case from last year so I could talk about it in a company Honor lecture."

"He was there when you went through the files?"

"Sure. I figured the best way to do it was to hide in plain sight."

"So what did you find?"

"Not much. I was going at it like we said, looking for patterns. I wanted to see which Vice Chairman forwarded the most charges to the full Honor Committee. You know how it works. If someone is reported for an Honor violation, the first thing that happens is, the company Honor rep talks to the person making the report, and the person who is accused. If he thinks there is reason to go forward with the charge, he turns it over to the regimental rep. He turns the case over to a Vice Chairman. The Vice Chairman . . . there are two of them. Favro and Reade. The Vice Chairman has the authority to dismiss the case or forward it to the Honor Chairman, who can order an Honor hearing."

"Favro and Reade were both at the party."

"Yeah. But here's the thing. Favro is in the Second Regiment, and Reade comes out of the Fourth Regiment. Rose is in the Second Regiment. I couldn't find any irregularities in the cases the Third Regiment has sent up through them. A couple of them they dismissed, and three of them went to a full hearing, one forwarded by Favro, the other two by Reade. Of those three, one cadet was found guilty, and the other two were acquitted. But what I'm thinking is, if these guys are pulling any funny business, they're doing it within their own regiments. I don't think I'm going to find anything unless I get my hands on the Second and Fourth Regiment Honor files."

"How can you do that without them finding out?"

He held up a set of keys. "We're going to have to do a little midnight research. Rose left the room today for about an hour and I checked the locks on all the cabinets. They're all keyed the same. My key to the Third Regiment cabinet will open the others."

"If they catch you . . ."

"If they catch *us*. I'm going to need some help. It's tedious, slow work going through those files, and I'm sure they figured out a way to muddy the waters and make everything look legit. We can get started Friday night. Everybody will be taking a long weekend leave to go to the Rutgers game."

"You're sure we can pull this off."

"There's no hundred percent guarantee, if that's what you're looking for. I mean, I don't think it's illegal to go through the Honor files. But if they get wind of what we're up to, it's going to blow the whole thing. We're going to have to be careful. We'll have to refile everything exactly the way it was. If they find anything missing or out of place, alarms will go off. These guys are smart, Jace. I think they've been getting away with this shit for at least a year. They know what they're doing."

She looked across the room at him. He was incredibly handsome. She reached for his hand. They sat there on the separate beds in the small cadet room, holding hands, and she looked in his eyes and said, "Thanks for helping, Ash. I've felt so alone in this thing. It's good to have you back."

"Have you talked to your father?"

"About Dorothy? Yeah, but it's so awkward. He's the court-martial convening authority. He can't be involved in the investigation."

"Yeah, but if this thing blows up your father's going to be the one *The New York Times* and the rest of them will be putting the questions to. I think you ought to tell him as much as you can. He needs to know what's going on."

"I will, but it's hard. He's the Supe. Whichever way things turn out, I don't want the Corps of Cadets to think that I went running to my father. Whatever we do, we've got to do on our own."

He gently rubbed the top of her hand with his thumb, the way he used to do in movies when they held hands. "I see your point. We can do it, Jace. We're cadets. When we graduate next June, we'll be grads. This place belongs to us. If these guys are up to something that's going to fuck up West Point, we've got to stop them."

"Do me a favor, will you?"

"Anything."

"Let me continue to handle Agent Kerry. That will keep the spotlight off you."

"I've got an idea. Why don't you tell Kerry to call me in and question me, along with the other guys who were at the party. That way it'll look like I'm being treated just like everyone else who was there.''

"Good idea. I'll tell him." She paused for a moment, looking into his eyes. "I don't think we should be seen together. If they find out you came to see me tonight, they'll know you're working against them. I want Rose to think I'm at least a little intimidated. He's not going to get that message if they see us hanging around together.''

"Okay." He held her hand for a moment, then let go and stood up to leave. "I'll send you an E-mail toward the end of the week and tell you where to meet me Friday night.''

"I'll be looking for it.''

He gave her one of his incredible, crinkly little smiles, unlocked the door, and was gone.

CHAPTER 33

HAVING LEARNED that the three cadets identified in the DNA screen had been questioned by Agent Kerry the day before, Slaight was hardly surprised when the phone rang at Quarters 100 and Melissa informed him that General Gibson had called the office early that morning requesting a meeting as soon as Slaight arrived. An hour or so later, he found General Gibson sitting in the outer office across from Melissa's desk when he walked up the stairs.

"Jack. Good to see you. Why don't you come in and we'll have a cup of coffee." The Commandant followed him into the Supe's office. Melissa had already put out the coffee tray. Slaight sat down on the leather sofa. "What's on your mind, Jack?"

Keeping his uniform jacket on, Gibson sat stiffly in the chair across from Slaight. "Your CID Agent in Charge called in three of my top cadets and questioned them. I'd like to know why these young men were called in and interrogated by a law-enforcement officer without my being informed."

"I wasn't under the impression you didn't need to be notified, Jack. You've been getting reports from Lieutenant Colonel Percival about every development in the investigation. I don't mind telling you that I don't like playing back-channel-ring-around-the-rosy with my subordinate commanders. I gave the order for the CID to proceed with the interrogation without notifying you.''

''General, that's against procedure, and I strongly object to it.''

Slaight poured a cup of coffee. ''I think you'd better have a look at the regs. I had Cliff Bassett give me an opinion. Your authority extends to cadet disciplinary matters, and right now, this is not a disciplinary matter. It's an investigation into the cause of death of Dorothy Hamner.'' Slaight handed him the cup of coffee and settled back on the sofa.

''The interrogation took place at the Provost Marshal's office. The cadets were not given the opportunity to consult with military counsel. That's another violation of procedure. And you violated Army regulations when you ordered battlefield DNA profiles to be used to identify the three cadets.''

''Wrong again. Regulations prohibit use of battlefield DNA profiles in criminal matters. We're not running a criminal investigation. If it develops that Agent Kerry has assembled evidence that a crime was committed, all of the protections under the UCMJ will be afforded to those suspected or accused. At this juncture, we don't have any suspects, and Agent Kerry had been ordered to work with Major Vernon to establish cause of death.''

''You are splitting hairs, General. My concern is for the rights of my cadets. The way I see it, they're getting jerked around. I've spoken to them. They have assured me that the sex was consensual. That's all you need to know to call off this witch-hunt and let them get back to running the Corps of Cadets.''

''Let me get this straight. Agent Kerry questioned them yesterday. I believe Mr. Rose was interrogated after supper. Just when did you speak with the cadets about their sexual encounter with Dorothy Hamner?'' Slaight took a sip of coffee and watched as Gibson came to the realization that he had stumbled into an admission that was going to be hard to back out of. He pulled at his shirt cuffs, straightening his uniform.

''I became aware that three cadets had sexual relations with Miss Hamner some time ago.''

''How did this happen?''

''Mr. Rose reported it to me.''

''Interesting to learn that you could have volunteered the names of the cadets. That would have made our battlefield DNA screen unnecessary, wouldn't it, Jack?''

"I didn't see how a sexual encounter was germane to an investigation into cause of death. The cadets have assured me the sex was consensual. It was a cadet party. You know what goes on. You were a cadet.''

"That's right. I was a cadet. And back when I was a cadet, we were taught that it's our duty to cooperate in official investigations. I must say that your silence in this matter speaks volumes.''

"Are you accusing me of obstructing the investigation?''

Slaight called to Melissa for more coffee, taking a moment or two as she came in and replenished the carafe. He waited until she had closed the door before he looked over at Gibson. As Commandant, Gibson was in charge of the administration of the Honor Code. He had weaseled around, trying to assert his control over his "top cadets," all of whom happened to be on the Honor Committee, and having failed at that, he was now offering up himself as the issue. It was an arrogant and reckless gamble. For the first time Slaight suspected that Jacey's instinct that the whole thing was about the Honor Code had been right. Gibson was trying desperately to protect the members of his Honor Committee, and from what? From being questioned about their involvement with Dorothy Hamner. Slaight found himself wondering if Gibson had even a clue how transparent were his motives.

He poured himself another cup of coffee and held the carafe aloft, offering it silently to Gibson, who shook his head no. He decided to play Gibson's game, if only to see how he played out his hand. "Let me ask you a question, Jack. When you learned that three members of the Honor Committee, including its Chairman and its Vice Chairman, had sexual relations with Dorothy Hamner in the hours immediately preceding her death, didn't that raise a red flag with you?''

"No.''

"You never considered that such an unusual sexual encounter might be of interest to the people charged with determining her cause of death?''

"No.''

"Why not?''

"Because the cadets assured me it was consensual.''

"How do we know for sure it was consensual?"

"I accept their word of honor."

"Let's think about this for a moment. We're dealing with young men who are twenty-one, twenty-two years old here. Unless I miss my guess, as Commandant you deal every day with young men and women who are accused of violating regulations. In the most serious cases, you authorize regimental and Commandant's boards to investigate accusations of wrongdoing. When cadets are found guilty of violating regulations, you authorize punishment. But you're telling me in this case, involving the death of a young woman, you decided to suspend normal procedures, and you decided to simply take their word that they did nothing wrong? Why the sudden relaxation of vigilance?"

"I know the cadets in question. They are honorable men. They don't deserve to have their names dragged through the mud because they had sex with a young woman who happened to suffer heatstroke the next day at a parade."

"But she didn't suffer heatstroke, Jack. That's why we're conducting an investigation. Because we don't know the cause of her death yet."

"Well, I can tell you one thing for certain, General. The entire matter would be behind us if it had been a young man who died out there at parade."

"What's that supposed to mean?"

"It means the Academy bends over backwards and jumps through hoops every time something happens to a female cadet. One of them flunks a PT test, they get extra training and more attempts to pass it. They turn up with a failing grade, they're counseled and tutored and tested again and passed."

"The same second chances are provided to male cadets."

"But they weren't before females were admitted to West Point. West Point used to be a place where young men were tested and the strong survived and the weak perished."

"You've been here two years. You've had ample opportunity to change the system if you found it lacking."

"You know very well that the climate of political correctness pervading the Army would never permit a return to the West Point we knew as cadets. That's why the Congress is considering a proposal to close the service academies. They have reached the conclusion that all we've got left at West Point is a glorified ROTC program with gray uniforms. It costs too much, it's ineffectual, and it's not producing warriors."

"It sounds to me like you don't want to be Commandant of Cadets at West Point, Jack. If you want out, I can certainly arrange it for you."

"I'm not going to sacrifice my career on the hollow altar West Point has become."

"Then I want you to listen to me closely. I'm only going to tell you this once. I'm going to run the investigation into the death of Dorothy Hamner my way, and you are going to back me up. If I get any reports that you are standing in the way of this investigation or not cooperating to your fullest, you are finished as Commandant. Have I made myself perfectly clear on this?"

"Perfectly."

"Very well. You're dismissed."

Gibson snapped a salute and left. As Slaight watched him go, he wondered what lay behind the bitterness Gibson had shown, his intractable conviction that the presence of women had somehow left West Point in ruins. And he wondered how far Gibson was willing to go to return the Academy to the glory he imagined it had once had.

CHAPTER 34

IT WAS later that afternoon, and Jacey was jogging along Mills Road next to Lusk Reservoir. She had just started down the hill toward the Cadet Chapel when a staff car pulled up next to her and the passenger window rolled down. It was Chief Warrant Officer Kerry.

"Jacey?"

She stopped. Her sweats were soaked from the exertion of coming up the hill leading to Michie Stadium. She was just about to cut behind the chapel to the path through the woods past the water tower that would bring her out right behind the barracks. She leaned forward with her hands on her knees, panting. "Agent Kerry. How's it going?"

"I have a few questions for you."

"Jeez, I'm pretty stinky. Maybe I should grab a shower and meet you later."

Kerry reached across the seat and opened the car's passenger door. "I don't think you ought to be seen down at the Provost Marshal's office. Hop in. We'll take a little drive."

Kerry drove down the hill and took the turn up Merritt Road leading to Delafield Pond. He pulled into the empty parking lot and cut the engine. "I questioned Rose, Favro, and Ivar yesterday."

"I heard."

"Really? I tried to keep it quiet, and I certainly didn't think any of them would leak the news."

"Ivar blabbed to some guy on the football team."

"That was stupid of him. Or maybe not."

"So what's the story?"

"They're stonewalling. They've coordinated their stories, and they're not deviating from the script. They admit to having sex with Dorothy, but they contend it was consensual."

"That's crazy! Dorothy would never have consented to that!"

"I know. But it's going to be tough to crack them. I need something I can wedge in there and split them."

"You know what's weird, Agent Kerry? These guys are acting like it was just another cadet party, and maybe it was. I've been to parties like that one. Everybody gets together and rents a bunch of rooms in a country motel or a hotel down in New York, and they get a bunch of beer and vodka and stuff, and there's a lot of drinking. I mean *a lot.* I guess it's a cadet thing, to see how drunk you can get and still manage to function. So let's say it was just another cadet party. Then why didn't they come forward and volunteer that Dorothy was at the party? The only reason there could be is that they had sex with her. But if it was like they said it was, that she, like, was willing, then what have they got to be afraid of? It doesn't make sense. They're not acting like guys act when they've got nothing to hide, nothing to be ashamed of."

"They're acting guilty."

"Yes, but guilty of what? Of rape? What if they raped her? They've got nothing to worry about. She never charged them, and now she's dead. There aren't any other witnesses. If it was rape, it was a perfect crime. They're home free."

"We're not at all certain she was raped. Major Vernon said the physical evidence in the autopsy was inconclusive. There's a chance they didn't rape her."

"Then that's even weirder. If they didn't rape her, why are they acting so guilty? It's got to be that they're covering up something else. Why did they steal the E-mail disks from my room? It had to be because they had to find out what was on them. That means they were afraid Dorothy had a secret. They were afraid she had told someone, maybe somebody who's not at West Point, like a friend back home, or her mom or dad. Maybe the secret was that she had been raped. Or maybe the secret was something else, something even bigger. Maybe the secret involved more than just the three of them. All I know for sure is, they felt vulnerable enough to take the risk of stealing the disks. That's the first big mistake they've made, because there was nothing incriminating in her E-mail. They ended up tipping their hand that they've got something to hide.''

"I could call them in and question them about where they were the night the disks were stolen, but they'll probably just cover for each other.''

"They can't cover for Rose. He followed me up to Captain Patterson's office, and then followed me back to the area of barracks. There isn't anyone who can account for his whereabouts but me and Captain Patterson.''

"Then the other two will cover for each other. It's a dead end either way.''

"Wait a minute. No, it's not. Captain Patterson saw Rose follow me down the stairs when I left his office, then a few minutes later, he caught up to me on Thayer Road. But neither of us saw him follow me to Patterson's office.''

"So?''

"I was in Patterson's office for an hour. If we assume he followed me down there from the barracks and left as soon as he saw me enter the office, that would give him plenty of time to make it back to the barracks and go through my room and get back to the fourth floor of Building 606 and wait for me to come out of Patterson's office.''

"You're right. He's got at least an hour he'll have a hell of a hard time accounting for. Does he know Patterson saw him?''

"I'm sure he doesn't. Patterson caught a glimpse of him going down the stairs. He didn't see Patterson.''

"So if he doesn't know Patterson saw him, he'll probably feel free to alibi himself any way he wants. This is what we'll do. I'll put him on the spot and grill him, and we'll see what kind of alibi he comes up with. If he says he was with Ivar or Favro, I'll know he's lying, but he won't have any way of knowing that I've caught him in a lie. So

I'll let him sit back and think he's beaten me. In the meantime, why don't you get a yearbook photo of him and check around your company and see if anyone saw him that night."

"What if I don't find a witness?"

"We've still got him, because we've got Patterson. He saw him following you. If Rose tries to say he was anywhere but the fourth floor of Building 606, he's fried. We'll have the Chairman of the Honor Committee caught in a lie. If that doesn't shake some leaves out of the trees, nothing will."

"Listen, I just thought of something. You know there were three other guys at the party."

"Reade, Prudhomme, and Lessard. What about them?"

"Are you going to question them, too?"

"I hadn't intended to. The three I'm interested in are the ones who had sex with Dorothy."

"I think you should question Ash Prudhomme. He's helping me—"

"You're sure you can trust him?" Kerry interrupted.

"We dated for two years. I know him better than my roommate. He was at the party, but he didn't have anything to do with Dorothy. I believe him."

"That's not what I'm talking about. He's on the Honor Committee. If he was at that party, he's got to be close to Rose and the others. How do you know he's not doubling on you and telling them everything you tell him?"

Jacey looked out the window of the car at the shuttered swim club across the parking lot. She and Ash had spent many afternoons lying in the sun next to the pond, getting up every once in a while to cool off in its icy spring-fed waters. How could she explain to Agent Kerry that even though Ash had told Rose about Dorothy's E-mail disks, she couldn't bring herself to mistrust him after all the time they had spent together? He would write her off as sentimental and warn her that nobody on the Honor Committee could be trusted. Unless . . .

"He's taking me into the Honor Committee office this weekend. He's got the keys. We're going to go through the Honor files together. He knows how the system works. If Rose and the rest of them are monkeying around with the Honor Code, it will turn up in those files."

"How can you be sure they haven't sanitized the files? It could be a setup to get you off their trail."

"I guess we'll know by next week, won't we?"

"You seem pretty certain he's okay."

"I am. And it's not just because I've been in love with him. There are some guys here at West Point who are . . . different. He's one of them. It's hard to explain. You haven't been a cadet . . ."

"No, but I've been a soldier. I think I know what you're talking about. I'll take your word for it. Besides, when we start shaking the tree, if he's thrown his lot in with Rose, he'll fall out. One way or another, we'll know whether or not your instincts were right."

"I know they're right, Agent Kerry. It was Ash who suggested you call him in for questioning along with Lessard and Reade. He wants to make sure Rose sees that he's being treated just like everyone else. If Rose figures out that Ash is helping me, it's all over. They'll close ranks and hide behind the cadet code of silence."

"I hadn't intended to question the others, but I see his point. Tell you what I'll do. I'll call all three of them down together, but then question them one by one, so the others are sitting out in the hall, waiting their turn. That'll make it look even-handed."

"Thanks."

Agent Kerry started the car and drove out of the parking lot. "Where do you want me to let you off?"

"Up there by the pumping station behind the chapel. There's a little road . . ."

"I know the one."

"You know what gets me about this whole thing, Agent Kerry? We're talking about the West Point Honor Committee. We're talking about how one of the guys on the committee probably stole the disks from my room, how they're lying. If they'll lie to cover for each other, if they'll steal to make sure Dorothy didn't rat them out, then they've really got something big to hide."

Kerry turned down the road behind the chapel and stopped next to the pumping station. "What do you think it is?"

"I think Dorothy knew something, and they killed her to shut her up."

CHAPTER 35

G ENERAL GIBSON had returned to his office from his latest confrontation with the Superintendent and immediately picked up the phone and called Cecil Avery down in Washington. He wanted a meeting with Congressman Thrunstone, and he wanted it *yesterday*. Avery asked for the morning to work on it, and sure enough, he had called back that afternoon with the news that Thrunstone would see him the next day at one P.M. Gibson had called in his secretary and told her to cancel his meetings for the following day. He told her he had to go to Washington on family business. His brother was going into the hospital for some tests and he wanted to be with him.

The next day he parked his car in the covered lot at La Guardia and hopped the D.C. shuttle. It wasn't crowded, and he managed to find a seat by himself next to a window in the back of the plane. As he settled back for the hourlong flight, he thought of the years he had spent climbing the proverbial ladder of Army success. He had had a single ambition since the first day he walked through the gates of West Point as an eighteen-year-old civilian on the first day of Beast Barracks: One day he would be Army Chief of Staff. The arc of his career had been established early. In fact, he remembered the day he knew he was on his way.

As a newly promoted captain, he was "snowbirding," waiting for the next class of the Advanced Course to begin at the Infantry School down at Fort Benning. Because he had just transferred from a duty station overseas, he was early. He had been on a division staff over in Germany and had achieved something of a reputation as a briefer, so with a month and a half to wait for his slot at the Advanced Course, the Army sent him up to the Pentagon, where a briefing slot needed to be filled temporarily because a female captain was on pregnancy leave.

He gained his footing quickly in the Pentagon. Part of his job was to brief politicians and captains of industry and dignitaries of various sorts who had an interest in defense issues relating to the Army. He had just given a late-afternoon briefing to a small group of governors from states with large defense industries when he was approached by a small man wearing an expensively tailored suit with the kind of featureless face you often saw in Washington. He recognized him as the man who had escorted the governors over to the Pentagon from the White House. Now the governors were off to an embassy party with a new escort from the State Department, and his duties were at an end. He had been very impressed by the briefing Captain Gibson had delivered, and since it was well past the end of the duty day, even at the Pentagon, he wanted to know if Gibson wanted to have dinner at a restaurant in Alexandria.

Gibson was staying at the Crystal City Marriott, just down Route 1 from the Pentagon, so he figured, why not? The small, rather fastidious man introduced himself as Cecil Avery. He was General Counsel to the National Security Council in the White House. Avery had a White House car waiting outside. They stopped at the Marriott and Gibson changed into civvies before they were driven to an Italian restaurant tucked away on one of Alexandria's Old Town alleys.

Cecil Avery turned out to be an impressively well-connected man. Before he was on the NSC, he had run the Washington office of a major West Coast electronics firm with enormous governmental contracts. Before that, he had taught at the Kennedy School of Government at Harvard, from which he had earlier graduated with honors. Before his Harvard professorship, he had been the chief legislative aide on Capitol Hill for an up-and-coming young congressman from Illinois by the name of Thrunstone, who had secured for himself as a freshman seats on both the Agriculture Committee and the National Security Committee, ripe political plums indeed. Avery explained that when he left the NSC, he was to be assigned as a deputy secretary of state, a position that awaited him when the President was reelected, for it was already obvious that he would be swept into office again by a healthy margin.

What, Gibson wondered, did Cecil Avery want with an infantry captain on temporary duty from Fort Benning?

Not much. He wanted to make friends with a young Army officer in whom he could see great potential. The dinner had ended with Avery picking up the check and dropping Gibson at the Marriott. As Avery drove away into the night in his White House car, Gibson recalled, he had stood there thinking that this had been a first: Every day of his life he had worked his ass off to gain what little advantage he could, and along comes a guy who had had all kinds of advantages, and he was willing to share them.

The next afternoon the phone rang at his desk in the bowels of the Pentagon. It was Avery calling from the White House, inviting him to a party in Georgetown. There were some people at the party he wanted Gibson to meet. He'd be picked up at the Marriott in two hours.

So that's it, he remembered thinking. One of the guys he had known at West Point, a real smart firstie, had once told him that when he got in the Army he should be on the watch for talent spotters. Avery was a talent spotter, and he had just been spotted.

So Gibson suited up again, went to the party in Georgetown, and found himself in the company of several congressmen, including the gentleman from Illinois, Mr. Thrunstone, as well as a healthy smattering of generals of the one- and two-star variety. About a year later, when he had graduated number one in his Advanced Class at the Infantry School, he found himself invited to Washington by a full colonel who was assigned to the personnel department in the Pentagon for the infantry. The colonel wanted to know where Captain Gibson wanted to be assigned. Gibson didn't even have to ask why he was being offered a choice of assignments, because he knew the answer: Cecil Avery had a made a phone call. Gibson respectfully asked the colonel if it was possible that he could get a company command in the 101st Airborne Division.

Done.

Cecil Avery had not looked over Gibson's shoulder at every single step of his career, but he had been lurking in the mists of Foggy Bottom when Gibson was picked to attend the School of International Relations at Georgetown, where he had been put into a fast-track program for a master's degree. And it had been Avery who had pulled the necessary levers in the State Department to arrange for Gibson to depart Georgetown, degree in hand, for an assignment as Deputy Military Attaché at the Embassy in Moscow.

Later, when the White House changed hands and the Democrats seized power, somehow Avery had yanked some very obscure White House permanent-staff strings to secure an appointment for Gibson to the NSC. With Gibson installed in the Democratic White House, it had been Avery who had made sure that Gibson and Congressman Thrunstone were reintroduced. That Thrunstone was now the senior member of the minority on the House National Security Committee hardly seemed a coincidence.

But there had always been a question lurking back in the darker regions of Gibson's mind about Cecil Avery.

Why?

A very powerful man in Washington had taken an intimate and attentive interest in his career. Over the years Gibson had learned a few things. One of them was that there were only three motives in Washington: sex, politics, or both. Gibson had realized fairly early on that Cecil Avery was a homosexual, albeit a very discreet one. This had not disturbed Gibson, because the best friend he'd ever had in his life, his cousin, had revealed to him that he was a homosexual. It had surprised Gibson that his cousin's sexuality hadn't really changed anything between them. They had still attended Army football games together, and during the summer, they had found the time to go bass fishing down in Alabama where his cousin lived.

So if it wasn't sex, it was politics, and if it was politics, what politics were involved, and whose were they? Well, they were Republican politics, because Cecil Avery was a Republican. But no political party was a monolith. The loyalty of men like Cecil Avery to a party with a right wing that was virulently antihomosexual was evidence enough of that.

Politics was about connections and friendships. Avery had become his friend. In fact, Gibson and his wife had named Cecil Avery as the godfather of their first son. That's how deep the friendship was.

And the friends of Cecil Avery had become his friends. These included Congressman Thrunstone, who was a rock-ribbed supporter of the military, even though he had never served a single day in uniform. And there was Ambassador Joseph Sweeney, whom he had served in Moscow. Sweeney returned from his post in a collapsed Soviet Union to the chairmanship of the company that had made him a very wealthy man, the one down in Alabama that Gibson's own cousin worked for, which made some kind of new superstable missile propellant that was going to revolutionize the battlefield weaponry of the twenty-first century. Sweeney had been a Republican, of course, because those were the days when the Republicans controlled the White House and all of the goodies that could be dispensed therefrom.

Gibson himself was a registered Republican. So were most of the officers he knew at West Point. It was almost a given. If you wanted to get ahead, you had opinions that followed close to the grain of the Republican Party. Nobody could ever determine how you voted, but they could sure as hell listen to your opinions, and opinions among military men, especially those of Gibson's generation, ran about ten-to-one Republican.

As an officer in the United States Army, General Gibson had long known that he was helping to push the Republican agenda, and what the hell was wrong with that? It was the agenda of a strong national defense. It was the agenda of those who claimed Jesus Christ as their savior. It was the agenda of the party that wanted criminals behind bars, not out on the streets free to commit more crimes. It was the agenda of a free and prosperous America.

Not even the tiniest grain of doubt had lodged within the soul of this man who was dedicated to his nation and the Army that served it. For hadn't he played the game the way it should be played? Everybody kissed ass. Everybody covered his own ass. Everybody took advantage wherever he could. Everybody made friends in high places and made sure the friends would come through for him. General Gibson was flying the shuttle to Washington because he had learned how to play the game, and he was good at it.

*   *   *

WASSERSTEIN ENTERED Congressman Thrunstone's private office
through an unmarked door. As Chairman of the National Security
Committee and a veteran of more than fifteen terms in the House,
Thrunstone rated one of the most spacious suites in Congress. It
occupied nearly half of one side of the Rayburn Office Building,
including the corner that housed the congressman's official office.
But that room, which had a vaulted ceiling and windows on two sides
overlooking the Capitol and the Mall, was deemed by the congressman to be far too accessible to staffers, constituents, and the lobbyists
who prowled the halls of congressional office buildings like packs of
rabid dogs. Thrunstone delighted in using an old and rather insult-
ing description of the German people to characterize lobbyists: They
were either at your throat or at your feet. So most of the time he
used the private anteroom behind the unmarked door.

When Wasserstein walked in, the congressman was sitting in a
wing-backed leather armchair going through an updated list of military procurement orders, making notations next to the contractors
and subcontractors with facilities in the districts of his committee
members. Capitol Hill politics was not often a zero-sum game, where
at the end of the day you could add up the columns and determine
winners and losers. There was way too much other stuff that got in
your way: ideological crap, and blathering about "values." Thrunstone believed that the real job of the Congress was to pass the laws,
and there were only two kinds of laws worth passing: those that taxed,
and those that spent. Sitting at the helm of the National Security
Committee, Thrunstone got to write one of the biggest spending bills
of them all: the budget for national defense, a gigantic pile of line
items that exceeded $260 billion at last count.

To the world outside the corridors of congressional power, Thrunstone appeared at times to be a politician of the old school who used
the power of the National Security Committee to slam through bills
and bring to heel the generals and admirals who inhabited the
armed services. In reality, he was as savvy a politican as had ever
operated on either side of the aisle. Like many congressmen of his
generation, he had started out as a Democrat and had turned Republican when he saw his party retreating from its commitment to

the nation's defense. He had learned from watching previous chairmen of the National Security Committee that if you wanted the committee firmly under your control, you had to pay for neutrality first and support later. At first, Thrunstone had not understood the value the system placed on neutrality, but it hadn't taken him long to see how it worked. He learned that you gain control over a committee when those who oppose you and those who back you comprise about two-thirds of the members. Support of the other third, the margin of victory, you pay for in the currency of Washington power.

The thing about Thrunstone was, as Chairman of the National Security Committee, he had to maintain two kinds of power: The first was power over his committee, and this could be paid for in the conventional Washington manner, with contracts and jobs. But the second kind of power was far more elusive: He had to maintain a firm grasp on both the support and neutrality of military men, but you couldn't use jobs or contracts for this purpose, because the power of military men lay outside the realm of money. Their loyalties could be won, indeed could be paid for, but only if you used a very different currency. They wanted the same thing Thrunstone and politicians like him wanted: the power to control.

Generals and committee chairmen were so much alike that distrust was immediate and visceral, thus gaining power over them was a complicated business, indeed. If you couldn't pay them off, you needed to win their hearts and minds, and in order to do this, you needed agents among them who would represent your agenda. It was just like operating on the Hill. You had to know as much about your enemies as you knew about your friends. Maybe more.

When Wasserstein walked into his private office, Congressman Thrunstone didn't look up.

"Did you bring the file on Slaight?"

"Yes sir." He handed the congressman a thin manila folder.

Thrunstone fingered it suspiciously. "This is it?"

"Yes sir. I put out feelers all over town. I got our people to turn the Pentagon inside out, and Gibson called in every IOU he had. There just isn't that much on Slaight, sir. He's been below the radar so long, he almost doesn't exist."

"Then how the hell did he get to be Superintendent?"

"Meuller, sir. He and Slaight were close as far back as Vietnam. I think you'll find in there that Meuller was Slaight's commander over there. The word is, Slaight pulled him out of a hot spot during the war. Meuller's term as Chief of Staff is up next year. He's paying off some old debts, and he owes Slaight.''

Thrunstone quickly leafed through the file's pages. ''Goddammit, this doesn't even show his political affiliation.''

''He doesn't have one, sir.''

''You mean to tell me this son of a bitch isn't even a registered Independent?''

''That's right, sir. As far as I could determine, he hasn't voted in the last twenty years. That's as far back as I could track him, sir.''

Wasserstein was still standing in front of Thrunstone. The congressman flipped a thumb in the direction of a chair, and his aide gratefully took it. He scanned the last page of the file, then tossed it on the table next to him and checked his watch.

''I thought you told me Gibson would be here at one.''

''Yes sir.''

''Then where the hell is he?''

''Avery just called from his car. They're on the way. Uh, sir, I think your watch is still on Illinois time.''

Thrunstone looked at his watch. ''You're right.'' He reset his watch. ''When did you say Meuller's term as Chief of Staff is up?''

''Next June, sir.''

''We can't wait to get him out of there. We're going to have to put a shot across their bow and do it in this Congress, or Meuller is going to put some stuff in place that will take a decade to correct.''

''Yes sir. I agree, sir.''

Thrunstone leaned back in his chair and loosened his belt a notch. ''Why is it this business never gets any easier? Tell me that, will you, Wasserstein? I mean, you read the Duke study. Generals and admirals are something like seventy percent Republican at this point, and still we've got to get down in the trenches and fight those bastards every day. Don't they realize we're all on the same side?''

''They don't exactly see things that way, sir.''

''What's their goddamned problem?''

There was a soft knock at the door. A secretary stepped inside. ''Sir, Mr. Avery and General Gibson are here.''

''Send them in,'' said Thrunstone.

Gibson followed Avery into the congressman's private office. The four men exchanged warm greetings and Thrunstone invited them to sit down.

"Cecil tells me you've been a great help with Meuller, Jack. We appreciate it. I've got to admit we've had our hands full with him and his crowd over there."

"Glad to be of service, sir," said Gibson.

"We've got a real fight on our hands. Cecil, why don't you tell us how it's shaping up."

For such a small man, Avery's voice was surprisingly powerful, and he knew how to command the attention of the men in the room. "I think we all know we've got a shrinking pot of defense dollars, and the battle is over how those dollars will be divided up between low-tech warm military bodies and high-tech weapons systems. I know all of us sitting here realize that the future of our national defense lies in the technological advances we make in hardware. The problem we've got with General Meuller is that he's fighting a rear-guard action, seeking to shore up his manpower resources at the expense of developing new hardware. And there's the rub. Manpower has not produced military returns commensurate with its costs. Even Meuller knows we get more bang for the buck with modern-day weapons systems. But he's got the political problem of heading up a service that is heavy with warm bodies and light on weapons systems. The Army has always had more political power because they have been better at playing the political game. The problem with the Army has also been one of its greatest strengths: There are lots of them, and they spend most of their time sitting around and waiting for conventional wars that are few and far between. Yet while they sit around and wait, they keep busy. They've got Reserve and National Guard units in every congressional district. There are major Army posts in nearly half of the states, and they provide tens of thousands of civilian jobs. There are more Army bands marching in parades every summer than there are days in the year. They're better at public relations than they are at drill these days. General Meuller presents a problem because right now, he's got a good piece of the defense budget and he's not going to let go without a fight."

Thrunstone turned to Gibson. "Is that about the way you see it, Jack?"

"Yes sir. Cecil nailed it."

"What do you think of Meuller?"

"He's smart, he's popular with the troops, and he knows his way around the Pentagon better than any other two service chiefs combined, sir."

"Every time we hit the ball over there, he hits it back," said Thrunstone. "I'm tired of playing budgetary paddleball with Meuller."

"Chuck, Meuller's got an Achilles' heel I think we can exploit," said Avery.

"Tell me he's got a mistress. Make it easy for me."

Avery laughed, joined by the others. "He's a West Pointer. That's his Achilles' heel. A piece of real estate up there on the Hudson."

"What do you think of Cecil's idea, Jack? You think we ought to go after West Point?"

"It's a good idea, sir. It'll put the fear of god in Meuller. I think you can count on that."

Thrunstone turned to Wasserstein. "Where do we stand with the bills on the service academies?"

"The senate bill would close down the academies and turn over their commissioning quotas to ROTC on civilian college campuses. The other bill is yours, sir. It would consolidate the three major academies—Army, Navy, and Air Force—into a single Defense Academy, located close to the Capitol, where we could keep an eye on it."

Thrunstone tapped his fingers on the arms of his chair. "I see only one problem with the scenario you're suggesting, Cecil. In order to make this thing work, we've got to make the threat credible. The fact is, there isn't much support in the Congress for closing down or consolidating the service academies. West Point in particular has a strong base of support on the Hill."

"I wouldn't worry about actually passing the bill, Chuck. All you have to do is call hearings and put them on the spot. They'll jump like you stuck them with a cattle prod."

"You really think it's that easy?"

"The academies are sacred cows. The only time they're supposed to get in the newspapers is when they win football games or serve as a backdrop for presidential speech-making at graduation. I guarantee that if you put West Point under a microscope at a hearing of the National Security Committee, Meuller will come crawling across the Fourteenth Street Bridge on his hands and knees begging your indulgence."

"What reason does he have to be threatened by hearings? From everything I saw when I was up there for the Southern Illinois game, West Point is in excellent shape. The cadets look good, their graduation rates are up, and they've never had so many applications for admissions. My own office is swamped. We have over a hundred applicants for two congressional appointments to West Point."

"I think Jack might have some ideas for you," said Avery with a thin smile.

Thrunstone turned to Gibson. "What do you think, Jack? Do you think hearings would bring Meuller to heel?"

"Yes sir, I do."

"What makes you think that?"

"Go after Slaight," said Avery, jumping in. "He's Meuller's star pupil. Put Slaight in the hot seat and fry him. Meuller will sue for peace."

"I can't believe it'll be that easy," said Thrunstone.

Avery nudged Gibson. "Tell him why Slaight's vulnerable."

"That female cadet who died recently, sir? Slaight is covering up the cause of her death because he's afraid it will hamper Meuller's plans to increase the number of females in the Army from fifteen to twenty percent."

"Tell him how she died," prodded Avery.

"She dropped dead at a parade. She couldn't cut it. Neither can most of the rest of the females. It's West Point's dirty little secret. They've reduced standards and softened training and done away with blood-and-guts stuff like bayonet drills and twenty-mile forced marches. Slaight and Meuller know the score, and even so, they are in full stride turning the place over to the women. Slaight has announced he will appoint a female brigadier general as Dean. It wouldn't surprise me in the least if he didn't replace me with a woman when I leave next year. They're feminizing the warrior culture. I have to tell you this, Congressman Thrunstone. As much as I love my alma mater, I would rather see West Point shut down than stand by and watch it being transformed by the reductive and politically correct vision of General Slaight and General Meuller."

"That's a pretty strong statement, General Gibson," said Thrunstone. "Would you be willing to tell the National Security Committee how you feel?"

"I would be honored to, sir."

Thrunstone turned to Wasserstein. "Very well. Notify the committee members and call a meeting of committee staff. Prepare a letter for my signature to General Meuller. The National Security Committee will hold hearings on the future of the nation's service academies, and we will start the hearings with West Point."

GIBSON STRODE quickly across Washington Avenue to a waiting limousine and heard a soft click as the door was unlocked from inside. Helen Messick was holding an icy glass of Absolut vodka.

"How did it go?" she asked, as he took a sip of his Absolut.

"Very well. Thrunstone is going to call hearings and put Slaight on the spot." Gibson took another sip of his vodka and chuckled. "Slaight will never know what hit him."

She reached for the overhead console and pressed the intercom button. "You can take us to Boonsboro, driver."

The limousine pulled away from the curb into traffic and took the first turn onto the Southwest Freeway. Soon they could see the Jefferson Memorial on their right and the Fourteenth Street Bridge just ahead. "This place in Bluemont, you're sure it's far enough away? We're not going to run into any familiar faces?"

She giggled. "First of all, it's a Motel Six. Secondly, it's two hours from here in the foothills of the Catoctin Mountains. Not a chance, in the middle of the week. We stayed there last April, remember?"

"I thought that was Berryville."

"We stayed in Berryville right after June Week, when you came down here for that conference on promotion boards, and I was able to get away because my sister was sick."

"Right. I remember now. What was your excuse this time?"

"My sister relapsed." They both laughed as he felt her fingers pulling at the zipper of his trousers. "What time is your flight tomorrow?" she whispered hotly in his ear.

"Eleven."

"Good. We can have breakfast in bed."

"So what do you call this?" he asked, sliding his hand under her thin sweater and cupping her breast, fingering her erect nipple.

"A late lunch?"

He leaned back against the rich leather of the limousine's seat and took a healthy swig of Absolut. This was turning into one of the better days he had spent as Commandant of Cadets at West Point.

CHAPTER 36

THE CALL from Agent Kerry came just before supper. Rose was to report to the Provost Marshal's office at seven P.M. Immediately he called Favro and Ivar and asked them if Kerry had called them, too. He had. They were to report at the same time.

The three of them left the mess hall and walked to the Provost Marshal's office together.

"What's this about, man?" asked Ivar. "I thought this shit was over."

"I don't know," replied Rose.

"I don't like this, man," said Ivar.

"Me either," echoed Favro.

"All you've got to do is keep your head on straight. He shot his wad the last time he questioned us. If they had anything more than the DNA evidence, they would have used it."

"What if he starts asking us about the Honor Committee?" asked Favro.

"That's not going to happen. Gibson told me Honor has been put off-limits for the CID. Gibson's the only one who can investigate the Honor Committee, and we all know that's never going to happen."

Ivar stopped on the sidewalk outside the Provost Marshal's office. "How can you be sure we can trust him?"

"Because if we go down, so does Gibson," Rose whispered. "Now listen. Gibson told me Slaight justified Kerry questioning us because they're conducting a cause-of-death investigation. We're not being charged with anything. If they had anything on us, they'd be reading us our rights and we'd be allowed to call a military lawyer. Gibson said we should cooperate and be friendly and forthcoming. The last thing we want to do is give them the idea we're uptight or scared."

"What if he reads us our rights tonight?" whispered Ivar.

"It's not going to happen."

"But what if he does?"

"Then keep your mouth shut and demand a lawyer and don't panic. They can't do shit to us if we stick by our story."

Rose opened the door and they went inside. An MP sergeant led them to an office at the end of the hall. He knocked on the door and Agent Kerry appeared.

"Mr. Favro, you are first. Mr. Rose, Mr. Ivar, have a seat." He pointed to chairs just down the hall.

Favro followed Kerry into the office. Ivar and Rose walked down the hall and sat down, their eyes fixed on the door at the end of the hall.

"What is this shit, man?" whined Ivar.

"Quiet. We don't know who's listening."

After about ten minutes, the MP sergeant reappeared and stood outside Kerry's door. A few more minutes passed, and then the door opened. Kerry stood in the doorway.

"Sergeant, give Mr. Favro a ride back to the barracks in your squad car, will you?" Kerry stepped aside, and Favro walked through the door. He traded glances with Rose as he passed the two cadets in the hall, followed by the MP sergeant. Agent Kerry pointed to Ivar. "You're next, Mr. Ivar. Step inside, please."

The door closed, and Rose sat alone in the hallway. He checked his watch, trying to gauge how many minutes it would take for Favro to reach his room in the barracks. He kept his eyes on the door as the moments ticked by. Finally, he stood up and walked down the hall to a secretary's desk. He picked up the phone and dialed Favro's room. The phone rang once, twice. On the third ring, Favro picked up.

"It's me," Rose whispered. "What did he ask you?"

"It was strange. He asked me some of the same questions he asked before, you know, about Dorothy, when I met her, stuff like that. Then right at the end he asked me where I was between eight and nine on Monday night, October third."

"What'd you tell him?"

"I told him the truth. I was at the library."

"Listen to me. If he calls you in again, tell him you saw me there."

"All . . . all right," Favro replied uncertainly.

"I'll tell you why later." He hung up the phone and hurried back down the hall and took his seat. He checked his watch. Ivar had been in there about fifteen minutes. He heard footsteps and turned as the MP sergeant walked down the hall and took up his position outside Kerry's door. It was obvious to Rose that Kerry was questioning them one by one and preventing them from comparing notes. He smiled a secret smile. Kerry had no way of knowing that he had checked with Favro and was ready for his questions. The door opened and Ivar passed him on his way out.

"Mr. Rose?" Kerry crooked his finger. Rose followed him into the office and stood at parade rest in front of Kerry's desk. "Have a seat, please." Rose unzipped his dress gray coat at the bottom and sat down.

"You know what's ironic, Mr. Rose? We've been trying to get our phone system updated down here at the Provost Marshal's office for about two years, and it was only last week they finally came around and installed a whole new system." Kerry turned the multiline phone on his desk around so it faced Rose. "You see this little light right here? It's the one for the phone on my secretary's desk down the hall. It came on a few moments ago, when I had Ivar in here. And you know what's funny? My secretary went home early tonight, around four-thirty. Her daughter twisted her ankle at soccer practice." Kerry ran his fingernail down the row of buttons on the phone and stopped at the bottom button. "You know what's neat about our new phones? We've got auto-redial. If I press this button right here, the one for my secretary's phone, and I hit this button right here"—he tapped his finger on the bottom button—"this phone will call the last number dialed. Tell you what. Just for fun, let's give it a try and see if it works. I'll put the speakerphone on, so you can hear, too."

Kerry pressed the speakerphone button, and the hum of the dial tone filled the room. He pressed the auto-redial button, and the phone dialed. It rang once, twice, and a voice answered. "Second Regiment, sir."

Kerry spoke slowly and clearly: "Mr. Favro, please."

"Speaking, sir."

Kerry pressed the speakerphone button and the hum of the dial tone filled the room again. He turned the phone around and leaned back in his chair. "I think it's a safe assumption that you and Mr. Favro spoke on the phone while I was questioning Mr. Ivar and that you got your stories straight. Am I right, Mr. Rose?"

"We didn't have to get our stories straight."

"Then let's cut to the chase, and I'll just pop the question you're waiting for. Where were you between eight and nine P.M. on October third? It was the Monday before last, Mr. Rose."

"I was at the library."

"I see. Did you happen to run into Mr. Favro there?"

"Yes, I did."

"Where would that have been?"

"What?"

"I mean, where did you see Mr. Favro? In one of the reading rooms? In the stacks? Down in the main lobby?"

"I don't remember."

"You don't remember."

"That's right, I don't remember. And I want to know why we're being questioned about our whereabouts. It was my understanding that you are conducting an investigation into the cause of Dorothy Hamner's death."

"We are, Mr. Rose."

"What does that Monday night have to do with it?"

"That was the night certain computer disks belonging to Miss Hamner were removed from Jacey Slaight's desk without her permission. You know anything about that, Mr. Rose?"

"No."

"I was certain that you didn't."

"If that's all you want to know, I've got classes to study for." Rose stood and moved toward the door.

"One moment, Mr. Rose." Kerry's voice boomed across the

small room, stopping him. Rose turned to face Kerry, eyes flashing. "You were seen on the fourth floor of Building 606 that night, down there at the end of the hall where the Department of Law has its offices."

"So? I'm taking an elective in international law this semester. I'm down there all the time."

"You were seen there at eight-twenty, Mr. Rose."

"I had to pick up a copy of the *Georgetown Law Review*."

"And then you went to the library."

"That's right."

"But first you stopped Jacey Slaight on Thayer Road and spoke with her. Is that correct?"

"I think I recall seeing her on my way to the library."

"I can assure you that she recalls seeing you."

"I don't know what this proves. I was down at the Law Department, and then I was at the library. So what?"

"It seems as if your recollection about the events of Monday evening, the third of October, have improved as we've gone along, Mr. Rose. Let's see if you can recall where you were between seven and eight P.M."

Rose's face froze, his lip curled in anger. "I'm tired of your questions. If you've got evidence that I broke into Jacey Slaight's room and stole something, go ahead and charge me. I will warn you right now that if you bring charges against the Chairman of the Honor Committee, you had better be prepared to make them stick, because if you don't, I'll file an Article One-thirty-eight against you, and I'll bring your pissy little career to a screeching halt and have you discharged from the Army for malfeasance, dereliction of duty, and bringing an improper prosecution."

"Are you refusing to answer my question, Mr. Rose?"

"You heard me."

"Very well. I'm going to send you back to the barracks with my sergeant. But before you go, allow me to explain a few details in military law of which you are obviously not aware. If you conspire with Favro, Ivar, or anyone else to falsify answers to questions in this investigation, that can be and will be construed as obstruction of justice and perjury. These are very serious charges under the UCMJ,

Mr. Rose. Each of them carries a punishment of more than five years in the Fort Leavenworth Disciplinary Barracks.''

"You are calling the Chairman of the Honor Committee a liar? Wait until the Corps of Cadets hears about this witch-hunt. We take our honor very seriously at West Point, Mr. Kerry. Maybe you've lost sight of that fact, sitting down here in your office, playing with your new phones.''

Rose reached for the doorknob. Behind him, he heard the scrape of Kerry's chair being pushed back from the desk.

"You've maneuvered yourself into a corner, Mr. Rose," Kerry called out behind him. "You know what a corner is? It's a place with only one exit. And you know who's going to be standing there waiting for you when you want to get out? Me.''

Kerry picked up the phone and dialed. "Jacey?''

"Yes sir.''

"It's Kerry. Rose just left.''

"What happened?''

"I figured he wouldn't recall what time it had been when he broke into your room, so I put my question to all three of them about the eight to nine o'clock hour. I questioned Favro first. Rose managed to get him on the phone when he returned to the barracks. Favro told him he had been at the library, so Rose was all prepared to alibi himself with Favro at the library.''

"What happened when you asked him where he'd been between seven and eight?''

"He refused to answer.''

"Jesus. He's the one who did it.''

"Yeah, but all I've got are a few scraps of circumstantial evidence. It's not enough.''

"What about Favro and Ivar?''

"I can squeeze them, but I'm positive Rose will stiffen their spines.''

"He will. But they're going to know he's in more trouble than they are now. They'll want to start moving away from him.''

"You're right. I got the distinct impression from both of them that they didn't have a clue what happened that night, which tells me that Rose stole the disks, and he never told them about it.''

"That can mean only one thing, Agent Kerry. All three of them might have had sex with Dorothy, but Rose is the one with something to hide. He's the only one who was so afraid of what might have been in her E-mail that he felt compelled to steal it."

"He'll crack. He's only begun to feel the pressure."

"I've been watching him for three years. I'd watch my step if I were you. He's smart, he's well connected, and he's popular with the Corps of Cadets. He's got more resources than the average cadet, and he knows how to use them."

"That may be so, but he's already made his first mistake. He's shown us where he's vulnerable."

"I'm not sure I'm following you," said Jacey.

"What could have been in Dorothy's E-mail that was so damaging to him that he would risk stealing it?"

"I really don't know."

"Well, think about it. If you come up with any ideas, let me know."

"Will do, Agent Kerry."

FAVRO'S DOOR burst open and Rose walked in, his face red from exertion. "Kerry knows I called you. He had auto-redial."

"But I don't get it. You called me on one number, and he called me on the other."

Rose looked confused. "What do you mean?"

Favro pointed to his phone. "I've got two lines, remember? One is my Second Regiment line, and the other's the Honor Committee hot line. He called me on the Second Regiment line. You called me on the hot line."

Rose slammed his fist on Favro's desk. "Goddammit! That bastard lied to me! How many calls did you get on the Second Regiment line?"

"Two. One of them was a hang-up. The other one must have been Kerry. He asked for me by name, then he hung up."

"The bastard set the redial by calling you and hanging up. He didn't know I called you!"

"Did he ask you where you were Monday night?"

"I told him I was at the library. He's going to check, so be ready to cover for me."

"What's that guy up to, man? I thought he was in charge of the Dorothy Hamner investigation."

"He's after the Honor Committee. Jacey Slaight is helping him." Rose kicked a metal trash can across the room. "We're going to do something about that bitch."

"Hey, man. She's not some dumb hair-rack like Dorothy. She's the goddamn Supe's daughter."

"Yeah," mused Rose, a smile creeping slowly across his lips. "That will make it fun."

"When are we going to do it?"

"Tomorrow night."

"Man, tomorrow's Friday. How can you be sure she'll be around?"

"I'll get Gibson to put her on Guard."

CHAPTER 37

GENERAL MEULLER called on Thursday afternoon, the moment his office received the letter from Congressman Thrunstone notifying him that the House National Security Committee would hold hearings on the future of the service academies. On Friday morning, Slaight took the Air Force C-21 the Chief of Staff had put at his disposal. It was a military-spec Learjet, which made the flight to Washington both comfortable and quick. A Pentagon Town Car picked him up at Andrews Air Force Base and deposited him at the river entrance to the Pentagon.

It had been a while since Slaight had walked across the sky-blue carpet in the office of the Chief of Staff. Out the window he could see the Potomac, and beyond, the Lincoln Memorial and the Washington Monument. To the southeast, he could see the dome of the Capitol.

General Meuller and the Chairman of the Joint Chiefs of Staff, the biggest of the big dogs inside the walls of the Pentagon and arguably the most powerful military man in the world, were waiting for him. General Douglas Drabonsky was a former commander of the 101st Airborne Division. He had also served in the 101st as a lieutenant in Vietnam. He was what they used to call "Airborne all the way." His hair was buzz-cut, shaved clean on the sides with only a half-inch left on top. He was square-jawed and his eyes were a chilly shade of blue-gray. If perchance you were a civilian who walked into a room and found him among those present, your first instinct would be to conclude that he was the perfect West Pointer. However, this was not the case. He was the third chairman in a row who had come from what were euphemistically called "other commissioning sources." This caused a measure of some pain among West Pointers, but it was of no concern to Slaight. Drabonsky served much the same function that other chairmen of the Joint Chiefs had served since the reign of Colin Powell. He was the voice of the Pentagon in the White House. He worked directly for the Commander in Chief. It was thus left to the chiefs of the individual services to actually get as far down in the trenches as they dared and run their respective organizations: Army, Navy, Air Force, and Marines.

Slaight saluted the two generals, and the three of them sat down, not in the informal gathering of sofa and armchairs where generals usually conversed with one another, but down at the other end of the office at the conference table. General Meuller presided, while deferring to General Drabonsky at key moments of the meeting. Slaight took immediate note of the fact that they were the only ones in the room. Aides, secretaries, and other hangers-on had been banished. The message Slaight got was that they were nervous about the hearings, but they didn't want their anxiety to leak into the corridors of the Pentagon where it would catch on like a bad flu.

There was small talk about Army football to break the ice. Slaight had often wondered what Army generals would do without the ease of talking about Army football. It was the one thing they all had in common, West Pointers and non–West Pointers alike. Everyone rooted for Army.

When the previous weekend's game had been adequately dissected, Meuller stiffened his back and cleared his throat in a manner that had probably gotten its start in Alexander's day, or at least Caesar's.

"Ry, I think I made you aware last night how concerned we are about these hearings."

"Yes sir. My transportation down here put quite an exclamation point on it."

All three generals chuckled at his remark, for indeed there was nothing like the expenditure of federal dollars, even the relatively few that had gone to buy gas for the Air Force C-21, to make a point quickly and forcefully.

Meuller glanced at General Drabonsky as if to receive his approval, and Drabonsky followed through with a squinty-eyed smile. "Here's the thing, Ry," said Meuller. "We have only a sketchy outline about what Thrunstone is up to with these hearings. We're counting on you to play your hand very carefully. Hopefully, we'll know more about Thrunstone's intentions when the press gets wind of what he's up to. Reporters will start sniffing around Capitol Hill. I think we can count on some leaks from Thrunstone's committee that will help us."

General Drabonsky stopped fiddling a fountain pen and faced Slaight. His squinty-eyed smile was gone, replaced by a grim, stony-faced scowl. "I don't trust this son of a bitch Thrunstone. We've been dealing with him on the budget, but every time we try to pin him down and reach a consensus, he shifts on us, and every goddamned shift has been away from us and toward the Navy and the Air Force. He wants manpower concessions from the Army. Our force structure has been cut to the bone. We've gone as far as we're going to go, and he's still leaning on us for concessions. He's trying to shove twenty more B-2's the Air Force doesn't even want through his committee. We could put five divisions on the ground and run them full force for ten years for that kind of money, and he knows it. This five-year budget plan has turned into a slugfest, Ry. I'm certain these hearings are a subterfuge. He's going after West Point, thinking we'll trade him the Military Academy for another division he wants us to mothball. I don't know who he's been listening to, or what he's been smoking, but Thrunstone is in for one hell of a rude awakening."

"Sir, do we know if he's called any other witnesses?"

"No, not yet," replied Meuller. "You're the only one on the docket for the first day."

"Maybe we ought to concentrate some of our resources on his agenda," said Drabonsky. "We find out who else he's been talking to, it'll give us some indication of which way he's heading with this thing."

"I'll put our Capitol Hill liaison people on it right away, sir," said Meuller, making a note.

"Anything we can do for you, Ry?" asked Drabonsky.

"I assume I'll be getting briefed by your liaison team," said Slaight.

Meuller looked up from his notes. "We'd like to hold that off until just before the hearing. That will give us more time to assemble our intelligence."

"How about if I come down the morning of the hearings and meet with your people for a couple of hours before I go in?"

"That ought to work. You've been called for a one o'clock appearance. That should give you plenty of time to be brought up to speed by the liaison staff."

Drabonsky straightened his tie, preparing to leave. "I'm glad we've got you up there at West Point for us, Ry. There isn't anyone I would rather have going up against Thrunstone."

"I met with him when he was up for the Southern Illinois game, sir. I think he's got a few points of vulnerability. One of them is the 4-F he pulled down that exempted him from the draft during Vietnam. A friend of mine called a friend of his and looked up Thrunstone's draft file. His record reflects that he was medically disabled by psoriasis. The day I saw him up at West Point, he looked like he had just stepped off the golf course. I don't think his psoriasis has put much of a crimp in his style since his draft eligibility ran out."

"He plays at Burning Tree at least twice a week, and I've seen him at the Army-Navy Country Club course many times," said Meuller.

"I'd be careful challenging the Chairman of the National Security Committee as a draft dodger," warned Drabonsky.

"I don't plan on calling him a draft dodger, sir," explained Slaight. "But I do intend to tell him that I know he pulled down a 4-F exemption."

"How do you plan on accomplishing that?" asked Drabonsky.

"I'll figure out a way, sir. I think it's time people learned how some of these drum-beating, flag-waving politicians served their country when duty called."

CHAPTER 38

J ACEY FOUND a pink phone message slip on her desk when she returned from class on Friday afternoon. The Cadet Regimental Commander had called. She picked up the phone and dialed his number. "Tommy? It's Jace. What's up?"

"I got some bad news. You're on Guard Duty tonight."

"What? Company Commanders don't pull Guard!"

"It's some kind of new policy that came down today. They want a four-striper in charge of the Guard Detail on weekend nights. You're the lucky duck who pulled down duty for tonight."

"Who called you?"

"Reade, Brigade Adjutant. He said the orders came down straight from Gibson this morning."

"Oh, man. That's going to blow my weekend."

"Tell me about it. I'm on the schedule for Friday night on Navy weekend."

"Okay, thanks, Tommy."

"Sorry, Jace. Orders."

"I've got you. See you around." She hung up the phone just as Belle walked in.

"What's up, girl? You look like you just flunked a test."

"Don't ask."

"C'mon, Jace."

"I've got Guard Duty tonight. It's some kind of new policy. They're putting four-stripers on weekend nights."

"Oh, God, I'm sorry."

"You're sorry! My weekend just went down the toilet."

"You can't get out of it?"

"No, but it cuts you loose for the weekend, Belle. Long as I'm pulling Guard, you may as well take the weekend and go to the game."

"Are you sure?"

"Your turn will come soon enough. When it does, you can take company duty officer for me."

"Okay. If you're sure . . ."

Jacey threw her cap at her roommate. "I'm sure! Get packed! You're out of here!"

Belle opened her closet and started going through her civilian clothes. Jacey walked out the door and down the hall. She stopped at Ash's room and looked through the open door. He was curled up under his comforter taking a nap. She tiptoed into his room and closed the door behind her.

"Ash."

He awoke with a start. "Jace. What's up?"

"I got put on Guard tonight."

"That can't be right."

"I haven't got time to explain. We're going to have to put off our little visit to you-know-where."

"You're sure there's not some mistake."

She held her finger to her lips. "Sssh. I'll call you later and tell you about it." She cracked the door and peeked down the hall. There was a plebe delivering laundry a few doors down. She stepped into the hall and closed his door softly behind her.

THE GUARD Room was a spare ground-floor room in Washington Barracks down at the west end of Central Area. As the ranking member of the six-person Guard Detail, Jacey set the tours for the night. Everyone went to early chow, and then it was two on and four off, pulling two-hour shifts until Reveille Saturday morning. One guard had to man the phones at all times, so the second person on the two-person team was given the responsibility of patrolling the area of barracks. Guard Duty at West Point was largely a ceremonial task, although when Jacey had been a plebe, a large number of computers had been stolen out of the barracks during a weekend when the entire Corps was away for a football game. After the computer thefts, locks had been put on the doors of cadet rooms for the first time in West Point history. The Rutgers game the next day in nearby New Jersey was another weekend when the entire Corps would be gone. It would be necessary to supplement the increased Military Police patrols that had been ordered for weekends.

Jacey's shift began at ten P.M. She began her rounds in what they used to call the Lost Fifties, a section of barracks tucked into a narrow corridor between a sheer rock cliff and the gymnasium. She continued through MacArthur Barracks and moved across North Area to do a turn through Scott Barracks. She thought of going through Washington Barracks, but reasoned that the presence of the Guard Shack on the ground floor would discourage intruders, and headed down Brewerton Road toward Grant and Lee Barracks instead.

It was dark behind the mess hall and very quiet. The clanging and banging of huge pots and pans you usually heard from the kitchens had ceased after the cleanup of the evening meal. Even the lights over the loading docks had been turned off. She was about to make the corner that would take her behind Central Barracks when she noticed something move in the shadows. She had just picked up her pace when she felt a hand grab her left arm. Then a thick blanket was thrown over her head and she began to scream, but she knew with the barracks empty, no one could hear her. She felt another set of hands lifting her from her feet and heard a voice say, "Gag her"; then something that felt like a belt was tightened around her head, covering her mouth. Someone reached under the blanket and grabbed her wrists. She felt the sting of rope wrapping them tightly together. They grabbed her arm, wrenching her elbow backwards. She cried out in pain, but the blanket and the belt muffled the sound.

She was dragged up concrete stairs. She heard a car engine and a trunk pop open. They pushed her into the trunk and slammed the lid shut. She was tossed violently to one side as the car turned sharply and accelerated up a hill. The car jerked to a stop, banging her against the seat back, and then accelerated again, turning left and then right, still going uphill.

Only a moment or two had gone by since they grabbed her, and now an icy chill of fear set in. She knew from the hands that grabbed her and the muffled voice she heard that they belonged to young males. Then it came to her. They were cadets! It had to be! Rose? Ivar? No, he was already down at Rutgers, getting ready for the game. Favro? These idiots actually thought they could blanket-party her and scare her? Fools!

She heard the wheels of the car leave pavement and begin to claw their way along a gravel road. The gravel gave way to a rutted, bumpy surface, tossing her around inside the trunk. Finally the car came to a stop. She heard the doors open. Footsteps. She could hear muffled voices. The trunk popped open, and they pulled her roughly from the trunk to her feet. They grabbed her arms and she stumbled forward. The ground was rocky and she fell. They yanked her to her feet and pushed her. Her back hit something. A tree. She felt a rope. They pulled it tight around her waist and legs. She couldn't move.

She heard footsteps rustling leaves, breaking twigs. They were somewhere in the forests surrounding the Academy. Not far. She'd been in the trunk only a few minutes. She heard them whispering, just out of earshot. Footsteps. Moving away. A car starter. The engine fired. Tires spun, spitting rocks into the bush. The engine, fading away.

Silence.

She thought for a moment she was alone. She struggled against the ropes. Then a crack split the silence of the forest like a thunderclap. Dry wood breaking maybe. One footstep. Two. She heard a whistling sound and a jolt of white pain shot up her left arm. She screamed. Another whistling sound, a hard shot in the stomach, doubling her forward. She couldn't get her breath. She could feel her mouth working desperately, trying for air. Finally, a wheezing sob, sounding very far away. Air rushed into her lungs. She knew the sob was hers. She sagged against the ropes, hanging limply from the tree. She could feel the wet heat of tears running down her face.

A footstep. A twig snapped. She could hear him taking deep, slow breaths. He swung again. Her leg snapped back, a hot barb of agonizing pain shooting up her thigh. She cried out, "Stop! Stop!"

She heard his breath quicken. A footstep. She felt him lift the blanket. The jagged end of something struck her bare thigh. She cried out in pain as he scraped it upward. She struggled, trying to cross her legs. He jabbed it into the soft flesh of her crotch.

"No . . . no." All she could do was whisper the word.

She heard his breath, fast little gasps. In horror, she realized he was masturbating. The gasps stopped. He jerked the branch back and stabbed. She screamed out in pain, writhing against the ropes, trying to pull free. He jabbed again. She struggled, trying to turn away. He pulled back, she heard that whistling sound, and he hit her again and again, whacking it hard against her legs, her ribs. Then there was a loud *snap* as it broke. She heard it hit the ground a short distance away.

A footstep. His voice, low, almost a growl. "Where's your daddy? Why don't you call for your daddy?" A footstep. Closer. Another. A rasping whisper. "I will kill you. Your daddy didn't stop me this time. Think about next time."

Footsteps. Leaves rustling. Growing fainter. Gone.

She struggled against her ties, burning her wrists with the rope. The pain in her arm was almost enough to make her stop, but she pulled and pulled against the ropes. It was no use. They were too tight. She screamed into the empty forest. "Help! Help me! Somebody! Help me!"

A cold wind hissed through the trees, and then it stopped, and there was only silence.

BOOK

THREE

AT THE Guard Room, the midnight shift arrived a few minutes early. "Where's Jacey?" asked one of the cadet guards.

"Making the rounds. Have a seat. She'll be here in a minute."

The cadets poured themselves cups of coffee from the urn in the corner and stood reading notices on the bulletin board. Finally one of them checked his watch. "Hey, man, it's almost twelve-thirty. What's going on?"

"She's late. Cool it. She'll be here."

"I think we ought to try to find her. Maybe she tripped and fell down some stairs or something."

"Okay. You guys go ahead and have a look around. I've got to stay here."

"Maybe we ought to call the third shift. I don't like this, man."

"Okay." The cadet behind the desk dialed the phone. "Hey, you guys better get down here. Jacey never showed up at the end of her shift. We think she might have tripped and fallen or something." He hung up the phone. "They're on their way."

"Where's the Officer in Charge?"

"Checking Ike Hall."

"Beep him."

The cadet dialed the phone, listened, and punched in four digits.

In a moment the phone rang. "Major Hall, Jacey Slaight never showed up. Yes sir. Right away sir."

"What'd he say?"

"He's on his way."

The Guard Room door opened and the third shift came in. "What's going on, man?"

"Jacey's like thirty minutes late. You guys take North Area. We'll start with South. Let's go."

The teams of cadets headed out the door. One of them broke into a jog. The rest followed suit. Leather-soled footfalls echoed across the darkened area.

"HELP! HELP ME! I'm over here!" Jacey's voice was hoarse from yelling. It was useless. They had left her way out in the woods, probably off one of the firebreaks that crisscrossed the hills above the parking lots north of Michie Stadium. Everything ached. Her ribs. Her leg. Her hands. Her arm. Her stomach. Her vagina felt raw and burned with a fiery itch.

She tried to yell, but her voice broke. What was the use? She knew no one could hear her. There was a thick blanket over her head, and a belt was tied around her mouth. It was hopeless. She tried to relax against the ropes tying her to the tree, but every time she tried, it hurt. She felt a numbness in her arm, and every time she shifted her weight from one foot to the other, one of her ribs popped, shooting a pain up her side. He must have broken it, she thought. She tried standing perfectly still, but that didn't work either. It was getting colder. Suddenly, she began wondering if she was going to make it.

Wait a minute. She heard the sound of tires on the firebreak, springs squeaking as a car crept slowly up the hill. She was about to cry for help, but then she thought it might be him coming back. She froze at the thought. There was no moon. Maybe it was so dark he'd forget where he'd stopped and he wouldn't be able to find her.

The car came to a stop. She heard a radio, then voices. A girl laughed. Silence. Then, "Jerry, wait."

It was a couple of kids parking in the woods! She struggled, trying to scream as loud as she could. "Help! Help! Down here!" She took a breath and tried again. "Help me! Help me!"

An electric window rolled down. "Did you hear that?" It was the boy. "Somebody's out there. We better get out of here."

"Wait! Help me! Down here!"

The car started. "Wait, Jerry, I heard it that time. It sounds like a girl."

A car door opened. Footsteps. "Help! Over here!"

"Look! Over there!"

She heard them running through the leaves. She felt hands pulling at the ropes. They undid the belt around her head and pulled off the blanket. "Oh my god. I'm so glad you heard me!"

"What happened?"

Jacey gasped in pain. "Careful. My arm. It hurts."

"Sorry."

The ropes came free. She turned around and they loosened the rope tying her wrists. She could see them. They were teenage kids from the post. "Can you help me? I don't think I can walk."

"Sure." The boy reached for her arm. She pulled away.

"Around the waist." He wrapped his arm around her, the girl gripped her hand, and they struggled up a leaf-covered hill to the car. The boy opened the passenger door and she eased herself onto the seat. As she sat down, she cried out in pain. "Oh God!"

"You okay, ma'am?"

She was breathing deeply, trying to gain control of herself. "Get me to the hospital. Quick."

The boy started the car. The headlights picked out a narrow dirt road through the forest.

"Where are we?"

"Up above Delafield, ma'am. We'll be at the hospital in a minute."

The car hit a rock, throwing her against the door. Tears filled her eyes, and she felt herself losing consciousness. She heard the car's engine, the tires squealed, and then there was nothing.

ASH LOOKED UP from a book as an MP car's whirling red light flashed through the window on the wall. He leaped to his feet and opened the window. MPs were getting out of a squad car. "Hey! What's going on?"

"One of the cadet guards is missing," an MP yelled.

"Who? Which one?"

"The Supe's daughter."

He was in his drawers and a T-shirt. He pulled on his trousers, stepped into his shoes, grabbed his gray jacket, and ran for the door. He was running across Central Area toward the Guard Room when he saw the Officer in Charge getting into a staff car. He ran up to the car and tapped on the window. "Sir, sir . . ."

The Officer in Charge rolled down the window. "We found her. She's been taken to the hospital."

"I'm in her company, sir. I'm . . . her boyfriend."

"What's your name?"

"Prudhomme, sir."

"Get in, mister."

"Yes sir."

The Officer in Charge whipped the wheel and sped across the area. He flew down the pedestrian walkway in front of the Library and turned left on Cullum Road. Ash reached for the dash, steadying himself. "Sir, does anyone know what happened?"

"She was kidnapped and beaten up."

"Oh, Jesus. Hurry, sir. Please."

"I'm going to put this thing in the ditch if I go any faster, mister."

"Yes sir."

LIGHTS. FLASHING LIGHTS. Lights flashing. Too bright. A face. A woman.

"Can you hear me?"

An echo, like thunder, somewhere over Storm King Mountain. A big white light. The face.

"Jacey! Can you hear me?"

Somebody's calling my name. The light. The light's too bright.

"Where are you? What's your name?"

Stupid. They're asking my name. A face. It hurts. Hurts. Hurts.

"Jacey! We're going to undress you!"

They're calling the uniform of the day. Dress gray. Hurts. Hurts! "No! No! Stop! Stop!"

"Jacey! We've got to remove your clothes!"

"No! Hurts! Hurts!" Hands. Lifting. Dizzy. Swimmy little things, bugs up in the clouds, stupid bugs in the clouds . . .

"She's out. Get her dress coat off. Give me glucose IV, push. Get a cuff on her. Get a pressure. Give me oxygen. Now."

Major Vernon was pulling her third emergency-room overnight shift since she arrived at West Point. Her first two shifts had been uneventful. She had stitched up a kid who fell on some glass and administered pressurized Albuterol to a young girl having an asthma attack. Tonight they had wheeled Jacey Slaight into the trauma room, delirious, eyes rolled back in her head, floating in and out of consciousness. Vacation over.

"She's coming around." An EMT shined a flashlight in her eyes. She blinked wildly.

"Jacey! Can you hear me!"

Doctor. I can hear her. "Yes."

"Can you tell me your name?"

Of course I can. "Jacey. Slaight."

"Do you know where you are?"

What is this? Twenty questions? "Hospital."

"Pressure eighty over thirty. Open the IV full. Let's have a look at those wounds."

Major Vernon moved the overhead light closer. There was a large contusion on her stomach, another on her left arm. Neither was bleeding, probably because the dress coat protected her. She moved down to her leg. There was an open wound just above her knee, and a violet-colored scrape up her leg.

"Jacey! Can you hear me?"

Stop shouting. I'm right here. "I can hear you."

"I'm going to remove your panties."

"No! No! Hurts!"

"Jacey, it's okay. Look at me."

Open your eyes. Open them! There. It's a woman. A doctor.

"Jacey, I'm Major Vernon. You're in the emergency room. It's okay now. I'm going to remove your panties. You don't have to worry. I'll be gentle."

Hands, pulling. Hurts. Hurts. "Hurts!"

"Morphine. One cc." She slipped the needle into the IV and pushed the plunger.

Warmth. Sun. Up on the barracks roof with Ash. He's rubbing suntan lotion on my back . . .

"How is she? Will she be okay?" Ash was at the foot of the trauma table, eyes wide, looking down at Jacey's nude body as Major Vernon worked on her.

"Get him out of here."

"No!" Jacey jerked her head, her eyes fluttering. "Stay."

"I'm her boyfriend, ma'am. My name is Ash Prudhomme. I'm in her company."

"Okay. Move back."

"Yes ma'am."

"Jacey, can you hear me?"

"Yes."

"I'm going to put some ointment on you. It's going to be cold. It's going to help you feel better. You tell me if it hurts, okay?"

"Okay."

She gently applied an antibacterial salve to the raw areas of Jacey's vaginal opening. "You okay?"

"Yes ma'am."

"Are you feeling the morphine?"

"It's like a beach."

"There you go."

"Doctor. Am I going to be okay?"

"You're going to be fine, Jacey. You've got some pretty good bruising, but you'll heal right up. What you need is some fluids and some rest, and you'll be better than new in no time."

"Can Ash stay?"

"Sure."

"It's so bright . . ."

"We're going to move you. Step back." Major Vernon and the EMT wheeled her out of the trauma room and down the hall.

Jacey could hear voices all around her. She caught a glimpse of a green officer's uniform and an MP armband. They turned into a room down the hall and pressed the stretcher against the side of the bed. She felt hands lifting her, and then she felt herself sinking into a soft mattress. She opened her eyes. There were two IVs next to her. Something was wrapped around her right arm. A blood-pressure thing. A sheet was pulled up to her chin. Ash moved close and took her hand.

"Everything's okay, Jace. You're going to be okay."

She squeezed his hand. "I want you to stay."

The Officer in Charge moved to the other side of the bed. "Jacey, I sent a chopper for your father. They're in the air on their way back from Rutgers right now. They should be here in fifteen minutes."

"Thank you, sir."

"Are you up for a couple of questions? There's someone here who wants to talk to you."

"I don't feel so good."

Ash squeezed her hand and leaned close to her ear, whispering. "It's Kerry."

"Okay."

The Officer in Charge stepped into the hall. Agent Kerry pulled up a stool and sat close to her bed. His voice was warm, reassuring. "It's just me and Ash, Jacey." He looked over at Ash. "Close the door. Don't let anyone in." Ash swung the door shut and leaned against it. "What happened?"

"I was on Brewerton Road. They threw a blanket over me."

"How many were there?"

"More than one. I could hear them whispering."

"What happened next?"

"They tied me and put me in the trunk of a car. They tied me to a tree, and then the car drove away. One guy stayed."

"Did you get a look at him?"

"No."

"Did he say anything?"

"Just a few words. He said, 'Where's your daddy?' He said, 'Your daddy couldn't help you this time.' Then he said . . .'" She started to sob.

Agent Kerry touched her hand. "That's okay. We can talk later."

"No. I've got to tell you what he said. He . . . he told me he would kill me."

"Did you recognize his voice?"

"No."

"Is there anything you can think of that will give us a start figuring out who did this?"

She thought for a moment. "I don't know if this helps, but he masturbated as he was beating me. I could hear him."

Kerry gave her hand a squeeze. "That's enough for now. I'll stop by tomorrow morning."

"Thanks."

He pointed at Ash. "Stick with her."

"I will." Ash waited until Agent Kerry had left. He put his lips close to her ear. "The Officer in Charge is going to come in here in a minute. You can tell me, Jace. Was it Rose?"

"I don't know."

"It was him. I can smell the sick son of a bitch."

"Let Agent Kerry deal with it, Ash. Don't do anything stupid."

"Don't worry."

She turned her head toward him. A dull pain ran from her neck down her left arm.

"Hurt?"

"A little." She reached up with her right hand and stroked his cheek. "You need to shave."

"I didn't bring my razor."

"I love you, Ash. I want you to stay here with me. I won't be able to sleep without knowing you're here."

"I'm here, Jace."

"Ash, is this what it's like?"

"What's like?"

"War."

"All I've done is read about it in books."

"It hurts bad."

He lifted his eyes and found a crack in the plaster on the wall over near the window. It looked like a creek running through a meadow covered in snow. "I don't know what war is, Jace, but what you've been through is close enough." He looked down at her. She was already asleep.

CHAPTER 40

T HE ARMY Blackhawk touched down in the parking lot behind the hospital. Slaight threw the door open and stepped out, turning to help Sam. "Duck your head," he shouted over the roar of the whirling rotors. They ran across the parking lot toward a clutch of cadets and officers standing on the sidewalk. The Officer in Charge saluted.

"Sir, Major Hall. This way, sir, ma'am." He turned and led them down the sidewalk through a back door into the hospital. They made their way up a narrow set of stairs and went through a door into a brightly lit corridor. The Officer in Charge led the way around a corner and down another corridor. He stopped before an unmarked door. "She's in here, sir."

Slaight pushed the door open, taking Sam by the hand. They walked together to Jacey's bedside. She was asleep. Sam touched her shoulder. "Jacey?"

"Mommy?" Jacey's eyes fluttered open. She turned her head, grimacing from the pain.

Sam rested her hand on Jacey's arm. "Jacey, are you okay?"

"Sort of."

Slaight walked around to the other side of the bed. "You look like you could use some water. Are you thirsty, Jace?"

She licked her lips. They were dry. "Yes, Daddy."

Slaight picked up a carafe and poured half a glass of water. He stuck a straw in the glass, held it next to Jacey's pillow, and helped her lift her head to get the straw between her lips. She drank deeply.

"Tastes good." Pain shot through her stomach, and she jerked forward involuntarily. Tears formed in her eyes, and her face contorted.

Major Vernon walked in carrying new IV fluid. "General and Mrs. Slaight, I'm Major Elizabeth Vernon. I'm the duty doc tonight." She moved quickly to unhook one of the IV bags and rehook the new one. "How are you, Jacey?"

"She's in pain," said Sam.

"I'll push another cc of morphine," said Major Vernon.

Slaight followed her into the corridor. "What can you tell me, Major?"

"She took a bad beating, sir. She's got some bruises and contusions. The wounds don't look grave enough to have caused internal bleeding, probably because she was wearing her uniform and they had thrown a blanket over her, but we'll X-ray her in a couple of hours. I want to get her stable and comfortable first. I don't think the X rays are going to show any additional damage, but you never know."

"I got a report over the radio on the way up here that she was sexually assaulted. Is that so?"

"Yes sir."

"In what way?"

"I haven't talked to her yet, but it looks to me like they used a piece of wood. She's got some contusions and swelling around the vaginal opening, and I removed two splinters from her upper thigh. I'm pretty sure she was not penetrated, sir, but we'll be able to tell more in the morning. She's traumatized. It's best not to press too hard under these conditions."

"I understand."

"General Slaight, she's a brave young woman. I haven't heard a complaint from her yet."

"The night is still young, Major," Slaight said, trying to lighten the moment.

Major Vernon smiled. "She'll probably want eggs instead of Jell-O when the food cart comes in with breakfast."

"You've got the picture."

"Excuse me, sir. I want to get that morphine." Slaight walked back into Jacey's room. In a moment, Major Vernon returned with a syringe of morphine and pushed it through her IV. Jacey's facial muscles relaxed almost immediately. "Better?"

"Thank you." She tried to lift her head, looking around the room. "Where's Ash?"

"He was here with you?" her mother asked.

"Yes." She looked up at her father. "Daddy. He's going to do something stupid. You've got to stop him."

"Do you know where he went?"

"He's looking for Rose."

Slaight walked out of the room and signaled to the Officer in Charge. He ran down the corridor. "Yes sir."

"There was a cadet here with my daughter, Ashford Prudhomme. Find him."

"Yes sir."

"Call the MPs. Turn out the Cadet Guard. I want him brought in. He thinks he knows who did the beating, and he's going after him."

"Right, sir." Major Hall saluted and ran back down the corridor, disappearing around the corner.

Major Vernon came out of the room. "Five more minutes, sir. She needs to rest." He nodded his assent.

At her bedside, Slaight hugged his wife close and said, "Jace, your mother and I are going to let you get some rest. Your mother's going to stay with you."

"Daddy, you've got to find Ash."

"We will."

"I'm afraid he'll kill him, Daddy."

"Don't worry, Jace. I'll take care of it."

"Try not to worry, Jacey. Everything is going to be all right."

"Okay, Mom."

Slaight leaned over the side of the bed and kissed his daughter on the forehead. Her eyes were closed. She was drifting off. He took Sam's hand and led her into the corridor.

"This is my nightmare," she whispered.

"Mine, too."

"We never should have let her go to West Point. This place is evil."

"If Jacey hears you say that, you will break her heart, Sam."

"But it's so wrong, Ry. I can't help it. She's my baby."

He held her in his arms. "She's going to be a lieutenant next year, Sam. There's going to come a day when she'll be sent far away, and she'll be out there with her troops, on her own. That's the way it is when kids grow up."

"I know, Ry. It's just so hard to see her in such agony."

"She's tough. She was tough when she was three years old. You were the one who saw that."

A sergeant walked up and saluted. "I've got a car for you outside, sir."

"One moment, Sergeant."

"I feel so helpless. I wish there was something I could do."

"Go in there and sit with her and be her mom. That's what she needs. She's going to come through this okay, Sam. She's strong."

AGENT KERRY called for his CID forensics team and sent them up into the woods with a generator and a brace of crime-scene lights to search for physical evidence. They took the two kids to lead the way to the place where they had found Jacey. Now Kerry was standing on the first floor of the MP barracks. Fifteen young military policemen were standing along the wall in front of him. Several were in uniform. Some of them had been pulled off weekend passes and were in their civvies. The rest had been asleep, and were in pajama bottoms and GI drawers and shower clogs.

He pointed to the uniformed MPs. "I want you five to form a team and get up there behind Delafield Pond and secure the crime scene. Nobody goes in or out of there without my say-so." The uniformed MPs took off. He turned to the others. "The rest of you, I want you to find this cadet. His name is Ash Prudhomme. Here's his photograph." He passed a Xerox blown up from the Howitzer, the West Point yearbook. "He's not a suspect. We think he's gone after the guys who kidnapped Jacey Slaight. Your job is to find him and bring him back here and hold him. Nobody sleeps until he's in our custody, understood?"

"Yes sir!" came the chorus from the MPs.

"Get moving."

The last of the MPs had left the barracks when Kerry heard the door open at the end of the hall. He turned to see Lieutenant Colonel Percival striding toward him.

"What's going on, Kerry?"

"I turned out the barracks. We're trying to locate Cadet Prudhomme."

"Prudhomme? He's a suspect?"

"No sir."

"Then why are you looking for him?"

"He's gone after Rose, sir."

"The Honor Committee Chairman? What for?"

"He thinks Rose did the beating, sir."

"That's absurd. Prudhomme's a more likely suspect than Rose."

"I'm going to be straight with you, sir. I haven't got time to talk right now."

"Are you being insubordinate with me, Mr. Kerry?"

"No sir. I'm just in a hurry. Now if you'll excuse me, sir, I've got work to do." He brushed past Percival and headed down the hall toward the exit.

"Chief Warrant Officer Kerry! Come back here!"

Kerry stopped. "Sir, you want to come along, that's fine with me. We can talk in the car."

"Goddammit, Kerry, I'm ordering you!"

Kerry stuck a finger in his ear and cocked his head. "I've got a buzzing in my ear, sir. Can't hear a thing. Must be an old war wound acting up." He opened the door and walked into the cold night air. He checked his watch. Three A.M. Rose would be holed up in some motel down near Rutgers by now, doubtlessly with his pals, probably with an alibi a mile wide and an inch deep. He climbed in his staff car and started the engine. He'd start with his company orderly room.

*　　*　　*

KERRY DROVE into Central Area and pulled up in front of Company B-2. The light was on in the first-floor orderly room. Prudhomme was way ahead of him. He jumped out of his car and ran inside. Weekend leave forms were scattered across the top of the Formica counter. He went through them. Rose's was missing. Prudhomme must have taken it. He looked around for the sign-out book, opening desk drawers. Nothing. He opened the closet and found the sign-out book jammed under a pile of manila folders. He ran his finger down the list of names, each with a contact phone number written next to it. There it was. Rose. A 201 number. New Jersey.

Kerry picked up the phone. "Thompson, get ahold of Atlantic Bell. Get me an address for this number." He read off the ten digits. "I'll be in my car."

As he passed through the main gate he reached for his red light and hit a switch; the light flashed, and he stuck it on the top of the dashboard and stepped on the gas. The rain had stopped and the road was clear. He blew through Highland Falls and turned on 9W.

Just before he reached the Bear Mountain Bridge, his phone rang. "Kerry."

"Thompson. I've got that address for you. Comfort Motel. Eleven-twenty North Main Street. Bound Brook, New Jersey.

"Got it. I want you to look up the license number for Cadet Ashford Prudhomme. I need the make and model."

"Wait one."

Kerry made the circle at Bear Mountain and picked up the Palisades Parkway headed south. "Thompson, you got that license for me yet?"

"One minute. Here it is: 1997 Toyota Celica convertible. Black. New York one, Y for Yellow, B for Bravo, six-six-two, N for Nancy."

"1YB662N. Got it. Patch me through to the State Patrol."

"Wait one. Okay, you're on."

"New York State Patrol, this is Military Police Agent Kerry. I'm headed south on the Palisades Parkway, and I've got a stop-and-hold for you. It's a 1997 Toyota Celica convertible, color black, license one, Y for Yellow, B for Bravo, six-six-two, N for Nancy. Driver is West Point Cadet Ashford Prudhomme, male, twenty-one, brown hair, six feet one inch, about one-eighty. He's wanted as a material witness. We need him picked up and held for West Point authorities. Repeat.

Prudhomme is not a suspect. He is not armed. He is not dangerous. He is to be stopped and held for West Point authorities. Copy?"

"Agent Kerry, this is New York Patrol headquarters, we copy. Stop and hold Toyota Celica convertible, black, 1997, 1YB662N. Ashford Prudhomme."

"He is headed south for Bound Brook, New Jersey. Can you relay my stop-and-hold order to New Jersey State Patrol?"

"Roger, Kerry. Do you need an escort?"

"It would help."

"Give me your location."

"I'm coming up on 17A."

"Roger. We'll have a patrol car with you shortly. Look for him coming up on your rear."

Kerry pressed his foot to the floor. The speedometer read eighty, eighty-five, ninety. A flashing blue light appeared in his rearview mirror. Headlights blinked him twice as a New York Patrol car passed him doing over a hundred. The patrol car pulled in front of him. Kerry's radio crackled.

"Agent Kerry, this is New York Patrol One-sixteen. I've got you to the New Jersey line."

"Roger, One-sixteen."

"It's coming up."

"Roger."

They sped past the New Jersey State sign, and Kerry spied a New Jersey Patrol car coming out of a rest area on the right.

"We're gonna pass you off to New Jersey Patrol. See you around. New York One-sixteen out."

"Thanks, One-sixteen." The blue lights of the New Jersey Patrol car rushed up from behind.

"New Jersey Patrol Alpha Five-eight. We're coming around you."

"Got you, Jersey Alpha Five-eight."

"Where we going tonight?"

"Bound Brook."

"Roger, Bound Brook. Follow us to the exit for 202. We'll take Route 202 and pick up 287 southbound."

"Roger, Alpha Five-eight."

"You got a name back there?"

"Kerry."

"We've notified patrols south of here to look for your Celica. If he's out here, we'll get him."

"Thanks, Alpha Five-eight." Kerry looked down at his speedometer again. He was right on one hundred miles an hour. The steering felt tight. The car was planted. They flew around a semi-truck, slowed for the 202 exit, and picked up a three-lane. The Jersey Patrol car put on his siren as they passed through Suffern. Ahead he could see the overpass for 287.

"Follow us. We're going right."

"Roger."

They swept the on-ramp and regained speed. "Any word on the Celica, New Jersey Alpha Five-eight?"

"Negative."

Kerry mentally crossed his fingers. Prudhomme had at least an hour's jump on him. He hoped there was time.

CHAPTER 41

ASH WAS about fifty miles ahead of Kerry. He knew the CID agent was resourceful and would have Ash's car license nailed in two minutes, so he had stopped in Jacey's room to pick up the keys to her Miata. A white sports car in the middle of the night on a nearly empty interstate . . . he was doing five miles over the speed limit, all he thought he could afford.

Rose had done it. He was certain of that. He had tried to put himself in Rose's place. What would he do? He would stick to his routine, that's what. He'd pretend he was going to the Rutgers game, check into his motel, drive back to West Point and commit the crime, and get straight back to the motel. He would claim he'd been there the whole time, and he'd have Favro and a couple of others to back him up. Hell, Favro was probably the other guy who had grabbed her. If Jacey never saw them, they would claim they'd been together the whole time, sitting around the motel watching TV and drinking beer.

Ash had taken Rose's leave form with the address for the Comfort Motel to throw Kerry a curve, but he knew Kerry would figure out where Rose had gone. West Point didn't like its Honor Committee Chairman being out of reach.

All he had to do was beat Kerry to the motel. He wanted just five

minutes alone with Rose. Five little minutes was all it would take. He
flipped on the dash light and checked his map. He was coming up
on the intersection for Interstate 78. Maybe twenty-five miles to go.
He checked his speed. Jersey still had the fifty-five speed limit. He
was doing sixty. Headlights appeared in his rearview mirror. They
were coming up fast. He dropped his speed to fifty-seven, fifty-six. A
New Jersey State Patrol car flew by him in the left lane. *Whew*. He
picked his speed back up to sixty. Twenty minutes, and he'd be there.

''THIS IS Alpha Five-eight. We've got Bound Brook coming up. The
Comfort Motel is a right turn at the bottom of the exit ramp.''

"Thank you, Alpha Five-eight."

"Follow me."

"I'm on you." The Jersey Patrol car turned on his siren and went
right through the stop sign at the bottom of the ramp, Kerry's staff
car right behind him. He could see the motel up ahead. The Jersey
Patrol pulled up, and the trooper jumped out as Kerry stopped under the motel carport. Kerry ran into the office followed by the patrolman. There was no one behind the counter. He started banging
on the counter. "Police! Police!"

The door behind them opened, and a middle-aged man walked
in. "Can I help you?"

"You've got a West Point cadet registered here. Jerry Rose."

"Right. There was someone—"

"Where is he!"

"Room Eleven-oh-nine. It's on the back—"

"Which way?"

"Around to the right . . ."

Kerry and the Jersey trooper took off running. As they came
around the side of the building, they could see an open door across
the parking lot. A white Miata had been left sideways, blocking two
cars parked in front of the room with the open door. Kerry sprinted
across the parking lot. "Wait outside!" he yelled at the Jersey patrolman. He burst through the door. There was no one in the room.
Then he heard them. The bathroom! He ran for the bathroom. He
tripped as he passed the first bed. Favro was unconscious, lying between the two beds. Kerry got up and ran for the bathroom door.

Prudhomme had Rose by the throat, bent over backwards, his head in the toilet. There was blood on the walls, on the mirror, on the floor . . .

"Prudhomme!" Ash looked up. He still had Rose by the throat, his face under water. Kerry grabbed him from behind in a hammerlock and Ash let go. Rose's head came out of the toilet spitting water. His face was a bloody mess, eyes swollen, nose pouring blood, lip split.

"Agent Kerry. I . . . want you . . . to arrest . . . him," Rose sputtered.

Kerry backed Ash out of the bathroom. Rose held a towel to his nose and looked at himself in the mirror. "I'm going to let you go, Prudhomme," said Kerry. "Don't touch him."

"He's lucky I didn't kill him."

"If I were you, I'd keep my mouth shut."

"He did it. He admitted it."

"I admitted nothing," said Rose. "Arrest him! I'm bringing charges!"

"Shut up, Rose," Kerry barked. He turned to Ash. "How long have you been here?"

"A few minutes."

"What in hell did you do to Favro?"

Ash pointed across the room where a steering-wheel lock lay on the floor.

"All right, I want you to walk directly out of this room. Do not touch anything. Do you understand me?"

"Yes."

"Do it. Wait for me outside." Ash walked through the door.

The Jersey patrolman was standing there wide-eyed. "What's this about?" he asked.

Ash pointed through the open door at the bleeding Rose. "He raped my girlfriend."

Kerry took Rose by the arm and led him out the door. He leaned him up against the motel wall. "Stand right there. Don't move."

"Are you going to arrest him, or will I have to call the civilian police?"

"You know something, Rose? For a big-time smart-boy cadet, you are the stupidest motherfucker I have ever come across. I told you to shut up, and I meant it. I told you to stand against that wall and not to move, and I meant that, too. You move, and I'll cuff your ass and throw you facedown on the ground. Your choice.''

"But—"

"Shut up." Kerry turned to the Jersey patrolman. "Keep an eye on him, will you?"

"Sure."

Kerry walked back inside and turned Favro over. There was a lump the size of a golf ball on the side of his face. He shook him, and Favro stirred. "Favro! Favro!" He opened his eyes. "Can you stand up?" He struggled to his knees. "Stand up." Kerry helped him to his feet and out the door. Favro's knees weakened and he slumped to a sitting position on the sidewalk. "Stay there. Don't move."

He signaled to Ash, and they walked down the sidewalk and turned into a stairwell leading to the second-floor balcony. "I need to know what you touched in the room, Prudhomme. Think."

"I knocked on the door. When he opened it, I pushed the door. I swung at Favro, and he dropped. I grabbed Rose and hauled him straight into the bathroom."

"Did he struggle?"

"He tried, but I had his thumb bent back. He went."

"You didn't touch the bed or the dresser?"

"No."

"You are certain? I'm treating the room like a crime scene. I'm going to do a forensics search. I need to know what I'm going to turn up that's yours."

"That's it, Mr. Kerry."

"Let me see the soles of your shoes."

Ash leaned against the motel ice machine and took off one shoe and then the other. They were clean.

"What are you looking for?" he asked.

"Dirt. Mud. Anything I can trace back to the woods where they held Jacey."

"So you think he did it, too."

"I'm not paid to think, Mr. Prudhomme. I'm paid to investigate. It's what I do."

"But you're treating him like a suspect."

"He made a threat against Jacey. He's gone from being a material witness to being a suspect, yes."

"You think you'll get him?"

"If he did this crime, I'll get him, Mr. Prudhomme. But I will tell you one thing right now. You just made my job about a factor of two harder."

"He confessed. He admitted he did it."

"That doesn't help me. You beat it out of him. Where do you think we are? Argentina? That's not admissible. It might even turn out to help him."

"I'm sorry, Mr. Kerry. I wasn't thinking about that. I was thinking about Jacey."

"I want you to sit in your car and wait for me. I'm going to need to talk to you later."

"Okay."

"Be a good boy. Don't cause me any more problems."

"I won't, Agent Kerry."

Kerry flipped his keys to the Jersey trooper. "Will you be so kind as to pull my car around?"

"Sure. Do you want backup? I can get you a couple of sheriff's deputies."

"That won't be necessary, but we could use an ambulance. Somebody ought to have a look at these wounds." The trooper headed toward the front of the motel. Kerry walked over to Rose and Favro. "You two are under arrest. You have the right to remain silent. You have the right to military counsel, which will be provided to you without cost; you have the right to civilian counsel, which you may provide at no expense to the government; or both. You do not have to answer any questions without the presence of counsel. Do you understand your rights?"

Favro nodded vacantly. Rose removed the towel from his nose. "Yes." He took a step forward. "This is absurd."

"Back up, Rose. If you want cuffs, I'll sure oblige you," said Kerry. Rose stepped back and stood against the motel wall. "You're being charged with assault and battery on Cadet Jacey Slaight last night."

"But we were here last night from ten o'clock on!" shouted Favro.

"Shut up, Favro," whispered Rose. He turned to Kerry. "We want lawyers."

"You're not going to arrest Prudhomme?" cried Favro. "He's the one who assaulted us!"

"You want military counsel, Rose?"

"I already said yes."

"You want military counsel, Favro?"

"Yes."

"All right, counsel will be provided for you when we return to West Point."

"We were here; we didn't do anything!" said Favro.

"Shut the fuck up," barked Rose. "We're not talking until we see a lawyer. I don't know what you're up to, Kerry, but you're in big trouble if you don't arrest Prudhomme. You're putting *us* under arrest! *He's* the one who committed a crime!"

"What Prudhomme pulled might be a crime back at West Point, but it seems like you've forgotten something, Rose. You're in New Jersey. Things are different here. People around here don't like guys who try to fuck a girl with a stick."

Favro's head swiveled up at Rose. The look on his face told Kerry all he needed to know.

CHAPTER 42

R OSE HAD a few stitches put in his lip and eyebrow at a local emergency room, and they X-rayed Favro's head, diagnosing him with a concussion. They returned to the motel with the state trooper and sat in the back of his patrol car while Kerry completed his forensics examination of the motel room.

He questioned the motel manager and a security guard and several of the motel guests who were staying on the back side of the motel. The guests hadn't noticed which cars were in the parking lot that night, but the security guard had. He carried a list of the license plates taken from the motel registration slips. The car belonging to room 1109 was a 1997 Dodge Intrepid registered to Cadet Jerry Rose. It had remained parked in the back lot of the motel all night. There was a light on in the room until late, and both the security guard and the motel manager had walked by the room and heard the sound of the television. Neither of them had seen either Rose or Favro leave the room except just after they checked in, and that was to get ice from the machine in the stairwell.

The room itself had yielded precious little in the way of forensics evidence. He lifted prints, which he figured would turn out to belong to Rose, Favro, and Prudhomme. He examined all of the clothing in the room, but found no obvious signs that any of it had been worn in the woods. No leaf fragments. No dirt. No mud. Same with the shoes. They were freshly polished and showed no signs of mud or leaves or dirt. He bagged the whole lot anyway. There was no telling what would show up under a microscope.

There were several ways they could have pulled it off. There could have been a third cadet who drove the car back to West Point who was staying somewhere else. They could have also rented a car and driven it to West Point and back and turned it in. That no one had seen Rose and Favro leave their room didn't mean they hadn't been gone. It simply meant no one had *seen* them leaving or returning to the room. Kerry made a mental note to come back down to the Bound Brook area and canvas the car-rental places.

As for the lack of obvious forensics evidence, they could have dumped the clothes they wore. There was no way every gas-station Dumpster between West Point and Bound Brook could be checked in time. Some of them had probably already been picked up and their contents were on the way to a dump.

Kerry drove back to West Point with Rose and Favro in the back-seat. Ash followed him in Jacey's Miata. When they reached the Pro-vost Marshal's office, Lieutenant Colonel Percival was waiting for them. He was less than thrilled when he saw Rose and Favro get out of the backseat of the staff car, and when he saw Rose's bandaged face close up, he flew into a rage.

"What is the meaning of this, Kerry? What happened to this young man?"

"It's a long story, sir."

"No it isn't," said Rose. "Prudhomme assaulted us, sir. I want to press charges under the UCMJ. I asked Agent Kerry to arrest him, but he refused."

"These two are the ones I apprehended, sir," explained Kerry. "They are suspects in the assault on Jacey Slaight."

"What evidence do you have that these young men committed that crime?" asked Percival.

"I'm developing the evidence, sir. Some of it is circumstantial, and we've got a mountain of forensics stuff to go through."

"Did anyone see them? Were they identified by Miss Slaight?"

"No sir."

"Then I want to know why you apprehended them instead of Prudhomme. It seems to me that we have victims, physical evidence, and witnesses in the assault Mr. Rose claims Prudhomme committed."

"Sir, I don't have any doubt that Prudhomme assaulted these men. But it's not that clear-cut."

"What's the complication, Mr. Kerry? I want Prudhomme apprehended. Where is he?"

"Here on the post, sir. He followed us back from New Jersey."

"I want you to apprehend him, and I want these men released forthwith."

"Sir, I don't think that's such a good idea."

"I don't care what you think, Mr. Kerry." He turned to Rose and Favro. "You men are released. You are free to return to your barracks."

"What do I have to do to press charges against Prudhomme, sir?" asked Rose.

"Don't worry about it, Mr. Rose. I'll see to it that it's done." Percival signaled to an MP who was leaning against his squad car. "Give these men a ride back to the barracks, Sergeant."

"Yes sir," said the sergeant. Rose and Favro got in the squad car and he pulled away.

"I'll see you in my office, Kerry. Now."

Kerry left the evidence bags in the trunk of his car and followed Percival. In his office, Kerry stood at parade rest while Percival paced back and forth in front of his desk.

"Do you know what you've done? You apprehended the Chairman and the Vice Chairman of the Honor Committee! How is that going to look? What do you think General Gibson's going to say when he finds out how you treated Rose and Favro?"

"I really don't know, sir, and to be frank with you, I don't care. I don't work for General Gibson. I work for General Slaight. His daughter is lying up there in the hospital. Someone used a piece of wood to rape her. I think Rose is that someone, and I think Favro helped him. I'm going to pursue my investigation. If you try to stop me, I'll go over your head to Colonel Lombardi, and if I don't get satisfaction there, I will report to the Headquarters Building to General Slaight himself."

"Your career is over, Mr. Kerry. I will personally see to it that you are discharged for refusal of my orders, insubordination, and dereliction of duty."

"You are entitled to take whatever steps you feel are necessary against me, sir. But I'm going to tell you something right now, and I think you'd be well advised to listen to what I have to say. I know you've been making reports to General Gibson about the progress of my investigation into the death of Dorothy Hamner. If you in any way hinder my investigation from this point on, I will file a report on your activities that will go right up to the Secretary of the Army. You want to talk about careers being over? If I catch so much as a whiff of you getting in my way, you'll need a flashlight to find your ass when I get finished with you. Think it over, Colonel. I don't know what your deal is with Gibson, but whatever it is, it isn't going to save you from the load of shit I'll pile on your ass if you start playing patty-cake with him and I find out about it."

Percival had stopped pacing and was standing there staring at Kerry's back as he walked to the door. He stopped and turned around.

"You want Prudhomme apprehended, Colonel, do it yourself."

Kerry got in his staff car. There was an upside to the confrontation with Percival. He had released Rose and Favro. That was going to lift their spirits and give them a sense of invulnerability. He was pretty sure they wouldn't be rushing to the SJA to get themselves military counsel now. That meant they would rest on the alibi Favro had blurted out. They were at the motel together all night. If he shot a hole in that statement, one or the other of them would crack, probably Favro. It was obvious from the look on his face that he had no idea of the assault Rose had committed on Jacey until the very moment that Kerry had described the rape with a piece of wood. That meant there was already a split between them. All Kerry had to do was give Favro a reason to let the split widen and he would turn on Rose.

Things weren't going so badly. The attack on Jacey had raised the stakes. He liked it when the stakes went up. That meant some players were wont to fold their hands and get out of the game, and who would be there to help them lick their wounds and recover their losses?

Chief Warrant Officer Jim Kerry, the nicest guy in the world when he wanted to be.

BY THE time Ash reached Jacey's bedside in the hospital, she was reclining against a pillow eating Jell-O.

"How are you feeling, Jace?" he asked. He took her hand and kissed it.

Mrs. Slaight was sitting on the far side of Jacey's bed. "Ash. We've been worried about you."

"You didn't . . ." Jacey let her words trail away, unable to finish the sentence.

"Rose is a little worse for the wear, but he's back in the barracks. So is Favro. Kerry arrested them, but Percival let them go."

"Why?"

"I don't know. Kerry told me Percival blew his stack at him. He thinks the Chairman of the Honor Committee is a water-walker, I guess. Kerry said Percival was worried about what Gibson would do if Rose and Favro were under arrest."

"Gibson? How is he involved?"

"Kerry said Percival's been reporting to Gibson about the investigation into Dorothy's death."

Jacey looked over at her mother. "Mom, what do you think of General Gibson?"

Sam took a deep breath. "Your father is having a very hard time with him. General Gibson came to see him a little while ago. He objected to his cadets being questioned down at the Provost Marshal's office."

"That was when Kerry questioned them about having sex with Dorothy, wasn't it?" asked Jacey.

"I think so."

"Why would Gibson be upset about that?"

"Your father said Gibson told him he already knew what the cadets had done."

"What?"

"Your father got really mad that Gibson hadn't reported it to him."

"Mrs. Slaight, did Gibson give General Slaight an excuse? I mean, did he tell him why he hadn't reported the sexual encounter between those guys and Dorothy?"

"He said it wasn't a disciplinary offense because the sex was consensual."

"Which is what Rose and those guys told him," said Ash.

"Ash, do you know what this means? Gibson's taking their side."

"It looks that way."

"Gibson runs the Honor System, Ash. He's in with them."

There was a knock at the door. "Come in," called Mrs. Slaight.

A uniformed MP walked in. "Cadet Prudhomme, I've been ordered to pick you up and take you to the Provost Marshal's office. You'll have to come with me."

"What's this about?"

"You have been charged with assault and battery. You are under apprehension."

Ash looked down at Jacey. Color was coming back to her cheeks, and she managed a little smile. "Go on, Ash. I'll call Captain Patterson. He'll meet you down there."

"He's probably at the game."

"I've got his cell-phone number."

"I'll be back, Jace. Don't worry about me."

"I won't."

He leaned over and kissed her. He felt a handcuff as it snapped around his wrist.

"Is that really necessary, Sergeant?" asked Mrs. Slaight.

"Orders, ma'am."

The cuff snapped around his other wrist. As the MP led Ash from the room, he heard Jacey's mother. "It's a miracle they can teach cadets to march in a straight line," she said. "Everything else in this place is crooked."

KERRY REACHED the firebreak up in the hills behind Delafield Pond and was pleased to see that his MP squad had done their job. An area one hundred yards in diameter was cordoned off with yellow crime-scene tape. Two MPs stood guard where the tape crossed the road. They picked it up and let Kerry's staff car through. He parked down the hill from where he could see his guys working.

His main forensics tech was a retired sergeant who had spent twenty years in the Military Police. Along the way he had picked up a degree at John Jay College down in New York. After he retired, he had held down a forensics job for several years somewhere in Pennsylvania, but as he described it, he got an itch to be close to the action and applied for a CID position. He'd been at West Point for two years. The fact that he'd been an MP there ten years previously was a great help. He was familiar with the lay of the place, and he knew the Academy ropes. His name was Lester Carl, one of those funny southern handles that sounded like two first names.

Kerry called to him from the road. "Lester! Lead me down there, will you?"

"Walk between those pieces of tape, Jim," he called back.

Sure enough, Lester had made a walkway out of two lines of yellow tape. Kerry walked down the path to a point about ten feet from the tree where Jacey had been tied. "What have you got for me?"

Lester and the other guy, a young sergeant he was training, were both wearing white jumpsuits, surgical gloves, and fine-mesh hair nets. They had white plastic bags wrapped around their feet and tied off at midcalf. Lester walked over holding something in his hand.

"We've taken plaster casts of damn near every footprint out here. This one belongs to Jacey Slaight. See the outline of the female cadet shoe?"

"Yeah. How about the kids? You got theirs?"

"Sure do. The boy was wearing cross-trainers. Easy to identify. The girl was wearing pumps with a short heel. We've already picked up their shoes and checked them against our casts. We can easily eliminate the kids' and Jacey Slaight's."

"How many others are there?"

"Two. Both male. One was wearing some kind of sneaker. We got one really good cast with a spotless tread on it. We'll have the make and size nailed today. The other was wearing shoes with a smooth bottom. If you gave me a guess, I'd say they were boat shoes, you know, moccasins. Top-Siders, maybe some other brand of boat shoe. They're gonna be hard."

"Did you get a size on it?"

"Yeah. It's about a nine and a half, ten."

"What about fibers?"

"See all the fallen branches? The place is alive with them."

"How does it look?"

"We got the kids' clothes, so we can do those matches. Same with Jacey Slaight's. We recovered the blanket. It was still here."

"Let's have a look at it."

Lester signaled the sergeant and he carried it over. It was an Army-issue olive-drab woolen blanket, fairly new.

"We also picked up this." Lester removed an evidence bag that he had tied to his belt. He reached inside and pulled out a man's leather belt. "Eddie Bauer. It's embossed on the back side. Size thirty-two."

"Must be five thousand of them."

"Yeah, but it's a start."

"Any prints on it?"

"Not a one."

"So where do you think we stand, Lester?"

"Depends on what you came up with, Jim."

"We won't know for a few days. I didn't get any dirt or mud or leaves. We might pick up some microscopic shit, but I doubt it. It looks to me like they ditched everything."

"Smart little fuckers."

"I've got to get going. They're picking up Prudhomme, on Percival's orders. I want to be there when they haul him in."

"We're getting ready to wrap up here. I'll talk to you later."

"Sure thing, Lester." The crime scene would provide one source of forensic evidence. The suspects would hopefully provide the other. Criminal investigation was like an equation. The one side was supposed to match the other. When the two sources of evidence didn't provide a match, there were problems.

Kerry knew he had his work cut out for him, because he could already tell that nothing he had found in the New Jersey motel room was a match for what Lester had turned up.

He was at one of those points in a case when you begin to wonder if you shouldn't throw out the assumptions you've made and start over. As he took the turn at the bottom of the hill, he made up his mind.

Those smart little fuckers are going down.

CHAPTER 43

W HEN SLAIGHT took the call from Sam and learned that Percival had ordered the arrest of Prudhomme, he came close to
driving down to the Provost Marshal's office and ordering his release.
But that would be command influence, which would run the risk of
blowing the entire investigation, so he did what generals do when
confronted with the various events that by law they are prevented
from controlling. He sat in the chair behind his desk and steamed
with frustration. Then he picked up the phone, called Bassett, and
briefly explained what was going on. Bassett drove straight to his
office.

"I heard about Jacey. How is she?" he asked.

"She's pretty shaken up, but she's stable. I think she'll be okay."

Bassett sat down in a chair next to the desk. Out the window,
clouds were gathering up the Hudson. There would be a hard rain
within the hour.

"I want to know what I can do about Prudhomme, Cliff."

"Nothing right now. Let Patterson handle it. He's the best guy I've
got down there."

"I've got to wait until the Article Thirty-two?" he asked, referring
to the military version of a grand jury hearing.

"If it gets that far."

"And then I could throw out the charges."

"You could."

"That doesn't sound like a ringing endorsement."

"It's not. You've got to watch your step, Ry. Prudhomme is charged with assault and battery. If Percival can convince Lombardi, he might get him to throw 'intent to cause grievous bodily harm' in there. I understand he used a steering-wheel lock on one of them."

"Yeah. Prudhomme's from New Orleans. Jacey told me he grew up over a grocery in the French Quarter. I get the impression that his idea of a fair fight is one you win."

"The boy sounds like an infantryman to me."

Slaight laughed. "We ought to let him teach hand-to-hand combat, is what we ought to be doing, instead of charging him."

"One thing you can do is order him released from custody and returned to the barracks. That is entirely up to the commander. In the case of officers, they are never held in custody, and are usually remanded to their quarters. I'd take the position that cadets fall into that category."

"I'll do it."

"After you issue that order, I'd pull in my horns. Everyone's going to know Prudhomme went after Rose and Favro because of Jacey. That she is your daughter is the most complicating factor you face. There may come a time, if things get that far along, that you'll have to remove yourself from the case and turn it over to higher authority."

"That's what I was afraid of."

"Have you heard from Gibson?"

"No, and that seems a little strange, doesn't it? I would have thought that he'd be all over this thing by now."

"Gibson is probably on the phone to Percival right now."

AN ICY rain blew in sheets against the window of room 112 at the Seaside Inn. Helen Messick threw back the comforter and walked to the window. "Hear that? It's really blowing." She parted the curtain. "Jack, I can see waves coming over the road!"

General Gibson came up behind her and reached under her arms, pulling her against him. "It's nothing. Let's get back in bed."

"Wait. I see something." She pressed her face close to the glass, looking down the street. "It's a fire engine. There's a police car right behind it."

"Come on, Helen. We haven't got much time. I have to be at the Chancellor's house in a few hours for the reception."

There was a loud screech and the sound of somebody testing a microphone. "Attention. This is the Seaside Fire Department. A mandatory evacuation has been ordered for all dwellings along Ocean Avenue. You have ten minutes to gather important papers and belongings and vacate. I say again. This is a mandatory evacuation order. You have ten minutes to vacate. A temporary shelter has been established at the Benjamin Franklin Junior High School on Pelican Avenue. Police Department personnel will conduct house-to-house inspections enforcing the evacuation. Get your belongings and move out."

"Jack, that's us," said Helen, pulling his hands from her breasts. She closed the curtain and turned to face him.

"You think I drove all the way down here from Rutgers for nothing? This is bullshit. Come on. Get back in bed. I feel good today. We pounded Rutgers's ass."

"Jack, they'll be knocking on doors. We've got to get dressed and get out of here. You saw those waves! They're swamping the street!"

"Fuck the waves."

"Jack, be reasonable." She leaned down, reaching for her panties.

"We've got time. I need you."

She pulled her panties on and looked next to the bed for her hose. "You're crazy. You don't need me as bad as you need to get out of here. If the police come in here and find you undressed . . ."

"Fuck them."

"You fuck them, Jack, 'cause you're not fucking me today. I'm getting out of here." She slipped her dress over her head and stepped into her shoes. She switched on the table lamp, looking for her purse. He was sitting on the bed, naked. "I'm getting the car, Jack. Get dressed."

He stood up. "What are you? Eager to get back to your husband and that queer boyfriend of his?"

"I don't know what I'm doing here with you. This is crazy."

"You want a real man. What's so crazy about that?"

She had her car keys in her hand. "I'm serious, Jack. Get dressed. I'm ready to leave."

"Are you threatening to leave me here?"

"What's wrong with you? Can't you see we're in danger? There's a storm out there!"

"Danger? You don't know the definition of the word." He put on his shorts and his shirt and stepped into his pants. He sat down to put on his shoes. "The problem with you is, you're forgetting what I told you about our arrangement. You come when I call. You do what I say, or your little world is going to come crashing down around you."

He was pulling on his coat when she threw the chain on the door. The nor'easter bearing down on the coast of New Jersey blew her purse off her shoulder, and a lamp crashed to the floor behind her. The tall spruce at the corner snapped at the base of its trunk, falling across power lines, sending a shower of sparks into the air.

He pushed her out the door into the driving rain. She opened the driver's door and got behind the wheel. He slid in beside her and grabbed her hand. "I'm just going to say this once. Move over. I'm driving. You're going to suck my big cock."

CAPTAIN PATTERSON was following standard defense tactics when he counseled Ash not to respond to Lieutenant Colonel Percival's questions. What he had not anticipated was the Provost Marshal's reaction.

"I will be making a report to Colonel Lombardi about your performance today, Captain Patterson. You might consider that you will still be an Army officer when the Prudhomme matter is disposed of."

"Are you threatening me, sir?" asked Patterson, trying not to show his astonishment.

"Let's just say I'm reminding you that as a captain, you have quite a few years to go before qualifying for retirement."

"I am well aware of my date of rank, sir."

"Then we understand each other perfectly."

"No, we do not, sir. You have attempted to intimidate me into encouraging Mr. Prudhomme to cooperate in his own prosecution.

Make whatever reports you want, Colonel Percival. I categorically reject your threat."

"I have not threatened you, Captain."

Patterson reached for his overcoat and hat. "Our business is finished, Colonel Percival. Good afternoon, sir."

On his way back to Building 606, Patterson ran into Colonel Bassett coming out of the Headquarters Building. He told Patterson about Percival's threat and was surprised when he laughed.

"Percival is a cop. He doesn't give a damn about your client's rights except as they interfere with his vain attempts to ingratiate himself with General Gibson. Percival is attempting to shield Gibson's pet cadet from prosecution. Sadly, Mr. Prudhomme has presented him with a wonderful opportunity to do so." Bassett buttoned the top button on his overcoat and turned up his collar against the wind coming off the Hudson. "Let's get upstairs, Harper. I'll teach you what little I know about criminal-defense strategy."

A few minutes later they were seated in Bassett's office. Late on the Saturday afternoon of the Rutgers game, the department was deserted. Bassett opened one of the drawers in his desk and withdrew a bottle of Scotch. He found two coffee cups, blew the dust out of them, poured a healthy shot in each.

"Percival made a crucial and rather silly error early this afternoon. He removed Chief Warrant Officer Kerry from the Prudhomme case. That means you can interview Kerry and get access to everything he's developed against Rose."

"Are you suggesting I use a diminished-capacity defense, sir?"

"No, such a defense won't provide you with much of an advantage before a military court."

"But Prudhomme's motive is obvious, sir. We won't even be able to contest it. Both Favro and Rose will ID him. I'm certain Prudhomme's prints are on the steering-wheel lock he used on Favro. I'm going to need a defense that mitigates his motive and gives the jury a reason to identify with him."

"I'm not talking about the facts of the case, Harper. They're against you. We agree on that. I'm talking about throwing the facts away and putting the victims on trial. Did you sleep through Cochran's masterful defense of O. J.? You can't expect to go in there and try a case like you've got and win. You've got to attack. And attack. And attack again.''

"I think I get you, sir. Kerry arrested Rose and Favro. Percival let them go and arrested Prudhomme for assaulting Rose. He's not after Prudhomme as much as he's covering for Rose.''

"Music to my ears, Harper. Pour us each another shot.''

"I believe I will, sir." Patterson tipped the bottle of Scotch, and Bassett raised his cup in a toast.

"I am pleased to see that New York University hasn't thrown its criminal-law courses away in favor of workshops on how to do the paperwork on a leveraged buyout.''

Patterson laughed. "Prudhomme says Rose did it. He told me Rose admitted as much, under a measure of duress, I would allow.''

"You're learning, Harper. There are times when motive works against you, and there are times when motive works for you. I hold that this is a case of the latter.''

"So you're saying we help Kerry get Rose, and Prudhomme goes free.''

"Harper, I feel comfortable alleging that it would not be possible to find a military jury on this planet that would convict Prudhomme of beating the living shit out of his girlfriend's rapist.''

"All of which assumes that Rose is indeed guilty of the attack on Jacey Slaight.''

"Prudhomme seems comfortable with that scenario.''

"It's a big risk, sir.''

"The risk is Prudhomme's. Perhaps the decision about how to proceed with his defense ought to be his as well. I suggest you present him with your theory and see how he reacts.''

"I'm not sure defense theories go over too well when you're in the post detention cell, sir.''

"He won't be there for long. General Slaight is going to release him about an hour from now. He will be returned to the barracks under room arrest pending trial.''

"That leaves us with the problem of timing. We are gambling that they will arrest Rose before Prudhomme is court-martialed.''

"What have you been taught concerning criminal procedure, Harper? From the standpoint of the defense, that is.''

"Throw down a basic load of defensive firepower. Delay. Evade.

Request investigative resources. Demand the right to travel to interview character witnesses."

"And when you are denied?"

"Heat up the keyboard and file appeals."

"You can tie up Percival and his prosecutor for months with a little imagination."

"Sir, I'm glad you recruited me to come back here and teach law. It's a little like clerking for a good judge."

"I will take that as a compliment, Harper."

"It was intended that way, sir."

"Bottoms up. I am hearing the distant call of a hot meal and a decent bottle of red."

Patterson laughed out loud. Outside of the tiny community of law professors at West Point, who in the world could have known that guys like T. Clifford Bassett still strode the earth? He was a dinosaur, huge and omnivorous and nearly extinct, and Patterson relished every moment he spent roaming the wilds of the law with him.

CHAPTER 44

A FTER HER emergency-room shift was over Saturday evening, Major Vernon went home, fixed a frozen pizza, and got some much-needed sleep. She returned to the hospital on Sunday morning to check on the tests she had ordered. Jacey's X rays were negative. Her blood work showed an elevated white-cell count, but that was to be expected. Her vital signs had returned to normal, and Mrs. Slaight reported that she had slept most of the night. Jacey's roommate and several other cadets from her company showed up to see her, but Major Vernon sent them away. She didn't want Jacey facing the kinds of questions her friends were likely to ask until later.

When she returned that evening, she found Jacey's father sitting alone in the room. General Slaight nodded toward the bathroom. "First time on her own. She's much improved, doc." The bathroom door opened and Jacey came out tying her hospital bathrobe.

"You're looking better, Jacey," said Major Vernon.

Jacey made her way slowly to the bed and her father helped her lie down. "I'm pretty sore, but I guess that comes with the territory."

Major Vernon took her pulse and listened to her heart and lungs. "Did you eat anything?"

"A little. It hurts to swallow."

"You've got some cramping in the stomach muscles. It'll go away pretty soon."

"I'm hungry, but I just can't eat."

"Hunger's a good sign. It means your adrenaline is leveling out."

"I don't want morphine. I'm starting to like it."

"It's like expensive wine, Jace," Slaight teased. "You've got to avoid the good stuff, or you'll develop a taste for it."

"I'll give you some Lorcet. It's effective and there are few side effects."

The bedside phone rang and Slaight answered. He listened for a moment, said, "Right, thanks," and hung up. He kissed his daughter and held her hand. "I'm going to have to leave you two alone for a while. They need me down at Headquarters. I'll bring your mother with me when I come back, Jace."

"Okay, Daddy."

He flipped his thumb, signaling Major Vernon to follow him outside. "Stay with her until I return, will you?"

"I'll be glad to, sir."

When she went back into the room, Jacey was bending her left knee. The look on her face said it was a struggle. "How long am I going to feel like this, doctor?"

Major Vernon sat down next to the bed. "Maybe now's a good time to talk, Jacey. Are you up to it?"

"Kind of."

"Why don't you start by telling me how you feel?"

"Sore. Everything aches. Like my knee feels like there's this weight holding it down."

"I understand that you're in pain. I was asking how you feel inside. You've been through something no one should have to experience. Can you tell me how you feel about it?"

Jacey's eyes wandered, finally settling on the television, which was showing CNN with the sound off. She was holding her sheet in one hand and twisting it with the other. "I guess I just can't believe it happened to me. I mean, you're not *ready*, you know?"

"No one is. It's not part of the curriculum."

Jacey stayed focused on the TV. "It's not like I'm suffering. I just feel so humiliated. I can't get the thought out of my mind that he did this to me. I can see his eyes. He's watching me, and I can't stop him."

"You're talking about helplessness."

"Worse. It's like I'm a little girl, and my mother's telling me to hold on to her hand, and I'm letting go and running away from her, and all of a sudden I can't see her and I'm scared and all I can think of is, I should have listened to her. I should have minded her. I should have been *nice.*"

"Are you thinking that there was something you could have done?"

"Not really." She let go of the sheet and pressed it smooth with her open palm. "It's like, violence is a bargain, it's always on sale, and West Point is Wal-Mart. What did I expect? Sorority teas and lawn parties? I mean, I'm a *customer.*"

"Guilt is a natural thing, Jacey. It's a warning mechanism. You feel guilty because your body is telling you to."

When Jacey dropped her eyes from the television, they had filled with tears. "I don't want anyone to see me like this."

Major Vernon took her hand. "Like what?"

She pulled her hand away. It was shaking. "Like *this.*" She threw back the sheet, exposing herself.

Gently, Major Vernon touched Jacey's shoulder. "Tell me what you see."

"I couldn't wipe myself. I couldn't look at myself in the mirror."

"Tell me why."

"Why? You're asking me *why?*"

"You're asking yourself, Jacey. It's like breathing. You take air in, and you exhale. Ask and answer. Ask and answer. In and out. In and out. Doubt is part of life's rhythm."

"I don't have any doubts. All I have is hate."

"Who do you hate, Jacey?"

"I hate my arm. I hate my stomach. I hate my knee. I hate my ribs. I hate my . . . vagina."

"Ask it. Do I hate myself?" She moved her hand from Jacey's shoulder to her wrist. Gently, she lifted Jacey's wrist and placed her hand on her thickly bandaged ribs.

Jacey looked down. Her fingers were bony, splayed like the rays in a child's drawing of the sun. She closed her fingers, feeling the coarse threads of her bandage. She watched, as if a spectator at a sporting event, as her other hand moved slowly from the mattress to the other side of her body, finding her rib cage. Her hands moved together, coming to rest on her sternum. She turned her head and found Major Vernon's eyes with hers. "I used to lie in bed at night when I was a kid, tapping my ribs with my fingers, counting one, two, three, four, five, over and over until I fell asleep. I can remember it like it was yesterday."

"It *was* yesterday. I came in here last night, and you were lying in this bed just as you are right now, sleeping. You are the same person you were, Jacey. You have your mother and your father and you have your friends and you have your life."

"Am I being ridiculous?"

"You are being yourself. All you have to do is heal and you'll get to know yourself again. I think you'll probably be surprised."

"At what?"

"How easy it is to love someone you've been with all of your life."

Jacey looked at her hands. She reached down and touched her thigh. A clear fluid leaked from her bandage. She lifted her finger and touched it to her tongue. It was salty. There was no pain, only the intimacy of self.

CHAPTER 45

BY THE time they released Jacey from the hospital on Wednesday, the entire Corps of Cadets knew about the events of Rutgers weekend and people were taking sides. While it surprised Jacey, it was no shock to Ash when they found out how many cadets, especially those in the Second and Fourth Regiments, had lined up behind Rose. Few of them were female, but support for Rose cut across class lines and included most of the firsties who lived in the north end of the barracks. Jacey at first wrote it off to sexism and the typical cadet tendency to follow the herd, but Ash felt differently. As Chairman of the Honor Committee, Rose had power. Cadets were in awe of the kind of power that carried Rose almost daily to the office of the Commandant of Cadets for one-on-one meetings. Ever since they were plebes, all cadets had been inculcated with respect for the Honor Code and those who administered it. Rose was their man. Guys in his company spread the word that Jacey had pissed off some punks in Newburgh in a traffic incident, and they taught her a lesson. Prudhomme was a pussy-whipped little fool. He was covering up for Jacey's misdeeds by attacking the Honor Chairman. The strength of the rumor campaign was remarkable. By the end of the week, Jacey swore to Belle that she could see people in their own battalion whispering at their mess hall tables when she walked by.

Belle told her she was crazy, but it was the truth. People in the Third Regiment had been gotten to. A friend of Belle's on the volleyball team who was from the Fourth Regiment told her that Rose was using the Honor reps to spread the rumors. Ash was friends with the rep from Belle's friend's company, and he called him to check out what Belle had heard. When the rep heard Ash's voice, he mumbled something about a Chess Club meeting and hung up.

Agent Kerry meanwhile was hitting dead-ends like they were lane reflectors on a highway. His microscopic examination of the clothes and shoes seized from the motel room produced nothing. The footprint casts didn't match any of the shoes belonging to either Rose or Favro. He tried a half-dozen Eddie Bauer stores within a hundred-mile radius of West Point, and no one recognized photographs of Rose or Favro. He tested the trunk of Rose's car for fiber and hair evidence, and found nothing that matched Jacey's uniform or the blanket that had been thrown over her. He was about to give up on the physical evidence when something caught his eye. He brushed past the olive-drab blanket and knocked it off the top of his filing cabinet. When he reached down to pick it up, he noticed that a triangular wedge had been torn from one edge of the blanket. On a hunch, he put the tear under the microscope. There was a tiny sliver of steel imbedded in the wool. He removed it with fine tweezers and isolated it on a slide. It was crescent-shaped and razor sharp. It reminded him of something, but he couldn't quite put his finger on it. It wasn't until the next day when his car failed to start and he lifted the hood that it came to him. He was checking the bolts on the battery-cable connectors when he felt a sharp pain in his thumb. He stepped back into the sun. A tiny piece of flashing from the end of one of the quarter-inch bolts was stuck in the soft, fleshy part of his thumb. When he got to the office, he took it upstairs and slipped it onto the slide next to the piece of metal from the blanket. They were almost exactly the same. Somewhere there was a triangular wedge of olive-drab blanket stuck to a quarter-inch bolt in a car trunk. He went back down to the parking lot and checked the trunk of his own car. It was probably one of the bolts that held the taillight assemblies in place. In his car, they were out of sight, tucked under the curve of the rear fenders, almost impossible to reach without a socket on a four-inch extender. If the car that carried Jacey up into the woods behind Delafield was anything like Kerry's, the little piece of fabric was probably still there.

It was literally a thin scrap of evidence to hang his hopes on, but it was all he had. Kerry took off and drove down to New Jersey, where he started canvassing the rental-car agencies around Bound Brook. By that afternoon, he had covered Piscataway, Middlesex, and Edison. He spent the next day working the area around Rutgers: New Brunswick, North Brunswick, Somerset, Highland Park. No one recognized the photographs of Rose and Favro. Most of the agencies let him check their records, and that didn't turn up anything either.

When Kerry drove back to West Point, his spirits were at an all-time low. He had a meeting with Captain Patterson scheduled for the next morning. There was nothing new to give him, other than a promise that he would keep looking.

ROSE HAD removed his bandages and wore the stitches in his face like a badge of honor. Guys he didn't even know came up and high-fived him. The plebes in his company paid him the singular cadet honor of short-sheeting his bed, and one morning made a production of presenting him with breakfast in bed on a silver tray they had pilfered from the mess hall. The members of the Honor Committee froze Prudhomme out of their meetings. Rose spent the better part of one day going through the regulations on Honor Committee procedure, trying to see if there was a way they could vote Prudhomme off the committee. There wasn't. He had to be voted off by his own classmates in his own company, and that was unlikely, given the fact it was also Jacey Slaight's company, and a vote against Prudhomme would be seen as a vote against her as well.

Rose felt especially gratified that Prudhomme's attack on him had derailed Kerry's investigation of the Monday-night theft of the E-mail disks. He knew he was vulnerable if Kerry kept after him. He had no alibi for the seven-to-eight-o'clock hour. Everyone seemed to have forgotten that Monday-night football was early that week due to a West Coast game. Nearly the whole company was downstairs in the TV room watching the game, which had made it easy to slip into Jacey's room, get the disks, and get out without being seen. He had seen one plebe coming out of the sinks when he was turning down the stairs, but it didn't look as if the plebe saw him. He had worn his white parade gloves while he was in her room, so he knew he hadn't left any prints.

The really delicious thing was, it looked like the whole Dorothy Hamner thing was being shoved on a back burner while Percival worked up his case against Prudhomme. He had set out to put the fear of God in Jacey Slaight, and the way things were turning out, he had succeeded beyond his wildest imaginings.

Favro was his only worry. He had avoided Rose ever since they were released from custody at the Provost Marshal's office. It was starting to look bad. Prudhomme had attacked both of them. Favro should have been basking in the support they were getting. Instead, he spent most of his free time in his room. Rose stopped by one night to ask him if he wanted to go to a movie. They were playing one of the *Lethal Weapon* movies, perennial cadet favorites. The theater would be packed. Some of the guys on the Honor Committee had suggested they show up at the movie. They promised to start an ovation when they came in. It would look great, a show of solidarity against that animal Prudhomme. But Favro wouldn't go. Rose asked him what was up. Favro just shrugged and told him he still felt a little dizzy from the concussion. Rose pegged that as top-grade bullshit. Favro didn't like what he had heard on the grapevine about Jacey Slaight getting raped. Rose thought about telling him to grow the fuck up, but he decided against it. Favro would either come around by the time Prudhomme was court-martialed, or Rose would remind him of that night at the lake with Dorothy Hamner and the role he had played. That would straighten him out.

Gibson was playing it very, very cool. They continued their Honor Code meetings every other day or so. Gibson never breathed a word to Rose about Jacey Slaight or Prudhomme or Dorothy Hamner. They were like two eagles soaring above the rest of the Academy on a warm current of clear air, free from the niggling worries and scrambling below them. Rose had learned a lot from Gibson over the last couple of years, but now he was learning something he would never have guessed in a million years. If you treat problems the right way they turn into opportunities. It was as if he and Gibson were being rewarded for keeping focused and calm in the face of adversity. Gibson had once warned him that the way of a warrior was a treacherous path only a few could negotiate without fear. That was where dignity and honor came from. You did what you had to do. Gibson said consequences were an empty scabbard. Your will, honed to a razor edge, was your sword.

CHAPTER 46

SAM HAD watched with amazement as Jacey recovered so quickly from what must have been an experience beyond any terror Sam could imagine. As a little girl Jacey used to climb trees and ride her bike along narrow trails in the woods, and during the winters when there was snow she would drag her little sled to the top of the highest hill she could find, come rocketing down, wreck the thing in a snowbank, and get up and do it over again. Her legs were always black and blue, and Sam couldn't recall a time when she didn't have a cut or a scrape bandaged somewhere on her little body.

Now she had rebounded from the kidnapping like it was a fall from a tree, or a spill on her bike. Sam didn't know whether to be proud of her or frightened that she seemed not to have absorbed the lesson a close call was supposed to teach you. Jacey seemed more worried about the charges Ash faced than her own injuries. Sam paid a visit to Major Vernon, who had continued to see Jacey throughout her stay in the hospital despite the fact that she wasn't her primary physician. Major Vernon explained that some young women react to trauma as if charged by it, and Jacey seemed to be one of them. She warned Sam to be on the lookout for a delayed reaction like depression, but also told her that Jacey might not suffer such a reaction at all. People were different, she said, and female cadets were sometimes in a class all by themselves.

The best thing to do, Major Vernon said, was to get back to the normal rhythms of life while keeping a quiet watch on Jacey. So Sam jumped back into the swing of Academy life. She and Ry had a reception planned for the Academic Board. The entire staff and faculty would be invited to Quarters 100 for cocktails. It was the biggest party they had planned to give yet, and it took quite a bit of organizing to get everything lined up.

It was the middle of the afternoon and she was in her study, sketching the way she wanted the buffet table arranged in the dining room, when she heard a knock at the back door. Standing outside on the back porch was Helen Messick. The strange thing was, it was a mild, cloudy day, but Helen was wearing dark glasses and a long winter overcoat, and she had a scarf wrapped around her head. Sam opened the door.

"Can I come in?"

"Sure, Helen."

She walked into the breakfast room. "I hope I'm not interrupting anything."

"Don't worry. I was just puttering around here. There's always something I've got to catch up on."

"I have to talk to you, Sam. Is there someplace we can go? Someplace private?"

"Of course." Sam led the way to her office and closed the door behind her. "This is my little sanctuary."

Helen looked around. "It's nice, Sam. It feels like you."

"Have a seat."

Helen sat down on the love seat and removed her glasses and scarf. Sam sat down in the wing-backed chair across from her.

"I'm leaving for my mother's today. I'll be gone for a while, Sam. I may not be coming back."

Sam knew she was building up to something, so she sat there listening and let her take her time.

She unbuttoned the long winter overcoat. She was wearing a simple blouse and a pair of black pants. "I wanted you to know, Sam. I felt like I had to tell you." She was holding the scarf in her lap. She folded it in half and then unfolded it, and then folded it again. "I've got to get out of here. Does this place get to you, Sam?"

"Sure it does. West Point can seem like a beautiful prison at times."

"I heard about your daughter. I'm so sorry for her. It must have been terrifying."

"It was, but she seems to be doing better every day."

"I've got something to tell you. I should have told you before, but I was afraid. It's so stupid, the way I was acting." She paused, looking beyond Sam out the window. Her lower lip quivered. She started to say something and stopped. Then it burst out of her. "I know who did that to your daughter." She started to sob, covering her face with the scarf.

Sam sat forward and reached for her hand. Helen's sobs came faster, and her hands began to shake. Sam moved next to her on the love seat and held her as she shook, crying uncontrollably. "Can I get you some water?"

"N-n-no." Her shoulders stopped shaking, and she dropped her hands to her lap. Her face was red, and only now did Sam notice that she wasn't wearing makeup. "I am so, so sorry. I don't know how to tell you how ashamed of myself I am."

"It's okay."

A couple of little sobs escaped from her, and she paused, taking deep breaths. "This is so hard."

"Helen, take your time."

"Ry probably told you that I have been seeing Jack Gibson. It was a couple of nights ago. He went to some kind of conference in Albany and called me and I drove up there. I was going to tell him it was over, that I didn't want to see him anymore, and then I was going to drive back. That was my plan."

She wiped her eyes with the scarf. "Can I get that glass of water, Sam?"

"Sure." She poured a glass of water, and Helen took small sips. It seemed to settle her.

"I told him what I came to tell him, and he flew into a rage. He was insane. He started threatening me, threatening my husband. He said he'd destroy his career. I got mad, and I told him I didn't care about my husband's damn career. That was when he started screaming about your daughter." Her eyes filled with tears and Sam reached for the Kleenex. She handed her some tissues, and Helen blew her nose. Her eyes were bloodshot, and she looked at Sam pleadingly.

"I've been such a fool."

"Helen, there is nothing you could tell me that would make me feel worse than how I felt when I saw Jacey. It's over. Both of us have healed. I know that people make mistakes. I've made my fair share over the years."

Helen reached for her hand. "It was so awful. He asked me if I wanted what Jacey got. I couldn't believe what I was hearing. He said your daughter was no better than a cur, and then he laughed, and he said Rose hog-tied her and whipped her like a bitch dog."

Sam gasped in horror. "Oh my god. Oh my god. What kind of a man is he?"

"He's not a man, don't you see? That's why I had to come here and tell you!"

Sam stood. "I'm afraid Ry is going to kill him."

"There's more, Sam."

"More? More?"

"He's laying some kind of trap for Ry. He was down in Washington, meeting with Congressman Thrunstone. He bragged that he had given Thrunstone the dirt on Slaight. He said the committee is going to put him under oath and expose West Point's weakness. They're going to call for his resignation. He said it will be all over the television news, and Meuller won't have any choice but to force him out." She looked up at Sam, tears running down her cheeks. "I was with him in Washington, Sam. I did this to myself. I walked into it with my eyes open, and I'm going to end up paying the price for my recklessness. But you have suffered enough. Jacey, that poor child . . ." She started sobbing again. Sam let her cry. Finally Helen looked up. "I have destroyed everything that was dear to me. He's going to hurt you and your family. You've got to stop him."

"I want you to talk to Ry. Tell him what you've told me. I'll talk to him first. I promise he won't get mad. You're a victim, Helen. He will see that. Will you do it?''

Helen nodded yes.

Sam picked up the phone and dialed the Superintendent's private line. "Ry, I want you to drop everything and come home at once. I've found out who attacked Jacey.''

SLAIGHT SAT next to her as Helen Messick told him everything she had just told Sam. He listened with an icy calm that made words gush out of her in a torrent. When she was finished, he left the room silently. Helen looked desperate. She was still fidgeting nervously when he returned carrying a tray with three glasses. He handed one to her and said a single word: "Vodka." He handed the other glass to Sam and the three of them sat in her study sipping the chilled vodka for several moments before he spoke again.

"You said you are going to your mother's. Where does she live?"

"Alabama."

"You may have to come back, Helen. We may need you."

"I don't know if I could do it."

"Helen, this is an Army post. This is federal land. Any crime committed on this land is a federal crime. You can be subpoenaed across state and national boundaries to testify in a federal criminal proceeding, which is what's going to come out of this."

"I'm scared of him, Ry! You should be, too! He's out to destroy you!"

"Do you want him to harm anyone else?"

"N-no."

"You'll be protected. I'll see to that personally."

"He's a dangerous man. You have no idea how evil he is."

"It's over, Helen. He's going to bring himself down. All I'm going to do is make it easy for him."

"What will she have to do, Ry?" asked Sam.

"She'll have to give a statement to the Agent in Charge, Chief Warrant Officer Kerry. She'll probably be subpoenaed to appear at an Article Thirty-two hearing."

"You can do that, Helen," Sam said encouragingly.

"I'll try."

"What about Dick? Does he know you're here?"

"No."

"Are you going to tell him?"

"There isn't much left of our relationship. It's probably better if I do what I have to do and leave for my mother's, and you have someone else tell him."

"It's going to turn into a huge scandal, isn't it, Ry?" asked Sam.

"I don't know yet. I don't know if we're going to get enough on Gibson to charge him with anything. He'll deny he ever said anything about Rose. It's Helen's word against his, and I'm not positive about the law, but I'm fairly certain anything he said to Helen is hearsay. If it's hearsay, it's not admissible in a trial."

"What about this monster, Rose?" Sam pronounced his name like it hurt to say it.

"Kerry hasn't got much. This is going to help, though. There may be some way Kerry can turn the other cadet against him. We'll have to see."

"Even if he does, Jacey said the other one left before Rose started in on her. There was no witness."

"You're right about that. I'm going to talk with Bassett when I leave here. I'm thinking about taking the whole thing away from Lombardi and Percival and letting Bassett handle it. If there's a clean way to get that kid, Bassett will find it."

Sam touched Helen lightly on the arm. "Where are you going when you leave here?"

"I don't know. I don't feel like I can go home. What there is left between Dick and me is complicated, but I have betrayed him, and I don't think I can face him right now."

"I'll have Melissa, my secretary, drive you down to Westchester

County for a few days," said Slaight. "We'll put you up in a hotel in Tarrytown or Dobbs Ferry until you've completed what you have to do here. We'll arrange for your airfare to your mother's."

"I hope you can forgive me, Ry. I can't tell you how badly I feel about Jacey."

"What happened to Jacey is not your fault. Both Sam and I understand what you've gone through. Life can be tough on you, Helen. You get to be our age, and you think the world should have somehow turned into a softer place. Then you wake up one morning and you see that the years haven't worn any of the edges off. It's still a big, bad world out there, but we've all got to live in it. The thing about Jacey that just amazes me is that somehow, she knows it already, and still she's hanging in there. She's a piece of work, just like her mother."

Helen drank the last of her vodka and put her glass down. "I appreciate what you're doing for me, Ry. You didn't have to, and I wouldn't have blamed you if you just threw me to the wolves."

"The first job I have is to protect my people, and I haven't been doing it too well so far. I don't want anyone else hurt on this Army post." He stood up and shook her hand. "I've got some calls to make. You stay put. Melissa will be over here shortly, and she'll take you where you've got to go."

"Thank you, Ry."

Sam followed him into the kitchen. He was standing at the sink, washing his glass. "What do you think our chances are with Gibson?"

"Fair."

"What about the hearing?"

"I can't worry about that. It's the other stuff that troubles me. Gibson is not going to make any more mistakes. When he finds out Helen is missing in action, he'll go into deep-bunker mode and batten down the hatches. He'll call in every IOU he's got. This is going to be like a Mafia war, his family against our family."

"Well, at least we're in the right."

"That and a token will get you a subway ride."

Sam didn't laugh. "I'm nervous, Ry. How is this going to affect Jacey?"

"It's already affecting her. The goddamned cadets are picking sides and I've heard Rose is winning that battle. Jacey is going to be smack in the middle of this whirlwind no matter what we do. She'll just have to ride it out, Sam. We can help her. We can love her, and we can pray for her, and we can give her all of the things that parents can give a daughter. But she's not a child anymore. At the end of the day, she is out there on her own."

"That's what scares me. Look what happened to her, being on her own."

"Gibson's not the only one who isn't going to make any more mistakes, Sam. That's one of the things about growing up. You learn to watch your back. A little paranoia will serve her well."

"I love her so much, Ry. I wish I could take her place. It's so sad to watch her innocence stripped away."

He hugged his wife close and whispered in her ear, "Our daughter was never innocent. She's a Slaight."

CHAPTER 48

THERE WERE two things holding Jacey together. One was the support she got from other female cadets, but the support she got from Ash was far more important. Patterson told him he was facing ten years in the Fort Leavenworth Disciplinary Barracks for his assault on Rose and Favro. Beating the shit out of Rose was the lesser of his worries. Using the steering-wheel lock on Favro had gotten him charged with assault with intent to cause grievous bodily harm. His prints were on the red plastic cover of the lock, and Favro had signed a statement identifying him as the person who assaulted him.

Ash seemed unconcerned about the charges. Even though he was supposed to be confined to his room when not going to class or attending to official duties, Ash spent every moment he could with Jacey and insisted on sleeping on a pallet at the foot of her bed every night, which also broke the rules. Patterson warned him that violating his confinement could send him back to a holding cell, but Ash ignored his entreaties.

Jacey had been back in the barracks for only a few days. Her wounds still ached, and the painkiller she was taking made her sleepy. It was an hour past taps. Jacey was asleep in her bed. Belle was studying at her desk, and Ash was reclining on Belle's bed, reading by the light from Belle's desk lamp. There was a knock at the door. Ash jumped from the bed and ran to the door.

"Who's there?"

"You don't know me," came a young woman's voice. "My name is Debbie Edwards. Can I come in, please? It's important that I speak with Jacey Slaight."

Ash unlocked her door. She was thin and dark-haired, wearing a hooded sweat jacket. "Come in," he said, checking up and down the hall. He saw no one. "Jacey's asleep. What's this about?"

She stood nervously in the semidarkness. "I'm in Company E-Four, over in the Fourth Regiment."

Belle walked over to get a better look at her. "Aren't you on the women's pistol team?"

"Yes, I am."

"I watched you shoot a match last year. You're good."

"Thanks."

"What's the story?" Ash asked her. "You're not out for a stroll at this hour."

"No, I'm not." She glanced nervously around the room before she spoke. "Can you wake up Jacey? I want her to hear what I've got to say."

"This had better not be a load of bullshit," said Ash. "She's not feeling too well."

"It's important. Really."

Ash gently shook Jacey's shoulder. She blinked, rubbing her eyes. "What's going on?"

"There's someone here to see you," Ash whispered.

"Who is it?"

"I don't know her."

Jacey got out of bed, and Belle helped her into her bathrobe. "I'm Jacey," she said, introducing herself to the stranger.

"I'm Debbie Edwards. Everybody's talking about what happened. I want you to know that women in the Fourth Regiment are behind you all the way. The guys who did it . . . they're shit."

"Thanks," said Jacey.

"I heard one of them was Favro."

"We can't prove it yet."

"What do you know about Favro?" Ash asked.

"I . . . I . . ."

"If you know something, spit it out."

"Give her a chance," said Jacey.

"I went out with him a few times. Then one night he dosed me with this." She took a small vial from her pocket and handed it to Jacey. "They call it fX, Cherry Bomb, Liquid Rush. It knocks you out if you take too much. That's what he did to me."

"Wait. Back up. You'd better tell me how this happened."

There was sadness in her eyes. "Favro is like this gorgeous *creature*. Every girl in the Fourth Regiment would *die* to get him. So one day after class, I'm walking back to the barracks and he falls in next to me and he asks me out. Just like that."

"What happened next?"

"We went out a few times. You know, a movie here on the Post, down to Highland Falls for lunch on a Sunday. I started seeing him around. He'd stop by my table in the mess hall and walk me back from dinner."

"When was this?"

"Last May."

"Did you go out with him again?"

"That's what I'm getting to. One night we're walking back from dinner and he tells me there's going to be this party, and he wants me to go. It was going to be up near Kingston. They were taking rooms in this motel and it was going to be, like, an open house. I said yes. That's where he dosed me."

"Was Rose there?" asked Ash.

"Yes. It was him and Favro and some other guys I didn't know. They all had dates."

Jacey held the vial under the desk lamp and opened it. "It looks like water."

"They sell it at a disco up in Newburgh right out in the open, 'cause it's legal. It's got no odor, no taste. It *is* just like water."

"How did he do it to you?"

"I wasn't drinking. I think he put it in a bottle of Evian. The next thing I knew, I was like, out there. It makes you lose your mind." Her voice turned to a whisper. "I mean, you'll do stuff you would never think of doing . . ." She was zipping and unzipping her jacket, up and down, up and down.

Jacey gave the vial another sniff and put the cap back on. "I'll bet this is what they gave Dorothy."

"That's why I had to see you. They think it's funny. They dose a girl and then they fool around with her. It's a big yuk. You've got to stop them."

"What happened after the party?"

"I was so crazy for him, even though I knew he gave that stuff to me, I was like going to forgive him and stuff, but it was like, he'd had his fun. He stopped calling me. I sent him E-mail a few times, but he never E-mailed me back."

"And you never told anybody?"

"I told him. I went to his room one night, and I told him it was wrong, what he did. I said I was going to my Tac. He just laughed. He said he was on the Honor Committee, and Rose was his best friend, and if I wanted to graduate, I'd forget about it. I thought he was bluffing. I said, I'm going to the Tac, I don't care what you say. He told me if I reported him, he'd get with the other guys who were at the party and they'd deny it. He said the Tac would believe them because they were all Honor reps. He told me I'd pay. They would get somebody to bring an Honor charge against me. He said Rose would make sure the charge stuck."

Jacey held the vial in her palm. "Can I have this?"

"Yeah, but like, keep me out of it, okay? I mean, I'm scared of those guys. They've got friends. I'm only a yearling. I've still got two years to go, and I'm afraid his friends might . . ."

"You don't have to explain," said Jacey.

"Did he tell you how they would fix the Honor hearing?" Ash asked.

"He just said Rose would do it." She zipped up her jacket. "I know you're facing charges. I hope this helps you."

"It helps. Thanks," said Ash.

"Jacey, I think your dad's a pretty cool Supe. A lot of us do."

"Thanks, Debbie. I'll tell him." She unlocked the door and Debbie moved silently across the darkened hallway to the stairs. Jacey relocked the door. "We've got to call Agent Kerry first thing in the morning. This is an incredible break."

"They're using the Honor Code to threaten people, Jace. We have *got* to get into those files."

"We can't take that chance, Ash. We should turn this stuff over to Agent Kerry and let them handle it."

"He hasn't been able to come up with anything on Rose or Favro. Sure, give them that joy juice and let them run another autopsy test. I'm going in the Honor Committee room tonight."

Jace stood there looking at him. He had his weight on his left leg, and his rangy frame crooked around like a gentle question mark. She loved him very, very much. "I'm going with you."

"Jace, you're not strong enough," said Belle.

"If he's willing to risk going back to the stockade, I can haul my aching butt up those stairs with him."

"Belle, have you guys got an empty laundry bag?" Ash asked.

"Sure." She rummaged around in the bottom of a drawer. "Here it is."

He took the bag and jammed it in the top of his sweatpants and pulled his sweatshirt over it. "If we find anything, we're taking it out of there."

"Do you really think you should?" asked Belle. "They'll know who did it."

"I'm in such deep shit now, a little more won't hurt."

Jacey was trying to pull on the hooded jacket of her sweats, but her left hand was still too sore. Ash helped her.

"Ready?"

"Any time you are."

"Let's go."

CHAPTER 49

THE HONOR Committee offices were on the fourth floor of the old First Division in Central Area. One of the rooms had been painted and outfitted with a semicircular table and served as the Honor Hearing Room. The American and Military Academy flags hung from flagpoles behind the center chair, where the President of the Board sat. The table was covered with felt the color of the cadet uniform. The walls were hung with black, gray, and gold bunting, the Academy colors. Rose had insisted that they needed something to designate the severity of purpose the room served, and so he had placed crossed sabers and a full dress gray hat at both ends of the table. A single witness chair was placed in the center of the semicircle. Ash had sat in judgment on his share of Honor Boards, and every time he did, he couldn't help but feel for the person sitting there in front of twelve cadets in full dress gray, their eyes locked on the accused.

Ash unlocked the door to the First Division. They made their way to the stairs and went up to the fourth floor. Ash unlocked the door to the Hearing Room. It was pitch-black. He told Jacey to wait by the door and felt his way around the table to a door hidden behind the bunting. He unlocked it and flipped on the overhead light, throwing a shaft of light across the table. He signaled to Jacey, she followed the light to the door, and they went inside.

It was a small, windowless storage room lined with filing cabinets, about twenty in all. Ash relocked the door and they stood in the center of the room looking at the cabinets.

"The ones from last year and this year are down there at the end." He pointed at two cabinets standing alone against the far wall. "Let's get started. You take this year. I'll take last year." They each opened the top drawer of a cabinet.

"The case files are organized like this," said Ash, holding open the first one. "The first thing you've got is a memo from the company Honor rep stating the charge against the cadet who's accused. The memo will name the accuser and detail the charge. Usually there will be a statement from the accuser attached. The next section is a report from the regimental Honor rep. He or she will hold an informal investigation using Honor reps who are not from the company of the accused. Based on what they hear from the accused, sometimes the regimental rep will dismiss the charges. When that happens, the rep has to detail why they found the charges groundless. If they're forwarding the charge to the Vice Chairman, the regimental rep will either sign off on the company rep's memo, or include another memo confirming the charge, including statements made by the accused. The next thing you'll come across is the report of the Vice Chairman. The Vice Chairman doesn't hold a hearing. He can dismiss the charge or forward it to the Chairman. If the charges are dismissed, no reason has to be given. Only a signature is required."

"That's a lot of power."

"It sure is. The weird thing is, the Honor Chairman can't dismiss charges. All he can do is forward the charges to the Commandant, who orders the Honor hearing. But the Honor Chairman picks the Vice Chairman. That's a major source of his power."

"So Rose picked Favro. What a lovely little couple."

"Favro's a mouthpiece. It's Rose calling the shots. If the charges lead to a full hearing, you'll find the names of the Honor reps picked to be the Board for the hearing, the minutes of the hearing, and the disposition. If the accused is found guilty, there will be a memo in there from Rose forwarding the results of the Hearing to the Com.

That's where the Honor Committee's job comes to an end. It's up to the Com from there on out. He's the one who recommends to the Supe if the accused should be dismissed or not. The Supe almost never overrules the com.''

"There's real opportunity for abuse here.''

"And real opportunity to do things fairly and honestly, don't forget.''

"Yeah. Let's do it,'' said Jacey.

Each of them withdrew a stack of case files, sat down on the floor, and began poring through them. Jacey checked her watch. It was 1:30. They didn't have a whole lot of time, and it was a complicated business. She pulled a pen from her jacket and began making notes in a little notebook. Ash did the same.

Jacey was working on her first stack from the second drawer when she slapped a page with the back of her hand. "Look at this!'' she exclaimed. "This is the third case I've come across where Lessard forwards a charge to Favro, and he signs off and sends it up to Rose, and a hearing is called, and who's picked to preside over the Board? Reade.''

"Let me see.'' She handed the case files to Ash. "Where is the list of reps who sat on the Board?''

"Right here.''

"Let me see the other two cases.'' She handed him the files. Ash read through them carefully. "The Board is listed in each of these cases, but something's not right. What's the case number on that other file?''

"Bravo 1241.''

"Go back through the last drawer of files. Check the case numbers on the Board lists.''

"Okay.'' She stood up and started pulling the files she had put away, checking the case numbers. In a moment she sat down next to him holding two case files. "Look at these. There's no number on them.''

"Let me see.'' He held up the Board list, examining it closely. Then he stood and held it closer to the overhead light. "They're copies. See how they're more blurred than the others?''

She stood next to him. "Yeah. They must have put a little piece of white paper over the number and then copied it.''

"Look at this. Eight or nine of the Board members are the same in each case."

"The verdict is guilty. And look at the accused. All three are females."

"I found two hearings that look suspicious. Rose appointed himself as President of both Boards. Let me check who else was on them." Ash flipped through the files. "Okay. Why am I unsurprised that these Board lists have no numbers on them?"

"They're switching lists, aren't they?"

"Yeah. Let me check back through my files and I'll see what I come up with." He went back to his previous drawer and flipped through the case files, checking the Board lists. He sat down with two new files. "I must have missed that there wasn't a number on these lists. Let me see yours." She handed him her unnumbered lists. "Here we go." He lined her Board lists on the floor next to his and checked off the names. "Okay. This is it. I see what they're doing. You've got three cases that went from Lessard to Favro to Rose, a hearing was ordered, they came down with a guilty verdict, and each time, the Board list is unnumbered. My two unnumbered cases went from Reade to Favro to Rose. Both are guilties. So we have a total of five cases with guilty verdicts, and each case file has a Board list that's unnumbered, and all five lists have different names of reps who sat on the Boards. Now let's take the five unnumbered Board lists we found scattered through the other case files."

Jacey handed him the five lists. "They're nearly the same, Ash. Look at them."

"Yeah. On two of yours, seven names match with two of my lists. On your third list, eight names match my phony lists. Every time at least two of the remaining seats are taken by Ivar or Reade or Lessard. And in my two cases, it's topped off by Rose presiding."

"Yours are guilty and guilty. One female, one plebe."

"Put your case files aside and let's keep looking."

They worked their way through another drawer and were starting on the third when Ash looked over at her. "It's almost five in the morning. How many have you found?"

"I've got my original three and two more that have no numbers on the Board lists."

"I've got the two I showed you and three more. Let's grab the whole bunch of them and get out of here. We've got ten cases they fixed. Every time, they swapped the real Board list with an unnumbered list in another case file. Make sure you get the other files, Jace.''

"Don't worry. Did you notice the verdicts in those other files?''

"Sure did. Not guilty.''

"They concealed the names of the Board every time they fixed a case, so it couldn't be traced.''

"This stuff would have sat in here gathering dust for years, and nobody would be the wiser,'' said Ash.

"How do you think they came up with this scam?''

"I don't know, but we've got enough heat to fry some asses, bigtime. Somebody's going to get theirs on the hot seat and want to get off. Somebody's going to blab.''

"You think so?''

"What did you say about guys when they're scared?''

"They'll do anything to save their ass.''

"There you go.''

Ash pulled the laundry bag from his belt and they shoved the case files inside. Downstairs he unlocked the back door and checked his watch. It was 5:15. "You go first. Jog. Try to look like you're out for an early run.''

"I can't jog. I'm too sore.''

"So shuffle.''

She grinned, kissed him, and headed out the door. He watched as she painfully moved down the hill in a halting half-step. He waited until she was out of sight and slipped out the door, locking it behind him. He broke into a run. As he came around the corner of the barracks, he ran straight into the Officer in Charge, a female major. It was dark, and a light drizzle had started to fall. He had the hood of his sweats up and hoped she couldn't make out his face.

"Morning, ma'am!'' he exclaimed, snapping a salute.

The officer was startled. She had barely said "Mister,'' when Ash sprinted past her through the barracks door and up the stairs, taking them two at a time.

"Halt, mister!'' the Officer in Charge called out from the area.

Ash stripped, threw the laundry bag of files and his sweats into his hamper, and got in bed. He heard her coming up the stairs. She started opening the doors of cadet rooms, ordering the cadets out of bed. She was next door. Ash heard her shout at the cadet and then slam the door closed.

The door to Ash's room flew open and the overhead lights came on. "Out of the rack!" she commanded.

A stark naked Ash Prudhomme leaped from his bed to the position of attention and saluted. The Officer in Charge stood there wide-eyed for an instant, then she backed out the door, turning off the light. "Excuse me. I'm sorry," she said. Ash stood at attention until she closed the door. Then he collapsed on the floor, laughing.

CHAPTER 50

A GENT KERRY went back down to New Jersey a couple of days later and checked the car-rental agencies in more towns near Rutgers, turning up exactly nothing. He was in his sixth rental office, about to give up and drive back to West Point, when he noticed the local news on a television in the corner. It was a live police chase. They were trying to recover a stolen car when the driver took off.

Then it came to him. What if they *stole* the car?

He started with the Bound Brook Police Department. He showed his ID and asked if there had been any car thefts reported the weekend of the Rutgers–Army game.

"Let me check our books," the desk sergeant said. He disappeared into another office and returned with a thick register. He turned the pages back and stopped. "One."

"Which night was that?"

"Saturday."

"That doesn't help me. I'm looking for a theft on Friday."

"Why don't you try the Edison PD? They've had some problems lately."

"Thanks." Kerry got back in his car and found the Edison Police Department about ten miles south of Bound Brook. He made the same inquiry and was referred upstairs to the car-theft division, where he was greeted by a genial plainclothes sergeant by the name of Browne.

"What was that date you were looking for?" asked Browne as he went though a stack of papers.

"Two Fridays ago. The weekend Army played Rutgers."

"Right. Gotcha." Browne leafed through the sheets and pulled out a handful.

"We had five that weekend. Let me see . . . here they are. Two on Friday." He handed the reports to Kerry. One car was stolen around midnight from the parking lot of a 7-Eleven. The other was a Pontiac stolen from a parking lot at a mall around six o'clock. That fit the time frame.

"Was the Pontiac recovered, by any chance?"

"Let me check." Browne walked over to a chalkboard on the wall and ran his fingers down a list of numbers. "What's the case number on that Pontiac?"

"Two-Two-Three-Eight Delta."

"Here it is. Yeah. It was recovered maybe ten miles from here, out behind a closed gas station. They found it two days after it was stolen."

"Where was it, exactly?"

"I'm not sure of the address, but they found it up there around Bound Brook."

"You don't think I could have a look at that car, do you?"

"It's been returned to the owner."

"Do you have the name?"

"It's right there on the theft report. Here, I'll make a copy for you." He took the theft report from Kerry and photocopied it on a machine in the corner. He checked the address as he handed the copy to Kerry. "Fourteen-sixty-six Meadowbrook. That's on the other side of town. You take this road out front of the station and go straight for about three miles. You'll come to University. Turn right and go two lights. That's Meadowbrook. Take a left. Should be on the first or second block. It's down there near the university."

"Thanks a lot," said Kerry.

The anticipation was killing him. Everything fit. American car. Good-size trunk. Dropped off in Bound Brook. Stolen in time to make the drive back to West Point. He found University and turned right. He made a left at the second light. There it was: 1466. The Pontiac was parked under the carport. Kerry pulled into the drive and got out. He knocked on the door. A middle-aged woman wearing a hair net came to the door. "What do you want?"

"Police matter, ma'am." He showed his ID. "My name is Agent Kerry, Military Police. I'm from up at West Point. I have been trying to find a stolen car that was used in a crime up there. I think your Pontiac might be the car. It was stolen a couple of weeks ago, right?"

"Yeah. I was in the mall. I came out, and the damn car was gone. They jimmied the steering column. Cost me three hundred bucks to get it fixed."

"Would you let me have a look at the car, ma'am? I'm looking for some evidence. If this is the car that was used in the crime, we might be able to get your money back for you. Pay for your damages."

"You're kidding me, right?"

"No ma'am."

"Let me get the keys." She closed the door and returned wearing a shopworn raincoat and slippers. She led the way to the Pontiac and handed Kerry the keys. He popped the trunk open. The light didn't work, so he got a flashlight from his car and shone it inside. He couldn't see from outside the car, so he climbed into the trunk and lay on his side, shining the light into the corners of the trunk. He checked the left taillight fittings. Nothing. He twisted himself around and shone the light into the right corner. There it was, caught on the shiny end of a bolt.

He got a case from the trunk of his car and removed a Nikon camera body and attached a micro lens. He plugged a Vivitar flash into the camera body and climbed back into the trunk. Holding the flash above his head, he focused the camera on the taillight assembly and fired off several pictures, moving the camera to get new angles. Then he put the camera away and using a pair of tweezers, he removed the scrap of blanket from the bolt and dropped it into a plastic evidence bag.

"I need to take a little bolt with me, too, ma'am. I'll put in a replacement for you. Is that all right with you?"

"If it will help you get the criminals who stole my car, it is."

"It'll help. I can assure you of that. I need to print your car now, ma'am. I'm trying to find out if the thieves left any fingerprints."

"Well, you go ahead. I'm going to wait inside. It's cold out here."

"All right, ma'am. I'd like to take a statement from you when I'm finished, if that's all right with you."

"What kind of statement?"

"Confirming this is your car and it was stolen that Friday night."

"That's okay with me. Just knock on the door when you're finished out here."

"Thank you, ma'am." Kerry went back to the staff car and got out his fingerprint kit. The chances he'd find their prints were slim, but he at least had to give it a try.

MAJOR VERNON had to wait two days before she went down to Walter Reed to test the vial of clear fluid Jacey had given her. Colonel Knight was out of town, testifying at a court-martial at Fort Bragg. When he got back, he called her and told her to come on down.

She called Melissa in General Slaight's office and arranged for a travel voucher. The Institute of Pathology already had a sample of Dorothy Hamner's blood on file from the tests they had run before. When she reached Walter Reed, Colonel Knight met her cab. They went straight to the lab.

She handed him the vial. "So you don't think we tested for this stuff first time around?" he asked.

"I know we didn't. We ran the standard drug screen, covering controlled substances. This isn't controlled. They're selling it right out in the open in New York State."

"It's some kind of designer drug, then."

"I'm sure that's what it is, sir."

He twisted off the cap and took a sniff. "Interesting. It's exactly as you described it on the phone. Odorless, colorless, and you said it was tasteless, too?"

"That's what they say. I haven't tried it myself."

Colonel Knight took a Q-Tip, dipped it in the solution, and touched it on the tip of his tongue, quickly spitting into a sink and rinsing his mouth with water. He smiled. "Tasteless. Let's see what we've got here."

They removed a portion of the contents of the vial and fed it into a mass spectrometer, which would break the substance down into its elemental chemical parts. From there, they could use the complex techniques of organic chemistry to reassemble the individual chemical elements found in the substance into the components of the whole.

The mass spectrometer did its magic, and they took its results to the lab computer and started running them through chemical ID programs. It took them less than an hour to arrive at what Colonel Knight called "a preliminary but astounding conclusion."

They were both huddled at the computer screen, going down the list of component substances that had been found in the clear liquid in the vial. "From the top, in general order of merit," he joked.

"You mean from the mostest to the leastest," she joked back.

"Yep. Okay, first we've got our old pal, H_2o. Plain water comprises about a third of the substance by volume. Then we have one-four-butanediol, taking up a second third. We have a good hit of old-fashioned caffeine, and as a final kicker, we've got a small amount of epinephrine, such as might be found in a common cold remedy. No wonder they call it Cherry Bomb. If you took enough of this stuff it would go off like a bomb inside your head."

"It's not an upper, and it's not a downer. . . ."

"It's both, an industrial-strength speedball. This stuff one-four-butanediol is very close in its chemical composition to gammahydroxy-butyrate, the stuff they call Bute. Butanediol is only a couple of oxygen molecules of GBH. I would presume it would have the same knockout-drop effects of GBH. Let's get these results to the blood lab and run a check on the sample you brought from Dorothy."

They made a computer printout and gave it to a lab technician, who disappeared through the door to the blood lab.

"GBH isn't a controlled substance in most states."

"You'll probably find that it's illegal in New York, which is why they punted GBH and put out this one-four-butanediol mix. The New York authorities are playing catch-up ball, trying to stay ahead of the chemists who dream this stuff up." A specialist in a lab coat approached Colonel Knight. "What have you got for us, Abby?"

"Sir, I've been in touch with New York City. They confirm there's a new party drug that's making the rounds. It's got a bunch of names, but its main ingredient is an industrial chemical they said is totally legal and easy to come by. It's called one-four—"

"Butanediol!" they chorused.

The specialist looked surprised. "Yes sir. There was a problem at one of those 'rave' all-night disco parties back in August in New York. Thirty people were taken to emergency rooms suffering from nausea, accelerated heartbeat, and respiratory problems. They all took it."

"Did they describe the respiratory problems, Abby?"

"Yes sir," she said, consulting her notes. "Labored breathing, sir."

Colonel Knight looked over at Major Vernon. "In Dorothy, this stuff would be deadly."

They went upstairs to the officers' lounge and had a cup of coffee while they waited for the blood results. After about two hours, a technician from the blood lab appeared in the door.

"Come in," said Colonel Knight. The lab tech handed him a computer printout. He tapped the page. "Look at this. There's an incredible quantity of this stuff in her bloodstream, considering that she apparently took it the night before."

"The amount of caffeine alone would trigger a reaction," agreed Major Vernon. "But in combination with one-four-butanediol, it overwhelmed the prednisone. It's no wonder her lungs were inflamed."

"I don't know how you account for the large amount in her bloodstream. It may be very slow to be expelled by the body. Whatever the reason, that's one hell of a lot of junk in her blood. It was a death sentence." He handed the printout to Major Vernon. "I think you'd better jump on a plane and get back to West Point. That young woman didn't die of natural causes. This stuff killed her."

Major Vernon tucked the results of both tests into her briefcase. It was Friday. She would get back to West Point too late to file her report, which she had been instructed to do with Colonel Bassett, since General Slaight had relieved both Lieutenant Colonel Percival and Colonel Lombardi from the Dorothy Hamner investigation. She was glad for the delay. Now that she had established Dorothy Hamner had been killed by a drug overdose, even if the drug was legal, those responsible would end up facing criminal charges, and her findings would come under attack. The weekend would give her the time to pull all her findings together and make her report a comprehensive document that would stand up to the toughest scrutiny.

T HE HEARINGS of the House National Security Committee were called for Monday at 1:00 P.M. General Slaight, Sam, and Colonel Bassett flew down to Washington on an Air Force C-21 that morning provided by General Meuller. Leroy Buck was waiting for them when their jet taxied to a halt on the tarmac at Andrews. All four of them climbed into the back of an awaiting Army van for the drive to the Capitol.

"I have some new stuff on Thrunstone and his committee," said Buck after the van started moving. He pulled a file from his briefcase and handed it to Slaight. "I took the data the Pentagon folks gave you on the concentration of defense industries in the districts of his committee members and ran it through my computer. Here's the way it comes out. There are defense contracts on about ninety-five billion dollars in their districts. That's one-third the entire budget for the Department of Defense. Eighty percent of those contracts are held on matériel being built for the Air Force, Navy, and Marines. The way I figure it, his committee is spending about eight percent of its time worryin' about the Army and the rest worrying about all that money and all those jobs comin' into their districts via contracts for the other three services."

"He's going to say there are Army installations all over the country, and lots of them are in the districts of his committee members, and they can hardly be accused of being hostile to the interests of the United States Army.''

''He ain't hostile to the Army. He's just more accommodatin' to the other guys, 'cause there's more money to be had with them.''

Bassett and Buck got reacquainted while Slaight studied Buck's figures. He was certain they were correct. He was less certain that the Secretary of the Army was going to want him to throw them in the face of the Chairman of the House National Security Committee. He studied the text of his opening statement to the committee, but by the time the van pulled to a stop on Capitol Hill he was still unsure about what he was actually going to say when he addressed the Congress of the United States.

They had a meeting in the office of a friendly congressman in the Cannon Building with the legal and public-relations teams from General Meuller's office. It was mercifully brief. They wanted to reemphasize Meuller's wish that General Slaight stick to the ''talking points'' that had been discussed over the past few days. Slaight nodded his assent without saying much. Then the whole bunch of them traipsed across South Capitol Street to the Rayburn Building.

Room 2120 was a rather large hearing room with a three-tiered dais, needed to contain the committee's considerable membership. Appointment to the committee was a coveted assignment. Nearly every congressional district in the country had a financial stake in the defense of the nation, so widely scattered were the military installations and defense industries paid for with defense dollars.

Buck prowled the corridors outside the hearing room, returning just as Thrunstone and the rest of the committee were filing into their seats from doors behind the dais. He studied the members of the committee and the staffers who hovered behind Thrunstone, feeding the chairman notes and whispering in his ear.

''See those two staffers on either side of Thrunstone?'' Buck whispered. Slaight nodded. ''I just saw them down the hall huddlin' with Gibson not ten minutes ago. This is gonna be a totally scripted performance.''

Thrunstone gaveled the committee into session and opened the hearing with the statement *The New York Times* had predicted he would make. The time had come to reassess the nation's priorities when it came to providing the leadership of the armed forces for the twenty-first century. The nation had entered upon a period of unprecedented peace and prosperity with the end of the Cold War. Because of a need to cut taxes and reorient budgetary priorities, the military budget would make up a smaller slice of the pie in the coming decade. The nation had always prided itself on fielding armed forces of "citizen soldiers." Perhaps, said Chairman Thrunstone, the time had come to close down the "elitist and unnecessarily expensive" institution of West Point. He noted that the number of West Pointers among the Army's senior three- and four-star general leadership had diminished greatly over the past twenty years, and that no West Pointer had served as Chairman of the Joint Chiefs in well over a decade. West Point was failing in its mission to provide the Army with leaders because large percentages of West Point graduates had resigned from the Army before becoming senior officers or reaching retirement age.

"If they cannot retain Military Academy graduates in the Army, why should the people of the United States be required to spend their hard-earned dollars on a place that is wasting scarce federal dollars? It appears that the Military Academy is providing the country not with top Army leadership, but with a bunch of money-hungry military yuppies instead."

"Wonderful," whispered Sam as the room buzzed. Thrunstone gaveled the committee into order. "That sets just the tone we were looking for."

"It ain't playin' back in Peoria, I can tell you that much," whispered Leroy Buck from behind them.

"I hope you're right," said Slaight.

Two new staffers showed up behind Congressman Thrunstone. One was a middle-aged man in a rumpled sport coat. The other was an attractive young woman with an expensive hairstyle.

Slaight turned around to the legal team from Meuller's office. "Who the hell are they?"

"Give me a minute," said one of the lawyers. She hurried across the hearing room. Slaight could see her whispering to a young woman seated in the press section. When she returned, she crouched behind Slaight's chair. "The one on the left is Basil Embry. He's a retired colonel, with a Reserve commission."

"What's he doing here?"

"The reporter from ABC told me a guy named Cecil Avery arranged for him to be a special advisor to Thrunstone for the hearing. His real job is defense manpower specialist for the Heritage Foundation. The woman is Sheila Rooks. She's the head of the Center for a Responsible Defense, the right-wing think tank that's done all the lobbying against women in the military."

"Thanks," said Slaight.

"Rooks runs one of Thrunstone's PACs," whispered Buck. "Embry raised big-time money for congressional Republicans in the last election."

"Great," whispered Sam. "Gibson's pal Avery is helping to call the shots. Talk about stacking the deck."

Thrunstone gaveled the committee into order. "The Chair calls General Rysam Slaight, Superintendent of West Point."

Slaight walked to the witness table, raised his right hand, and was sworn in. Thrunstone peered down at him over his half-glasses.

"General Slaight, welcome to the hearing. Do you have an opening statement you wish to make?"

"No sir. I am prepared to take your questions."

Thrunstone looked momentarily confused. "I was told by staff people from the office of the Secretary of the Army that you would be making an opening statement. You are certain you do not have any remarks you wish to make to the committee in advance of the questions we have for you?"

"Yes sir. I am ready for your questions, sir."

Two staffers hurriedly conferred with Thrunstone as members of the committee whispered. Finally Thrunstone hit the gavel.

"General Slaight, I have become aware that there is a culture of weakness and political correctness which has infected West Point in recent times. I have been receiving complaints from officers all over the Army, many of them West Point graduates, that the Military Academy standards have fallen, and the effectiveness of the Army is being compromised because of this. These complaints are coming to me from all over the country. That's why I called this hearing. Have you heard any complaints from Academy graduates, sir?"

"I've heard the usual grumbling that West Point went to hell in a handbasket since the day we did away with reveille formation, if that's what you mean, sir.''

The gallery erupted in laughter, and Thrunstone had to gavel the room to order.

''I'll assume you did not intend that remark as a joke, General Slaight.''

''It's not a joke, sir. A great number of graduates object strongly to the changes that have been made at West Point. There is an especially strong objection to the presence of women in the Corps of Cadets. But I am certain that you are not here to question the wisdom of that decision, sir, since it was this committee which wrote the law allowing women into the nation's service academies.''

Thrunstone removed his half-glasses and glared at Slaight. ''General, you do not appear to be aware that there is a large body of opinion in this town that West Point is failing to serve its traditional role in setting high standards for the nation's Army. I have seen some Army studies which show that less than forty percent of enlisted soldiers have confidence in the officers who lead them. The same studies indicate that only thirty percent of our young soldiers would feel confident going to war under their current leadership. West Point is charged with training the leaders these young soldiers have lost confidence in. We on this committee believe West Point is falling down on the job, and I'll tell you why.'' Thrunstone pointed a fat finger at Slaight. ''West Point is bending to feminist pressures. You are demilitarizing the system at West Point, General. I have heard you have some female officers up there who are talking openly about eliminating the blood-and-guts aspects of West Point training. You've got separate standards for men and women. In the opinion of this congressman and a majority of this committee, West Point has been coddling women. That is why standards are being brought down across the board. I have heard from Army officers who have been on the staff and faculty up at West Point, and they have told me that West Point has become so politically correct that they don't even recognize the place anymore. I do not like what I'm hearing. West Point is supposed to stand for something, General. It's supposed to stand for duty and honor and country, but from what I've heard, the West Point of today stands for kindness and respect for others and harmonious cooperation. To me, that doesn't belong at the Military Academy, it belongs at a civilian college that is not enjoying the support of taxpayer dollars. The way I see it, West Point is damaging the morale and effectiveness of our Army, and it's damaging our nation's defense, and we on this committee are not going to stand for it."

Slaight looked straight at Thrunstone and spoke loudly into the mike. "Sir, I don't know who you've been listening to, but I'm afraid that you have been misinformed."

"Misinformed? About what?" Thrunstone growled.

"Sir, let's begin with physical standards for cadets at the Academy. It may interest the commitee to know that female cadets today are required to do more push-ups, sit-ups, and pull-ups than male cadets did back in the sixties when I was a cadet. Their minimum time for the two-mile run is faster than it was when I was a cadet. We haven't lowered standards, Congressman. We've raised them."

"They still don't have to meet the same standards as the males, do they?"

"No sir, they do not. But they are meeting a standard that is tougher than it was. The same is true for academics, sir. We've got a tougher academic program at West Point today than we did even ten years ago, and far more comprehensive than it was twenty years ago. The same is true of military training. Cadets get more intensive military training during their summers than they ever did in the past. When I was a cadet, we didn't get the chance to go to Airborne School until after graduation. Now we've got male and female cadets going to Benning every summer. I see jump wings on dress gray coats every day, sir. We've got male and female cadets going through jungle-warfare school every summer. We've got cadets assigned to Army units all over the world every summer. We've got plebes going through an indoctrination and training upon entering West Point that is far tougher than the one I went through. If you want facts and figures, sir, I can arrange for them to be sent to the committee. But you can take it from me right here, right now that your assessment of cadet training at West Point is dead wrong."

"So what you are doing is defending the status quo. Is that right, General?"

Slaight was looking straight into Thrunstone's eyes. You couldn't read this guy even if you spent months trying. It was no wonder he had ended up chairing the National Security Committee. He was a pro.

"Congressman, I believe you're wrong on every count, and if you want me to, I'll prove it to you."

"We are up to our ears in facts and figures here at the National Security Committee, General. What those figures tell me is that we have an Army today that is being feminized, and much of the responsibility for this trend lies with West Point."

"Congressman, West Point started instituting policies to facilitate the integration of women into the Army beginning with the first class of women at West Point. We have carried out the laws passed by this Congress, and we have done a good job of it. Unless and until the Congress changes its mind and passes another law removing women from the Army, we're going to continue following the letter and the spirit of the law."

"Are you trying to tell this committee when the Army falls down it is the Congress of the United States that pushed it?"

"No sir."

"Then what are you telling this committee, General Slaight?"

"I'm telling you that West Point is a better Military Academy today than it's ever been, and we're turning out classes of young officers who measure up to the class in which I graduated and every other class that has graduated from West Point, sir. What you are hearing from these sources of yours does not comport with my experience either at West Point or in the Army."

"You are telling this committee that our military is just as effective today as it was fifteen years ago?"

"More effective, sir."

"It is remarkable, General, that we could differ so greatly on this very basic point."

"Congressman, there was a great line in one of my favorite movies, *Cool Hand Luke:* 'What we've got here is a failure to communicate.' "

Titters of laughter broke out around the hearing room. Thrunstone banged his gavel. "Are you trying to test the patience of the Chair, General Slaight?"

"No sir. But there is a communication problem if what you are hearing differs so markedly from what I have experienced in more than thirty years of service in the Army."

"Why don't you point out where you think the communication breakdown is, General."

"I'll be glad to, sir. The Army has changed greatly over the years, and it continues to change every day. Fifty years ago, we had a segregated Army commanded entirely by white men. Today we've got an Army which is integrated by race and gender, commanded by men and women, many of whom are not white. As we move into the next century, the makeup of our Army will change even more. The year I graduated from a West Point class which was one percent black, eighty-three percent of Americans were white. That was twenty-eight years ago, sir. As we sit here today, seventy-three percent of the population is white. By the middle of the next century, less than fifty percent of Americans will be white. The Army will reflect those figures, and I would posit that the Army will also undergo further changes along gender lines as well. The complaints I heard about the Army twenty-five years ago were about race. The complaints you're hearing today are about gender. Somebody is always complaining about the Army, Congressman. That's just one of the things soldiers do, and if I may say so, they complain better and louder than any class of people I've ever come across."

"The issue before us today is not whether the Army and West Point have changed, but whether they have changed too much," said Thrunstone. "The purpose of West Point is to train leaders to win our nation's wars. I can tell you right now that this Congress is not going to stand for engaging in social experiments in either West Point or the Army."

Slaight pulled a sheet of paper from his inside jacket pocket. "Congressman, I'd like to read you a quote from a congressional hearing which was called to review President Truman's executive order integrating the Armed Forces in 1948. The witness was General Omar N. Bradley, who rose to five-star rank, and was one of our country's great leaders during World War II. General Bradley was asked what he thought about Truman's order integrating black and white military units. He responded, 'The Army is not out to make any social reform, Mr. Chairman. The Army will not put men of different races in the same companies. It will change that policy when the nation as a whole changes it.' "

Slowly Slaight folded the sheet of paper and stuck it back into his jacket pocket as the hearing room buzzed around him. Thrunstone banged his gavel, silencing the room.

"If you are comparing me to Omar N. Bradley, I can assure you right now that is a comparison I will gladly accept, General Slaight."

"Very well, sir, but I would point out to you how wrong General Bradley was when he testified before the Congress. The Army he grew up in was a white male institution, and he thought it should remain that way. The Army did not remain the same. Neither did West Point. You are hearing from constituents who do not identify the West Point of today with the West Point they have seen in old movies on television. West Point is different. So is the Army. They are both far better institutions for having faced up to the problem of race in our society. We are not finished facing up to the gender problems which we have encountered since women were integrated into the services twenty years ago. West Point and the Army have led the way on race, and now we're leading the way on gender."

Thrunstone's face was red. He turned to Sheila Rooks, the young woman Cecil Avery had lent to his committee. They whispered for a moment. She reached into a briefcase and handed him a document.

"Since you brought up women at West Point, General, let's stay on that subject for a moment. It has come to the attention of this committee that a young woman died recently at West Point. Is that true?"

"Yes, it is, Congressman."

"Why hasn't this information been made public, General?"

"We have been conducting an investigation into the cause of her death, sir. When the investigation is completed, we will make a full report to the Pentagon, and to this committee, if you so desire. We are not concealing anything at West Point, Congressman Thrunstone. In the interest of conducting a thorough and complete investigation, we have attempted to prevent the kind of circus atmosphere the media can create. We don't want a media feeding frenzy, sir. We want an answer as to how and why this young woman died while marching in a parade at West Point. We need to learn this in order that it never happens again."

Behind Slaight, a cell phone vibrated. One of the lawyers from General Meuller's office answered. He listened for a moment and passed the cell phone to Colonel Bassett. The lawyer stood up and hurried out of the hearing room. Bassett was whispering into the phone as Slaight poured himself a glass of water and took a long swig.

"I'm not satisfied with that answer, General Slaight. I don't like cover-ups, and I smell a cover-up here. What is the name of the young female cadet who died?"

"Her name was Dorothy Hamner, sir. She was a first-class cadet, an excellent student, and one of the top women in her class in physical aptitude. That's why her case is so confounding. We're having a hard time figuring out how a young woman of her abilities simply dropped dead on a parade ground."

"It was hot that day, wasn't it, General?"

"Yes sir. It was ninety-six degrees."

"That was the parade welcoming you as Superintendent, was it not?"

"Yes sir."

"As hot as it was, why didn't you reschedule, or call it off?"

"Sir, we don't call off wars because it's too hot to fight. We don't call off parades because it's too hot to march. I thought you were concerned about standards, sir. Are you suggesting that we set a maximum temperature, and if it exceeds that temperature, we should call off parades and training?"

"Of course not."

"No cadet has ever died on parade at West Point until Dorothy Hamner died, sir. That is why we have conducted an extensive investigation into her cause of death."

"Isn't it obvious she died from the heat?"

"That cause was ruled out in the autopsy, sir."

"Then what killed her, General? What is it that you are covering up from this Congress?"

Slaight was about to answer when he felt a hand on his shoulder. He turned his head. It was Bassett. "Sir, if I may take a moment to consult with Colonel Bassett."

"Go ahead."

Slaight covered the mike with his hand. Bassett whispered in his ear for a moment and then sat down. Slaight turned to face Thrunstone.

"Sir, Colonel Bassett is in charge of the investigation into Dorothy Hamner's death. He just reported to me that the final report was filed with his office this morning by Major Elizabeth Vernon, the pathologist who conducted the autopsy. We have a cause of death, sir. One of my staff has left the hearing room to receive a fax at an office down the hall. We'll have the written report in a moment."

"Do you know how she died, General? Have you been told what's in the report?"

"Yes sir."

"Why don't you enlighten this committee, General Slaight."

"All right, sir. Dorothy Hamner died of a drug overdose. We have reason to believe that the overdose was administered to her by another cadet. The investigation into who gave her the overdose of drugs is continuing, sir."

The hearing room buzzed at the news. Thrunstone covered his mike and whispered with Rooks and Embry. Embry got up and rushed out a side door. In the back, Buck got up and left through the main door to the hearing room. In a moment, he came back and whispered in Slaight's ear.

"Embry ran down the hall and talked to Gibson. He's been sittin' in the next office, watching the hearing on C-span."

"What are they up to?"

"I wish I damn well knew."

"This guy is pissing me off, Leroy."

"Keep your head, man. Play it cool. If he's listening to Gibson, he's gonna be stepping in shit pretty soon."

Up on the dais, Embry had returned and was whispering in Thrunstone's ear. He listened for a moment, nodding, then he turned around and gaveled the hearing to order. He put on his half-glasses and consulted the papers that had been given him by Sheila Rooks. He took his time. When he was finished, he looked up at Slaight with a dimpled smile.

"The young woman who died was in your daughter's company, H-3. Is that correct, General Slaight?"

"Yes it is, Congressman, but I hardly think that has any bearing on the question of how she died."

"Oh, but it does, General Slaight. There are drugs at West Point, General, and the drugs are being used in the company under the command of your daughter, Jacey Slaight. This is a matter of great concern to this committee. If there's a drug problem at West Point, we need a superintendent who can deal with the problem, not a father who is covering for his own daughter's failure of command."

Slaight sat there for a long moment, gathering himself. He knew there was no use going into the details of the investigation, explaining to the committee that Dorothy Hamner had overdosed at a party far from West Point, and that she had gone as the date of a cadet who wasn't even in her own regiment. Thrunstone had no interest in the facts. What he wanted to do was hang the Superintendent of the United States Military Academy in front of about a dozen TV news cameras. He saw his hands were bunched into fists. He relaxed his fingers, and pressed his open palms on top of the witness table.

"You have dragged my daughter into this, Congressman, and you have wronged her in a most cowardly way. I take exception to your characterization of my daughter's professionalism and character. It will delight me no end to supply every member of this committee with a full report on the death of Dorothy Hamner which will exonerate my daughter and establish the facts as they have been revealed by our investigation. Gentlemen may disagree, Mr. Thrunstone, but they do not denigrate one another's families, a lesson in manners and honor which you obviously never learned."

There was a loud buzz behind Slaight. People were whispering, pointing at Thrunstone. He banged his gavel, red-faced.

"I am accusing you of running a lax Military Academy, General Slaight. It appears to me that you are not up to the job of Superintendent. I will propose that this committee hold a vote on whether or not to recommend to the President that he ask for your resignation."

"You're the Chairman. You can hold any vote you want. But before you vote, I want to point out to the members of your committee that every member of Congress on Capitol Hill, every senior commander at the Pentagon, and probably most of the reporters covering this hearing can see right through your motives. They know that this hearing is being held under false premises. You are attacking West Point because you want to bring the Pentagon to heel on the fight over the defense budget. This Congress has cut the United States Army's manpower strength by one quarter, and you are not finished. You want to strip four more divisions from the Army. You plan to take the money you save on paychecks for soldiers and spend it on a mess of B-2 bombers the Air Force has told you it doesn't even want. You've been listening to complainers in the Army? Well, I've heard a few complaints myself. I've heard complaints from soldiers and citizens that the members of this committee represent districts with defense-industry contracts totaling ninety-five billion dollars. That is one-third of the total budget of the Department of Defense. By a huge majority, those contracts are for weapons systems and hardware. You don't care about West Point, Congressman Thrunstone. You don't care about the Army. All you care about are the defense jobs you deliver to your districts and the campaign contributions you suck down from the contractors who are getting rich off those contracts. It's obvious to those of us in uniform that you don't care about soldiers. You care about money."

"You have accused the members of this committee with false charges of corruption, General. I think you had better reconsider your words. You owe me, and you owe the members of this committee, an apology."

"I don't owe you or your members anything other than the solemn commitment I made when I took an oath as an officer in the Army to defend the Constitution and to lay down my life, if necessary, to defend this nation. How many of you on this committee have taken that oath, Congressman? How many members of this committee have served as much as one day in uniform?"

"That is an impertinent question—"

"I know the answer to that question when it comes to you, Congressman Thrunstone. When your nation needed your service during the war in Vietnam, you were awarded a 4-F draft status because you had a *skin condition*." He slurred the words derisively, and before Thrunstone could react, he raised his voice, thundering, "You want to try and pass a bill in this Congress to cut the funding for West Point and shut the place down? I can tell you as I sit here today, Congressman, it's not going to happen. Not at West Point, and not on my watch. See how far you get without the young men and women from West Point who have set the moral standards for the Army of duty and honor and country for nearly two hundred years of our nation's history. See how far you get without the West Pointers who have fought and died for their country in every war since its founding in 1802. See how far you get with all those parents out there in your congressional districts when you tell them there won't be a West Point offering worthy students from every state in the Union the opportunity to serve their country. See how far you get when your constituents learn you will no longer be making the congressional appointments to West Point which each of you make every year. See how far you get telling the American people they can forget about the Army–Navy game, they can forget about visits of the West Point choir to their churches, they can forget about driving up the Hudson to see a parade, or watch their college play Army in soccer or basketball or lacrosse or wrestling. See how far you get with this President, or any other for that matter, when you tell him you want to destroy West Point in order to save it."

Thrunstone glared at Slaight. "Do you think you can come before this Congress and lecture us about our duty to this nation?"

"Congressman Thrunstone, you saw your duty to your nation when you turned eighteen and registered for the draft, and you shirked it. Every person in this room has seen photographs and television footage of you playing celebrity golf tournaments. They've seen you swimming in the ocean down there on the Gulf Coast where you have your condo, and they've watched you skiing at Aspen with movie stars and corporate moguls. And I can tell you this, Congressman. Every young woman in the Army, every young woman at West Point—all of those female troops who you think can't measure up? Every one of them knows if you can golf and swim and ski, you could sure as hell have done the push-ups and sit-ups and other physical tests necessary to qualify for military service. You want to talk about standards, Congressman? Why don't you tell the members of your committee why you couldn't meet the minimum standards for the draft. Why don't you explain how itchy skin prevented you from wearing the uniform of the United States Army."

Chairs scraped behind Slaight as reporters ran for the exit. TV cameramen spun their lenses, getting a close-up of Thrunstone's face, a Vesuvius of bulging blood vessels and quivering flesh. He banged his gavel, and still the room did not come to order. The senior Republican on the committee leaned over, covered Thrunstone's mike, and whispered to him. The faces of senior Democrats seated to the left of the Chairman wore satisfied looks as Republican committee aides scurried wildly behind them.

At the rear of the room, television correspondents could be seen madly making notes for their stand-ups, which would lead footage of the hearings on the nightly news. A half-dozen committee staffers left the dais and were busily spinning the correspondents, seeking to control the damage they could already see had been done. The hearing had backfired. The most panicked faces in the room were those of committee members who did not look forward to the ocean of faxes and E-mails and phone calls that would flood their offices in the morning. Deep down in their political bones they knew the television news was going to show them as complacent pawns of a chairman who had led them in a charge against a foe who sat there before them unvanquished. He had waved their dirty laundry before the cameras, and there was not a thing they could do about it.

Several younger Democrats seized the opportunity and began loudly calling "Mr. Chairman! Mr. Chairman!" with raised hands, seeking to question Slaight. Thrunstone ignored them, huddling with his deputy chairman and other senior members of his party on the committee. Finally he turned to face Slaight and gaveled the committee to order.

"I have been informed that we have a vote on the floor of the House. This committee will stand in recess." He struck his gavel once and hurried out one of the side doors behind the dais.

Slaight turned around and faced a forest of microphones and cameras. He answered a few questions, then he elbowed his way through the pack. Bassett and Buck and Sam were waiting for him near the door. Sam took his hand and squeezed hard. "Jacey will be so proud of you."

"I'm afraid the boys across the river at the Pentagon aren't going to be too happy with me. I did what they told me not to do. I picked a fight with a powerful committee chairman."

One of the Pentagon lawyers walked up and handed Slaight a cell phone. "It's General Meuller, sir. For you."

Slaight took the phone. "General Slaight, sir."

"We've been watching you on C-Span. Drabonsky wants to say

something to you." There was a brief pause, and then General Drabonsky came on. "Slaight, goddammit, we're going to be dealing with the fallout from your appearance today the rest of this year, but let me tell you this. You ate his lunch. That man won't be able to get his phone calls returned over here. There isn't a person in uniform who doesn't owe you a debt of gratitude, Slaight. *Damn,* that was fun to watch." He handed the phone back to Meuller. "Ry, we'll talk tomorrow. You broke every rule in the damn book, but maybe it was about time we threw the book away and slugged it out with that bastard. Good job."

"Thank you, sir."

"You don't have to have any worries about the President asking for your resignation. He's already weighed in. He called a few moments ago. He was laughing so hard I could barely understand him. He said he'd been waiting for someone to chop Thrunstone down to size for years."

"I didn't set out to stir things up, sir. But when he went after Jacey . . ."

"We know. Go home. Get some rest. Tomorrow's another day. Damn fine job, Supe."

Slaight handed the phone back to the lawyer. Bassett patted him on the back. "Masterful," he said. "Just gorgeous." Buck came alongside as they walked out of the hearing room, heading for the street.

"That reminded me of a slugfest I saw one time when I was a kid. There was a county chairman back in Illinois . . ."

Sam took his arm, and they walked out on South Capitol Street listening to Buck spin his story of down-and-dirty county politics in Illinois. Buck was just warming to his tale. It was going to be a great flight home.

CHAPTER 52

J ACEY AND Ash took the laundry bag full of Honor Committee files to Captain Patterson late Monday afternoon as her parents were on their way back from Washington. They had missed the C-Span coverage because they were in class all day. Patterson had seen most of it, and he filled them in on how Thrunstone had accused Jacey of condoning drug use and how Slaight had counterattacked Thrunstone for dodging the draft. Jacey high-fived Ash when she heard how her father had stood up for her.

Then the three of them went down the hall to a conference room, spread the contents of the case files across the table, and went through them in minute detail. The deceptions that were employed by Rose and the others went far beyond concealing the makeup of Honor Boards. All ten of the cases fit a pattern. Two of the charges were brought by the same person. Jacey called Debbie Edwards over in the Fourth Regiment. She checked company records and discovered he was a former roommate of Favro's. Another charge was brought by one of Rose's former roommates. The fourth was brought by a guy who had gone to high school with Rose on Long Island.

Even the charges preferred against the accused had similarities. Three of the women were accused of falsifying an official document.

What document was that? The card they signed certifying their PT test results.

Other attempts had been made to conceal the way they fixed the Honor hearings. The minutes of the hearings were signed by different Honor reps, but it looked like all of them had been written by the same person. The same word was misspelled on seven of the ten minutes, and the sentences recording the testimony of witnesses were unvarying from one set of minutes to the other. It looked as if either Rose or Favro had run the minutes off on their computer and handed them to an Honor rep to sign.

One thing about every hearing that produced a guilty verdict could not be concealed. General Gibson signed every case file, recommending dismissal for each person accused. Four of the other case files they had carried out of the Committee storage room had guilty verdicts as well, but in two of those cases, General Gibson had recommended suspension for a year, and in the other two cases, Gibson had reversed the findings of the Honor Board and recommended that the accused cadet be retained in the Corps and given extra Honor training.

It seemed like the only cases where there was a rush to judgment by both the Honor Committee and the Commandant were the ones that were fixed.

When they were finished going through the case files, Patterson sat down and put his feet up on the conference table. "I'll tell you what this stuff proves to me. They were using the Honor Code to remove certain cadets from the Corps. The question is, on whose orders? We don't know if it was Rose who was fixing the cases and handing them off to Gibson, or Gibson telling Rose to get a certain cadet, and then Rose went off and fixed the case on Gibson's orders."

"Maybe it was a little of both," said Ash. "Maybe they were in close enough agreement that the decision could come from either source."

"That's very likely," said Patterson. "Gibson might not have known enough about every cadet to have a reason to want them out of West Point."

"I don't see Rose setting up the system and taking it to Gibson," said Jacey. "I think Gibson picked Rose and he taught him how to work the system. It made Rose feel like a big man to have the equivalent of life-and-death power over the Corps of Cadets. He's getting off on it."

Patterson got up from his chair. "You guys take this stuff down to Kerry. I'll go down there and see him later today. He's going to have to be briefed on just exactly how the system worked in order for him to use the evidence against Rose and the others."

"I don't think I'm up to walking all the way down there," said Jacey.

"I'll bring you down with me in my car later, then," said Patterson.

"Do you want me to show him what we found out today?" Ash asked.

"Sure. I'll come down and back you up and clue him on how it adds up to violations of the UCMJ. We'll have to separate out all the moves they made and determine which of them fit which crimes. Like, making a false official statement is one crime. Conspiracy to violate the legal rights of an accused person, even in an administrative hearing like an Honor Board, is another crime."

"This is what Kerry has been waiting for," said Ash. "He's come up dry on them assaulting Jace. Maybe he can use this stuff to split them."

"Yeah, Kerry will know exactly what to do with it," agreed Patterson.

KERRY WAS having more luck than they knew. That day he had received results back from the Army crime lab at Fort Gillem, Georgia. He had FedExed the olive-drab blanket to the lab, along with the scrap of blanket he had taken from the stolen car, the taillight bolt, and the sliver of steel he had removed from the blanket.

They had conducted a microscopic forensics examination of the evidence and reached the conclusion he had hoped for. In a thick report, the lab confirmed that the scrap of fabric had come from the blanket, and the sliver of steel had come from the taillight bolt.

Kerry had lifted two partial prints from the dashboard. One was a fingerprint he had found on the power button for the radio. The other was a partial palm print that came from the rocker panel on the driver's side. He had talked the lady into letting him print her, and neither of the partials came from her. The one on the radio button almost certainly belonged to Favro. He had sent the print down to the FBI lab to get their opinion. The partial palm he kept. When he arrested Rose again, he would print his whole hand and compare them.

Ash arrived just as he finished typing up a summary report detailing how he had found the stolen car. When Kerry told him of his find, Ash leaped from his chair.

"I can't believe it! You found the car!"

"It was luck. I never would have thought of going after the stolen cars if I hadn't seen that chase on the news."

"That wasn't luck, it was detective work," said Ash. "Man, you are the best!"

Kerry managed a smile. The kid was right that sometimes good old-fashioned legwork paid off.

Ash laid out the Honor Board case files and went through them one by one, pointing out the deceptions and Xeroxed Board lists and the other methods that had been used to conceal the cases that had been fixed. Now it was Kerry's turn to rejoice. He gave a low whistle when Ash explained how they'd done the minutes.

"You guys did some fine five-finger detective work of your own. That's good. That's very good."

"Can you use this stuff?"

"You're damn right I can."

"What about the evidence rules?"

"We'd be screwed if I went up there and snatched those files. But you're on the Honor Committee. You can make a case that you are entitled to remove the files and examine them. If you voluntarily turn them over to me, I can accept them, and they are valid and legal evidence."

"Well, I'm volunteering them."

Kerry shook his hand. "And I'm accepting them."

It was well after dark when Jacey and Patterson showed up. Patterson and Kerry sat down and went over the possible charges. Since Patterson wasn't the prosecutor, they didn't have to nail every little thing down. They settled on three major charges they figured would stick: Conspiracy to wrongfully interfere with an administrative proceeding, making false official statements, and dereliction of duty.

They were serious charges. You could get less jail time under the UCMJ for negligent homicide than you could on any one of the other three.

Kerry decided he shouldn't waste any time. He would haul in Rose and Favro and Ivar on the Honor Committee charges the next day. There was no way Percival could spring them when confronted with the mountain of evidence Ash and Jacey had amassed. Once he had them in the interrogation room, he owned them. Even if they lawyered up he could go after them hard on the Honor stuff. One of them was bound to get scared and talk, and he knew just who that would be.

CAPTAIN PATTERSON dropped Jacey off at Quarters 100 when they were finished with Agent Kerry. She found her parents where she usually did, in the kitchen, standing around, drinking wine and talking. Leroy Buck and Colonel Bassett were there when she walked in. Sam rushed to the kitchen door, took her hand, and kissed her forehead.

"Did you watch it on C-Span?"

"I couldn't. I had class."

"Fran taped it," said Bassett. "I'll get you a copy. It was a spectacle I won't soon forget."

"I heard," said Jacey, breaking away from her mother. She went over to her father and kissed him on the cheek. "Thank you, Daddy. There aren't many kids whose fathers would do what you did for me today."

"There aren't many fathers who would get the opportunity," said Slaight, laughing. "Besides, he was using you to attack West Point. I wasn't about to let that go unanswered."

"Who dropped you off?" asked Sam.

"Captain Patterson. We just came back from Agent Kerry's office. We turned over a huge pile of Honor records to him. Ash and I . . . well, let's say we removed them from the Honor Committee files. It turns out Rose and Favro and some of the others have been using the Honor System to run cadets out of the Corps."

"With the eager connivance of the Commandant, I'd bet," said Slaight.

"Who the hell is this guy?" asked Buck. "He thinks he's this big savior of West Point, and he's down there feedin' shit to Thrunstone, and now we find out he's been messin' with the Honor Code?"

"I think he's crazy," said Sam.

Bassett chortled. "That is always the great question, isn't it? Who is he?"

"I'm afraid Gibson has made the mistake of wanting power for its own sake," said Slaight. "Power is expensive. You had better have something you really want to use it for if you're going to pay the price to get it. Gibson has confused getting power with exercising it. Bad move. Power is like electricity. It wants someplace to go. If you don't know what to do with power once you get it, it's going to arc the gap and shock you. Gibson is about to get the jolt of his life."

CHAPTER 53

A GENT KERRY didn't want to give the Honor Committee any more time to discover that Ash and Jacey had removed the case files. He wanted to arrest Rose and Favro and Ivar before they had a chance to compare notes and line up behind a stone wall of denials. The rest of them—Reade and Lessard were two, and there were others—could wait. Kerry wanted Rose, and the way to get Rose was to turn either Favro or Ivar against him. Kerry had to find a way to erode some of the mortar in their wall of denial, break a few bricks loose. Then all he had to do was sit back and watch it fall.

Kerry went down to the barracks when it was still dark and woke up six of his best MPs. When they had gotten dressed, he briefed them on the mission. They were going into three cadet rooms before reveille. They were to arrest Cadets Rose, Favro, and Ivar.

One of the MPs clicked his tongue against the roof of his mouth in astonishment. "You mean the football star Ivar?"

"One and the same."

"Man. This is gonna ruffle some feathers."

"That's why you can't screw it up. I want their rights read to them twice. Have them sign off on DA Form 3881. No cuffs. Let them get dressed and bring them straight back here to the MP barracks."

"We're not taking them to the Provost Marshal's office, sir?" asked one of the MPs.

"Negative." Bassett wanted Percival cut completely out of the picture, so Kerry had cleared out rooms in the MP barracks. Three of them would be used to hold the cadets. The other would serve as the interrogation room.

"I want these assholes kept separated at all times. We're going to use those free rooms in the basement to hold them. I want them treated right. No rough stuff, no snide remarks. I don't want anything for them to hang a complain on. Got it?" The MPs nodded. "I'll be going along on the Rose arrest. He's the one who did the assault on Jacey Slaight. I want him bad."

They piled into squad cars and took off down Thayer Road, heading for the barracks. Two cars went into Central Area to the Second Regiment barracks. The other car headed down Brewerton Road for North Area after Ivar in the Fourth Regiment. Kerry jumped out of his car and sent one team after Favro. He and his team went up the stairs for Rose.

Kerry knocked on the door. There was no answer at first, so he tried the handle. It was locked. He knocked harder. He heard a voice. "Who is it?"

"Military Police. Open up."

"What do you want?" Rose asked from behind the door.

"I want you, Mr. Rose," said Kerry as plainly and clearly as he could. Rose opened the door. When he saw Kerry, his lip curled into a sneer. "What are you? A fool? You've been told to leave me alone."

"That was then. This is now, Mr. Rose. Get dressed."

IT WASN'T hard to decide where to begin: Ivar. As a star athlete, he would naturally believe himself to be the one with the most to lose. Ivar had played only a minor role in the Honor conspiracy, but his name was found on several of the kangaroo court Honor Boards, and he had signed one of the phony sets of minutes. He was vulnerable to all three charges, even though he had probably not been one of the instigators and had just gone along with the program.

Kerry had Rose and Favro fingerprinted and made sure they both had access to telephones. He stood guards outside their rooms so they couldn't communicate. Both Rose and Favro immediately placed phone calls. Kerry had Army lawyers standing by, and when Favro asked for a lawyer, he sent them in.

Ivar, on the other hand, was under the impression that there had been a mistake. He wanted to talk to Agent Kerry, so he had Ivar brought straight to the interrogation room. He told Ivar to sit down at the small metal table in the middle of the room, while he remained standing. Ivar's nervousness was obvious. This time the interrogation came with no warning. This time Ivar hadn't been prepped by Rose or anyone else. This time Ivar was on his own, and he didn't like it a bit. He was by nature a team player. Going solo went against the grain of the big running back.

Kerry began by laying the pages from the Honor case files that contained Ivar's name on the table before him.

"What are these?" he asked.

It was just as Kerry had thought. Ivar was a participant but hardly a conspirator. He had done what he had been told to do and signed his name where they pointed on the page. Kerry was certain that he had never read a single document he signed and had probably barely listened to the testimony at the Honor hearings he sat on.

"These are the documents that are going to determine what you do with the rest of your life, Mr. Ivar. I want you to read them."

Ivar looked confused. "I don't get it. I thought you were bringing me down here to talk about Dorothy Hamner again."

"Mr. Ivar, you are under apprehension. The MPs told you that. They read you your rights and had you sign DA Form 3881, did they not?"

"Yeah, but I thought it was just a formality. I heard Percival told you that you couldn't talk to us anymore, so I figured you had us apprehended so you could get around his order."

"Not so, Mr. Ivar. I had you arrested because you are facing the charge of conspiracy to deprive cadets accused of Honor violations of their rights to due process. You're also being charged with signing false official statements—"

"Where's that? I never signed anything."

"Is that your signature right there?" Kerry pointed to a set of Honor Board minutes.

"Yeah, but I didn't take that stuff down. They told me it was just a formality. They do it all the time. Somebody's got to sign the minutes.''

"Those minutes were falsified, Mr. Ivar. You signed a false statement. You're also charged with signing false charges against a cadet.''

"I never did that.''

"Your name is on this charge sheet right here.'' He pointed to another document.

"That was written up by the regimental rep, Reade.''

"Yes, but you brought the charge to him.''

"No, I didn't. He came to me. He told me this girl in the company cheated on her PT test. He said because I was the company rep, I had to sign off on the charge.''

"So you didn't have personal knowledge that the young woman had cheated?''

"No. I didn't even know her. She was a plebe.''

"Mr. Ivar, do you realize how serious this is? You're facing more than five years in Fort Leavenworth prison on each of these charges.''

"What?''

"That's right, five years.''

"That's not right. All I did was do what an Honor rep is supposed to do. I went to the Boards. I listened and I voted. We didn't find everybody guilty. Lots of people got off.''

"I know that, Mr. Ivar. But whether they were guilty or innocent, it is illegal to conspire to deprive someone of due process.''

"They got their rights. They called witnesses. They got to testify.''

"That is not all there is to due process, Mr. Ivar. You can't have due process if the charge itself is fabricated.''

"When did we fabricate charges?''

"You did the day you signed the charge handed to you by Mr. Reade. That's five years right there. Unless we can find a way to make the prosecutor understand that you were just going along and doing things the way you were told they should be done.''

"That's what happened.''

"So maybe we can get the prosecutor to understand.''

"What can we do to make that happen?''

"He's got to know that you're sorry, and that you understand the mistakes that you made. And he's got to be able to get the guys who led you to believe that what you were doing was right.''

"Who's that?"

"Mr. Rose, for one. And Mr. Favro for the other."

"Man, I can't do that."

"Okay, then, I'll just call the prosecutor and tell him to start draw-ing up the formal charges. You're going to have to read and sign the charges. It's going to take a while. Do you want some coffee?" Kerry reached for the phone and started dialing.

"Wait. Are you calling the prosecutor?"

"Yes."

"But I thought you said we could talk to him."

"We can. But only if you are willing to tell him how you came to sign these false statements."

"Man, Favro never told me anything. He just put stuff in front of me and I signed."

"Was it only Mr. Favro? Didn't Mr. Rose hand you the minutes to sign? He was the one who presided over the Honor Board that night."

"Yeah, I guess he did."

"See, already you are being cooperative. Why don't I sit down with you, and we can go over these documents, and you can tell me who handed them to you, and what they told you when you signed them."

"I guess . . ."

"It's either that or I call the prosecutor, and you're going to be signing a whole new stack of documents, Mr. Ivar: the charges he's bringing against you."

It was funny how it happened when they folded. It actually looked that way. Ivar's shoulders seemed to sag, and he put his hands in his lap, as if in prayer. Kerry sat down and slid the first page in front of him. Ivar looked at his signature and read a few lines of the docu-ment.

"Favro called me one day, and he said he needed to see me up at the Honor offices, so I went up there, and he handed me this and told me to sign it. He told me the guy who was supposed to sign was on leave, and all they needed was an Honor rep's signature."

"And you signed, just like that."

"Just like that."

* * *

FAVRO WAS next. When Kerry walked him out of the room where he was being kept, he made sure to parade Favro past the open door of the office and give him a look at Ivar sitting there as the clerk typed up his statement.

Favro had quickly lawyered up, taking one of the JAG lawyers as his defense counsel. Kerry called in the trial counsel from the SJA's office who would prosecute the case. The defense counsel, Captain Fleiss, sat next to Favro and listened as the trial counsel, Major Harriman, read the three charges: conspiracy to wrongfully interfere with an administrative proceeding, signing false official statements, and dereliction of duty. Kerry sat down at the table across from Favro to explain his situation. With Ivar's confession, Favro was facing a very grim reality. It would be difficult if not impossible to convince a military court-martial that the star running back on the West Point football team was lying to cover his own ass, when in fact his ass wasn't covered, but fully exposed.

Then he laid out the case files that Favro had forwarded to Rose. All ten of them. His name was everywhere. He had even signed one of the sets of phony minutes. Kerry explained what Ivar had told him. He started with the meeting in the Honor Committee office, when Favro had lied to Ivar, telling him one of the Honor reps was on leave and all they needed was the signature of an Honor rep. Ivar had signed a trumped-up charge against a female yearling. It was another one of the PT test charges, accusing her of lying when she gave her time in the two-mile run.

"That's conspiracy, Mr. Favro. It's falsifying official statements, it's depriving a cadet of due process, and I think we can even make a case that you solicited Ivar to sign the charge by lying to him, and if we want, we can throw in a charge of conduct unbecoming." Favro's face fell. "What have you got to say, Mr. Favro? Ivar's in there right now making his statement. He's going over every one of the things you got him to sign, and he's telling the clerk what you said to him, how you got him to do it. This is some serious business here, Mr. Favro. You're looking at the kind of prison time that will have you out of Leavenworth about the time we put a man on Mars."

The defense counsel whispered to Favro and asked for some time, so Kerry escorted the two of them into a private office. When they returned to the interrogation room, Favro's face had lost its color.

He was shaken up. They sat down. "What's the deal?" asked Captain Fleiss.

Major Harriman was blunt. "The deal is, Mr. Favro gives us everything he knows about the Honor Committee and we'll see what we can do about the charges in the death of Dorothy Hamner."

"What charges are those?" asked Fleiss.

Kerry put the vial containing the rave drug down on the table in front of Favro.

"Recognize this?"

Favro looked at the vial, then at Kerry.

"You should. You used this substance to render Miss Hamner so drunk and incoherent that you and Rose and Ivar could have sex with her, knowing there was a good possibility she wouldn't even remember it the next day."

Kerry pulled up a chair and sat down across from Favro. "With the permission of your counsel, I would like to tell you what I think is going through your mind right now, Mr. Favro. Can I do that for you? Can I help you out here?"

Favro looked up at the lawyer. Fleiss leaned down and Favro whispered something and Fleiss nodded. "Go ahead, Mr. Kerry. We'll listen, but we're not making any promises."

"Good enough. All I want to do is tell you honestly where I think you're at. Okay, let's start with what I believe you're thinking right now. You're sitting there and you're wondering, How come it's me? How did I end up sitting here, when it wasn't even my idea? Hell, look at you, Favro! I've heard about your reputation! You've got girls coming out your ears! What do you need with this kind of stuff? So maybe one of the other guys, they suggested it, because it was a little something extra, something different. A goof. And here's the great part, they told you. It's *legal.* You'd get in more trouble for screwing a plebe than you would for this stuff. Am I helping you out, Mr. Favro? Are we getting anywhere?"

Favro nodded. "Yeah," he said flatly.

"You want me to go on, Mr. Favro? Or do you want me to stop?"

"Go ahead."

"That's good, because the thing is, I happen to agree with you. I don't think you should be the one sitting here looking at this vial of semilegal drugs. You want to know why?"

"Yes."

"Because in fact it *wasn't* your idea. You were just along for the ride. The whole thing wasn't your idea, was it?"

"No."

"Do you want me to tell you why you're sitting here looking at this drug vial, Mr. Favro? There's a reason, and I can tell it to you."

"Yes. I want to know why."

"Because I have a witness who can put a vial just like this one in your hand. Somebody ratted you out. Now you're thinking, was it Rose or was it Ivar? That's what you're thinking, aren't you? Here's the other thing, Mr. Favro. I don't believe it was your idea to snatch Jacey Slaight. And I sure as hell don't believe you were the one who assaulted her. I think I know you better than that by now. You're just not that kind of guy. But I think you know who *is* that kind of guy. And I think I can do something for you here, something that will make it go a hell of a lot easier on you when this whole thing is done with. I'm going to help you out if you help me out. Do you understand where I'm coming from here? If you can help me out, then I can help you make it clear to Major Harriman here that you weren't the ringleader, and it wasn't you who had the idea to pull this kind of shit. When Major Harriman listens to you being cooperative, and when he knows that you really helped us out, then Major Harriman, he's going to step up there and he's going to recommend that some of these charges against you are dropped, and that you should be shown leniency, because you were a good soldier, and you stood up and you admitted that what you did was wrong, and that you are sorry for it. I'll be honest with you. The charges are not going away completely, but at least you will not be facing the great many years behind bars at Fort Leavenworth that you are facing right now."

"We're disadvantaged here," said Captain Fleiss. "You clearly didn't get anything out of Ivar about the Jacey Slaight incident, or you wouldn't be offering a deal to Mr. Favro. Yet I can't counsel Mr. Favro to cooperate unless we know what charges he'll face."

"This will take us a minute or two. Please relax," said Kerry. He and Harriman went across the hall and called Colonel Bassett. He was waiting for the call in the Superintendent's office. Harriman explained the situation and made a recommendation, and Bassett said he would get right back to them. Bassett would consult with the Superintendent, the court-martial convening authority for West Point, because the decision to take a plea in any case under his jurisdiction was his. After a few moments, Bassett called back with the news that the Supe concurred. They could proceed.

Kerry and Harriman went back into the interrogation room. Harriman did the talking, addressing the defense counsel. "You're looking at involuntary manslaughter and rape in the death of Miss Hamner. We'll take manslaughter off the table, and we'll take away rape and make it indecent assault. But negligent homicide stands. We've got your client dosing the girl. He had no way of knowing what the condition of her health was, but lack of knowledge is no excuse here. Giving someone a drug, *any* drug, even a legal substance as innocuous as aspirin, without their permission is negligent behavior. If Mr. Favro had informed Miss Hamner that she was drinking some kind of so-called party drug along with the Evian, and she had agreed to take the substance, we would have another matter before us. But we'll put a witness on the stand who will state that Favro has used this drug in such a manner previously, that he dosed her without her knowledge. That's a pattern of behavior, and that's negligent homicide. I personally think we can make manslaughter stick, but we're willing to deal it away, along with the rape, if Favro opens up and tells us everything he knows about the Hamner case and about the assault on Jacey Slaight."

The defense counsel whispered to Favro, who listened intently. Then both men looked across the table. "What are you looking for in terms of jail time?"

"You're looking at three years max for negligent homicide and five years for indecent assault. We'll go for a year on the homicide and two years on the assault and you'll serve two years. The Supe has authorized me to offer you these terms."

"I want it in writing."

"You've got it," said Major Harriman.

Kerry couldn't keep himself from rubbing his hands together as he dug into Favro's story about the night at the lake with Dorothy Hamner, but what he really wanted to hear were the details of how they pulled off the kidnapping of Jacey. When Favro was finished, it was almost noon. They broke for lunch, and afterward, Kerry and Harriman called for Rose. He had retained two lawyers, Captain

Lamb, a JAG from West Point, and a civilian by the name of Hoff-man. Both men had been with him all morning.

When Rose and his lawyers reached the interrogation room, Rose whispered to Hoffman, who turned to Agent Kerry. "I'm going to make a suggestion that we take this up tomorrow. We need time to consult with our client."

"I'm going to respond by saying that we will go forward with our business right now," said Agent Kerry.

The military lawyer whispered to Hoffman, apparently explaining the rules that prevailed on an Army post, and Hoffman nodded. "Very well."

Major Harriman read the Honor Committee charges against Rose. Then he read the charges in the death of Dorothy Hamner. Rose's face was unresponsive. He had been expecting the Hamner charges, and now here they were.

Kerry stepped forward when Harriman was through running down his set of charges. "Now comes the part you've been waiting for, Mr. Rose. I've got you on kidnapping Jacey Slaight. That's a life term. I've got you on indecent assault of Jacey Slaight. When you tie that in with the rape charge in the Hamner matter, you are looking at life without parole. How does that sound to you?"

"You haven't got shit," said Rose.

"I told you to be quiet, Mr. Rose," said Hoffman. He turned to Major Harriman. "We want to know the deals you gave the other two."

"New man, new deal," answered Harriman.

"No way. We want to start with at least the same thing the others got."

Agent Kerry addressed the civilian attorney: "Let me explain something to you, Mr. Hoffman, so you can explain it to your client here. It's my way, or it's a highway heading straight to Fort Leavenworth. You're at West Point, Mr. Hoffman. People believe in the ideals of duty, honor, and country here. They tend to believe that individuals like your client Mr. Rose would best serve their country by serving lots of time. You're not going to run across any O. J. juries at West Point, Mr. Hoffman. You won't find any bleeding hearts at this little outpost on the Hudson. Perhaps you should consult with Mr. Rose. I'm sure he can enlighten you."

Hoffman and Rose leaned close together. Rose did the talking. When they turned around, Hoffman addressed Major Harriman. "No deal. My client had nothing to do with Dorothy Hamner's death, and he doesn't know what you're talking about when you refer to Miss Slaight."

Kerry gave Rose an indulgent look and turned to Captain Lamb, the military defense counsel. "Captain, I'm going to explain this to you, because I know that you've tried cases here at the Academy. We've got two cadets who will take the stand and tell a military court-martial jury that your client not only had knowledge that Miss Hamner was dosed with a chemical substance, but that, in fact, it was your client's idea. The star running back on the football team, Mr. Ivar, will get up there and testify that your client masturbated while he had sex with Miss Hamner. Both men will testify that your client insisted that they dose Miss Hamner with drugs so that she was nearly unconscious because he could not stand the thought of a woman looking at him. He will tell how Mr. Rose pleasured himself and then at the last minute penetrated Miss Hamner, which is how his semen ended up being identified in the DNA analysis. Now Captain Lamb, I'm not going to try to tell you how to do your job, but if I were you, I would advise my client just how successful a defense at a court-martial here at West Point would be, facing testimony such as I have just described to you. Major Harriman and I will give you a moment or two if you'd like." Kerry and Harriman stood and exited the room.

"What do you know about Hoffman?" asked Kerry.

Major Harriman answered, "He's from Poughkeepsie. He's defended several murder cases around here. He's good, but he's no Johnnie Cochran."

They walked upstairs to the MP lounge and had a cup of coffee. About an hour passed before Captain Lamb walked in on them. "We're ready to discuss terms," he said dryly. When they got back downstairs, Captain Lamb did the talking. "The fact of the matter is, Mr. Kerry, you need Mr. Rose far more than he needs you at this point, because without Mr. Rose, you're not getting anywhere near the Commandant of Cadets."

Harriman whispered in Kerry's ear and spoke to Lamb: "What kind of deal are you proposing, Captain Lamb?"

"Rose will give you Gibson, but you've got to drop the rape charge. My client doesn't want to leave the federal prison system with a rape record, because that would subject him to sex-offender registration laws in an increasing number of states, thus limiting the places he could choose to live, even limiting his ability to travel within the country."

"I'm going to do you a favor, Mr. Rose. I want you to listen closely to me. I'm going to tell you the unvarnished truth so you can get a grip on where you actually stand. I don't give a rat shit about the Commandant of Cadets. It's your ass I want, and I've got it. You can clam up about Gibson for the rest of your natural life, as far as I'm concerned."

"You can't touch me on Jacey."

"Really? Why don't we see about that. Gentlemen, excuse me for a moment." Kerry left the room and returned a moment later carrying two thick files. He sat down at the table across from Rose and the lawyers and opened the file.

"You really fucked up when you stole the car down there in Jersey, Rose. I don't know when you did it, probably right when you were snatching the car out of the mall parking lot, but you reached down and leaned on the rocker panel and left an amazingly clear palm print. Want to have a look at it?" He shoved a copy of the print he had lifted from the Pontiac across the table. "Here's the palm print we took from you this morning." He pushed another sheet over. The lawyers looked at them closely.

"So I stole a car. That's six months with no record down in New Jersey. Fuck you."

"Good for you, Rose. You admitted to the car. Here's where it really gets good." He removed the plastic bag with the scrap of blanket from the file and held it up. "I found this little piece of blanket in the trunk of the car. See? I took pictures." He pushed them across the table. "It was hiding down there under the taillight assembly. That's why you missed it. Took me ten minutes to find the sucker. Happens that this little piece came from the blanket you threw over Jacey. It's a match, Rose. That means you've got to find some shyster expert to refute the report from Fort Gillem that says the scrap I found in the car you stole came from the blanket used on Jacey."

"We'd like a few moments," said Hoffman.

"Take all the time you want," said Kerry. "Time's cheap. At least now it is, anyway." He and Harriman left the interrogation room. Outside in the hall, Harriman grinned and high-fived Kerry.

"I think you got him when you told him you didn't give a shit about Gibson. It was so believable."

"That's the thing. I don't give a shit. Gibson's a corrupt asshole, but the Army is full of creeps like him, especially with stars on their shoulders. He'll get branded whether Rose rats him out or not. His career is over. That's all that ever happens to general officers anyway. Did you know that since the Uniform Code of Military Justice was codified in 1951, not a single general has been court-martialed?"

"Are you sure about that?"

"Positive. I don't care if Gibson walks, 'cause he's not going very far. He will be remembered as being in charge of the Honor Code at a time when maybe the biggest Honor scandal of them all hit West Point. He's rotted trash headed for the Dumpster. I don't give a shit about sniveling creeps like Gibson. They're a dime a dozen. I want that sick fuck Rose."

CHAPTER 54

CAPTAIN LAMB emerged from the interrogation room looking like he had just encountered the ghost they said lived up in the Fifty-fourth Division, in the Lost Fifties. Kerry and Harriman were standing at the end of the hall talking with Captain Patterson. He had stopped by to see how things were coming along. The fate of his client, Ash Prudhomme, depended on Kerry breaking Rose. Even though they had Favro's confession, if Rose didn't give up something on the assault of Jacey and opted to go to trial on that charge, there was a chance that Ash would have to face a court-martial. What Patterson needed was even a minor admission by Rose that he had been involved in the assault on Jacey.

"Hi, Harper," said Lamb without enthusiasm.

"How are you doing?" Patterson replied.

Lamb turned to Kerry and Harriman. "We're ready."

Kerry led the way back to the interrogation room. Rose was sitting right where he had been when they left. The look on his face had not changed. Even his body language was insolent. He had his arm slung over the back of the metal chair and his legs were crossed as if he were sitting in a club somewhere, instead of facing an interrogation in the basement of a Military Police barracks at West Point.

Kerry had to restrain himself from spitting on him, his contempt for Rose was so overwhelming.

Harriman noticed Kerry's attitude and stopped him. He closed the door and walked him down the hall. "Get a grip, Jimbo. It ain't a game, but it ain't a war either. We use guns in wars, remember? All we've got here is words, and you're my word man with this punk. Keep it together. Can you?"

Kerry tried to shake it off. Harriman was right. He was just another shitbag. "Yeah. I'm all right."

Harriman opened the door and they went in. Rose was still reclining in the chair. He gave Kerry a little grin. "Here's the deal, asshole. You win and I win."

"Doesn't work that way, Mr. Rose," said Kerry.

"How about you let me go and I wear a wire and talk to Gibson. You knock down the kidnapping on Jacey Slaight to unlawful imprisonment and drop the rape, and I'll set him up for you in spades."

"Why should Gibson even agree to meet with you? The word is all over the Corps that you've been arrested. Gibson's got to know that you're facing serious charges. What's in it for him?"

"You arrested me before and Percival let me go, and I went back to the barracks and got right back into my old routine. I meet with Gibson on the Honor Code nearly every day."

"It's different this time. Favro and Ivar have both copped pleas."

"So return them to the barracks and tell them to keep their mouths shut or their plea deals go down the toilet. Gibson's got to meet with me. I know too much for him not to."

Captain Lamb spoke up. "It's a good deal, Mr. Kerry. Rose sets up Gibson for you. We'll plead to negligent homicide, we'll plead to all of the Honor Committee conspiracy charges, we'll take the unlawful imprisonment, as long as you leave aside the rape. You've got him for twenty years on the charges we'll plead to. Twenty years isn't bad, considering you're not looking at a trial. We can probably keep the whole thing quiet and West Point won't suffer unduly. I think you should talk to your boss."

Kerry found himself acting like a suspect, picking out a spot and staring. He was gazing at a pipe that took a funny curve around a floor joist. Looked like the nose on his first wife. He almost laughed out loud.

"You will excuse us. We've got work to do," he said.

Harriman called Colonel Bassett, who in turn called the Supe. Slaight agreed to the plea deal, but he insisted on the advice of Colonel Bassett that Rose sign a stipulation admitting to the facts of the case.

Harriman and Kerry returned to the interrogation room. Harriman spoke rapidly. He was losing patience with the process, but most especially with Rose. "You've got your deal. We'll throw out rape and take the unlawful imprisonment and the other lesser included charges. But we're going to insist that Mr. Rose signs a stipulation admitting to the facts of the case as we've presented them."

"What does that mean?" asked Rose.

"I will tell you what it means," said Kerry. He leaned forward with his hands flat on the table, face-to-face with Rose. "It means you sign an affidavit admitting that you set it up for Miss Hamner to be dosed with a chemical substance. You conspired in every one of the Honor Committee charges, bar none. And you threw a blanket over Miss Slaight and hauled her off to the woods and tied her to a tree and beat her. Your stipulation will become a part of the permanent record of your case."

"Does that mean I'll be listed as a sex offender?"

"Not unless you commit another sexual offense. In that case, your stipulation could be used against you in another trial."

"Will it be publicly released?"

"We'll ask the military judge to seal it."

Rose and his attorneys whispered for a moment. Captain Lamb responded: "You've got a deal, Major Harriman."

"There is one further matter," said Kerry. "We've told this same thing to the other two. We're going to return these men to the Corps of Cadets until the disposition of their cases is complete, and until then, none of them, and that most especially includes Mr. Rose, will communicate anything that has happened here today to anyone. That applies especially to Mr. Rose. The only persons Mr. Rose will be permitted to speak with concerning this matter will be his defense counsels."

His attorneys whispered to him for a moment, and then Rose slowly nodded his head.

"The stipulation and agreement to remain silent will be part of the written plea, Mr. Rose," said Agent Kerry. "If you are found to have broken the agreement and have talked to anyone outside of this room, the deal goes out the window, and you go to trial on all charges with Ivar and Favro testifying against you. We'll get you on rape, Mr. Rose. And we'll insist on the maximum penalty for kidnapping, which is life without parole. Do you understand me and agree to this?"

Again Rose nodded.

"Speak up, Mr. Rose," commanded Major Harriman.

"Yes, I understand, and I agree."

"Then let's get down to business," said Agent Kerry.

Kerry and Harriman listened with a kind of horrible fascination as Rose folded back the thick blanket of secrecy that had covered the workings of the Honor Committee and his conspiracy with General Gibson to corrupt the Honor Code and make it do the bidding of the Commandant of Cadets. He admitted to drugging Dorothy Hamner, and he admitted to the assault on Jacey. By the time they were finished, it was late afternoon. Rose had dropped his aggressive air of defiance and had adopted the far more subdued manner of a man in the dock. Not many young men get an advance look at their future, but now Rose had his. He was going to the Federal Disciplinary Barracks at Fort Leavenworth and he would emerge as a middle-aged man with a felony record and a dismissal from the Army.

RIGHT AFTER the deal with Rose was sealed, Colonel Bassett drove to the Provost Marshal's office. There was one last bow that had to be tied in the package they were preparing for General Gibson.

Bassett walked to Percival's door and entered without knocking. Percival looked up from his desk.

"Colonel Bassett. What a surprise. Come in. Sit down."

"I don't need a chair to say what I've got to say to you, Percival. I've just come from the Supe's office, and I am speaking for him. We've arrested Cadets Rose, Favro, and Ivar. They have been charged with some very serious offenses, including manipulation of the Honor System, manslaughter, rape, and a passel of lesser charges. General Slaight ordered me to inform you that you will be relieved of your position as Provost Marshal within the month. In the meantime, General Slaight has ordered you to take an immediate leave and not return to your office for at least fourteen days. You are ordered not to communicate with General Gibson in any fashion whatsoever. You are ordered not to reveal the nature of the charges against any of the cadets. You are ordered to stay completely clear of the prosecution of these or any other cadets until you depart this post. If you violate any of the Superintendent's orders, you will be charged with disobedience of a direct order, interference with an official investigation, and obstruction of justice. Do you understand the orders which the Superintendent has given you?''

Percival looked up at Bassett uncomprehendingly. "I don't understand.''

"Allow me to clue you in, Percival. Slaight knows you've been a back channel for Gibson. He could court-martial you right now for dereliction of your duties as Provost Marshal and interfering with the investigation of the death of Dorothy Hamner. But he's going to let you slide, Percival. I don't why. He just is. However, if you violate either the letter or the spirit of his orders from now on, I will personally put you under arrest, and I will personally supervise your prosecution. Now do you understand?''

Percival's hand shook as he took off his glasses. "Yes sir.''

"Good. Sit in that chair and keep your goddamned mouth shut and you'll survive this thing. But if you breathe a word to Gibson, you are going to Fort Leavenworth, and not as a student.''

Bassett left Percival sitting behind his desk and walked outside. That felt good, he thought as he got in his old clunker.

I T TOOK Gibson until the following day to learn that Rose, Favro, and Ivar had been put under apprehension and returned to their barracks under room arrest. The first thing he did was call Percival. He was surprised to learn that Percival had taken a fourteen-day leave. Then he called Colonel Lombardi, only to discover that Lombardi as well had taken a leave. He asked Lombardi's secretary where he had gone, and she told him Lombardi had taken his family to Vermont to see the foliage.

It was the middle of the afternoon before he reached the point that the only person left to call was the Superintendent himself. He thought it over for only an instant before he decided not to. He couldn't call Slaight after the humiliation he had visited upon Thrunstone at the hearing. One of Thrunstone's aides had told him that Slaight's friend Leroy Buck had seen him huddled with Embry during the hearing. There was no way Slaight was going to listen to his entreaties on behalf of his Honor Committee Chairman and Vice Chairman now. No way at all.

Things were closing in on Gibson. He didn't have many places left to turn. He picked up the phone and called Cecil Avery. His old friend was very distant and cold with him on the phone. He told

Gibson that Thrunstone was livid over the fact that Gibson had not informed him that female cadets now met physical standards that were tougher than the standards in Gibson's day as a cadet. Gibson tried to make an excuse, but Avery cut him off.

"You did not serve well the interests of Congressman Thrunstone and his committee, Jack. Your representations to Thrunstone and myself were full of holes which Slaight was able to exploit with impunity. I suggest that you lie low and bide your time and hope like hell that Thrunstone doesn't tell his pals in the Senate to withhold their votes when you come up for your second star. *If* you get promoted, that is."

Gibson tried to smooth the waters, but Avery cut him off, saying he had to take another call. It seemed as if his Washington patron was leaving him to fend for himself.

He went home that night and fixed himself a double manhattan. Helen Messick was history. His wife was down in Pennsylvania visiting her mother. Both of his kids were away at college. The halls of Quarters 101 echoed hollowly as he walked to his study at the rear of the house. He picked up *The New York Times* and scanned the front page. Congressman Thrunstone had addressed the Republican caucus on the negotiations regarding the defense budget. The story said that Thrunstone was digging in his heels, but Gibson could read between the lines. The Republicans had called him before the caucus because his hearings had turned into such a debacle. He was weakened, and the Speaker of the House was trying to prop him up. There was a photograph of Thrunstone and the Speaker down at the bottom of the page. They were standing out on the Speaker's balcony at the Capitol, arms around each other, smiling. It looked to Gibson like a picture of the kiss of death for the congressman from Illinois.

Gibson was startled by the doorbell. He wasn't expecting any visitors. He was heading for the front door when he saw Rose standing outside the side door on the stoop, wearing his dress gray uniform.

"Rose, what in the hell are you doing here?" he asked when he opened the door.

"I had to come and see you, sir. I think they're tapping my phone. I couldn't call."

Gibson looked around. The street behind his house was empty. "I think you'd better get back to the barracks. Aren't you under room arrest?"

"Yes sir. That's what I want to talk to you about."

"I don't think I can help you, Rose. Not now."

"Sir, I would rather come inside. I think I can explain what the problem is."

Gibson looked up and down the street again. "All right, but you'd better make this quick." He led Rose back to his library and sat down.

"May I sit, sir?"

"Yeah. Sit. But get with it, Rose. I don't want you seen in my quarters. That wouldn't serve either of our interests."

"I agree, sir."

"So why did they arrest you again? Did that CID agent get them to hang that dead bitch around your neck again?"

"It's not Dorothy Hamner, sir. It's the Honor Committee."

"What!"

"Slaight's daughter and that piece of shit Prudhomme got into the committee files. Kerry is charging me with conspiracy to deny due process—"

"I'll charge them with theft! They're using illegally obtained evidence! They can't do that!"

"Prudhomme has his keys, sir. He's Third Regimental Honor Rep. Any Honor Committee member has free access to the files."

"They can't prove anything. Those files are clean."

"Not exactly, sir."

"I thought I told you to sanitize the cases we fixed."

"I did, sir."

"Then they can't show any violations of procedure. They can't prove this due process shit. I showed you how to fix the case files so every 't' was crossed and every 'i' was dotted."

"I did everything you told me, sir. The problem is your recommendations for separation and dismissal. They've established a pattern in the guilty verdicts you signed off on, sir. Every time we fixed a case, you recommended dismissal. In the other cases, you recommended dismissal only sixty percent of the time. In three other cases, you reversed the findings of the committee, and in two more, you recommended suspension for a year."

"You didn't meet the proper standard I set in those cases, Rose."

"In the three cases you reversed, those guys handed in term papers they didn't even write."

"You think I give a shit about term papers? Those three men are warriors. All three of them stand at the top of their class in leadership. I did what was best for the Army when I reversed those verdicts."

"The problem I've got is, your reversals of those verdicts and your suspensions of the other two are what tipped off Prudhomme and Slaight and Kerry. They were looking for inconsistencies, and they found them. Now I stand accused of fixing the cases you didn't reverse."

"That's a problem you and your counsel will have to deal with, Mr. Rose."

"I need your testimony, sir. I need you to explain to the prosecutor that my actions were consistent with the standards you set."

"I'd love to see you try to convince someone of that." Gibson got up from his chair. "You're on your own now, Rose. This will be the last time you and I speak."

"No, it won't, General Gibson. You and I are in this together. I kept written records of every conversation we ever had. Every time I left your office, I went back to my room and typed up notes on what you told me."

Gibson froze. "What did you say?"

"I said I kept notes. Kerry doesn't know about them—"

Gibson started at him. "You little shit, I ought to—"

Rose held up his hands defensively. "You don't know where the notes are. I do. You're not cutting me loose, General Gibson. If I go down, you're going down with me."

Gibson stopped, sinking back into his chair.

"You think you've got it all figured out, don't you, Rose? You've been listening to me, and you've been watching me, but you haven't learned the lessons I've tried to teach you. What happened? I made you Honor Chairman. I promoted Favro to Regimental Commander and made him Vice Chairman. I put everything in place. I made you the most powerful man in the Corps of Cadets, and what did you do? You listened to your cock instead of me. That Honor Committee crap is the least of your problems. You don't need me testifying for you. You need a lawyer who knows a good headshrinker who can go in there and explain that you didn't know what the hell you were doing."

"Oh, but I did, sir," said Rose. "I took lessons from the master."

Gibson sat there staring at Rose. He thought he heard a banging noise. It sounded like someone was knocking on the door. He turned his head. Colonel Bassett and Agent Kerry were standing in the door of his library.

Bassett crossed the room and stood next to his chair. "General Gibson, please stand, sir."

Agent Kerry opened a brushed-aluminum box. Gibson could see a reel-to-reel tape recorder. The tape was running. "You are under apprehension, General," said Kerry. He turned to Bassett and grinned. "That felt good."

CHAPTER 56

SLAIGHT ACCOMPANIED General Meuller and General Drabonsky when they traveled across the Potomac to meet with the Speaker of the House of Representatives in his private office in the Capitol Building. Slaight handed the Speaker a list of the charges that had been filed against General Gibson.

"We are going to make history at West Point, sir. There has never been a court-martial of a general officer until now, but General Gibson will face a jury of his peers in two months' time."

General Drabonsky was standing next to Slaight. "Mr. Speaker, I will deal with Congressman Thrunstone in the budget negotiations for the time being because the law says that I have to. But I want you to understand that your Chairman of the National Security Committee has been listening to General Gibson ever since you gave him the committee. The brutish manner in which he treated General Slaight in the hearing was a direct result of General Gibson's involvement in those hearings. I want Congressman Thrunstone instructed that he is to issue an apology to General Slaight and to his daughter. If that apology is not forthcoming, I will cut off negotiations and report to the President. I am certain that he will take my case to the American people. The United States military will not put up with the kind of behavior your National Security Committee Chairman exhibited to General Slaight."

The Speaker pledged that he would talk to Thrunstone and was certain that General Drabonsky's demands would be met. If there was one thing a politician didn't want, it was to lose a fight with men in uniform.

Slaight and his bosses left the Capitol that day feeling pretty good about the future of the Army and most especially about the future of West Point. The Speaker had asked them if he could join them for the Army–Navy game. They had said yes, of course. That's what you do with politicians. You take them to ball games and you show them a good time and then you get back in the trenches and go at them with everything you've got.

Back at West Point, Slaight called for an assembly of the entire Corps of Cadets in Ike Hall. When they were seated in the huge auditorium, he had all the doors closed and ordered that MPs stand guard outside. The only people in the auditorium were the cadets and General Slaight.

He walked out onto the stage and spoke to them without notes. "You people have just gone through a pretty extraordinary couple of weeks, haven't you?"

The cadets stirred in their seats. Slaight heard a few hundred "yes sirs."

"Each of you is entitled to take your own lesson from what you've witnessed here at West Point. That's part of being a cadet. You watch and you listen and you figure things out on your own. But I want you to understand something about West Point from my point of view as well. It's hard when you reach my age and rank to go back in your mind and try to see things as you saw them when you were a cadet, just as I'm sure it's hard for you to imagine how I see things as a general. I have spent quite a bit of time since I became Supe trying to imagine my way into your shoes. They're the same shoes I wore, and this place is not so very different from the West Point I remember from thirty years ago. When I was a cadet there were officers who I did not respect, and there were officers I thought the world of. The same was true of cadets. I had guys in my company who I wouldn't have followed across the street to McDonald's, and there were guys I would have followed through a ditch filled with burning oil. That's the way people are. There are good ones and there are bad ones, and it's up to you to take example from those you respect. You cadets are free to consider my performance as Superintendent any way you want. I am certain there are those of you who think I'm a flaming asshole."

There was a good deal of laughter, which Slaight allowed to subside before he continued. "And there are those of you who think I am without fault. I am standing here to tell you today that I am neither. I am a man. I am a husband. I am a father. I am an Army officer. I try to meet my obligations in each of those roles as well as I can, but I know that sometimes I fall short. I thought for a time that I failed my daughter in not protecting her from harm, but I realize now that I did not fail her, because she is out there in this auditorium today among you. Today she is a cadet, as are you all. Soon, you will be officers, and, much sooner than you think, you will be husbands and wives and mothers and fathers. You are part of a great continuum, ladies and gentlemen of the Corps of Cadets. West Point is no more or less than the Corps of Cadets makes it. I am the Supe, sure. But I am merely a temporary custodian, pushing a broom behind the Long Gray Line. It's up to you cadets to keep West Point alive by making over your lives in its image, carrying its history and its honor into your futures. I wish each of you the happiness in your lives that I feel right now, as I look out at this sea of gray."

Slaight turned on his heel and took two steps toward the wings of the stage. Then he stopped and turned his head. "Oh, yeah. I almost forgot. *Beat Navy!*"

The Corps rose as one, filling the auditorium with a deafening cheer. Back in the next-to-last row, Jacey turned to Ash, smiling. "Isn't he great?" she said.

"Yeah," Ash replied. "He sure is."

Slaight left Ike Hall with Sam, and they walked back up the hill toward Quarters 100.

"Is Helen going to have to come back for Gibson's Article Thirty-two hearing?" she asked as they reached Washington Road.

"I don't think so. The stuff we got from the cadets will put him away for a long, long time."

"What about her husband?"

"We're keeping him on until the end of the academic year; then he's going to retire."

"I'm glad things worked out for them," said Sam. "Gibson left such destruction in his wake. It would have been sad to see them taken down with him."

The Hudson River Valley was ablaze with color. Sam suggested they walk out on Trophy Point. They were standing there, watching the Hudson making its way south toward the Atlantic, when Slaight turned to his wife and said, "Isn't it amazing? I remember this view from my first day as a plebe, back in 1965. I was standing right on this spot when I took the oath. We swore to defend the nation against enemies both foreign and domestic."

"I guess the ones we've been seeing lately have been the domestic kind," Sam mused.

He laughed. "I wonder what happened to that guy who was standing out here on Trophy Point with freshly cut hair itching his neck in the hot afternoon sun that day so many years ago."

Sam shook her head slowly. "That's easy. He's the same guy he was then. He's got the same old haircut. He's even got the same old wife."

Slaight hugged her, brushing the graying hair from her forehead so he could see her eyes. "I've got a hankering for a bottle of Côtes du Rhône and a steak that's black on the outside and blue in the middle."

"Me, too."

They turned and walked back toward Quarters 100, passing the spot where Dorothy Hamner had fallen. Slaight took a quiet pride in the knowledge that her death had not been in vain. Her memory lived on in his daughter and every other cadet at West Point.

Like the memories of those who lay in the cemetery behind the Old Cadet Chapel, the Corps of Cadets carried the memories and the honor of the fallen.

EPILOGUE

THE NEW Brigade Adjutant made an announcement from the Poop Deck in the mess hall some days later. Walking the area—the ancient form of West Point punishment that had recently been banned in favor of work details, whereby cadets picked up trash and policed the area and worked on projects around the Academy as punishment for their various sins—would be reinstituted on a one-time basis by the Superintendent. The Adjutant then read the Supe's orders: "For gross lack of judgment, i.e., assaulting fellow cadets and causing bodily harm by use of a steering-wheel lock and fists: fourteen demerits, fourteen hours walking the area, awarded to Cadet Ashford Prudhomme."

A gigantic roar went up from the Corps of Cadets, as several plebes at a table toward the rear of the mess hall raised an upperclassman on their shoulders and began parading him up and down the aisles between the tables.

The next afternoon, a lone male cadet could be seen walking back and forth down at the far end of Central Area wearing the dress gray uniform, carrying an M-14 rifle on his shoulder. If you were there in Central Area and you got close enough, you could see that when he reached the far northwest corner of the area and stopped to execute an about-face, a hand emerged from one of the barracks windows, holding a fat Creole po'boy sandwich. The cadet walking the area took a huge bite before executing his about-face and marching off once again across the area.

If *you* were the lone cadet walking the area, what you could see was that the anonymous hand holding the sandwich belonged to a young woman, unlined and slender and as beautiful as anything you'd ever seen in your life.

Except maybe the po'boy.